"MENACING . . . IMPRESSIVELY
MOODY."
—*Kirkus Reviews*

Sixteen-year-old Sarah Miller was no virgin. But
she definitely was a sexual victim. The question
was: *Whose?* To search out the answer, Chief of
Police Carroll Howser had to sort out the dirty
secrets of the squeaky-clean citizens of Rivertown.
What he uncovered was so blood-drenched, it
was unimaginable—even to himself. . . .

Down by
the River

"Monte Schulz has an ear for dialogue and a
talent for kaleidoscopic storytelling."
—*The New York Times Book Review*

"Succeeds in conveying small-town class
structure and the doom-laden atmosphere
that develops as violent events multiply."
—*Publishers Weekly*

SPELLBINDING THRILLERS ...
TAUT SUSPENSE

Monte Schulz

Down by the River

⊘

A SIGNET BOOK

To a dancer, rising

SIGNET
Published by the Penguin Group
Penguin Books USA Inc., 375 Hudson Street,
New York, New York 10014, U.S.A.
Penguin Books Ltd, 27 Wrights Lane,
London W8 5TZ, England
Penguin Books Australia Ltd, Ringwood,
Victoria, Australia
Penguin Books Canada Ltd, 10 Alcorn Avenue,
Toronto, Ontario, Canada M4V 3B2
Penguin Books (N.Z.) Ltd, 182–190 Wairau Road,
Auckland 10, New Zealand

Penguin Books Ltd, Registered Offices:
Harmondsworth, Middlesex, England

Published by Signet, an imprint of New American Library, a division of Penguin Books USA Inc. Published by arrangement with Viking Penguin, a division of Penguin Books USA Inc.

First Signet Printing, May, 1992
10 9 8 7 6 5 4 3 2 1

Grateful acknowledgment is made for permission to reprint excerpts from the following copyrighted works:
  "Desert Moon" by Dennis De Young.
  "Boys of Summer" by Don Henley and Mike Campbell. © 1984 Cass County Music and Wild Gator Music. Used by permission. All rights reserved.
  "She's So Fine" by Kris Moe and Lyn Phillips. By permission of Lotsa Music (BMI).
  "Nobody Loves Me Like You Do" words by Pamela Phillips, music by James Dunne, © 1983, 1984 by Ensign Music Corporation. Used by permission of the publisher.
  "The Road and the End" from Chicago Poems by Carl Sandburg. © 1916 by Holt, Rinehart and Winston, Inc. and renewed 1944 by Carl Sandburg. By permission of Harcourt Brace Jovanovich, Inc.
  "My Little Town" by Paul Simon. Copyright © 1975 Paul Simon. Used by permission of the publisher.

I shall foot it
Down the roadway in the dusk,
Where shapes of hunger wander
And the fugitives of pain go by. . . .

The dust of the traveled road
Shall touch my hands and face.
                              —CARL SANDBURG

In my little town,
I grew up believing
God keeps His eye on us all.
                              —PAUL SIMON

ACKNOWLEDGMENTS

I would like to thank Roger Archambault of the Los Angeles Police Department for his conscientious reading of this manuscript and his limitless patience in responding to the many questions I had concerning law enforcement attitudes and procedure.

Although writing is a solitary art, the truth is that few of us get here entirely on our own. Therefore, I would also like to thank Steven Allaback, Lawrence Willson, Gerald Rosen, Don Emblen, Geets Vincent, Gary Doudna and, of course, my family now and then.

Green River

Prologue

The body shone a pale silver in the moonlight between the two cattle cars. The corpse wore a uniform and the earth around it soaked the edges of the blue cloth in black, framing the shaft of light as a kind of extraterrestrial spotlight on the battered form. The first tramp moved forward into the light. He bent to touch the dead man behind the left ear where the head was cocked oddly away from the shoulders. A second tramp spoke from the edge of the light. "You don't have to touch him to see he's dead."

A quarter of a mile away, a train whistle sounded. The April sky was clear and warm. Traveling weather in early spring.

"Didn't even have to see him to know it was happening. Shit, you could hear him halfway to the junction. Sounded like he was getting his head torn off."

His old shoulders slumped from fear, the first tramp backed out of the light, whispering, "Got to ride."

The other tramp knew what the old man was whispering without having heard a word. It was a familiar monologue. "We wouldn't have to leave if you turned him in."

Hiding his face in the shadow, the older tramp closed his eyes. "He's just a boy."

"Every place that's comfortable we got to leave 'cause of him," said the younger tramp. "Cut him loose, goddammit. Cut the kid loose."

The old man sighed and leaned up against one of the

cattle cars. He wiped the back of a hand across his mouth and drew a rag from his back pocket. The night wind was on the rise now, blowing dust out along the tracks that led to the boxcars. The old tramp moved back into the light. He spread the rag out and placed it over the dead man's face whose eyes were reflecting the moonlight from a vacant gaze. Then he moved off into the shadows again, walking down the line between the cars. He stopped in the middle of his stride to turn around and call back, "Don't even know where he is. Might be gone already."

The old tramp wandered off into the warm darkness as the echoing of his voice trailed off in the vast railyard.

Before he'd disappeared completely, the second tramp shouted after him, "You sure as hell know where he is. So do I. He's waiting for us in the UP going west. Just like always."

1

The river grew still in the twilight. Wild rose petals, blown
free from the shore, fell onto the water and were carried
gently off downstream. The river cooled and the splintered
shade of the cottonwoods sunk and vanished into the current. A relentless droning of insects replaced the human
sounds in the murky air. The river ran south by southwest,
rolling past one little town after another on its way through
the delta. Electric lights burned and flickered on and off
streetcorner to streetcorner, town by town. Dogs barked
behind empty lots and harsh voices shouted out after hurried
footsteps passing rapidly into the dark. A stink of fresh
sewage clung to the wet grass by the river. The current
spread it south. A warm night breeze came up, washing
across the cold face of the water, rippling in the tule. Mosquitoes rose on the heated air and brokenhearted lovers
drove out alone to the river where they wept over the levee
and scattered paper remnants of recent betrayals into the
muddy drift. The river flowed on without them.

Earlier (much earlier), the river was quieter still. Only
the rain, and an occasional wind, made a sound on the deep
water. Then the tule bundles and balsa rafts split the lapping
tide of riverwash in summer crossing and brought strange
upright shadows and guttural echoes to the water in an ever-
widening wake. And the smoke of night fires drifted between
the shores like a reeking fog. And the river rose and fell,
flood season and dry, the shallow boats gliding in the

15

stream. And the summers went by, and again, and again, until lamplight glowed in the damp reeds along the waterline and the soundless quaking of deepdraft vessels was felt in the lower delta. Travelers come to stay entered the river and slid upstream. Engines whistled and howled, daylight and dark. Waterfronts grew beneath the cottonwood shade while the river muddied and churned under barge and side-wheeler and chugging scow, plying from landing to landing, high water and low. One night an entire town came out to watch a large passenger steamer, the elegant Ophir Princess, burning furiously stern to bow from a fuel-oil explosion as she drifted by downstream, people screaming and jumping overboard from her ruptured decks into the black ash-littered water. Another time, two store ships collided and sank in midstream, clogging the river with baskets of fresh fruit and crates of live squawking chickens and expensive spice tins and velvet draperies and Continental wedding dresses destined for summer brides up and down the delta. Then the highway reached the levees, and the trucks came and crossed, and the watertrade went away, and the barges ceased their visits to the slumping jetties. The empty river hissed quietly in the night.

Near Rivertown, summer stars shining like thousands of blue fireflies on the smooth surface of the river wheeled slowly westward across a clear and quiet sky. And shadows, green and ragged, sagged and waved on the cold water, and the refuse of another season floated in the stream or caught in the soggy grass by the riverbank and bled. Half a mile away on a narrow service road the headlamps of automobile traffic illuminated the mosquitoes in the air. White dust rose in following. Car horns echoed out and back across the dark. Radios blared at speed. The mosquitoes were swept away. The cars passed on into the night and the horn echoes and radio sounds faded. Afterward the dust swirled around a while and the mosquitoes came back. The honey scent of a young girl's perfume trailed briefly in the road. And there were voices whispering somewhere by the water. And laughter. The river looked old.

2

In the woods beside the Green River railyard, a teenage girl with thick dark hair and china-blue eyes danced barefoot in the dirt with her blouse off. Sarah Miller was naked above the waist and her breasts bounced as she moved. A pocket cassette player dangling from a tree limb played Sarah's favorite song: Bruce Springsteen's "Dancing in the Dark." She moved with enthusiasm. She'd been dancing for her boyfriend Jamie but he was gone now, so she performed for his friends. They cheered her every move. Jamie had picked his way through the thicket into the long grass and manzanita brush bordering the railyard. He didn't need to watch her dance. He'd already seen Sarah completely nude earlier in the day. In fact, he'd screwed her twice—once under the bleachers behind the old backstop at the high school in the morning and then again after lunch on the living room sofa at her folks' house. He'd seen enough of Sarah to last a few hours, so he'd left her with his friends and climbed up onto a tree branch at the eastern edge of the woods and stared out in the direction of the railyard where he'd found something more interesting to look at.

A hundred yards away, past the cyclone fencing and empty boxcars, small skillet fires glowed where the raggedy men made camp in the summer dust. Every spring they drifted to Rivertown, jumping off the AT & Santa Fe and staying until the weather cooled in late September. In the last century, the flats along the river bluff had served as a loading station for the riverboats and freight trains from Sacramento and Oakland. Now the old loading docks were lost in a fifty-nine-year growth of blackberry bushes, and the railroad ties on both sides of the highway had vanished beneath the wildflowers and rattlesnake grass. The last cars to use the old river line spur, a circus train abandoned in the late fifties when its operators declared bankruptcy and skipped town, sat now in the dense woods a quarter mile from the water, entombed and forgotten. The railroad maintained the original line—every Thursday the freight trains passed near Rivertown five miles north of the old railyard—but, ignoring the loading-dock spur and bypassing the river, it did not attract the attention it had a century earlier. No longer did crowds gather on Saturday mornings to see the huge steam engines thundering to the riverfront and back. These days, when a train whistle shrieked in the blue air, it summoned only brakemen and bums out along the rusty tracks in the noon hour, and the old Green River yard gradually deteriorated into an iron graveyard and a tramp jungle: dirty, isolated, and unsafe—particularly after sundown. There was talk every few years of bull-dozing the whole yard—cars, tracks, shacks, tents, and all—and building an elaborate hotel development with art galleries and ice cream shops and quaint boutiques selling plastic riverboats and keychains embossed with miniature steam whistles and paddle wheels, maybe even a restaurant called the Mark Twain or the John Sutter that would serve small pieces of fried chicken rolled to look like gold nuggets. However, the financing of a project that large was thought to be unrealistic for a community the size of Rivertown, so the jungle remained while the old tracks and the abandoned piggybacks and boxcars aged in the sun and the tramps came and went as they pleased and the town did its best to pretend they weren't there at all.

Sarah's tape ran out and the woods were quiet again. Jamie stood on his toes on the tree branch and studied the tramps shuffling soundlessly from one section of the railyard to another. In the dark, their faces appeared black and indistinguishable. Ash flew from burning cigarettes waved about in mumbled conversations. A warm draft carried to the trees an odor of filthy clothes (traveling clothes) and sweat. Sarah called out for Jamie, and a peal of laughter followed from the woods somewhere behind him. He ignored it. Two tramps were wrestling now in the dust. Jamie heard his name again in the darkened woods. He climbed down from the tree and slid to his knees in the dry grass. The fight continued in the jungle with an increasing ferocity. Eyes were gouged and a nose bitten, all blows directed now at vital areas. Several other tramps rushed in to break it up. An aluminum pot was overturned, spilling hot coffee into the dirt. The two combatants shouted obscenities at each other as they were dragged apart. Jamie crept forward from the underbrush up to the cyclone fence and watched. One of the sparring tramps rolled over in the dust and gave the finger to the other and got to his feet and stumbled away into the shadows. There was yelling after him and an object thrown that looked like a shoe. Then the coffeepot was replaced and the fighting ended. Jamie curled his fingers tightly in the wire fencing. Behind him in the woods his buddies had added their voices to Sarah's, calling his name in sing-song, *Ja-mie, Ja-mie*, over and over like bored children.

Emerging from the thicket, he saw Sarah pressing her breasts together for the towheaded fifteen-year-old Long twins. They were seated in the grass at her feet, both wearing the same white T-shirts and Sears blue jeans they wore every day. They looked like idiots, thought Jamie, with their summer freckles and new crew cuts, the stupid-ass grins they had on their faces. The fact that his girlfriend was doing a striptease for them seemed all the more grotesque.

"This is called cleavage," Sarah told Howie Long. And there was more laughter. Jamie kicked a branch out of his path and walked past her and sat down on a log.

"Put your shirt on," he said to her, and fished a can of Coors from the cooler. He opened it and took a sip.

"Sarah's got the greatest tits," said Ernie, the other twin, staring relentlessly. His brother grinned broadly in agree-

19

ment. This was the first either had seen a grown female in so advanced a state of undress and they were both impressed.

"Am I embarrassing you?" she asked Jamie. Her feet crunched in the grass as she danced in a slow circle. Jamie's older friends, all four seniors sitting on the fringes of the light from the two six-volt Coleman lanterns, watched him intently. Knowing him since grade school, they realized he wasn't amused. Roy Lee drew another joint out of his shirt pocket (he had given the first one to Sarah—in retrospect, a big mistake), lighted it, took a short hit off it, then passed it over to Jerry Hardisty and then on to Calvin Arnold and Cal's cousin Raymond Maddox. Roy figured that if this was going to degenerate into another one of Jamie's performances, the rest of them would need to witness it in an appropriate state of mind.

Jamie drained the can of beer and tossed the empty into the brush. Then he pointed at Sarah's blouse, folded over a log a few feet away.

"Danny," he said, addressing the third fifteen-year-old, "give it to me." Shaggy-haired Danny Williams bent over and picked up the yellow blouse and tossed it to him. Jamie grabbed it, and in the same motion threw it at Sarah. "Put it on."

She caught the blouse. Then dropped it.

The Longs giggled. Jamie glared at them and they stopped. Sarah picked up the blouse and shook the dust off. She frowned.

"Look what you did," she said, holding the blouse out at arm's length so Jamie could see it. "You got it dirty."

"Just put it on and shut up."

"Mom's going to be so pissed when she sees this."

"Fuck your mom. Just put the goddamn thing on!"

Reluctantly, Sarah slipped the blouse on over her head. "Happy now?"

Jamie looked away. He could still hear the tramps shouting in the yard. Were they fighting again? They were shouting about *something*. He thought about getting up and taking another look. Sarah walked over to the cassette player and rewound the tape. Then she pushed up the volume and punched the play button and Bruce came pounding back, drowning out the tramps.

"Turn that off!" screamed Jamie. He got to his feet. ·

"Screw you. It's my tape."

"I said, turn the fucking thing off!" Jamie leaped for the cassette player. Sarah reached over quickly to switch it off, then took two steps backward. Jamie snatched the tape player from the tree branch and pegged it like a rocket into the brush. Then he stared at Sarah, standing before him half-stunned.

"What'd you do that for?" she asked.

"Why are you always so stupid?"

Jamie tried to listen again to the tramps. Had they heard Sarah's tape? They weren't supposed to know anyone from town was spying on them, and if they found out there was no telling how they'd feel about it.

Quietly, Sarah picked up one of the Coleman lanterns and walked over toward the thicket where Jamie had chucked the tape player.

He frowned as she angled the beam. "What do you think you're doing?"

"What does it look like?" She swept the thicket with the light, searching for a way in.

"Put the lamp back where you found it."

All she could see were branches and leaves and shadows. "Why?"

"Because it's mine, and I don't want you using it."

She swung around, banging the lamp against her thigh. She saw the familiar Danielson smirk on Jamie's face. "Why are you being such an asshole?"

"I don't know, why am I?"

She set the lamp down in the grass. "You are so fucked up!"

He snapped off the end of a twig. "I'm hurt."

Roy's joint was burning now down to the nub. He had it pinched in a silver roach clip and was sucking out the last of the smoke, letting it cook in his lungs. Danny Williams, perched on a flat stump just behind Jamie, held his head hangdog and was blowing out of the corner of his mouth at a long strand of hair. The Long twins kept their eyes on Sarah, who was obviously still mourning her lost cassette player. She hadn't moved from the spot at the thicket where it had disappeared.

Howie got up. "We'll go get it."

Jamie shook his head. "Just leave it where it is."

Howie glanced at Sarah, thought a moment, then re-formulated his proposal. "How about if we get it, but don't turn it on?"

"How about if you just sit down and shut the fuck up, huh?"

"I'm going home," announced Sarah. She tied the bottom of her blouse closed, fastened the waist snap on her jeans and headed for the old fire road, a few hundred yards away in the brush, where they'd parked their vehicles. Since the main entrance had been fenced off a few years back and the gate shut tight and padlocked, the firebreak was the only way to get a car in close to the railyard. They'd discovered it by accident, screwing around with an old Jeep in the woods two summers ago.

"It's a long walk," said Jamie. "Have fun."

"Who said anything about walking?"

"Taking the train?" he laughed as she waltzed past him.

"No," she said. "I'm taking your truck." And she showed him the keys she'd snuck from his backpack earlier in the evening, jingling them once above her head for maximum effect, and bolted for the truck. Before Jamie could react, she'd entered the thicket and the woods had swallowed her up.

"You bitch!" He jumped up and ran after her into the brush. "Get back here!"

Her laughter dwindled away in the dark. Roy Lee flicked the dead roach from the clip, snuffing it out in the dirt beneath his shoe. He could hear Jamie shouting his lungs out as he chased Sarah down toward the fire road. "Give me those fucking keys!"

"She's so stupid," said Cal, shaking his head. Sarah's voice had joined Jamie's now in the warm air. They were both screaming like crazy people in the distance. Half a minute or so passed. Then Jamie's screaming stopped and Sarah's became louder. A metallic bang shot out of the woods, followed by a shriek and another bang. The Longs sat mouths agape, facing the thicket where Sarah and Jamie had entered the woods. Another shriek echoed across the night air and an engine starter whined briefly, then shut off.

"He caught her," said Roy.

They waited. Down on the fire road, a car door slammed.

"He's pissed off now."

Sarah shrieked again and Roy buried the joint with the toe of his shoe. Somewhere out in the woods now, Jamie was punishing Sarah for running off with his keys. He was hurting her, forcing her to apologize, bruising her. Later on, she would take those bruises home as a reminder of the mistake she'd made that evening. Once again, Sarah Miller was bawling in the dark. Her sobbing filtered through the woods in the warm air and made its way to the boys sitting in the small clearing at the edge of the Green River railyard. She cried out in pain and they heard that, too. Jamie was yelling at her, taunting her mercilessly. He was dragging her up the fire road now, back into the lamplight where his friends sat wishing that either Jamie or Sarah would just break things off and end the relationship and simplify all their lives.

"Let go of me!"

Grasping Sarah firmly by the wrist, Jamie pulled her from the brush into the clearing. As they passed through the last few branches she stumbled. He caught her and held her up by seizing a fistful of her hair with his free hand. Then he tugged and she screamed and he kicked her in the bottom, urging her forward. She collapsed into the grass, still trying to work her arm free. He was too strong for her, though; all she could manage to do was hurt herself further, so she gave up and hung there like dead weight in his grasp, crying both from pain and frustration. When finally he released her, she rolled over onto her back and lay there sobbing. Meanwhile, Jamie stuck the keys to the truck into his jeans, walked to the log, and sat down again.

"Stupid bitch."

Jamie took a slightly bent cigarette from his shirt pocket and a book of matches and lighted up. The smoke spun upward, invisible in the dark air. Ernie Long had his trusty pocketknife out now cutting arcane designs in the dirt at his feet while his brother Howie watched. Roy scraped the sole of one gray tennis shoe back and forth over the buried joint (wishing like hell he'd brought another) and exchanged empty glances with Cal and Raymond and Jerry. Danny Williams hid his own vacuous expression under a shock of sweaty brown hair. Nobody but Sarah made a sound, and she cried almost steadily for the next ten minutes.

When she finally did stop, the mascara she'd put on after supper ran on her face in sea-blue streaks and her eyes were bloodshot and swollen. She rolled onto her knees and began brushing herself off. Jamie made faces at her but no one laughed. Sarah finished wiping the dust off her blouse and jeans, coughed once, sniffled, and got up.

"Having fun yet?" asked Jamie, watching her.

"Oh yeah," she replied, fixing her blouse. "I'm having a swell time." She bent down and picked up the comb that had fallen out of her pocket when she stumbled out of the thicket.

Jamie looked around at his friends and saw that he was still the only one appreciating all this. Far off to the east, a man's voice (a tramp's) echoed across the night air. Jamie switched his attention away from Sarah to listen. Somebody hundreds of yards away was shouting, or calling, to somebody else. What they were saying was unimportant; it was the tone that mattered, and it was an angry one. Jamie considered hiking back to the railyard for another look-see, but decided against it. Spying on the tramps was one thing, accidentally running into one of them was another. He didn't know what the hell would happen, but the idea of it made him a little nervous.

Sarah interrupted his eavesdropping, saying, "I want my tape player."

Another shout flew across the darkness. Jamie wondered if the voices belonged to those two tramps he'd seen fighting earlier. Probably. He'd heard that tramps had memories like elephants and if you ever wronged one, they'd follow you wherever you went to get their revenge. The cigarette he'd been smoking burned out and he dropped the butt into the dirt.

"Did you hear me?" said Sarah. "I want you to go get my tape player."

"Shut up a minute." Were there more than two voices out there now? He pictured dozens of tramps shuffling in the dirt and gloom along the line of boxcars, gathering for a fight.

"I want it!" she yelled.

"Would you shut the fuck up!"

"Not until you go find my tape player!"

"What is it with you?" he screamed. "Are you crazy?"

The noise from the railyard increased, swelling into the summer night like a flock of birds in flight.

"Sarah, why don't you just go home," said Roy, trying to ameliorate an already shaky situation. "Here"—he tossed her a pair of keys on a black plastic ring—"you can take my truck."

Sarah let the keys fall untouched at her feet.

"I don't want your truck. I want my tape player, and I want Jamie to get it for me."

"Kiss my ass," her boyfriend said, his thoughts reverting again to the railyard where, he was certain, something extraordinary was about to happen.

Sarah walked over and kicked dirt onto him. As she did, another round of shouting roared from the railyard, much louder now (or perhaps closer) than before—wordless and unintelligible shouting, angry shouting. The Long twins rose together, their heads swiveled toward the tramp jungle. Roy forgot about the joint he wished he had and saw Jerry and Raymond and Cal scramble off into the thicket in the direction of the yard. He thought, briefly, about following.

Two more gritty kicks in the dirt and Sarah had regained Jamie's interest in her problem. His eyes flashed and he sprung at her, swearing and snatching her blouse at the shoulder, ripping the fabric along the sideseam clear down to her hip. In the same instant, Danny Williams slipped off alone into the dark toward the fire road and the trucks. Jamie wrapped his arms around Sarah's waist and hoisted her off her feet while she beat on his head with her fists. Roy watched them struggle. Howie Long became sick to his stomach, but it was his twin brother Ernie who vomited unexpectedly as several loud voices bellowed from somewhere inside the railyard, filling the night woods with a strong, violent echo. Jamie dropped Sarah into the grass. And yelled out: "What the *fuck* is going on?"

3

The streets in Rivertown were quiet at mid-evening. Stores had closed at six; parking lots emptied by suppertime. Cars traversing Main and Front streets were minutes apart now. Most of the traffic was on foot. The night air was warm and dead. At the courthouse downtown there was a single light on in a fourth-story window, the only light showing above the first floor. It glowed a soft yellow high up in the summer dark. Standing behind the shut glass and blinds at the small window, Carroll Howser looked out from his office into the center of town and yawned. He watched the signals on the corner change. A Chevy pickup shaded the red and went on by. A black dog trotted past on the sidewalk below. A girl carrying a leash gave chase. She yelled out, but the dog ignored her and continued into the shadows. The lawn sprinklers in the park across the street went off. The traffic lights changed, then changed again. The girl disappeared under the trees up the street. Howser came away from the window. He studied the lamplit office and frowned. His desk was a mess, littered with cold scraps of supper and week-old magazines and stacks of paperwork unsorted. The paperwork didn't bother him nearly as much as did the half-eaten cheeseburger. Where had his appetite gone? He'd always heard that fresh country air made you hungry, yet he'd been heavier when he lived in the city. It made no sense. Since he'd been in Rivertown, he'd lost twenty pounds. That put him under 210. He hadn't been that light in twenty-eight years. Not since high school. Pretty peculiar. Then again, maybe he had it backward. Maybe it had been the stress of being on the job in San Jose that had made him gain all that weight in the first place. Some people eat when they're bored, others when they're nervous. He'd always been one of the latter—eating to hide the sweat. And now, two years in Rivertown had cured him. He'd probably never overeat again.

He sat down and shoved all the supper garbage off to one side. Then he picked up the copy of *Time* magazine with the "Star Wars" defense system on the cover and leafed through it for a third time, skimming over the same articles on Alaskan holidays and unrest in South Africa and the nuclear meltdown at Chernobyl. When he was done, he tossed it into the trash can beside the desk and yawned again. Apparently his interest in reading had gone the way of his appetite.

The door to his office was cracked open to the hallway and a draft from the corridor outside circulated in the small room. A stale odor of dust and ancient leather exhaled and lingered. A few papers fluttered on the wooden filing cabinet. The sweat on Howser's face cooled. The light seemed dim.

The intercom buzzed, and a woman's voice came on the speaker.

"Chief?"

Howser leaned forward.

"Yeah, Jane."

"Corey wants to know if he can go home early."

"Why?"

"Personal reasons."

"What does that mean?"

"He says he's sick."

"Why didn't he call in himself?" asked Howser.

"He was afraid you'd talk him into staying out there the rest of the night."

"Where's Beef?"

"They're both still at the high school."

The traffic signals changed again and an old flatbed Ford roared past down the street.

"Is Beef going to stay out?"

"Yeah."

Howser thought a few moments, then asked, "When does Corey want off?"

"Eleven o'clock. Ten-thirty, he said, if you're feeling particularly generous. He says it's pretty slow out there tonight."

"I'm sorry he's bored. What about the reserves? They all go home, too?"

"Craig and Dennis are out at the river. They're staying on till midnight."

"And Alfie?"

"South side."

"When did he report in last?"

"Ten minutes ago."

Howser fished in the greasy yellow wrapping paper for a cold french fry. He found one and pulled it out and ate it. What he had to be nervous about now, he didn't know.

"What should I tell Corey?" asked Jane.

Howser glanced at his watch. It was twenty after nine. He looked up at the clock on the wall beside the door. It read half-past.

"Chief?"

"Tell him he can go home at eleven. But have him get off his butt out there now." Howser set his wristwatch forward ten minutes. "He's still got an hour and a half and I want him rolling. That goes for Beef, too."

"Okay."

"And Jane?"

"Yeah?"

"Keep smiling. It's a slow night."

"I'll try to remember that."

Howser punched the off switch on the intercom and tried again to get comfortable in the chair. The whole office felt cramped and claustrophobic. They had offered him a larger one downstairs off the lobby, his predecessor Lou Hudson's old office, but he had turned it down, preferring the quiet and solitude of the fourth floor. And in the daytime, with the sunlight bright in the windows, the filing cabinets and the chairs, the bureau and the big oak desk never seemed to take up space the way they did after dark. He poked at the paperwork stacked under the brass lamp.

29

Reports. What else? Files and forms. The bureaucracy that justified the badge. He opened the top desk drawer and snuck a magazine out from inside a sealed manila envelope. It was the June issue of *Penthouse*, left there earlier in the week as a joke by one of his patrol officers. He opened it and leafed his way through to the centerfold "Pet of the Month." Then he rotated the magazine to vertical and let the photograph fold open on Miss June. He stared at her. She was beautiful. Sexy and exotic. Nude. He smiled. She was staring back—at him. His face flushed. Then he saw that she was just a kid, a girl young enough to be his daughter, a child. He lowered his eyes. When he was sixteen, a shot like that would have provided jerking-off material for six months. Now it only embarrassed him.

"Cute, isn't she?"

Howser looked up and saw Alfie leaning in the doorway, wearing an outsized grin on his face and carrying his shoes in his hand. For some reason he got a kick out of sneaking up on people.

Howser laid the magazine on the desk and slid the drawer shut with his knee. "Yeah. Cute."

Grinning, Alfie put his shoes back on and stepped into the office. From the neck down, Officer Alfie Cox was the stick-boned man who dried up and blew away in a faint wind. His physique showed little muscle and less body fat. He could have been a walking advertisement for the undernourished in America. From the neck up he was a turtle, sloe-eyed and sallow. A laughing turtle, though, one with many funny stories to tell. Everybody in town liked him. In the city, they'd say the guy was more popular than air. Rivertown would probably elect him mayor the day he turned in his badge.

"I thought you were out on patrol," said Howser.

"I was." The patrolman smiled. "I had to come back in."

Howser watched Alfie walk quietly across the hardwood floor to the window and peel back the blinds.

"What for?"

Howser was beginning to wonder if anyone in Rivertown was interested in police work besides himself. Alfie peered down at the street below. It was empty again and the lights at the intersection were green.

"I wanted to tell you we got your unit up and running again."

Howser slipped the *Penthouse* into one of the stacks of paperwork.

"Oh yeah? What was wrong with it?"

"Busted fuel pump. No problem at all. Took her down to Redmon's and swapped your old Bendix for a new one. Runs like a champ now."

"What about the air conditioner?"

"Had to order a new condenser. It'll be in next week."

Howser let himself lean back in the old swivel chair until it creaked. On his first day at work in Rivertown, Alfie had assured him that the police chief's unit was the strongest-running vehicle in the department. *It's a Ford, Chief. They run like trains.* So when a hose burst or the generator quit or a tire went flat, Alfie made it his personal responsibility to get the thing fixed as quickly as possible.

"Thanks. I appreciate it."

Alfie let the blinds close.

"No problem."

The light from the street signals shimmered like green vaporous neon through the clear glass where Alfie stood hands in pockets making a dumb clicking noise with his tongue. Howser shifted anxiously in the chair.

"You going to go back out on patrol?"

Alfie came away from the window as the lights switched to red.

"Corey's taking off early tonight."

"So I heard."

He walked over to the desk and stopped behind the brass lamp. His shadow arched up across the office wall at his back.

"He never did get over to the east side like he was supposed to. He's been out at the high school with Beef since suppertime. I doubt if anybody's been on the east side all night."

"Really?"

"You can ask Jane."

"No, that's all right," said Howser, "I believe you."

He smiled. Every evening it was the same routine: Alfie would come into the office and point out that the east side needed a patrol and Howser would assign it to him. Alfie was always too embarrassed to come right out and ask for it himself. The Walcott Hotel was on the east side, managed by a woman named Ellen Kelleher with whom he had just that spring fallen desperately in love. It was no great secret; everybody in Rivertown knew. Alfie was almost forty and this was apparently the first woman who'd ever shown a serious romantic interest in him. Ellen was only twenty-six, but she'd grown up in Fresno and had already been married once before. They made a perfect match. Each night on the job he'd stop by the Walcott to spend an hour or so hanging about the hotel lobby or whispering with her and kissing outdoors in the porch swing next to the flowered arbor. When he had to go back out on patrol again, she'd give him a plate of cookies to take along in the car. Later on, they'd send coded messages back and forth to each other through the dispatch. Somehow the laughing turtle had found another heart in town.

"You wouldn't want to take a run over there for me, would you?"

Alfie looked up over his shoulder at the clock. It showed a quarter to ten. He shrugged. "Yeah, I suppose I could do that."

"Of course, if you have something more important to do, I can probably send somebody else."

"No, no, no," said Alfie, waving off that last suggestion. "I can do it. When do you want me to go?"

"How about right now."

"Okay, sure," said Alfie, walking to the door. "I'm on my way."

"Good."

Alfie wandered out into the dark hallway and disappeared down the corridor toward the rear stairwell. His footsteps echoed in the old walls. Half a minute later Howser heard the steel door to the city parking lot down below bang closed.

He reached forward and readjusted the lamp, tilting it

down from his eyes. Then he sat back again and looked out through the blinds. Rivertown was a great deal farther away from San Jose than it seemed on a map. The true distance could not be measured in land miles. How else was somebody like Alfie Cox able to wear a uniform and a badge and ride around in a black-and-white on a Saturday night? He was a nice guy, but guileless and frail—wrong for the job. The same was true of the other officers. Not one of them would've been able to buy a shield on a city force. They were amateurs—lazy and unprofessional in their day-to-day work. Corey Harris called in sick at least five nights a month; Eddie "Beef" MacAlister wanted to club everyone he arrested. They both drank and fooled around on patrol. In Rivertown, however, familiarity counted for at least as much as professionalism, and the two of them had been high school football heroes for the Rivertown Hornets on a rainy evening in some autumn long ago. The town had shown its gratitude by giving them jobs when they graduated. Now, twenty years later, when the glamour of wearing the badge had worn away and the job had turned into a grind, they'd become indifferent to the privilege and obligation that came with it and drove their patrols solely to justify two paychecks a month. The excitement had gone; the town was too slow and predictable. They no longer cared how fast the kids ran their cars on Mustang Road after school let out or how a power lawn mower and nine sacks of fertilizer were stolen from a locked garage on Willow Street or who threw that empty lunch bucket through Tony Martin's bedroom window at three o'clock in the morning. It meant nothing to them, beyond the fact that they had to listen to another sob story and fill out a report or two. They were worse than the new guys. While it was true that Rivertown's five reserve officers consistently mishandled the simplest assignments—grammar-school crossings, junior high turnabouts—at least they showed a little enthusiasm for the work from time to time.

Howser listened to a carload of noisy middle-aged softball players late for a distant celebration passing north through town. A couple of minutes later the street was silent again. He brushed his fingers across the nearest stack of reports, tracing his own shadow on the wood. He had never been a law enforcement junkie, not in the way he had known them in San Jose. He had never seen himself as one of Joseph Wambaugh's "new centurions" standing guard against the barbarian hordes. On the other hand, neither was he a mercenary collecting his paycheck for writing traffic tickets on rolling stops at the edge of town or busting teenagers for smoking joints in the rest rooms of gas stations and movie theaters. He had no idea what sort of reward he was looking for in the job, none whatsoever. But he knew that if the job was a grind, it was also what you made of it.

The door to the office squeaked and eased open a little wider. Howser leaned down to his right to have a look. A dark gray tabby stopped in midstride and sniffed the air.

"Hi, Jim."

The cat crossed the room at an angle, tracking a curious odor in the draft. Passing under the desk at Howser's feet, he came out on the other side under the corner where the cheeseburger lay in its greasy yellow wrapper. Then he stopped and sat there, looking up at Howser with wanting eyes glassy and night-black. Jim owned the courthouse. He'd been there longer than most of the staff. Consequently, he was shown the proper deference around the building upstairs and down wherever he chose to stalk. Howser made sure to leave his own door propped slightly open whenever he was in the office, particularly after twilight when Jim did most of his prowling.

"You don't want that cheeseburger."

The cat stretched forward and up on his hind legs and reached for the top of the desk but came up a few inches short.

"I'm telling you, you don't want it."

Jim made a sound like a rusty door hinge and blinked slowly. Howser smiled at the cat and Jim meowed again. Howser leaned across the desk and snatched the dried cheeseburger from the wrapper.

"All right, but I don't want to hear from you later on." He placed the food down on the cold floor beside the desk. The cat crept forward over it, licking the bun and chewing noisily. Outside, the street signals burned a fluorescent red in the dark. The downtown was empty and the evening air purple and still. Howser watched the cat tear the food apart and eat it. Eventually he closed his eyes and drowsed a while.

4

Across town, in another room, a man named Jack Clayton sat on a half-made bed reading a small magazine and breathing the sweet green scent of a summer arbor close by. The windows on the south and east corners of the room were open to the outdoors and dozens of brown dust moths pattered casually at the screen. There was an electric fan on the bureau top, but its blade was bent and the motor broken and the room was hot. He was looking through a back issue of *Reader's Digest* he had just found under the mattress. The bed was not his own, nor was the room; he was renting both for an indefinite stay. He had only the night before driven to Rivertown from the desert near Scottsdale, Arizona. He'd checked into the Walcott Hotel the hour he'd arrived and unpacked in a corner room on the top floor. An old cowhide Oshkosh suitcase was shoved under the bed and an empty army-surplus duffel bag slumped on the high shelf in the closet. He had his toiletries stuck in the medicine cabinet in the halfbath and his clothes sorted and put away in the bureau and the newspapers he'd saved during the trip were stacked up on the square desk by the south window—some read, some not. The sheets he sat on were rumpled and sweaty and a green cotton blanket was piled up at the foot of the bed. Lately, he'd been having trouble sleeping.

He finished the *Digest* article on the threat of Communism and was reading a few jokes in "Humor in Uniform" when a car entered the driveway and stopped outside the hotel. The motor shut off and Clayton heard somebody get out and walk up the front stairs into the lobby. He stuffed the little magazine back under the mattress and went to the window. A black-and-white police car was parked in the gravel down below. Its headlights were off. Beyond the driveway there was nothing to see but stars and darkness. The air at the screen was cooler than indoors; a light breeze was circulating in the trees above the arbor. Leaning forward, Clayton could hear voices from the lobby—small ones and quiet. The walls of the old hotel were thin and the property was narrow and ringed with fenced vegetation and any sounds inside or out were sucked up and cast about like bird echoes in the dark.

His van was down there somewhere, parked in a stand of bougainvillea by the gate. It needed a new muffler and a coat of paint. He didn't have the money to spend, though. There were other priorities. He'd get around to it later. The yellow light from the lobby threw shadows on the rose beds flanking the stairs. The dust raised by the police car was settling only now. Clayton listened to the voices. One of them belonged to the woman who worked downstairs at the front desk. He had met her when he checked in. Her name was Ellen something. The other voice he didn't recognize, but he assumed it belonged to the cop. They were speaking too softly to be overheard outside of the lobby, so Clayton quit trying and decided to go out for some fresh air instead. He went to the closet to change shirts. The one he had on was sweatsoaked and it stunk. He tossed it into a corner of the closet with his dirty underwear then took an old denim work shirt off a wire hanger and looked around for his shoes. He'd bought a flashy pair of Florsheims at a yard sale in Tempe and they looked so good on him he'd been wearing them everywhere but in the shower. He found them under the nightstand and put them on and went into the bathroom to wash his face. His hair was damp and stringy. The water ran lukewarm from the tap. He slipped his hands under the faucet. The water was cooling now, so he stuck the plug in the drain and let the sink fill. He rolled up his shirtsleeves and sunk his forearms into the white basin, then cupped his hands and brought water up to splash onto his face and neck. He ladled water into his hair and let it drip down his shoulders. The lightbulb above the mirror buzzed and flickered as he washed. Water droplets splattered onto the floor. When the sink had filled to the overflow, Clayton reached in and removed the plug. He splashed his face once more as the water drained, then grabbed a hand towel from the rack above the toilet to dry his hair and beard. Putting the light out, he walked back into the bedroom. The draft through the stormscreens cooled his skin now and relieved him. He buttoned up his shirt and went to the desk by the window and switched the lamp off, damping the room into shadow. The dahlia pattern on the pink wallpaper tossed in rhythm with the trees outside.

There was a television set on in another room. It had been broadcasting one program after another since the hour Clayton arrived. The volume seemed stuck on high. The noise hummed in the walls. The night before, on his way up from the lobby after checking in, he'd passed by the room where the idiot box blared. The door had been open to the hallway and inside a man dressed only in blue flannel pajama bottoms sat in a Morris chair across from an old black-and-white Philco set. He'd had a wet dish rag draped over his bald head and an empty TV tray in his lap. The shimmering screen had provided the sole light in the room; *Remington Steele* had boomed from the box. The man in the chair had been sound asleep. Lying in bed an hour afterward, drifting casually between dream and reverie, Clayton had imagined the old man in the chair to be his own father sitting up late in front of the television set waiting for his son to come home from another evening out. How long, though, would a father wait when his son hadn't been home in seven years?

Clayton stood at the stormscreen, listening. A few miles away to the west, the interstate highway would be flooded with light and sound. The draft off an eighteen-wheeler could blow like a storm if it happened to catch you downwind, perched unprotected on the edge of the blacktop. And the thunder never quit, either, day or night, because the highway had no end, no terminus. It just ran and ran, violating one horizon after another. And for everyone it carried home, there was somebody else it was leading farther away.

A little after half past ten on his second night in Rivertown, Jack Clayton left the sweltering room he'd rented on the third floor of the Walcott Hotel and went back out into the dark.

5

The first call came through thirteen minutes after midnight, catching Howser in thought at the office window, his face striped by the light passing through the blinds. He'd been thinking about something his ex-wife Kathy had said to him the day he'd accepted the job in Rivertown (the day she'd moved out of the house, the day they'd stopped being married), something about his wanting to be a small-town hero, solving rural crimes by day and chasing lonely small-town women by night. He hadn't argued the point at the time because, for some reason, two years ago the idea hadn't seemed quite so preposterous. Lately, however, he'd been doing more napping than sleuthing, and the little black book he kept in the nightstand beside his bed hadn't seen a new phone number in eight months. He had to admit, though, Kathy had been right about his fantasy; that was precisely how he'd considered things then.

When the intercom buzzed, he left the window and took the call from the dispatch standing at the desk. "Go ahead, Jane. What's up?"

"There's been some trouble out at the railyard."

"What kind of trouble?"

"An assault complaint. Kids and tramps."

"Who's making the complaint, the kids or the tramps?"

"The kids. They claim some tramps attacked them in the woods outside the railyard. Looks like one of the kids, a teenage girl, was raped. She's at the hospital right now."

Howser moved around to the back of the desk and opened the drawer beside his right knee and took out a legal pad and an old blue ballpoint. He sat down and started writing immediately.

"Where are the rest of them?"

"The kids?"

"Yeah."

"In the emergency room at City Memorial."

"Anyone hurt besides the girl?"

"Don't know. Emergency notified us as soon as the girl came in. All they reported was the rape."

Howser was scribbling notes as quickly as he could. "Anybody besides the kids witness the attack?"

"Not as far as we know."

"All right," said Howser. "Send whoever's out near the river over to the railyard. Have them close it up. Nobody in, nobody out. Tell them to wait there until I call, okay?"

"Got it."

"Where's Corey?"

"South side, coming in."

"Get him for me."

Then he signed off and finished his notes and sat back and closed his eyes. The noise off the street (what there was of it) increased inside his head: another car, some voices, lusty dogs roaming about.

The second call came in half a minute later. He hadn't even gotten comfortable in the chair before the phone rang. There was a loud voice on the other end.

"Chief?"

"Here."

"It's Ed Miller."

"What do you need, Ed?"

"Goddammit, Chief, my daughter Sarah, she's in the hospital. They hurt her, those bums out there. They raped my little girl."

"I just heard," said Howser.

"My wife's with her, but Sarah's not talking to anyone, won't say how it happened."

"She's probably in shock, Ed."

"Some of us are going out there. We're going out there and find the ones that did this."

"Ed?"

"They raped her. My little girl. They raped her."

"Ed? Where are you? Are you at home or at the hospital?"

"Those stinkin' bums."

"Ed?"

"Goddammit!"

"*Ed!*"

There was a pause followed by an audible sigh from the other end of the line, the sound of anger subdued and replaced, at least momentarily, by patience and reason.

"Where are you now, Ed?"

"Hospital."

"Okay, listen to me," said Howser, trying on his most diplomatic tone. "Stay right there. Can you do that? Just stay where you are and wait for me."

"I don't—"

"Just wait there, okay? Stay put a few more minutes. I'm coming down."

"Well . . ."

"Good," said Howser. "Thanks."

An instant after getting off the phone with Ed Miller, Howser rang the dispatch. "Jane, I'm going over to the hospital. When Corey calls, patch him straight through. I'll take his call in the unit."

"Okay."

"Who'd you send to the railyard?"

"Craig and Dennis," she said. "They were still out by the river."

"Have them call me, too."

"All right."

"And listen, I'd like you to call Charley Horton's office in Sierra Springs and let him know what's going on over here. The railroad junction is in his jurisdiction and it'd be a big help if he could either notify security there or send a unit out in the event our suspects have already decided to run."

"Got it."

"I suppose Alfie's still playing house at the Walcott, huh?"

"Last I heard."

"Well, tell him the party's over," said Howser. "I want to see him downtown in five minutes."

"Okay."

Howser switched off the intercom and got up. He found the keys to the black-and-white and went back to the window and looked out. Across the street, a soft wind fanned the trees in the park. He could see the branches stirring slightly through the shadows. The grass, still moist from the sprinklers, glistened under the streetlights, and fallen leaves, wet also, shuddered and blew. The park was quiet but outside of town there were sirens wailing, and he wondered, *Would there be fugitives now, too?*

Jack Clayton sat at a booth in a downtown diner picking over dessert, a stale slice of strawberry pie, with a crooked fork. He, his waitress, and the fat cook in back were the only ones left in the place. Everybody else had gone across the street to join the large crowd gathering in the parking lot of City Memorial hospital—apparently a local girl had been raped by the transients who camped out near the river. Clayton's waitress, a homely redhead in her forties, had tried to sneak out, too, but had been nabbed at the door by the cook. They'd argued there for a couple of minutes, then retired to the kitchen together to tell off-color jokes and laugh like giddy teenagers. Clayton swallowed another piece of pie and watched the traffic running slowly by outdoors.

After leaving the Walcott Hotel at ten thirty, he had headed downtown. The sidestreets of Rivertown were silent and unlit but Clayton had walked along as though he had lived there for years and had each neighborhood committed to memory. Entering an alleyway off North Street, he'd heard music coming from an open window and saw a short man singing along with the radio at a kitchen sink. Next door, a green nite-light glowed in an upstairs bedroom betraying the outline of a child's face pressed to the screen. Farther down the alley and beyond, where porch lights were extinguished and the houses dark, Clayton had imagined hundreds of small-town people fast asleep dreaming peaceful and rosy small-town dreams. He'd crossed town alone in the moonlight, the scent of honey-suckle and nightblooming jasmine wherever he went. In the dark, the town looked pretty. The angles of light in the trees and the perfectly cut shadows in doorways and eaves and latticed gateways flattered like a simple portrait in white and black. It seemed so pretty, in fact, that Clayton had wondered, as he walked, how Rivertown would appear in the daylight. He'd seen so many towns, at night-time looking like picture postcards, exposed at sunrise heat-shrunken and bleached, weathered to an impossibly ugly midsummer drab. And he'd spent weeks in those places marveling how complete the transformation could be, how quickly and shamelessly the carriage could revert to a pumpkin by daybreak. Now he'd been walking for almost an hour and still the night sky was hidden by dense old shade trees leaning over the sidewalks, only enough light filtering through to convince him there were stars up there somewhere. Black grass crickets chirruped. *The Tonight Show* played low in blue bedrooms. Then five more blocks in the fragrant dark and Clayton had crossed out under the streetlights along North Main where he'd found Andy's Grill and had his first decent meal in a week.

Now two police cars entered the hospital parking lot. The crowd parted to let them through. Clayton got up from the table, left a tip next to his plate, and took the check to the cash register. The waitress came out of the kitchen to ring it up for him.

"Seven forty-six, please." He handed her a ten-dollar bill. "Out of ten." She opened the register and gave him his change.

"Thanks."

Clayton pocketed his change and walked outside. There was more traffic. He stood on the curb waiting for a dusty station wagon, a Dodge Dart, and a Mazda pickup to pass before he crossed. None were moving better than fifteen miles an hour. He looked behind him and noticed the waitress and cook sitting at the window inside, observing the growing crowd—well over a hundred now. Over-head, the diner's lighted neon winked yellow and green. When the street cleared, Clayton ambled across toward emergency.

They were becoming restless. An hour had gone by since the girl had been brought in from the woods and nothing new had occurred. How long were they supposed to wait? The engines were still running in about half of the thirty or so vehicles parked haphazardly around the lot; conversation was inevitably loud and pointless ("Nothing that man does surprises me anymore" . . . "Do you like it? I got it on sale" . . . "Hell, I'll kick his ass any day of the week" . . . "You bring anything to eat?"). There were a few women about, mostly younger, dressed in cotton blouses and skin-tight blue jeans and colored tennis shoes, each looking like somebody's kid sister. Four perky blondes sat shoulder-to-shoulder in the cab of a half-ton Chevy pickup laughing themselves silly over a rude, sexy joke one had heard earlier in the evening. The men, standing by stiff-legged and bored, apparently failed to share the same humor. Many had come in off the countryside, straight out of bed half-asleep or fresh from the embrace of a familiar, accommodating lover, and none looked thrilled; it was long past midnight and a little late for a tailgate party.

Nor did they pay any attention to the stranger killing time with the rest of them. Jack Clayton drifted in their midst with the cigarette smoke and the country-and-western music piped in from radio station KRAK Sacramento. His Levi's and denim work shirt, the scruffy beard and the dark, allowed him to appear part of the crowd. Walking casually about, listening to the talk and admiring the shiny chrome tailpipes and rollbars on a couple of those new four-by-fours and the fancy pinstriping on that blue '68 Mustang fastback by the sidewalk, he made eye contact with a pretty brunette wearing a green-and-white high school varsity sweater who smiled coyly (so he imagined), and held her smile even as he moved on.

A third patrol car, light bar blazing red and blue, pulled into the driveway, forging a path through the crowd. Clayton recognized the thin police officer who climbed out of the cruiser from the lobby of the Walcott Hotel. The cop rushed through the double doors, chased into the hospital by catcalls and insults laced with laughter. Clayton walked around the perimeter of the crowd and slipped under a metal railing to the right of the entrance. He quickly saw why the crowd was milling about outdoors rather than inside the building where, presumably, all the action was. A pair of young security guards stood elbow-to-elbow at the hospital entrance, one of them talking to a woman at the front of the crowd, the other gazing out across the parking lot, seemingly indifferent to the conversation taking place beside him. An old green-and-primer GMC flatbed and a yellow International Scout with the roof sawed off drove up out of the dark and stopped at the curb. The brunette in the varsity sweater dashed over to the Scout and leaned in through the passenger side to give the driver a kiss. An air horn went off somewhere back behind the crowd causing a shriek and more laughter.

"Tom come out yet?"

The voice startled Clayton. Just off to his left stood a short, stocky man in a Giants baseball cap, a greasy red T-shirt and an old pair of brown corduroys; the skin on his face was dark with shiny beads of sweat. He spoke again, "Tom still inside?"

Clayton, eyes fixed on the two security guards, had no idea what the guy was talking about. Before he could ask a third time, Clayton shrugged and answered, "I don't know."

An engine raced at the rear of the lot and somebody shouted an obscenity. Part of the crowd had spilled out into the street now, forcing passing cars to slow in the southbound lane.

"Gonna be a hell of a party."

Clayton looked at him and the guy grinned and took a pack of cigarettes from his back pocket. He offered one to Clayton. Clayton shook his head and the guy lighted one for himself and blew a nice round smoke ring into the air. "Yeah," he repeated, "hell-of-a-par-ty," accentuating each syllable.

The neon sign above the diner winked once more, then went out for the night. The shade was drawn down in the glass door. A few minutes later Clayton's waitress emerged. She checked her makeup briefly then stepped off the curb, and was nearly run over by a northbound LTD. The driver punched a fist into the horn and swore at her. She waved, sheepishly, and hurried on into the crowd.

"You ever met the chief?"

Clayton shook his head again. The door to emergency was open partway now and one of the guards was talking to somebody on the inside.

"Nice fella." The guy laughed. "He-is-going-to-shit-his-pants, though, when he gets wind of this."

At the hospital entrance, the security guard nodded and pointed to his wristwatch and the door swung shut once more. Another truck engine roared in the back of the lot. The girl in the varsity sweater was alone again out on the sidewalk, now with a near-full bottle of beer in her hand. She sat down on the curb, her back to the security guards, and began sipping the beer. A black sedan went by. The girl's hair blew in the draft. Behind her, the hospital door opened just long enough to allow a tall man in a dirt-brown Stetson out into the front of the crowd. He spoke briefly with somebody there then reentered the hospital, squeezing between the two guards. When he came out again half a minute later, he nodded once to the person waiting for him at the door then made a wide circling motion with his right hand in the air above his head. This produced a great roar throughout the parking lot. Immediately, the crowd began breaking up, hustling toward the pickups and the larger flatbeds. Engines seemed to turn over everywhere at once, filling the night air with exhaust. Traffic out in the street came to a reluctant halt as the hospital parking lot cleared, one vehicle at a time. Starting away from Clayton, the man in the Giants cap took one final drag off the cigarette he'd been smoking and flicked the butt to the pavement, then asked, "Got a ride?"

Upstairs on the hospital's second floor, where the corridors smelled of industrial-strength disinfectant and the fluorescent lighting in the ceiling panels tinted the white walls a pale electric green, a gathering of another sort had taken place. Howser stood outside room eighteen on the north end of the building waiting for Sarah Miller's girlfriend

Annie to finish her visit. He had allowed her to go in ahead of him for a few minutes, hoping she might relax Sarah enough to make his own visit easier if not more productive. Three doors away, Officer Alfie Cox whispered with Sarah's parents. They were both obviously upset, yet also looked distracted and distant. What was their daughter doing in this place? Why wouldn't anybody give them any answers? What the hell was going on? Farther down the corridor, past the nurses' station and the elevator, seven dusty teenage boys sat crammed together on one long brown leatherette couch, trapped uncomfortably in heated conversation with Officers Harris and MacAlister. Howser checked his watch. It was almost one o'clock.

At five after, the blond teenager came out sobbing and ran off down the corridor. Sarah's mother tried to stop her but failed. Before the sound of the girl's running footsteps had faded away, Howser entered the room. It was nearly dark inside, the only light coming from the small table lamp by Sarah's bed. With the windows closed to the outdoors, the familiar medical odor of wrapping gauze and bandages and alcohol made the air in the room stuffy to the point of nausea. Howser watched the girl settle in the sheets, barely moving from the position she had assumed on the gurney downstairs in emergency. She lay with her head facing the closed door, eyes cheerless and blank. Howser walked over to the bed and stood there a few moments before beginning with the questions his job demanded he ask. He knew she had been waiting for him. The vacant gaze she held on her face was for him, though she was refusing just then to acknowledge his presence at her bedside. He tapped her lightly on the shoulder. She blinked. He touched her again and her eyelids flickered briefly below her bandaged brow.

"Sarah?"

She tilted her head slightly, staring now at the cream-colored fan rotating slowly clockwise overhead.

"Sarah, what happened out there tonight?" he asked. "Who hurt you?"

She bit on her lower lip where the skin was lacerated and swollen, tasting the blood. Howser repeated his question: "What happened, Sarah?" She avoided his eyes and did not speak. That was fine. He could be patient. He knew how to wait, though he would not leave without getting some sort of statement. Ten stacks of reports from a hundred eyewitnesses were never a substitute for even a few words from a victim. She shifted in the sheets and averted her gaze from the ceiling fan to the front wall where the silent television set mounted there stared back at her.

"Sarah?"

When she spoke it was with a dull, almost guttural masculine tone.

"Ask Jamie," she said. "He knows."

"I already did."

"And what did he say?"

Even in the near-dark Howser could see the deep bruises on her face and neck. "He told us some railyard tramps did it, that they attacked you in the woods."

"That's right," she said. "Uh-huh. It was tramps. They grabbed me, beat me up, and raped me. In the woods. That's exactly what happened."

"How many of them were there?"

"How many did Jamie say there were?"

"I'm asking you, Sarah."

"Well, to tell you the truth, I forgot to count. How stupid of me." Her eyes moistened. "There were a lot of them." Tears welled up and ran on her cheeks. "Do you have any idea what that feels like? Any idea at all?" She looked away. "It hurt *so* bad." She began to cry.

Howser looked out through the window at the warehouse on the corner. "I'm sorry," he muttered. "I don't enjoy this any more than you do." He lowered his eyes to Sarah again. "But we need your help. Understand?"

She nodded, freeing more tears. "Sure," she replied. "I understand. Of course I understand." She feigned a smile. "Do you?" Then, before he could answer, she rolled over, putting her back to him, cutting him off. He watched her slide crying under the sheets where she appeared smaller, more vulnerable than before, as though the effort of talking had literally deflated her. Trying to hide, she looked more like a child than ever. Howser walked out of the room.

Four miles outside of town, where the great silent acres of dry grass west of the river stirred under a stiff breeze, a long procession of trucks made its way north up the county road. Riding in the rear of one of the flatbeds, Jack Clayton stood with his ribs jammed against the sideboards and his head hung out into the wind. His was the last truck in the column, so there was nothing to see but the road disappearing behind in the dark. Leaning out, watching it go, smelling the dusty hay-scent on the draft, evoked in him an old memory of wagon rides at summer camp and city children singing by firelight in a distant canyon. Talk had quieted considerably since they had left the town limits, and the laughter had diminished. Most of the men were armed with shotguns or hunting rifles, weapons they gripped tightly, barrels pointed toward the stars. There was no traffic coming from the north so the trucks drove down the center of the road using the white line as a guide. The flatbed lurched on the bumps but the men were packed so closely together they had little trouble keeping their balance. The radio was on in the cab and one of the men sitting up front had an arm stuck out the window and was banging rhythm on the door panel with his knuckles. Three riders near Clayton shared a fifth of Jack Daniel's and bitched about the lateness of the hour. Somebody closer still was smoking a cigarette. At every bump in the road, glowing ash, like fiery sparks aloft, flew past Clayton's face. A porch light almost a mile away to the west shone like a faint star in the open field. Riding along, gripping the sideboards with his fingers, ignoring the swirling cigarette smoke and the muttered conversation and the loaded weapons, Clayton watched the light flicker and gradually diminish as the trucks slowly crossed the valley and passed on into the woods near the river.

The flatbed braked, then listed into a turn. He dug his fingers into the wood to hold on. The trucks were leaving the highway now, angling onto a service road; he could hear the tires crunching and sliding on a gravel surface.

They descended a short grade. The transmission howled and the truck bumped hard over a rut and Clayton heard somebody fall in the flatbed. He looked up in time to see an empty Jack Daniel's bottle, hurled at close range, shatter against a tree trunk. Overhanging branches scraped the roof of the truck. The riders ducked as the trucks rumbled forward. Somebody belched. The twin chains dangling from the tailgate, holding it shut, banged erratically on the undercarriage. The road widened and the trucks sped up. Clouds of exhaust filled the woods. Conversation had slacked off in the flatbed but up ahead in the forward trucks loud voices still echoed in the trees. The breeze was cooler here and Clayton supposed they were close to the river. A fistful of .00 shotgun shells clattered to the floor of the flatbed and rolled about underfoot. The trucks passed a bent and tarnished aluminum signpost reading: GREEN RIVER DEPOT. Tacked onto it was another sign: CLOSED. Overhead, the trees were opening up again now exposing a clear black sky. Night birds darted shadowlike beneath the stars. The trucks came out of the woods and rolled up onto a long unbroken stretch of pavement. Wild grass blew in the draft. Someone in the cab switched off the radio. In another truck, somebody whistled. A quarter of a mile up the road, a car horn sounded in the dark. The driver in the lead truck, a red Chevy Blazer no more than five hundred yards now from the railyard gate, flashed his high beams and shifted down two gears. A second horn echo followed. He hit his brakes and one after another the line of trucks behind him rolled to a gradual stop on the warm pavement, engines idling. A moment later, two uniformed men, both of them armed, came walking out of the darkness ahead grinning and waving flashlights.

Loose garbage blew across the empty hospital parking lot. The last car had long since driven off. The street, too, was quiet. The town had all but closed up for the night. Only the dogs stayed out. Howser stood under the light at the door to emergency, watching two of them chase a torn and empty paper bag into the road.

"I told you," said Alfie, stepping out into the lot and

closing the hospital door behind him. "Everybody's gone."

"I can see that," replied Howser, his eyes fixed hard on the dogs. They had caught up with the bag now on the sidewalk across the street and were ripping it apart. "I don't suppose it occurred to you to let me know they were leaving."

"You were still talking to Sarah."

"Yeah?" asked Howser, walking over to the cruiser parked at an angle beside Alfie's in the emergency driveway. "So?"

"So, you told us not to disturb you."

He leaned inside his car, grabbing the mike. "I appreciate the consideration." He switched it on. "Jane?"

The dogs had stopped clawing at the paper bag, their attention shifted to a point farther up the street.

"Go ahead, Chief."

"You better tell Craig and Dennis to expect some company."

"They just called in. Company's arrived."

Howser dropped the mike to his waist and looked at Alfie. "Did you hear that?"

"No, what'd she say?"

"They're already there."

"Oh."

The dogs were running now, chasing up the road into the next block, barking at something there in the dark. Howser climbed into the unit and pulled the door closed. He rolled the window down and gazed out across the parking lot, the mike resting in his lap. It was getting late now. He was feeling drowsy, and his feet hurt. His bedtime had come and gone a couple of hours ago. Alfie walked over to the car and leaned against the front fender. Howser, fighting off the desire to nap right there in the front seat, picked up the mike again. The wind gusted across the lot.

"Jane? Are you still there?"

"Yes, go ahead."

"I'm leaving for the railyard right now. Call Craig and Dennis back and let them know I'm coming. Remind them that under no circumstances are they to allow *anybody* inside that gate." Howser looked directly at his officer while starting the engine. "Alfie's going to follow me out

52

to the river. When Corey and Beef finish up with the kids' statements, send them out, too. And wake up another one of the reserves. We're going to need someone to take patrol for a couple of hours."

"Okay."

"I'll call in again when I get out there."

Then he signed off and hung the mike back on the dash. Alfie came over to the window. "You think the guys'll be able to keep 'em out until we get there?"

"Is there any way we can reach the yard in five minutes?"

"Nope."

"There's your answer," replied Howser, and he dropped the gear lever into reverse and backed past Alfie out into the empty road. Then he switched on the light bar, put the transmission into drive, pointed the cruiser north, and slammed his foot down on the accelerator.

Most of the small skillet fires were doused when the first trucks crossed the old railroad tracks into the Green River yard. Nobody there bothered to run. The glare from the headlamps flooded the camp like klieg lights at a Hollywood premiere while the raggedy men stood wordlessly by in the smoke and shadows. As the column rolled in, each truck took up a position in a wide arc east to west at the southern perimeter of the yard blocking exits back to the service road and the railroad tracks toward the old boxcars and the open countryside and the river. From the west to the northeast, a quarter mile of ten-foot cyclone fence separated the yard from the woods. Tailgates were sprung as the trucks came to a halt, letting the riders in the flatbeds down into the dust where they took up positions in a loose skirmish line across the yard. The drivers left the engines running to keep power up for the headlights. The tramps did not move.

Somebody's supper had apparently been cooking when the column roared up the road—the odor of burnt food was still strong in the camp. It carried with the rising smoke beyond the trucks and the headlamps. Sitting alone on the fender of one of the half-ton pickups, Jack Clayton recognized the smell of fried onions and kidney beans or badly overcooked Texas chili. Not much of a meal but a lot more filling than a cup of coffee and a cigarette. He watched the tramps, caught in the dust and glare outside of their canvas tents and tarpaper lean-tos, faces dry and expressionless like those of seasoned scarecrows. Familiar faces, too, somehow—even from a distance. Faces he'd seen all over America the past few years, wherever he'd looked.

Clayton slid off the fender and took a walk in the shadows behind the trucks. Through the spaces between trucks, he watched the tramps framed in the light. A few of them were sitting now and he noticed their hands wrapped tightly about valuable possessions: bedrolls, packs, burlap sacks, coffeepots, jugs, slender brown paper bags—items not quickly surrendered to anyone. As he watched, one of the tramps came forward into the middle of the yard and started yelling at the men on the line. Shading his eyes from the glare of the lights with his right hand, the tramp gave them the finger with his left and grabbed at his crotch, then unbuckled his pants and mooned them. Though most of the men laughed, Clayton saw more than one dummying a shot at the angry tramp.

The cops from the gate walked past, heading down the railroad tracks to where the closest group of boxcars loomed in the dark. Clayton stayed with the trucks long enough to let the two of them get a short lead, then trailed along behind. Forty yards from the tramp jungle, the noise from the trucks was cut in half. He could just hear the cops' shoes now in the dirt and gravel up ahead. The tracks ran three or four hundred yards east into the black, intersecting the old freight graveyard of deserted boxcars, cattle cars, grain cars, flatcars: iron and wood dinosaurs shrouded in starlight. Somewhere near that first group of boxcars, he lost sight of the two cops. One second they were in front of him, walking side by side, the next they were gone. He stopped and listened. A breeze was starting up and it swept high in the woods a hundred feet or so off to his left. He took another few steps forward, convinced the cops were close by. Dust swirled at his feet. He stared at the boxcars staggered apart on parallel tracks. The cargo doors were rolled wide open for anyone to crawl right up inside and make themselves at home if they so desired. A horn blew in the air and the echo carried down the tracks. Clayton looked back in the direction of the camp. From a distance, the bright glow of the camp, and the darkness surrounding it, reminded him of the setting for that great last scene in the movie *Close Encounters of the Third Kind*.

Then he smelled a cigarette burning and knew for certain *somebody* was nearby. Clayton walked quickly to the first boxcar and slipped underneath it, hoping to get a better view of the yard from the train cars to the woods. Just as he got situated, something much more interesting than cigarette smoke caught his attention. There were voices now or, rather, one firm voice coming from somewhere near two big cattle cars parked on an amputated section of track forty yards from the woods.

Sliding out from under the first boxcar, Clayton crossed the gravel between tracks to the corner of the second car where he paused to listen again. The location of those two cops still concerned him. He assumed they were over by the cattle cars, but that was not an absolute certainty and he had no desire to get arrested for trespassing (or whatever they'd decide to call it) and end up spending the night in the tank downtown with the local drunks. He looked down the tracks to the east and got an idea. The corridor between boxcars was empty far into the dark. He walked to the end of the car, took a quick look around, then cut across the railyard in the direction of the woods. Halfway to the cyclone fence, he circled back along the ties and ducked in under a flatcar just up the track from the cattle cars. He looked out. Standing less than thirty feet away, facing the two cops, was the same tall guy in the dirt-brown Stetson Clayton had seen at the hospital. This close, he looked older than he had back in town. Even in the moonlight, Clayton could see the liverspots and budding skin cancers on his face and hands. He had a cigarette in his right hand now that was burning down to the filter as he spoke:

"One other thing—don't try to bullshit him, all right? Just go ahead and admit you fucked up. Tell him you got scared and didn't know what else to do. He'll believe you because he'll be thinking the same thing himself."

"He's going to kill us," said one of the cops.

"After he cans us," said the other.

"No, he won't. He knew you wouldn't be able to handle this by yourselves. He'll just assume it was his own fault for not sending some help out a little earlier." The guy in the Stetson dropped the cigarette butt into the gravel and rubbed it flat with the heel of his boot. "Think of it this way if it'll make you feel any better: He's not paying you guys to be heroes. We all know that. You did the best you could. Things just got out of hand."

A siren could be heard now wailing faintly in the distance, still somewhere out on the county road, but coming fast.

"That's him."

A flurry of dust kicked up along the tracks. The guy in the Stetson drew another cigarette out of his shirt pocket, waited for the breeze to die down again, then lighted up.

"All right, why don't you two go ahead and get back to the camp. I'll follow you in a few minutes." He flung the spent match into the dirt. "Have Ed look for me, too. Tell him I'd like to talk to him before he sees the chief."

"Yes sir."

Then the two cops disappeared into the dark. After they'd gone, the tall man removed his hat and took a drag off the cigarette and exhaled the smoke into the night air. He stared blankly at the sidewall of the cattle car. When he'd finished his cigarette, he dropped the smoldering butt into the gravel next to the other one, put the Stetson on his head, and followed the cops back toward the camp.

Clayton slipped out from under the flatcar. The siren had quit finally, leaving the railyard quiet again; a light wind rustled in the grass nearby. He headed back across the open tracks between train cars toward the south section of the yard. Halfway there something to the east caught his attention and he stopped. A bedroll landed in the dust by one of the boxcars. A couple of seconds later two big burlap sacks dropped to the ground beside the bedroll. Clayton sunk to his haunches and watched three dark figures appear in the long doorway of the boxcar. One after another they climbed down into the yard and looked around. Then, apparently deciding it was clear, they grabbed up their things and hurried off down the tracks.

He knew where they were headed—the junction, which meant transportation out of the area. That was smart. By morning, they'd be out of the state. Twenty-four hours after that, halfway across America, jumping off into another empty railyard on the darkened outskirts of another small town or city. He smiled. That's how it always was: no place would ever be home, but neither would anywhere else be too far away.

The carnival of lights was visible clear down to the service road, but for some reason the brilliant glow above the treeline failed to register on Howser until he'd already passed through the front gate and was halfway up to the camp. That's when he cut the siren and brought the unit to a stop. Alfie hadn't prepared him for what was on the high ground up ahead: twenty or thirty vehicles parked side by side, headlamps and spotlights glaring, dozens and dozens of armed civilians wandering about doing who-knows-what to the vagrants up there. The light bar on his own vehicle was still operating but he doubted anybody was paying attention. He shook his head: describing this as a colossal screw-up would be an understatement. Where were the two reserve officers he'd stationed out here? Their unit, a white Dodge, sat down by the gate, keys still in the ignition, emergency flashers running. He got back on the radio and called in.

"RP1 to base."

In the rearview mirror he saw a pair of headlights coming up the road behind him and hoped they belonged to Alfie. His patrolman wasn't using the light bar but the grill configuration resembled a Rivertown police car.

"Go ahead, Chief."

"Jane, it looks like we've got a situation out here."

"I know, but Corey and Beef ought to be there anytime now."

"Yeah, well, we may need a little more backup than that. I'd like you to put in a call to county dispatch advising them of our situation. I'm not sure that we're going to need anyone, but I don't want this getting any farther out of hand than it already has."

57

The unit Howser had been watching in the mirror came up through the gate and stopped behind his own. Alfie got out. Howser waved at him, showing him the mike; Alfie stayed by the car.

"I'd also like you to wake Doc up for me, if you could. He'll understand. Have him wait for us downtown. Alfie's here now so the gate'll be closed after I sign off. Let everyone know they'll be parking down on the road and coming up on foot."

"All right."

"Thanks, Jane."

He stuck the mike back on the dash and climbed out into the road. "Alfie, you drive like an old lady."

"Sorry."

"We're going to close the gate and seal off the road," said Howser, walking past his patrolman. "We'll use your unit here as a roadblock. You can ride up to the yard with me."

Howser went down to the gate, kicked the rock out that was holding it open, and let it swing closed. Then he latched it and refastened the padlock his two reserves had unlocked. Meanwhile, Alfie was positioning his car sideways in the road, preventing anyone from driving past without first entering the thicket on either side. Howser returned to his own car and started the engine. Alfie caught up with him and slid in on the passenger side. Then they drove the last hundred yards or so up the road into the Green River railyard.

Idling truck engines droned from one end of the camp to the other where the armed men stood silhouetted in the dusty light. Leaving Alfie to monitor the radio, Howser got out of the unit and slammed the door. As he searched the yard for his two delinquent reserves, a familiar face appeared out of the darkness to the east.

"Evening, Chief," said the tall man in the dirt-brown Stetson, striding down the slope toward the cruiser.

"How're you doing, Tom?"

The two of them shook hands. Even at sixty-two, Danielson had a grip that easily matched his six-foot-four frame.

"Just fine, thanks. Yourself?"

"Well, seeing as how it's four hours past my bedtime and I'm still on my feet, I guess I'm doing all right."

"That's good."

Howser watched the flashing red and blue light color Tom Danielson's mottled face in stroboscopic patterns. "Mind telling me what's going on?" he said. "What are all these people doing out here?"

"They're friends of mine, Chief. I invited them."

"Why?" asked Howser, keeping one eye on the lookout for his officers.

"Ed Miller's girl got raped out here this evening. Some of the people responsible for it are in that camp up there and we're going to make sure they don't go anywhere until we can identify them."

"And just how are you planning to do that?"

A man wearing a camouflage hunting jacket and cap strolled up out of the shadows. His face was dark and streaked with sweat and his watery eyes blinked uncontrollably. Howser nodded at him. "Hello, Ed."

" 'Lo, Chief," the man said. "Did you talk to my girl?"

"Yes, I did."

Ed Miller wiped a jacket sleeve across his forehead and glanced at Alfie, who was still waiting patiently inside the unit, radio in hand. The patrolman looked up and gave him a wave but Miller didn't notice.

"Did she tell you what they looked like, the ones that did it?" he asked.

"No, she didn't, Ed," replied Howser, feeling the tingle in his chest now, the sort of thing he got whenever his nerves began kicking up. "I'm sorry but she couldn't give us much at all in the way of a description. Then again, your daughter's pretty beat up, so I'm not really expecting her to be much help for at least a couple of days or so."

Danielson removed the Stetson and placed a hand on Miller's shoulder. "Why don't you go back to the truck, Ed. Tell the boys I'll be along shortly." Miller smiled weakly at Howser and strolled off again into the long shadows behind the trucks. After he'd disappeared, Danielson turned back to Howser and said, "Ed Miller's a good man, Chief. I've known him a long time. Most of the men here tonight count Ed among their closest friends. It's my impression that if he asked, they'd do just about anything for him. But—"

Howser interrupted him. "Look, Tom, let's get something straight. I don't care whose friends these people are or why they came out here tonight. Fact is, I don't need thirty carloads of gun-carrying idiots to help me carry out an assault investigation. I don't work that way. Understand? These people don't belong out here. None of them. I want you to send them home, Tom. Okay? Send them home and let me do my job."

Two more police cars were approaching from the lower road now, light bars flashing, engines cranking hard. Any second now, they'd be at the gate.

"Nobody's trying to do your job for you, Chief."

"Like hell they're not!"

"Anyhow, it seems to me you're missing the point," said Danielson, taking a cigarette from his pocket.

"Oh yeah, and what's that?"

"We're already here, whether you want us or not. And we're not leaving until we're sure things are getting done the way they're supposed to."

Alfie rolled down the car window and stuck his head out. "Corey and Beef are down at the gate."

Howser kept his eyes locked on Danielson while he asked his patrolman, "Are the kids with them?"

"Yeah."

"All right, tell them to come up."

"Right," said Alfie. He ducked back inside the unit and grabbed the mike off the seat.

"What did you think you were going to do out here anyway? Line everyone up at gunpoint and try to scare them into fingering the guilty parties for you? Huh? Maybe shoot a couple for emphasis?"

Danielson walked off into the dark.

Howser kicked the unit's front tire.

Alfie leaned out the window. "What's wrong?" He searched for Danielson and realized he wasn't there any longer. "Where'd Tom go?"

"Never mind," said Howser, staring down the road. "I thought you said those guys were on their way up from the gate. Where the hell *are* they?"

"I don't know. They told me they were coming straight up."

"Which kids did they bring?"

"Ray Maddox, Jerry Hardisty, Roy Lee, and Jamie Danielson."

Howser glanced at his watch. It was almost two. He climbed back inside the black-and-white and took the mike. "RP1 to base. Jane?" He waited.

"Go ahead, Chief."

"What did you hear from county?"

"They'll roll if we need them. Ten minutes tops."

"Okay," said Howser, drumming his fingers on the dash. He looked through the windshield at the trucks and the lights. It was decision time now. Should he call for the backup or hold off? As he saw it, bringing in outside help offered the opportunity for both greater crowd control—more officers to monitor the idiots—and greater trouble. Outside help, regardless of how experienced and professional they were, would have no larger stake in keeping the situation under control than was defined by the job. And they would also be considerably less inclined to show much patience or restraint if things did deteriorate. On the other hand, his own people had grown up next door to the guys up there by the trucks, went fishing with them on the weekends, were teammates in Rivertown's Saturday softball leagues. If push came to shove, there might be a lot of harsh language traded about, but that'd probably be the extent of it. So, did he or did he not ask for help? It was a coin-toss either way he looked at it. The decision was all his. The problem was that he doubted he'd get a second chance.

Corey and Beef were coming up the road now, trailed by four teenage boys. Both patrolmen were carrying flashlights. The kids wore smiles. One was laughing. *Some*body was having fun tonight.

"Chief?"

"Okay, Jane, advise county that we're going to try to handle the situation ourselves, right? But have them stand by. Keep them monitoring. Let them know that if anything changes we'll call them in. I'm going up right now."

He signed off and climbed out of the car. He was still

amazed at how warm the night air felt, even this late. Alfie sat on the hood of the unit, looking up in the direction of the camp. There was sweat on his face and his shirt was damp. Since it wasn't *that* hot out, he guessed Alfie, too, was feeling his nerves.

Officers Harris and MacAlister led the four kids to the unit and parked them side by side along the rear bumper. Howser came around to address them. It was a short speech.

"You don't say a thing when we get up there, understand? You keep your mouths shut and let me do the talking. I'm going to ask each person a few questions. Maybe they'll give each other up, maybe they won't. What I want from you boys is to study their faces, their clothes, the way they talk. The sound of their voices. You don't say a thing yourselves. Nothing. Not a word, got that? No matter what you hear up there, you keep your own mouths shut. Okay? Do you understand?"

He looked straight at Jamie Danielson when he asked the question. All four of the boys nodded, but only Jamie retained the smirk he'd brought with him up the road. Kid's just like his old man, thought Howser. A cocky little son of a bitch. His girlfriend gets raped and he's still having a good time. What a heart.

"Alfie, you stay here with the radio and watch the road." Howser turned to his other two officers. "You guys come with me. Corey, I want you to find Craig and Dennis and post them over there on the railyard end of the camp. After that, you can help me with the interrogation. Beef, you're in charge of crowd control. Keep 'em back by their trucks and keep 'em cool. I can't have a hundred guys with shotguns leaning over my shoulder while I talk to these people. They can sit there as long as they like and do whatever, but I don't want any interference, got it?"

"Got it, boss."

Then Howser waved the kids off the rear of the unit and opened the trunk and took out a bullhorn. "Let's go."

Only a handful of tramps still stood. Leg-weary and blinded by the spotlights, many of the raggedy men were prone in the dust, caps pulled down over their eyes, heads propped up by dirty elbows. Each of the skillet fires was dead now and the smoke dissipated in the dry breeze. Stony faces, passionless and dark, regarded the midnight intruders. Nor was it the guns that held the raggedy men in place. A railyard was a refuge. Even one violated in the night. The sole virtues of true value on the traveling road were patience and a short memory.

"Keep your people back, Tom," said Howser, pushing his way through the line of men into the yard. As Danielson tried to follow, Howser stopped and faced him. "That means you, too."

"Don't tell me what to do."

The light from the headlamps was intense. At this range, it hurt Howser's eyes. He wondered how the people over there by the tents had been able to put up with it for this long.

"You want me to cuff you, Tom? In front of all your fans? Is that what you're saying? Because that's just what I'll do if you try to interfere now." He reached behind and took the cuffs off his belt and held them out to Danielson. "Want to try 'em on? One size fits all."

Howser started away from the trucks. Danielson stayed put. As they broke eye contact, Danielson said, "Don't make any mistakes, Chief. There's a whole lot of people watching."

Beef brought the boys through. Howser hooked the handcuffs back onto his belt and surveyed the camp. Tents and dirt and bedrolls and dirt and people and dirt. A couple of empty brakemen's shacks. High cyclone fence sealing the camp off from the woods. A dense treeline and a black empty sky above. Stars and darkness. Not much of a breeze now. The trucks droned behind him. His eyes fell on the tramps. Like ghosts, he thought, made visible in the white light. Dozens and dozens of ghosts, caught in a crude trap. Calmer than he'd expected them to be. And quieter. It had been years since he'd busted a jungle. He'd always felt awful about it afterward. Rousting drunks and vagrants anywhere wasn't exactly a joy but he despised busting broken people for trespassing on abandoned property.

He waited for Corey, his fingers squeezing the trigger ring of the bullhorn over and over. Directly behind him, the four boys shuffled restlessly in the dust. Farther back, voices were rising. He stared at the tramps across a haze of cigarette smoke. One of the tents. Something about one of the tents. Corey passed through the crowd and came up beside him.

"We're ready, Chief."

Howser nodded once and brought the bullhorn up to his mouth. He drew a last deep breath, and said, "All right, everyone. Listen up. I want—"

At the extreme rear corner of one of the tents directly across the camp from Howser, a canvas flap shook and the tent lurched violently backward. A loud ripping followed and the canvas tore top to bottom. The tent fell open toward the cyclone fence. Somebody burst free into the wire. Two strong hands tugged furiously at the lower half of the fence. Links snapped and shattered. The wire broke apart and the fencing separated from the support pipe. A huge dark form slipped through into the woods.

In the same instant, another figure emerged from the split canvas. As the small baldheaded man crawled out into the light and got to his feet, a cry went out from somewhere behind Howser. "They're getting away, goddammit!"

Before he could utter a word, gunfire erupted simultaneously from every truck along the line. The camp blew apart with a roar. Those unfortunate enough to be caught standing upright in the line of fire were hit immediately and knocked down. Others dove wildly into the dirt or scattered left and right for cover. The tents were shredded with .00 buckshot and high-velocity rifle rounds. Sparks flew where the wire fencing was struck. Bark splintered in the woods. Five tents collapsed in clouds of dust. The burnt odor of cordite smothered the camp. Screams mixed with the blast echoes. Howser's voice, coming to life now and amplified by the bullhorn, became audible above the cries of the wounded.

"Stop shooting! . . . Goddammit! . . . Stop shooting!"

Ten, fifteen, twenty seconds passed in the frenzied roar, Howser shouting repeatedly for a ceasefire. The gunfire was deafening at that range. Officer Harris and the four boys he'd been escorting lay flat on the ground nearby, hands over their ears. Crouching beneath the line of fire,

Howser began frantically waving his arms to stop the fusillade. The glare from the headlights was cut almost in half by the smoke. Beside the tents near the fenceline, all motion had ceased. In half a minute the tramp jungle was reduced to dust and thunder. Then the shooting slowed. Whether from Howser's efforts or the fact of ammunition running low, it suddenly wound down. A few last shots flew into the trees. Spent shells were ejected. The firing stopped.

Howser lowered the bullhorn. "Good God!" Ears ringing badly from the gunfire, he could barely hear his own voice. His eyes swept the yard. People were lying everywhere: some moving, some not. Black stains soaked the clothing of those fallen closest to the wire. Dust and blue smoke hung like haze in the spotlights.

A voice spoke from somewhere nearby, "One of them got away. Somebody go after him."

Danielson again.

Howser turned back toward the headlights. The glare was blinding. He shouted, "Everybody stay put!" Then he called for his officers while searching for movement in the shadow beneath the headlights.

"Everybody stay right where they are. Nobody goes *anywhere* until I say so!"

He looked again at the camp, the scattered bodies and flattened tents, the shocked faces cowering in the dust, the gaping hole in the cyclone fence. "Good God!"

By three thirty a.m. all but one of the ambulances from Rivertown had come and gone. The yard was almost empty. After their release by the police, many of the tramps had wandered off down the tracks toward the junction. Those who had chosen to stay until daybreak sifted among possessions left by the others. Ruined tents lay in the dirt like huge canvas rags. The last of the paramedics shuttled from one small group of tramps to another, treating surface lacerations and mild shock. The caravan of trucks and men and guns had gone. Only the police cars, the City Memorial ambulance and a paramedic van from Sierra Springs remained.

Howser sat in the front seat of his unit monitoring the radio. Alfie poked his head through the open passenger window.

"We've got 'em all squared away."

"How many did they identify?"

"Six," said Alfie.

"That's all?"

"Uh-huh."

"Not counting the wounded and the fatality?"

"That's right."

"How many are up there now?" asked Howser, pointing his pen in the direction of the camp.

"I don't know. Maybe forty or so? I didn't count. Should I go back?"

"No, it's not important. You want to take off?"

"Unless you need me for something else."

"No, go ahead," said Howser. "I'll see you in the morning. Thanks."

"Yep."

Alfie walked off down the road toward the gate. Howser reached across the seat and picked up the notepad he'd been scribbling in and made another note. He rubbed the sweat from his eyes and put down the notepad and watched the last ambulance pull out of the yard, emergency lights blazing. The radio squawked and he flicked it off. His eyes ached and he closed them. All he could think of now was climbing into bed and getting some sleep. Another vehicle pulled up beside the black-and-white. A car door opened and closed; he heard footsteps approaching in the gravel. He assumed it was Alfie until a fist rapped on the roof above his head. When he opened his eyes, he saw Tom Danielson leaning in at the door. Before Howser had a chance to say anything, Danielson announced, "One of them got away."

Howser stared at him, half-disbelieving the man was still there jabbering at him in the middle of the night.

"Did you hear me?"

Danielson's shirt was stained dark with sweat. Its sour odor fouled the unit's interior.

"Thanks," he said, flatly, hoping Danielson would go away. "I'll look into it."

"Maybe you *didn't* hear me." Veins bulged on Danielson's forehead. "I said one of the tramps who raped the girl got away."

Howser wondered whose nightmare he'd just stumbled into—Danielson's, or his own. He straightened up in the seat. "It's my problem, Tom. Not yours."

"I think you ought to go after him."

"I said, it's my problem."

The paramedic van was leaving now. As it drove past the black-and-white, the driver honked. Howser waved in return, then watched it disappear in the rearview mirror. Maybe, if he was lucky, when he woke up in the morning he'd discover the whole evening had been just a bad dream. He started the engine and switched on the headlights. Maybe if he was *really* lucky—

"You're not listening to me."

"Tom?" he said, putting the car in gear. "Go home."

6

For the four days following the shooting at the railyard, Howser shut himself inside his office and waited for the endless assault-with-deadly-weapon reports, coroner's reports, witness statements, ER slips, and civil complaints to descend onto his desk. By the middle of the afternoon of the fourth day, he had cleared off a fairly large space and sat there sorting stacks of paperwork riffled by the electric fan on the filing cabinet. Not that he needed to actually read the reports to know what they said: One female transient and twelve males shot and wounded, mostly shotgun wounds, mostly arms and legs, mostly minor injuries. Of the thirteen, three showed injuries from rifle rounds: one shot through the shoulder, one with a flesh wound just above the right knee, and one (the female) nicked in the ribs. The others had been hit by .00 buckshot in a variety of places. Eight were released from emergency after treatment, five were kept overnight for observation. Ordinarily, this kind of situation would result in legal action on a scale only slightly smaller than Bhopal. Not in Rivertown though, and not with tramps. They'd bitch and moan and threaten like everybody else—but then, after cooling down some, they'd become practical and accept a free ride to the town limits with a few extra bucks in their pockets (courtesy of City Hall), well aware, after all, that they were lucky to be alive.

Of course, the one in the morgue downstairs wouldn't

be complaining at all. The single gunshot wound he'd taken in the neck had settled that. The victim, a John Doe in his mid-to-late sixties, had died more or less instantaneously from a rifle round that severed both the carotid artery and his spinal cord, producing an exit wound the size of a tennis ball. Who fired the fatal shot? Nobody was saying. And with the woods providing a vast backdrop to the camp, there'd be little chance of locating the slug for a ballistics match. Howser could still hear the blast echoes in the air and the startled cries of those caught in the crossfire. He could still see bodies falling in slow motion, torn by steel, falling into the dust. One dead, thirteen wounded. Dozens of others scared out of their minds. A gigantic fuck-up.

Alfie knocked at the door and peeked his head in.

"Chief?"

"What do you need?"

"Got a minute?"

"Sure."

Alfie walked in holding a folder. He slapped it down on the desk in front of Howser and stepped back.

"What's this?"

"Statements from everybody in the trucks."

Howser opened the folder and skimmed the first page. "There's not even thirty names here."

"Twenty-six."

"You're telling me only twenty-six people admitted to being out there? I counted at least eighty myself."

"Well, since nobody's really sure who killed the old guy, nobody wants to say they were there."

"How'd you get this many to sign?"

"Most of the names are guys I saw myself, or ones Beef and Corey talked to. You know, guys we knew were there."

"Look, I need a complete list, okay? For my own record. Officially, the case is closed. We're not pressing charges on the shooting. Christ, we'd be arresting half the town. Just explain to them that the bullet wound in the old guy's neck was made by a round that probably buried itself out in the woods somewhere and the odds against locating it are only a thousand times slimmer than finding a needle in a haystack. So, we're not even going to try to make a match. It's over. I'll be the guy taking the heat. Nobody else."

"If we're not going to prosecute, what do we need the list for?"

"Just get it, all right? Did Corey head out to the river yet?"

"He left about ten minutes ago. I still think the guy must've come out of the woods farther up the tracks and headed for the junction like the other three."

"Except those three got picked up by Sierra Springs and our guy didn't."

"That's true."

"Which means he's still in the area, don't you think?"

"Maybe."

"Right," agreed Howser. "Who knows? Anything's possible, isn't it? Personally, I think the son of a bitch, if he's got any brains at all, is at least four states from here and we're never going to see him again, but let's keep looking anyhow, okay? Just for the hell of it."

"What do you want to do about the guys downstairs?" asked Alfie.

"Spring 'em."

"You read the report?"

"Yeah. Zero-for-six. No blood-semen matches at all. What would you've bet on that?"

Alfie stuck his hands in his pockets and shrugged. "I don't know."

"Neither do I."

"So, we're just going to let them go?"

"Hard to keep people in jail for dressing badly. This report tells me that the suspects we're holding didn't rape the girl. They were at the yard, but they probably weren't the ones who assaulted her."

"Maybe the kids got mixed up when they identified them, huh?"

"You think so?" said Howser, facetiously. "You think we might've been deliberately misled?"

"Well, maybe they were just confused about who they actually saw, you know? It gets pretty dark out there."

"Alfie, I have no doubt those kids are confused. But

that's our problem now, not those guys' downstairs. Just show them the door and thank them for their cooperation. Arrange for any transportation they might need. The sooner we get them out of town, the better."

A driver over on First Street across the park from the courthouse laid into his horn. The noise reverberated through the office windows. Alfie walked to the window and stared outside for a few seconds. The horn stopped. The patrolman glanced at his watch and turned back to Howser. "I was on my way to lunch. Want me to bring you back anything?"

"From Andy's?"

"Yeah."

"How about a cheeseburger and a Coke?"

"You got it."

Alfie closed the door on his way out. Howser got up and went to the window and looked out across the park. The sky was a perfect blue above town. Heat rippled off the roofs. Atop the Bank of America building, the big thermometer read 107. Down on the streets, traffic had picked up considerably in the last day or so. Locals, he guessed, sneaking back into town again. Most of the downtown stores stayed open late now. The drugstore on Main sold record amounts of skin lotions and sunscreens. Sears did strong business in sprinkler heads, table umbrellas, fishing lures and baseballs. Ray's barber shop filled with customers seeking summer haircuts. Only Ed Miller's hardware store had the green CLOSED sign in the window. Word had it that he'd open again at the end of the week, though nobody had seen him in town since Sunday. Apparently he was keeping close to home to look after his daughter. Since being released from the hospital, Sarah had refused to leave her room and there was some concern that she ought to see a professional, a psychiatrist perhaps or a counselor from one of the outpatient clinics in Stockton. She'd showed no interest in the identification and arrest of the six men accused of raping her. Why not? Why didn't she care? In all his experience with rape victims Howser had known few who did not thrill to the jailing of their attacker. In some cases, they'd call the station several times a day for reassurance that the suspect wasn't getting released accidentally. For just that reason, Howser felt he ought to drive out and have another talk with the girl even though Sarah's father had asked that they be given another week alone together. *She needs healing now, by her family.* It was a strange situation, one that bothered him, and what made it worse was the fact that, like everything else connected to Sarah's rape, he was stuck square in the middle of it.

Jack Clayton closed the van door and walked up to the gate. It was shut with a chain and combination lock wrapped around the bolt. The sun glinted off the chrome. The lock was new. Clayton turned it over in his hand. Probably just four days old. He let it go and took a look at the fence, evaluating his chances of getting over it. Not bad, he decided, and grabbed at the wire, hooking his fingers tightly into the mesh. He shook it once. It was firm. He jumped up, scaling it like the pegboard in gym class, hand over hand, until he reached the top where he balanced briefly, the fence swaying beneath him. Then he drew up his courage and swung first one leg then the other over the top and more or less allowed his body to slide down the face of the wire until he struck the ground, rolling onto his shoulder into the dirt and gravel.

When he got to his feet, he slapped the dust from his jeans and examined his fingers. They'd been scraped nearly raw from the mesh but he hardly noticed the pain. He looked up the narrow road. Dust and glare. Weeds growing in the dust. Insects buzzing in the hot sun. He walked up the empty road toward the yard. When he reached the rise and crossed the half-buried railroad tracks, he cupped a hand over his brow and studied the yard. No trace was left of the jungle that had been there five days before. Even the scraps of shredded tents had been carted off. Only the tire marks remained in the thick dust. Otherwise, the ground was bare. It had not looked so barren, so desolate at night. Now, a grader could not have scraped it any cleaner. No wonder they'd been left alone out here for so long. There was only one water faucet he could see and nothing at all resembling a toilet. Maybe they'd dug a pit in one of the two empty brakemen's shacks and used it as an outhouse. He squinted in the sunlight. Even with the proximity to the woods, shade was scarce. And how far was the river? A couple of miles, at least? And the junction? Maybe three or four? In the daylight, with this sun, that would make a long walk. Searching the fence, Clayton noticed the gap in the wire was erased, too. He strolled across the yard to the fence and examined it. Somebody had tied the hole shut with small bands of wire. They'd done a neat job: all the ends twisted tight by a wrench or a pair of pliers. Rivertown police, probably. Or railroad security guards.

Tramps raping a townie. Incredible. He'd never heard of it happening before. Not this close to a community. It had to have been some mistake. Either that or somebody had lied. Regardless of how belligerent tramps might be to each other, rarely would they mix it up with people from town. It didn't take a genius to figure out what a huge mistake that could be. Few communities enjoyed the presence of tramp jungles, even outside the city limits, and invariably sought excuses to drive them out whenever possible. Trouble, then, with anyone from town, especially school-age kids, would be just the excuse they'd need to clear out every drifter within a five-mile radius and, as had happened four nights ago, to do it with a genuine vengeance.

Somewhere off to the north, bird cries echoed across the summer sky. Clayton stood and watched overhead. Nothing. He waited. The echoes faded away. He listened to the air breathe in the heat. Nothing but a long quiet.

He headed east a hundred yards or so across the bleached lot of dirt and brittle grass toward the boxcars shimmering motionless and rusty-red in the afternoon sun. An interminable column of ants were using the same rails he'd followed four nights ago, using them like a great iron highway between the entrance road and the train cars. Flies and yellowjackets crossed in the heat above the tracks.

That night, after the shooting, he'd ridden back to Rivertown with three other men in the back seat of an aquamarine Buick. On the way, they'd pulled over to the side of the road so that the driver could get out and relieve himself. While pissing into the ditch, he'd spoken excitedly about the people he'd shot at—ones he'd missed, and ones he was sure he'd hit. Bragging about it like some weekend softball player reliving recent heroics.

Clayton reached the boxcars and stopped in the shade of the closest one. His four-day-old footprints were still visible in the dust. Or ones he supposed were his. In the daylight, the boxcar loomed even larger than it had at night. Somewhat more dilapidated, too. Rust and weather had been taking their toll season by season, year after year: the SOUTHERN PACIFIC lettering on its outer wall was barely identifiable; the wood siding was gnawed and splintered; rattlesnake grass grew between the iron wheels. He glanced at the other cars nearby and found the same sad prognosis—death by entropy. Neil Young was right: Rust never sleeps.

The boxcar doorway was open and Clayton swung himself up and in. It was cooler inside, though not much. Dirt and birdshit littered the floor. Bent bottle caps were scattered about. Tiny shreds of paper, torn candy-bar wrappers and such, lay here and there. An old green wool blanket, caked in dirt and badly frayed, was bundled in one corner. He walked over and picked it up. He shook it once and pressed it to his nose and found the blanket stinking of sweat and mildew. He dropped it and sat down, back to the wall, facing out. The boxcar still felt familiar, the odor (stuffier than he remembered), the dull brown light, the absence of comfort (the floor was already hurting his butt). When had he last ridden in one? Nebraska, summer of '77? It was coming back quickly now: the dark tramp jungles, the garbage, the boozing, the noise, the anxiety of being on the road, the constant hunger, a fear of sudden violence, paranoia-induced insomnia, the unrelenting fatigue, the daily effort of keeping his confidence up while coming to the inevitable realization that few creatures on the planet manipulate their personal environment more shabbily than does the human being.

Sixteen months he'd spent on the rails, riding with emotional cripples, hiding from railroad cops, scrounging day-old food from the filthy bottoms of dumpsters with other tramps, just surviving. He'd lived with them, ridden with them, and shared—too long, probably—the dubious freedom and frustration of a tramp's poverty. Traveling with wounded strangers back and forth across the country, city to city, jungle to jungle, always on the lookout for part-time work or a one-night flop or, that failing, the schedule of the next freight moving farther on. And what was it about anyway? He'd never found an answer. In the end, he'd wrangled a job passing out leaflets for an Italian restaurant in Berkeley and wound up sharing a basement room in the same apartment building he had occupied during a brief stint at the university six years before. But living on the road had taught him a few things both about himself and the America through which he had moved: as much as he'd wanted to think of himself as an optimist, a believer in the "Dream," he'd discovered instead a dark cynicism within himself about the very people with whom he had come into contact. And worse, wherever he went there seemed to be, in fact, thousands even more desperately cynical than himself. Cynical and angry. Some dangerously so. Sitting now in the boxcar, remembering, made him realize just how filthy and lonesome the whole experience nine years earlier had been.

Using the back of his hand, he brushed loose a layer of dirt from the wood above his head. It fell onto his shoulders and he shook it off. Looking up the side of the wall, he saw sunlight in the cracks at the roof of the car. In the rainy season this boxcar would be damp and cold and ugly. Uninhabitable by normal people. Clayton reached over and grabbed up the blanket, then crawled back to the doorway and dangled his long legs out over the side, something he'd rarely had the nerve to do when he was riding the rails. He stared out into the sunlit yard and played the blanket over in his hands. Bits of dirt fell into the grass below his feet. Why had he come back here? Curiosity? For four days now, he'd been driving around, touring, taking day trips into the foothills and out into the Big Valley. It seemed like he'd been everywhere but back here. Using his fingernails, he picked clean a section of the blanket then moved on to the next. If not curiosity, then what? Something else, something he could not get straight in his mind. The tramps were gone. They had been gone for days

75

now, driven out, kicked out—some more enthusiastically than others. One was dead. Clayton had seen a body four nights ago illuminated in dust and blood. And the other guy, the one who ran? He looked down at the blanket in his lap, a good blanket. He'd had a blanket a lot like it nine years ago. This one still had a few seasons left in it, too. Clayton shoved himself forward off the boxcar and landed softly in the gravel. He folded the blanket and laid it up in the doorway. Shading his eyes again, he looked back across the railyard toward the cyclone fence and thought about the one who'd gotten away. What did it matter? Wasn't the important thing that the town had finally done what for years it had obviously wanted to do? Now a hard sun bleached the grass where only four nights earlier something irreversible had been put into motion.

7

The statements were useless. Howser flung number twenty-three onto the pile. Alfie had fed 'em the questions and they'd fed him the bullshit. He picked up number twenty-four and skimmed it. Burt Kaiser:

> We didn't go up there looking for trouble. We were just seeing to it that nobody got away until you guys took care of things . . . then some of them went and made a break for it . . . we fired over their heads but it didn't do any good . . . I guess one of them got in the way of somebody's gun. . . . It was a bad break. You know?

He tossed the sheet onto the desk and tried number twenty-five. Pete Duff:

> . . . tell you the truth, I didn't even know where the hell we were going until we got there. . . . What was I supposed to do, walk home? We're talking ten miles! . . . I wasn't paying much attention because I didn't even know the girl . . . we smoked, had a couple brewski's, you know . . . fuck it, I said, let's go home. . . . So I'm off taking a piss and suddenly everyone's shooting. . . . It was fucking crazy, but it wasn't my fault. I didn't fire a shot.

Howser flipped Pete Duff's statement onto the desk. What the hell was Alfie thinking when he was taking this shit down? As he reached for number twenty-six, the intercom buzzed. Howser pressed the button on the speaker phone and leaned forward.

"Yeah, Jane."

"Just wanted to tell you I'm going home."

He looked up at the wall clock—it was nine thirty—then at the window. Behind the closed shades, it was dark out. He'd been so busy reading reports and statements, he hadn't noticed the daylight go away on him.

"Oh yeah. Right. Go ahead, Jane. Thanks."

"You need anything before I go?"

"No, I think I'm going to get out of here, too." He pushed his chair back from the desk and stood up. "Wait! Jane?"

"Yes?"

"There is something you could do."

"Shoot."

"Could you leave a note for Corey? Have him call me at home if he gets in from the river before eleven."

"Sure thing."

"And you can have Susan file the paperwork I've got up here, too. I'm done with it."

"Anything else?"

"Is there any way you can hurry Doc up with our John Doe? I'd like the guy ID'd and out of here this week, if possible."

"He sent the dental charts and fingerprints to Stockton this morning. We should hear something from their computer in a few days."

"Good. Tell Doc I owe him a lunch."

She laughed. "I'll make a note of it."

"One more thing. If you can arrange it, I'd like to see the kids again who were out at the yard that night with the Miller girl. And maybe you could try Sarah's folks again, too. I know they've been avoiding us, but we've got to talk to her sooner or later. Can you do that for me? Tomorrow morning?"

"No problem."

"All right," said Howser. "That'll do it."

"Chief?"

"Yeah, Jane?"

"Get some sleep, okay?"

Howser smiled. God bless her. He leaned toward the speaker. "Thanks, Jane. I will indeed."

Half an hour later he pulled the black-and-white into the garage behind the little yellow one-story on the west side he had been occupying since he'd arrived in Rivertown. He got out, locked up and stepped back into the dark beneath the trees, closing the garage door behind him. The light at the back door was burnt out. Big surprise. Even when he was married it was always Kathy changing bulbs, replacing fuses and fixtures, and generally keeping their lives in order. Without her he was a hopeless bachelor, barely staving off domestic indigency. He fumbled with the keys in the dark until he found the right one and opened the door. Once inside he groped his way to the switch over the kitchen sink and turned on the light. The dishes were still where he had left them at eight a.m., egg hardening on the enamel, a burnt crust of toast stuck in the half-empty cup of cold coffee. He pulled the toast out and threw it in the garbage beneath the sink. He poured the cold coffee down the drain and scraped the dried egg from the plate before rinsing it under the faucet in hot water. The phone rang. He reached to his right and lifted the receiver from the hook.

"Hello?"

"Carroll?" The voice was female.

"Here."

There was a pause on Jane Crockett's end of the line. Then, "Um, I was just calling to see if you're okay."

Another pause. This one Howser filled himself. "Thanks, I'm fine. Except for disgusting myself with my own domestic habits, yeah, I'm okay." He leaned over and turned the water off so he could hear more clearly.

"Kathy hasn't called, has she?" asked Jane.

Howser stared out the window into the darkened driveway. "No, she hasn't. But then she never said she would, so I suppose that means I probably shouldn't expect her to. What do you think?"

"I don't know," said Jane. "I just don't like the idea of

you sitting by yourself in the dark, night after night, hoping for a phone call that's already two years overdue."

"Well . . ."

"I hurt for you, Carroll. You know that, don't you?"

He was silent, watching the water swirl down the drain in the sink, trying to understand what she was saying to him, and why she was saying it at all.

"I'm sorry. I just wanted to see if you were okay, that's all."

"I appreciate it, Jane."

"I know you do."

"I should go. Got a mess here to clean up."

"Okay. But call me, please? If you need to talk? About anything, all right?"

"Sure, Jane. I will. Thanks."

"Okay. Otherwise I'll talk to you tomorrow."

The water finished draining completely from the sink basin as he hung up. Leaving the dishes where they were, Howser turned off all the lights and made his way through the dark to the bedroom at the back of the house, where he removed his shoes and belt and lay down. It felt good to be off his feet. He closed his eyes and saw Jane. She always knew when he was feeling the worst. He'd never felt so transparent to a woman before. Not even Kathy had seen into him so clearly. He undid the buttons on his shirt. She was the first person he'd met in Rivertown, introducing herself five minutes after his arrival in town. She'd shown him Green River that very afternoon and brought him home for dinner and sat up with him until two in the morning, talking about everything under the sun—including Kathy. Jane Crockett had helped him find this house. She'd picked out most of the furnishings, helped him set up housekeeping, and cooked the first meal he had ever had in the place. It was a small roast and there had not been so much as a scrap left over for lunch the next day. They became friends immediately, lovers afterward, and still later, when he found it somehow too difficult to forget he was no longer married to Kathy, they stopped sleeping together and settled on a careful friendship that was as awkward at times as it was heartfelt.

It might have been more had it not been for Kathy. She

was always there somehow, hanging in his thoughts. He wondered where she would be tonight. A dozen dark scenarios filled his mind. Somewhere in a bedroom in greater San Jose, she'd be sharing wine and crackers with a guy who'd never put anything on the line in his life. Touching each other. Intimately. He pulled back. It hurt. Even after all the time gone between, it still hurt. He could not imagine seeing her with another guy. Which was one reason he had not returned to San Jose since the day he left. It was his hometown, but he knew now that he might never go back.

But it had changed a lot anyhow. Especially since he'd grown up. When he was a kid, San Jose was still basically a sleepy little town in a quiet valley. That was the place Dionne Warwick sang about. He remembered the orchards and the crop dusters in the summer sky. When he was nine years old, butterflies still flew on the roadside in south San Jose. That was a long time ago and a lot had changed since then. Zoning regulations were overturned. Houses sprang up everywhere. The postwar boom took off like the Communists on the Chinese mainland. Overnight, a world turned upside-down. The Russians set off their first atomic weapon, and the orchards were shoved farther and farther from the center of town, taking the butterflies with them. Television antennae sprouted on rooftops all across the valley, Truman beat Dewey in the dark, the Reds took over Hollywood, and his own mother died alone in a car accident on one of the few remaining shady country lanes in the middle of a beautiful April afternoon. He was at his first Scouts meeting and did not know what had happened until twilight when his father came to get him in the black Studebaker. Neither of them cried much: he, because it was not yet something fully understood, his father because he was unable to allow himself the comfort. Which was something Howser did not see in his father until years later when it no longer mattered. By then, sharing the same house, they were less father and son than roommates: one older than the other, one defeated and the other bored. He had never known his father to be much more than what he was: more often than not sullen and down, suspended on a pair of wooden crutches or a steel-tipped bamboo walking cane. He'd lost his right leg, the strong one, his kicking leg, in the war: blown off and disintegrated during a mortar attack on the second-to-last day of fighting for Kwajalein atoll in early 1944. He'd never let anyone forget the sacrifice he'd been forced to make. *Could've gone to college on a football scholarship, could've been on the team, too. I was pretty good once.*

Davis Howser had wanted his boy in Scouting. He'd signed him up when Carroll was only six and had made him attend every outing. After that, it was hunting and Pop Warner football. It never ended. Nothing could please his father, especially after his mother's death. In high school Carroll went out for football because his father had wanted him to, but when he could do no more than play second string on the freshman squad, he felt shunned at home. On the morning his father expected him to go downtown and enlist in the Marine Corps, he joined the police force. No more comparisons. His father had spent half his life living in a past that had let him down. His son refused to make the same mistake. Thus, he spent every waking minute of Jack Kennedy's thousand days living and breathing squad-car patrols on San Jose's east side. He was drinking coffee in the unit on the day the call came through that the "Big Chief" was "down" in Dallas. Too late to radio for a backup on that one. He cried, but only later on in the evening when he was away from both the force and that one-legged imposter masquerading those days as his father. He drove the Falcon wagon up into the foothills above Hollister and drank a six-pack of Hamm's while listening on the car radio to the NBC news description of Dealey Plaza, the swearing in of LBJ, and the tragedy of Camelot undone. He slept in the car that night and did not get home, in fact, for three days. When he finally did, it was only to find that his father had followed the slain president into the sky. Massive heart attack. The ambulance and coroner had come and gone two days earlier. A note had been pinned to the screen door. It was the first he knew of it. In any event, he discovered that he had run out of tears to shed, even for his father, and what he felt for this death made crying again seem oddly out of place.

Three years later to the day, he made sergeant. Three weeks after that he met Kathy. Good things, his mother had always told him, came in threes. In this case, he hadn't even felt the need to wait for the next surprise: the second had done him quite nicely. When they'd met at that Christmas party, she was a prom queen, six years his junior, a kid. Sweet, though, and considerably less innocent than he. She surprised him in virtually everything she did. She smoked Winstons by the carton, drank tequila sunrises like lemonade, stole lipstick from K mart and drove her father's Impala like she was on the last lap of the Indy 500. She made him play records for her until three a.m. on weekdays, even when they both had to work in the morning. She was in love with the idea of being in love and she infected him with her own fever. They were married in the backyard of a local community center on the morning of the Fourth of July 1968, and rode a 707 to Waikiki at sunset on the same day.

Howser rolled over onto his stomach and hung his head over the side of the bed, staring blankly at the hardwood floor. What kind of marriage had they had? Just like everybody else's—the good and the bad pretty much equally distributed through the years. They had tried having kids. Daniel Edward Howser died in childbirth. The doctor said it was a death from natural causes, but what was natural about a kid not even getting the chance to breathe free, even once? His son. He and Kathy hardly spoke to each other for almost a full year afterward. Yet when they did, it was with none of the harshness and recriminations there might have been. Rather, it was with a kind of resignation to the unknown that they went on with the lives they had made for themselves.

Of course, he was a cop and a cop's marriage always ends in disaster. Right? So everybody told him. Nothing new there. That was fine as a statistic, but in real life it stunk. What it left out was the fact that cops are people too, real people with genuine emotional needs and desires, few of which are satisfied going solo. Living on the dark side every day only makes you yearn for the other, the brighter part, even more. The longer he was on the force the more he came home to Kathy spent and vulnerable, and the greater was his need to have her simply be there with him.

The first night they had lived together as a couple, the night she strung her clothes along wire hangers in his closet, was the best time he had ever had. Moving Kathy into the house he had shared last with his father five years earlier changed the way he thought about everything good and bad in the world he knew. So, when she left him sixteen years later on the eve of their anniversary, the emptiness her departure brought about swelled over him and left him paralyzed both with anger and bewilderment.

He felt the sweat beading up on his brow and wiped it off with the back of his hand. He sat up. The bedroom felt like an inferno. He got to his feet and without even bothering to turn on a light took his clothes off and fell back naked across the bed, hanging his feet at an angle over one end. Lying nude on top of the white sheets in the heat, Howser wondered what would have happened to Kathy and him had it not been for the 7-Eleven fiasco. Would there have been a difference? He could still see those kids drawing down on him, the sawed-off shotgun and the Saturday night special gleaming under the fluorescent lights of that twenty-four-hour convenience store. They were shaking, but not worse than he. And they had him, too. Dead. He'd been a fool not to see them when he walked in. You'd think that at three in the morning on the east side he'd have paid more attention. A customer dead already along the aisle in frozen foods, doughnuts scattered on the floor in front of the cash register. He had not noticed until it was too late to do anything about it. An instant later they'd shot the clerk in the face and turned toward him when Roy Becerra (a kid in his first night out on patrol), coming from nowhere, literally nowhere, took them both out while he, the experienced cop, stood there with his jaw locked permanently open. Humiliated, but still breathing. Thank God for that, huh? His ass was saved by a rookie, but his career, his confidence and credibility were ruined. By the time he realized what he had to do, get out of the city and start over, it turned out that Kathy had already been planning her own escape. *I have a life, too, Carroll, and I can't live like this forever. What do I*

have that's mine? Nothing, that's what. You think every-
thing you do is so God almighty important and all I have
to do is sit around all day waiting for you to come home.
I want something else besides just being your wife. She
wouldn't even wait to see what the people in Rivertown
had to say about his application. *Rivertown, CA, seeks*
experienced law enforcement officer for position of Chief
of Police—that ad he'd seen in the listings, the perfect job
at the right time. But by the time he got it, she was gone
and he had not spoken to her since the afternoon she left.

He rolled onto his back and stared at the ceiling where
a trio of daddy longlegs had stretched a web across the
width of the room above him. He'd knocked it down nine
times already and they'd built it up again. It was a test of
nerves, he decided. And patience. They seemed to have
lots of that. And persistence. Hanging upside down day
after day, doing nothing but spinning webs and waiting for
the dust moths to flutter into the room at night. He watched
the spiders suspended there in the shadows and imagined
they were probably as hot and tired as he was. He closed
his eyes again. The phone. No, he would not. One thought
entered his mind and remained there, circling. *She could've*
called at least once.

Three miles out of town, inside the old green-and-white
Victorian two-story off County Road 18, seventy-nine-
year-old Amy Johnson sat in her chair beside the tall cop-
per lampstand and watched the silvery images of the hour
flicker across the television screen. Beside her, at the bedroom window, the yellowed and cracked shades flapped
noiselessly against the screen where the mosquitoes had
been gathering since dusk. Amy had been alone since supper. She had eaten with her brother and sister at seven
and now they had gone and she had the house to herself
again. She reached forward and changed stations. She
found the late news. Since *Perry Mason* had gone off the
air, the news was all she cared to look at. She leaned over
and poured herself another cup of coffee. She drew the
warm cup to her lips and drank slowly. Though it had been
unbearably hot all evening, she preferred her coffee like

this—lukewarm and mixed with milk. The shades flapped and another face came flickering across the television screen in black-and-white. She turned the volume up and sat back. Only the slightest breeze fanned through the screen and into the room. Sissie and Elrod had left cake in the refrigerator for her midnight snack and she would have some at the first commercial message. It was angel cake with dark chocolate frosting. She'd had only a thin slice with dinner. Afterward perhaps she would take a bath. That might be nice. Sissie and Elrod wanted her to move from the old house in the orchard into Stockton with them, but she would not even allow conversation on the subject. This was her home. Why should she leave it? Amy slid the chair forward and turned the volume up again. She would continue to do so until it sounded right. The set was old and needed to be replaced. Some nights she could hardly hear a thing. Perhaps she would even buy one with color next time. Amy sat back again and listened. There were tornadoes near Joliet. She'd seen a tornado once when she was a little girl.

Somewhere down below her, outside in the dark, a figure moved through Amy Johnson's yard, sliding under the laundry she had hung on the line out back. Had she been in the kitchen just then, the figure would have appeared to her through the window as the swiftest shadow thrown by some big dark bird passing before the moon on an errant crossing of the night sky. But she was not downstairs and she did not notice a thing. A moment later the shadow had gone from her yard and passed away into the darkness toward the south leaving an old cotton blouse, damp and wrinkled, in the grass.

The same breeze fooling with the window shades in Amy Johnson's bedroom tore loose a section of the spiderweb hanging over Howser's bed. By three in the morning, the daddy longlegs were scrambling to make repairs even as the nude figure lying on the white sheets below twisted in a dreamless sleep. It was too hot for dreams, too hot for deep slumber, so the phone that began ringing in the kitchen at four minutes past the hour woke Howser on the third pulse. Sweat burned in his eyes as he forced them open. He leaned over onto his shoulder. The sheets beneath him were damp. The phone rang again. He rolled out of bed. The hallway leading into the center of the house was black as a cave. He entered it on faith, groping his way along the walls until he found the light switch in the living room. The phone rang twice more. *Who the hell calls in the middle of the goddamned night? Kathy? Yeah, sure it's Kathy, right.* On the seventh ring he grabbed the receiver.

"Hello."

"Chief?"

"Yeah. Who is it?" He didn't recognize the voice. Sleep still fogged his mind.

"Uh, Chief, sorry to disturb you."

The voice sounded familiar, though. "Who's calling?"

"Alfie."

Now it made sense. "Yeah, Alfie, what do you need?" Howser switched on the light above the sink and glanced over his shoulder at the stove clock. "Christ, it's three in the morning. What're you calling for?"

"Redmon's Garage, Chief. Out on the north side."

Howser was trying like hell to wake up enough to have a conversation and not having much luck.

"Chief?" asked Alfie. "You still there?"

Howser shifted the receiver to his left ear.

"Yeah, I'm still here. What kind of problem are we talking about?"

"Looks like somebody broke into his shop and went crazy, ripped everything up. Whole place is a mess. All the windows are busted. You got to see it for yourself."

"Okay. It'll take me a few minutes to get dressed. I'll be there as soon as I can."

Howser hung up the phone. *Damn this town*, he thought as he opened the refrigerator and took out a quart carton of Minute Maid orange juice. He drank what was left, then crushed the container and stuffed it into the trash bag beneath the sink. *What the hell's going on out there?*

Even at three-thirty in the morning it was mild out, as though the earth were still giving off warmth absorbed in the daytime. Howser swung into a parking stall on the righthand side of Redmon's service garage and climbed out of the unit. He drew a handkerchief from his top pocket and wiped the perspiration from his forehead. His officers, Alfie and four of the reserves, were lurking in the shadows by the rest rooms, awaiting his instructions. He took a casual survey of the surroundings. The three service-bay doors were closed and the big neon GAS & AUTO sign was out. He looked at the gas pumps; the padlocks were still fastened. That was a break. The last thing the town needed was a big fire. He checked the parking lot. Mike's tow truck was gone, but nothing else seemed out of the ordinary. The trash bin appeared empty. He guessed inside the building it was a different story, otherwise he'd still be in bed sleeping.

"Alfie?"

The figures stirred in the dark and one of them approached. "Yeah, Chief?"

"Where's Mike?"

"He's not here."

"I can see that," said Howser. "Where is he?"

"Don't know. He hasn't been here all evening so far as we can tell."

"Well, did anybody call him?"

Alfie turned around and yelled, "Hey, did any of you guys call Mike?"

Howser shook his head. Some police force he had under him. Very methodical. Painstaking in their pursuit of an investigation. Dennis walked into the light. He said, "I called him twenty minutes ago."

"What did he say?"

"What would *you* say if you got a call telling you someone had trashed your place? He was pissed off. Said he'd be right over."

"Well, then where the hell is he?" asked Howser. As he spoke, a pair of headlights shone up the road behind them, approaching quickly. Howser squinted his eyes, trying to see who it was. As the vehicle closed on the garage, the amber lights on the roof became visible. The blue tow truck swung in off the road and roared past him to a screeching halt in front of the service bays. The words REDMON'S GAS AND AUTO were etched in white on the driver's door. It flew open and a gaunt, gray-haired man in his early fifties leaped out shouting, "What the hell is this shit? Somebody busted into my garage? Who was it?"

Howser intercepted Redmon on his way into the garage. "Mike?"

Redmon shoved past him into the service garage where the interior lights had been switched on by the officers during their initial investigation. Ignoring the rest of the garage for the moment, Redmon went directly to his office and found it smashed open. "Goddammit! Look at this," he yelled, pulling the shattered door off its damaged hinges. "I just got that thing installed six weeks ago. Had my name on it and everything."

Howser entered the garage behind him. Alfie trailed after, walking across into the service bay and jotting information down in a small notepad. Inside the office, Redmon kicked through receipts spilled from a dumped file cabinet. The desk had been rifled, too; all the drawers were on the floor, empty. A floor jack lay on its side in the middle of the room.

"Mike, we're going to need to determine whether this was a burglary or vandalism. Do you keep a list of the tools and equipment you had in the shop so we might know whether anything's missing or not?"

"Hell no," Redmon shouted, leaving the office. "What do I need one of those for? I bought everything in the place myself. I'll know if anything's gone!"

The garage's three service bays were a shambles: an oscilloscope and battery charger were knocked over and the Sun scope's screen cracked, workbenches and tool cabinets were thrown down, old tire irons and shiny Snap-on wrenches and ratchets flung about, particleboard racks pulled down to the concrete floor and their contents—nuts, bolts, screws, headlights, fuses, alternator belts, brake-pads, sparkplugs and socket sets—strewn in broken glass from one end of the building to the other. An oil drainpan and drum had been overturned, splashing one large section of the concrete floor with a heavy brown grease that made walking precarious. Even the old candy-bar vending machine beside Redmon's office had been broken into, its glass viewing panel bashed-in, its contents pilfered.

Howser picked up a torn air filter half-drenched in oil. Redmon stalked by, shaking his head in obvious anger and disgust. Alfie tapped Howser on the shoulder.

"Look up there," he said, directing Howser's attention to the top of the back wall just below the ceiling where the glass in the window panes had been painted an opaque green to seal out the light. "Every single one of them's busted."

Howser tilted his head back and saw the moon shining through one of the broken panes. All the windows were broken; the only painted glass left was around the frames. He put the air filter down and said, "Alfie, go around back and see if you can find what was thrown through those windows."

The patrolman dropped the crankcase he'd picked up. It struck with a heavy metallic thud on the concrete.

"Sure thing."

Redmon was refastening a length of heavy chain to an engine block lying in the pool of oil. Howser approached, smiling weakly.

"Some mess you got here, Mike. Any idea who might've done it?"

"You think I'd be standing here"—he tugged on the chain, raising the Dodge 318 V-8 a few feet into the air and suspending it there in the sling—"if I had any idea at all what sons of bitches did this to my shop?"

He walked off toward another corner of the garage, wiping his hands with a dark rag. Howser scraped a glob of crusted oil off his left shoe with a pair of pliers and followed behind. Redmon gave a kick to the spilled oil drum as he passed it; more black fluid oozed out.

"Sons of bitches! I'll kill whoever it was did this to me. I'll break their fuckin' necks. Look at this place!"

Both of them stared at the expensive carnage of auto-motive tools and equipment that mixed with thousands of shards of broken glass littering the oily floor. Alfie stepped inside the doorway and motioned to Howser. The chief nodded. Redmon lifted the oscilloscope from the floor and pushed it over against the workbench. He wiped some oil off and stared at it.

"Don't go anywhere, Mike. I'll be right back."

"Where am I going to go?" Redmon angrily hurled the rag at the Snap-on toolchest. "Who else's going to clean this up?"

"I'll be back in a few minutes."

Howser went out behind the garage to where his men were searching in the grass aided by the light from indoors shining into the backyard through the four broken windows. Redmon's Garage fronted a wooded knoll that sloped down from a grassy stand of live oaks toward the road. Two of the reserves, Dennis and Al, were working the knoll, raking the rattlesnake grass by hand up into the dark beneath the oaks. The other two, Craig and Archie, had traded ends of the yard, searching the shadowed flanks with flashlights. The grassy dust beneath the four windows had been showered with fragments of smashed glass. Apparently the windows had been broken from the inside. Twice as much broken glass as lay soaking on the cement floor of the garage sparkled outside in the dirt under the shop light.

Alfie walked up and slapped a socket wrench into Howser's palm. "Think you could break a window with one of these?" he asked, proudly.

"Where'd you pick it up?"

"Over there in the grass. Saw some footprints there, too, right where the grass was mashed."

"How about fingerprints?"

Alfie looked at the wrench he'd given him and nodded. "Yeah, I don't see why not. We ought to be able to lift one or two."

"Yours, mine or the other guy's?" asked Howser, with a half-smile.

Alfie looked back down at the smudged wrench handle. His face flushed with embarrassment. "Sorry, I wasn't thinking."

Howser examined the wrench and handed it back to him. "We'll need Corey's print kit out here. We're going to want to dust whatever we find."

"I'll go call him right now."

"No," said Howser. "I'll do it. You stay out here and keep looking. We've got four broken windows up there and only one wrench." He watched the two reserves moving up under the live oaks. They were on hands and knees, sweeping the grass with the palms of their hands. "What about the other guys? Any of them bring evidence bags?"

"I don't know," replied Alfie. "I doubt it."

"And if they happen to find something?" Howser gestured toward the wrench in the patrolman's hand.

"I'll go tell them right now."

"Good."

Howser went back around through the weeds to the unit parked by the big trash bin. The road in front of the garage was pitch dark. Indoors, Mike was banging away with a hammer on a severely bent oil pan. The noise echoed across the blacktop. Sliding in behind the steering wheel, Howser grabbed the mike off the console and called town. "RP1 to base." The hammering from within the shop went on unabated. A breeze rustled the eucalyptus on the west end of the garage down past service bay number three.

"Base here."

"Susan?"

"Yes, Chief. Go ahead."

"I need you to wake Corey up for me and send him out here to Redmon's Garage with the print kit."

"Will do."

"And you'd better tell Randy to fill a thermos full of coffee. We're going to need him on patrol until at least seven or eight."

"Yes, sir."

"That's all, thanks. Out."

He hung the mike on the console and went back into the garage. Redmon had gotten the spilled oil drum upright and was tossing his tools onto the long workbench where he'd sort them out later. Howser watched him work. Mike owned the best gas and service garage in Rivertown. His reputation for good, fast work and reasonable rates attracted repeat customers from twenty miles around. He'd built that business with long hours and lots of sweat. It would take more than midnight vandalism to drive him out.

Mike noticed him and stood up. "Will you look at this shit? It's going to take me a fuckin' month to clean it up. The bastards." He threw a hammer across the room. It thudded off the wall and dropped in a corner beside an open cardboard box full of metal washers. "You find anything out there?"

"Not much."

"Of course not. The bastards never get caught."

"We'll catch them, Mike."

"Sure you will."

Redmon went back to picking up tools and giving them the short heave onto the workbench.

"Listen, Mike," said Howser, "I've got to get back outside." He could hear his officers laughing out behind the garage. Redmon fished another socket extension from the oil, wiped it off, and flung it over his shoulder onto the bench. "If you find anything that doesn't look like it belongs, let me know, okay? We're going to need your help on this one."

Redmon grunted a reply and Howser left the garage to wait for Corey outdoors where the night air was fresher and the world did not look so broken up and beaten. Down the road, half a mile to the west, a rooster crowed vigorously in the darkness. Howser checked his watch. Quarter after four. It would be another hour and a half or so until sunrise. He looked east toward the black-sky horizon and saw stars still shining above the hills. The rooster crowed again and Howser smiled. Dumb bird was early.

8

By eleven in the morning, the temperature downtown had reached 104 degrees and was still rising. In the suffocating heat, asphalt felt sticky underfoot, glare from the storefront whitewash hurt the eyes, the Stars and Stripes above the courthouse hung limp in the windless light. Windows all over town were closed tight, sealing in the cool air that had collected during the night. Dogs and people alike congregated in scattered pockets of tree shade where temperatures barely more tolerable hovered in the high nineties.

In Howser's office, the fan on the filing cabinet clattered noisily. His door was left open in anticipation of a draft that had not yet materialized. Out in the corridor, the distinctive click of a woman's heels on polished concrete ascended the stairwell. Howser replaced the newest set of reports inside the folder marked *Redmon's Garage*. Two wrenches, a disk brake assembly, and the recently welded gearshift lever to Dickie Strebel's '72 Chevy Camaro were what they had discovered in the grass behind Redmon's Garage. The Snap-on wrenches had been the easiest and best bet for dusting; they'd lifted prints from both and Jane had sent them on to the FBI's Stockton office as soon as she'd arrived in the morning. With any luck, they'd get a hit by the end of the week.

A woman stuck her head in the doorway and smiled. Howser didn't bother looking up; he knew who it was.

Charlotte Burkie, forty-two, redhead, columnist for the *Rivertown Courier*, the mayor's sister, laughed and walked into the office. Her white blouse fluttered as she passed by the fan.

"Good morning, Chief," she said, pleasantly.

He looked up at her, the translucent blouse, the slim navy blue skirt cut three inches above the knees, the overdone makeup, the not-so-subtle perfume she wore. Charlotte Burkie was not only a professional journalist, but a full-time manhunter. Three Reno divorces and Joe Burkie's fatal heart attack in a Stockton cocktail lounge had not diminished her enthusiasm for the game, a fact Howser hadn't recognized until he'd found himself alone with her in the upstairs of her brother's house last Halloween night. Only an act of God, the accidental downing of a power line on the south side, had allowed him to sneak away in the dark with his dignity still intact. Somehow, even weakened by passion, he'd sensed that sleeping with her was a no-win situation regardless of how much he might enjoy it at the time. Yet it wasn't as if he disliked her. She wasn't a *bad* person. Since they both worked downtown, their paths crossed weekly, allowing them to spar and even flirt occasionally when it served some obscure purpose. Why, though, he wondered, couldn't she just get married again and do them both a favor? Was he the only eligible bachelor in town? God, there had to be somebody else.

She sat on the corner of his desk and adjusted her skirt at the thigh. Pretending not to notice, Howser opened the drawer beside his right knee and took out a copy of the *Courier* dated three days ago. He skimmed the front page, right column, lead story. "This was some piece you wrote. Very inventive. Let me see . . ." He ran a finger down to the bottom of the page. "Oh yeah, I especially liked this part, 'Only the alertness of the deputized volunteers prevented the escape of more suspects.' Nice story, Charlotte. Very nice."

"Thank you."

"Of course, you made heroes of all those idiots by ignoring the fact that the shooting was not only stupid but illegal. And by calling them heroes, you made my officers and myself look like accomplices to the rape. That's just bullshit. Why'd you do it?"

She gave him a pouty smile. "Do you hate me?"

Howser left the desk and went to the window. He peeled back the blinds and looked out on downtown. Chrome flashed brilliantly from passing cars. Picnickers lunched in the shaded park. He heard the chair behind him creak as Charlotte sat down at his desk. He cringed, realizing his whole office was going to smell now of Valentine Surprise.

Keeping his eyes locked on the street, Howser said, "Do you understand what went on out there the other night?"

"That old railyard's been a breeding ground of nastiness for years now."

"That's not what I'm talking about, Charlotte."

"Guilt is so pointless," she said, her voice just audible above the whirring fan. "I think it's a rotten emotion."

"No, Charlotte. What's rotten is the attitude that if you can get away with something, then doing it must be okay."

"A girl got raped, a suspect got killed. Who's to say anyone got away with anything?"

"I read your story, Charlotte."

"A lot of other people have, too, and so far you've been the only sourball in the group."

Howser turned from the window and stared at her. "What's that supposed to mean?"

"It means," she said, getting up from the chair, "that I wrote precisely what this town wanted to hear about a very unpleasant situation. Now, you can dispute the point of view I took in the article, but nothing I wrote was unfactual—"

"Deputized volunteers?"

"You're just angry because I didn't consult you before writing the piece. Don't be. It wouldn't have made any difference." She went and stood in front of the filing cabinet, letting the fan blow in her face for a few moments.

Howser came back over to the desk, swiveled the chair around and sat down again. "What'd you come up here for today? It's obviously not business."

"You need to ask?" she replied, warming her smile up again.

"Forget it, Charlotte. I've already eaten."

"You know, I'm surprised you've let these few idiosyncrasies about our little town upset you so much. I assumed you'd thoroughly researched us before moving here, examining our dirty laundry and such."

"Only the information concerning available women in town. I spent months on your file alone, Charlotte, and you know what? I decided to come here anyway."

She opened her purse and took out a small compact and a gold tube of pink lipstick and began going over her lips, slowly. "I'll bet you don't talk to Jane Crockett like this, do you?"

"No, I don't."

"Of course not." Charlotte finished freshening her lipstick and checked her makeup once more. "You've always preferred her, haven't you? Don't answer that." She closed the silver compact and smiled. "Why are you so hostile anyhow? No one's holding you responsible for the other night. We realize you're doing the best you can. We're all aware of your limitations, Chief. Nobody blames you for them."

Howser looked up at the clock on the wall. It showed a quarter to twelve. Lunchtime. He had no intention of spending it in the present company. "Well, Charlotte, I've got to get back to work," he lied, "so, if you have some complaint you want to file against your manicurist, I'll get you some forms to fill out. Otherwise . . ." He let his voice trail off, hoping she'd get the point.

"How about fixing a couple of parking tickets for me?"

"I thought your brother took care of that."

"He does." She walked over to the filing cabinet and let the fan blow in her face again, sweeping the hair back off her neck. "It's stuffy in here. You should open a window."

"I prefer it stuffy."

"What on earth for?"

"Discourages visitors."

"Very funny." She walked over to the door and put a foot out into the hallway. It was dead as a tomb; they were the only two people on the fourth floor at the present time. She came back inside. "So you were out at Mike Redmon's place last night? I heard it was an awful mess."

"Yes, it was."

"But you have no idea who the vandals were?"

"Not at this moment, no. We're working on it."

Four stories below, outdoors, a car honked loudly. Angry yelling followed in the heat, a man's voice carrying clear across downtown.

"Same thing with the Miller girl rape, I suppose?"

"Excuse me?"

"You're still investigating?"

"Of course. How else do you think we catch the bad guys? It's not all that often they turn themselves in." He saw her take a notepad from her purse, flip it open and begin scribbling in it. "What is this? Are you interviewing me now?"

She looked up briefly, smiled, then continued writing as she talked. "And how long do you expect these investigations to take?"

"How should I know?" he said, a little irritated now. "What difference does it make?"

"Oh, I don't know. It just seems to me that by the time you get it all worked out, we'll have forgotten what it was you were working on."

He stood up at the desk and pointed to the door. "Get out!"

She closed the notepad and replaced it in her purse. Then she took out a pair of sunglasses and walked to the door, pausing there at the threshold just long enough to ask, "How about dinner tonight? My treat?"

"Out!" he yelled.

She propped the Ray-Bans on her forehead, then blew him a kiss. "Bye-bye!"

She disappeared into the corridor. Two steps down the stairs, she stopped and called back loudly, "In case nobody's told you, Chief, that poor John Doe from the railyard? I'd suggest you look in the files." Her voice echoed out of the stairwell. "He wasn't the first."

At ten past noon, Jack Clayton entered a small grocery store across Sutter Square Park from the courthouse. The ceiling lights had been turned off inside to cut down on the heat, so the store was dim but packed, people coming in for lunch and cold drinks and to get out of the heat. At the delicatessen in the rear of the old brick building, he ordered a ham and cheese on whole wheat. A freckled teenage blonde working the deli made the sandwich, wrapped it in heavy white paper, scribbled the price on the paper, and slid it to Clayton across the stainless steel counter. She moved on to her next customer as he went after something to drink. He found a soda cooler in another corner of the store and drew out a cold Dr Pepper, then brought the sandwich, a bag of corn chips and the soda up to the line at the cash register. After paying for everything, he went back out into the white noon. He located an empty space beneath one of the huge willow trees and sat down, unfolding the sandwich and laying it out on the grass. He took a bite and stretched his legs out and watched lunchtime traffic cruise lazily around the rectangular perimeter of the park. A century of summer sun had faded the downtown storefronts. Winter rain and wind had done the rest. Rust and wear prevailed in every corner. Yearly face-lifts of fresh whitewash could not hide that fact.

Clayton opened the Dr Pepper and took a drink. The carbonation burned in his throat but in this heat the cold felt good. He drank half of it, then tore open the bag of corn chips and ate a handful and washed them down with more cold soda. Across the lawn, a woman wearing blue jeans and the tan and olive-green shirt of the Rivertown Police Department came out of the courthouse. She paused for traffic, then jogged across the street. Her smooth brown hair, parted neatly in the middle, fell nearly to her slender waist in back, reminding him of folk singer Judy Collins in a sixties photograph. She stopped briefly to chat with a trio of old men seated on a park bench in the shade of a live oak just off the sidewalk. Clayton noticed how she carried herself—head up, eyes forward and alert. Most women adopted the slightly defensive posture of averted eyes, the natural reaction to the constant attention they elicited involuntarily from men. This one was different: she demonstrated a clear refusal to be cowed at all in that way. She crossed the lawn and strolled into the

99

grocery store and came out five minutes later eating a green salad from a cardboard plate. She chose a shady spot under another willow nearby and parked herself cross-legged, her back against the trunk. He felt guilty staring, yet found it difficult not to. Her sea-blue eyes were bright and lively, and her face, lightly tanned, framed and narrowed by her long hair, was beautiful. He watched her as she ate. After a few minutes, she caught him watching and smiled once before casually shifting her gaze elsewhere. Embarrassed, he looked away, too, toward the street where two women yelling and banging shopping carts like bumper cars at a fair had stopped traffic in the center of a crosswalk. Pedestrians on both sides of the street slowed to watch. One of the carts tipped over, spilling groceries onto the hot pavement. By then, Clayton had summoned up enough courage to return his attention to the woman under the tree. When he looked again, she'd gotten up and was walking toward him, still eating salad from the cardboard plate. He watched her approach, wondering if he was about to get a ticket for violating some obscure ordinance against sitting in the shade on a hot day.

"You're Jack Clayton," she said, stopping in front of his feet.

"I am?"

"Uh-huh. At least I think you are." Looking down at him, she smiled. "Are you?"

"I was this morning."

"Good, then you still are." She stuck her hand out. "I'm Jane Crockett."

He leaned forward and up. "Glad to know you." They shook hands.

"You're staying at the Walcott."

"Right again." He stuffed the last of his sandwich into his mouth and finished it off.

She stuck her fork into the salad. "Ellen told me about you."

"The girl at the desk?"

"Uh-huh."

"What did she tell you about me?"

"That you're extremely quiet and well mannered and hardly ever in your room—she thinks you deliberately

100

sneak in and out when she's not looking. Is that true?"

"Where'd she get that idea?"

Jane shrugged. "That's just what she told me."

"I never sneak around."

"I believe you." She smiled. "Mind if I sit down?"

"Please do."

Jane set the cardboard plate down and seated herself in the grass beside him. "Where are you from?"

Clayton drained the rest of the Dr Pepper and screwed the cap back on. "Lots of places."

"Such as?"

He laughed. "Are you always this nosy?"

"I try to be."

"All over. Scottsdale, Pittsburgh, Wichita, Oakland, Albuquerque, Atlanta—among others."

"You like traveling, huh?"

"I'm just restless," said Clayton. "What about you?"

"I'm a hometown girl. I was born four blocks back that way in City Memorial Hospital," she said, gesturing up the street to the north. "I have three cats, a mouse in the attic, a brother in Bakersfield and a mother in Cleveland. What else would you like to know?"

"And you're a cop."

"Police dispatch. Six years last April."

"So you don't get to carry a gun, huh?"

"No, but I know how to use one." She smiled. "Any more questions?"

"Just one," he said. "Is there anyplace to get a decent meal in this town? I've had everything on the menu at that diner by the hospital. I'm sick to death of chicken pot pie."

"And you'd like me to recommend some place? A little upscale on the quality index. Is that it?"

"If possible."

"Great food, but inexpensive, right?"

"You got it."

"How about my house? Tonight, eight o'clock?"

"Is that a dinner invitation?"

"Yes, it is."

The clock tower at the courthouse chimed for the half hour. Jane glanced at her watch. "I have to get back to work." She got to her feet and brushed grass from her jeans. "I don't get off until seven thirty, but if you can survive until then I'll fix you something I think you'll like."

Jane picked up her plate and walked over to the trash barrel a few feet away and dumped it in. Clayton jumped up and followed her, tossing his own trash in on top of hers.

"How do I get to your house?"

Walking off backward, Jane smiled and said, "Ellen'll give you directions from the Walcott, okay? And listen, I'm a great cook, so don't be late."

She waved once over her shoulder as she headed off across the lawn toward the courthouse. Wearing a large grin on his face, Clayton watched until Jane crossed the street and disappeared into the building. Then he walked back to the hotel to shower and lie down for a couple of hours, away from the heat.

Down by the levee a mile and a half below Rivertown, two men, Mike Henry and Vic Walton, were fishing from the riverbank, hanging their lines in ten feet of green water. The current was swirling and circling at this place, and small air bubbles were bursting the surface out in the middle of the river. The two men were spending their lunch break doing something they remembered from an earlier time: playing hooky. Leaving high school after fourth period to go fishing. Leaving work now. Fishing on the river at noon.

The surface of the river was warm. Sunlight, bright and unrelenting, had heated the first foot or so down into the murky green. Vic reached into the water to rinse his hands off. He shook them, splashing mud up onto Mike's blue trousers. Mike kicked at a mound of dust, sending up a cloud. Vic splashed again. Mike took off his glasses, laid them carefully on the ground, then kicked hard into the dust and retreated along the shore. Vic chased him. They were both laughing now, giggling like two idiots at a circus. They began wrestling in the grass and dirt, slapping at each other with open palms, goosing. Vic pulled free and tried to stand up. Mike lunged forward and shoved him off balance. Vic fell into the river, taking both their poles with him.

Soaking wet, Vic dragged himself back onto the shore to remove the soggy clothes weighing him down. Mike's lay folded in a neat pile under a bush a few feet away. He had already dived into the river, skinny-dipping like a nine-year-old, in pursuit of the blue two-hundred-dollar rod and line his kids had bought him for Christmas. Vic wanted to join him before it was too late, before both poles were recovered and he had no excuse to reenact his adolescence on one of the hottest days of the year. Mike disappeared around the leaning branches of the large willow whose trunk had sunk into the base of the riverbank. Vic undid his belt and shoes. Then he had his shirt off and his pants down to his ankles. He had to hurry. Mike was calling.

Then Vic was in the river swimming, too. Actually he was doing his own version of the dog paddle, moving as much with the current as under his own power. The sun was flashing off the surface of the water blinding him so that he had to make his way along using one hand as a visor. He let the current take over every few yards or so, but the river was sluggish in June and Mike was urging him to hurry. Vic arrived around a dark bend in the river where more willows hung out over the water, distilling the sunlight into thousands of brilliant threads sparkling on floating leaves. He slid through a narrow conduit to the south where Mike had gone. Then the calling stopped.

The river angled downward into a wide and shallow basin where the trees formed a tent over the water and twenty-five years earlier a much younger Michael and Victor had made a game of inviting teenage girls down to take their clothes off out of view of the riverbank. Passing now into the shade, Vic saw Mike standing still on a soggy log beneath a long tree branch. He was staring into the water below his feet. Mike was not speaking any longer, nor did he seem to notice Vic approaching slowly with the current. At the same time, looking up at Mike, wondering what he was standing there staring at, somehow Vic did not notice the girl submerged in the water—not until he swam straight into her, dislodging her bruised and bloated body from the sunken roots. As he struck her beneath the surface of the

103

river, and before he became sick from the sight of her eyes rolled back lifelessly into their sockets, he heard Mike burst out with a fit of laughter that echoed up and down the river.

An hour and a half later, the pool was quiet again. Only the sloshing of a police officer's boots carried over the soft trickling of the river current snaking by. Bodies discovered in water were called floaters. It had been years since Howser had seen one. The officers had hauled the girl up onto the shore and laid her down in wet grass beneath the broken willow where mosquitoes swarmed in the dank air. Her father, Ed Miller, stood off to one side, lost somewhere within himself. The two men who had found the body were waiting silently by the police cars parked under the black cottonwoods at the back of the clearing. Howser watched the waterbugs, skeeter-eaters, dance across the surface of the pond and off into the mud under the riverbank. He had no desire to look again at the girl—floaters never failed to make him ill—but it was his job to get her away from there and to do it soon.

His officers, their uniforms soaked and muddy from the effort of dragging the girl out of the river, were folding a blue blanket around the body, beginning with her ankles and moving upward to her thighs, waist and shoulders. Howser studied the odd angle Sarah Miller's body had assumed in rigor mortis. How could she twist like that? He glanced at Ed Miller, who was staring motionless at his daughter lying there in the shade. His gaze was empty, eyes not even blinking back visible tears. He was just staring, caught in the helplessness of shock and horror. *Was that his little Sarah lying in a heap like so many soiled clothes on wash day? She had never looked that way to him alive. The river had changed her forever, and somehow he could not bring himself to touch the thing she had become.* After photographing the body for the second time, the patrolman folded the blanket over the girl's face.

Howser put his hand on Ed Miller's shoulder. "I'm sorry, Ed. This is the last thing anyone wanted to happen. We're all sorry for you."

The water from Sarah's body was beginning to soak through the blanket while Miller stared at her, his eyes glassy and vacant. *Was that stench of wet rot his daughter?* He spoke with a flat tone. "We didn't know she was gone. Didn't even know. Mary went up to call her for breakfast and she was just gone. Window open. Screen pushed back. She crawled right off the roof and down the drainpipe like I used to when I was her age."

"You couldn't have known, Ed."

"My little girl, Chief. My little girl. Who'd want to do this to us?"

Howser found it impossible to drive from his brain the picture of Sarah Miller hiding half under the sheets in that hospital bed five nights ago, her arms bruised, her face streaked with tears. The humiliation had been unmistakable in her voice. He'd left her alone so she might find her own recovery but now that she was dead, he wondered, like her father, what had gone wrong.

"Do either you or your wife have any idea what time she might've gone out last night?"

Miller shook his head slowly. "All I know is that Mary and me turned in at nine. When my wife looked in on Sarah, she was already in bed."

Howser swatted a mosquito away and looked at his watch. It was a little after two-thirty. Doc Sawyer had examined the body when they'd first dragged it out of the water and had guessed she'd been dead at least eleven or twelve hours. That left more than four hours unaccounted for. Where'd she gone?

"Did she get any phone calls last night?"

"Annie called after supper. That'd be around seven."

"Annie Connor?"

Miller nodded. Now the two officers lifted Sarah's body and lugged it away from the riverbank to the clearing where the coroner's station wagon was parked in the shade of the cottonwoods. Doc was sitting behind the wheel, waiting to take her back to town.

"I don't suppose you know what they talked about, do you?"

"My daughter's business is her own. We've always believed in allowing her some privacy, Chief." He watched

105

the officers slide the body into the rear of the station wagon. "I have to go with my girl."

Miller walked off.

It was just a coincidence that Ed Miller had been on the river when those two men had discovered his daughter. He'd been driving by on his way back from the Purina feed store and had seen them on the roadside, directing the police to her location. Miller had screamed when he'd seen his child floating beneath the willow. They'd had to hold him down to prevent him from going in after her.

Howser looked over the shady pool and the surrounding woods one last time. Doc had guessed that Sarah had been dumped in the water postmortem farther upriver. How much farther up was anyone's guess, though it was unlikely they'd be able to determine the exact spot her body had entered the water. There was just too much territory to cover. However, when they'd pulled her out she'd been nude so there was always the chance they could get lucky and have an item of clothing turn up somewhere along the riverbank. Determining the precise cause of death would have to be done at the lab but the severely fractured skull she'd apparently suffered would be the place to start. There were also superficial ligature marks on her wrists and ankles, and massive bruises about her face and upper torso. It appeared as though whoever had killed the girl had tied her up and beaten her in a genuine frenzy of violence.

Fighting off more mosquitoes, Howser walked back to the clearing. One of his officers was already on the radio to dispatch. Doc had wanted an SID forensics team from Stockton to aid in preparation of the autopsy report. Knowing how and where she'd died might help uncover who'd killed her. Howser stopped by the station wagon and poked his head in at the window.

"This is a rough one."

"They're all rough," said Sawyer, setting his clipboard aside. The coroner's eyes shifted to the rearview mirror. "Look at that." Howser swiveled his head. Ed Miller was sitting stonefaced in the cab of the white Dodge pickup, hands squeezing the wheel. "What do you suppose's going on in that man's mind right about now?"

Howser shrugged. "It was a mistake letting him come down here. We should've kept him away."

"He'd have seen her sooner or later, and the morgue isn't a big improvement." Doc started the engine. "How about you and me getting together later this afternoon? Say around four? I'll get her squared away for the Stockton crowd and you come down and see me. We'll talk."

"Fine."

The two patrolmen drove off.

Doc put the station wagon in gear. "Four o'clock."

"Yeah."

Then Doc Sawyer left, too, driving out the dirt road toward the highway. Howser walked back to his own car. Just as Ed Miller's Dodge pickup began rolling, a red Chevy Blazer, trailing a roostertail of dust, roared down into the clearing. The old pickup stopped and the Blazer skidded up alongside and Tom Danielson, his face red and sweaty, jumped out into the midday heat, slamming the door behind him. The noise disturbed the crows in the tree line and several took flight above the river.

"My God, what the hell's going on around here?" he yelled.

Howser got into the unit and started the engine.

Danielson strode to the cab of the pickup and put a hand on Ed Miller's arm. "Was it your girl, Ed?"

Miller lowered his head.

Danielson gave him a pat on the shoulder. "Well, I'm sorry as hell to hear that."

He stepped away from the old Dodge and pointed a finger at Howser. "It was that tramp from the railyard, goddammit!" His voice echoed down to the river. "That goddamned tramp *you* let get away!"

But Howser's attention was still focused on Miller, a man who had only recently seen his daughter dragged dead from the river. This was the wrong time and the wrong place for arguing. Anyhow, who was blameless? Ed Miller's pickup rolled forward again, sliding past the police car and the four-by-four, away from the black cottonwoods and the cool green water. They let him go.

As the rumbling of the old pickup passed from the shaded clearing, Howser spoke to Danielson.

"Tom, the next time you do anything to interfere with my job, *anything at all*, I'll make you sorry you got out of bed in the morning, and I mean it."

"Don't threaten me, Howser."

"I'm not threatening you, Tom. I'm just stating a fact." Holding his right foot on the brake, he slipped the transmission into drive. "Understand? Do us both a favor. Stay out of my way. Now if you've come down here to do some swimming, be my guest. But I'm going back to town."

Then, without looking back, he let off the brake and drove slowly out of the clearing and up through the quiet woods to the highway.

9

The Walcott Hotel was a grand and elegant lady from an era when the freshwater streams and quiet foothills east of the Central Valley still held enough gold to make a lucky man rich in an afternoon. Rivertown's first mayor, Ben Walcott, had constructed his mansion on the corner of Fourth Avenue and Day Street as a testimony in architecture to his own fortune. His money bought him a three-story country Victorian with a steep mansard roof, sculpted eaves, handcarved spindlework and gingerbread, ornate Italian beveled glass in tall bay windows, and a long broad sunporch for tea and conversation on windless summer evenings. Early Rivertown society (what there was of it) celebrated occasions of merit in the octagonal ballroom. Political issues and agendas were debated in the library. Rich and influential guests were welcomed and entertained on the mansion's upper floors. Both Leland Stanford and Collis P. Huntington spent pleasant evenings there during early stages of construction on the transcontinental railroad. So did Adolph Sutro, en route to drilling his famous tunnel through Virginia City's Mount Davidson. Ben Walcott saw his youngest daughter, Carrie May, married to cattle rancher Harlan Danielson on the mansion's front lawn in the summer of 1921. A year later, Walcott was dead from the sleeping sickness and his widow had given his mansion to the town and moved back to Sacramento. The town remodeled and repainted the mansion, turning it into a luxury hotel as the centerpiece for steamboat tours on Rivertown's section of Green River. At midcentury, when steamboat traffic ceased and the jetty closed, the hotel became a boardinghouse. The last two guests to check in, Mr. and Mrs. Edgar Holloway of San Francisco, made themselves at home in the old bridal suite on the top floor and never left. During Eisenhower's final year in office, the Walcott was repainted once more and the lawn and gardens resown. By 1966, the mansion was the last remaining structure within Rivertown's city limits from the days when the town had meant something on the river. In the spring of that year, the town showed its love and respect for the grand old lady by voting it a historical landmark.

In the summer sunset, the white clapboard walls on the west face of the Walcott burned with roselight. The old glass in angular windowframes flashed and glowed. To cut the glare in his corner room on the third floor, Clayton pulled the canvas shade down on the window facing west. As he did, the shade went amber. A little light still seeped in around the edges but Clayton tied the cord to the sill and left it as it was.

Downstairs, the lobby doors were propped open to the porch and the yard and gardens were quiet. A brass ceiling fan above the front desk whirred silently, creating a slight breeze in the potted palms by the staircase. Colored sunlight slanted in through the bay windows, illuminating a shadowed lobby. Coming down the stairs from the third floor, Clayton found Ellen and her police officer squeezed together in the chair behind the desk, sharing a bottle of Coca-Cola and talking. When Ellen saw Clayton approaching she squirmed out of the cop's grasp. Her blouse was wrinkled and the top three buttons were undone. She rapidly fastened two of the buttons. Her cheeks were flushed. Pretending not to notice, Clayton glanced around at the empty lobby. The tabletops had been cleared, the magazines and ashtrays put away, and the kitchen door at the far end of the entry hall closed for the evening.

As he approached the desk, Ellen smiled at him. "Hot up there?"

"Very."

She took a sip from the Coca-Cola bottle and passed it to the cop. "Does the fan help much?" she asked.

"Not anymore. It stopped working last night."

"Oh, I'm sorry," she said. "We'll have to fix it for you."

"Don't hold your breath," said the patrolman, studying Clayton. "Nothing gets fixed around here unless you sue somebody."

"Mr. Clayton," said Ellen, "this is my boyfriend, Alfie Cox. Alfie, Jack Clayton."

The cop leaned up out of the chair and Clayton reached forward over the counter to shake hands. "Glad to know you."

Alfie pointed a finger straight up. "Hardly any insulation up there at all. This time of year, heat goes right through the roof."

"It's bearable."

The draft from the fan tossed in Clayton's hair. He was still sweating underneath his shirt. "Everybody go out?" he asked.

"Everybody except you," replied Ellen.

"I was on my way."

The telephone rang in the office behind the desk.

"Excuse me." Ellen slid off the chair and ducked into the office, grabbing the phone on the second ring. Clayton watched her. Ellen had a round pretty face, deep brown eyes and thin brunette hair clipped short at the shoulders. Her skin was tanned and pleasantly freckled. She was cute.

"What do you do for a living, Clayton?" asked the cop.

Clayton answered while switching his attention to the front door where the light was the strongest. "It depends."

"On what?"

"On where I am."

"Huh?"

"I'm not doing anything right now," said Clayton. He watched Ellen hang up the phone. "Just bumming around for the summer."

"Must be nice."

"Yeah," replied Clayton. "It's nice."

Ellen came out of the office and took the Coca-Cola from Alfie. "Like a sip?" she asked, offering the green bottle to Clayton.

He shook his head. "No thanks."

Ellen wet her lips with the tip of her tongue. Her eyes shone. "So, I hear you have a date tonight." She shoved the slip of paper with the directions to Jane's house across the desktop.

"Word gets around quickly here," the cop said to Clayton. "This whole town's nothing but a big pair of ears and a set of flapping lips."

"I admit it," replied Clayton, picking up the piece of paper. The light outdoors was changing hue, pink into red. "I have a date."

"Jane's fixing the man dinner," Ellen told Alfie. "What do you think of that?"

"When was the last time you cooked me dinner?" the cop asked.

"When did you take me out last?"

"Well, you two have a nice evening," said Clayton, leaving the desk.

"Have a nice dinner, Mr. Clayton," said Ellen.

Clayton walked out of the lobby. On the veranda, he looked at his watch. Only a quarter after seven. The sun was in his eyes, the last heat of daylight on his face. From the top step he could see the fields of grass outside of town, running on to a red horizon in the west. Without tractors or those big Rainbird sprinklers to occupy space in the distance the vast emptiness isolated the town, made it an island on the land. *So what sort of tide sweeps a person to a place like this?* After sticking the directions to Jane Crockett's house into his shirt pocket, Clayton took the keys to the van from his Levi's and descended the stairs.

By dusk, everyone in town knew what had occurred out on the river that afternoon. Even as the heat faded in the dark, an irritated restlessness began to manifest itself among all those involved with the handling of the girl's death. No one was supposed to die like that in Rivertown. That it should happen to a native daughter little more than a week before the town's celebration of Independence Day only made it worse. Since bringing Sarah back from Green River, Howser had not been able to find the patience to talk with anyone outside of the courthouse. He sat in his office with the chair swiveled toward the window at the same angle he'd had it all summer long, brooding about a girl beaten and raped in the presence of her friends and half a week later murdered and dumped into Green River on one of the warmest evenings of the year.

Howser went over the notes he'd made since returning from the morgue. Ed Miller had refused to say anything after they'd brought his daughter's body back to town. He'd helped the officers carry her out of the station wagon and down into the courthouse basement that served as the city morgue where his wife had been waiting for most of the afternoon. Miller hardly acknowledged her presence, and left the morgue with his wife trailing thirty feet behind him. When the Millers had gone, Howser'd sat down with a cup of coffee in Doc Sawyer's office and listened to the coroner tell him something about Sarah Miller's rape he hadn't wanted to hear. *The pathology of the genital region showed evidence of multiple intercourse but no bruising, no lacerations, no serious injury. What does that tell you? Those were grown men and she was a sixteen-year-old girl. Have you ever heard of a gentle gang rape? Neither have I.* There was a stack of files on his desk waiting to be read, the ones he'd requested from downstairs concerning prior fatalities in the railyard/river area. They still had no ID on the John Doe in the morgue and nothing on the prints lifted from the tools found outside Redmon's Garage. Neither had their phantom runaway from the railyard been spotted anywhere. Howser'd had his officers going door-to-door, asking the usual questions, but nothing had been turned up. Tomorrow they'd begin searching the riverbank for Sarah's clothes.

Now there were sounds in the street, voices from the sidewalks, loud and strident. Howser got up and went to the window. He saw a large crowd on the sidewalk outside the old Roxy theater two blocks away to the north on the corner of Main and Pine. They were waiting to buy tickets to the eight-o'clock showing of a Clint Eastwood movie.

Across the street from the courthouse, a teenage boy and girl walked arm-in-arm through the lazy shadows in the park. Now they embraced and were kissing. A pale green Buick drove by, arms hung out the front windows on both sides of the car. Exhaust funneled in the draft as the Buick passed on up the street. The movie crowd formed a line that stretched three-quarters of a block long beside the darkened storefronts of the local State Farm office, Sears, Rexall drugs and the Bank of America on Main. The two kids on the park lawn slipped away into the dark. Another few cars came and went. As the noisy moviegoers entered the theater, the street slowly became quiet again. Though there was nothing to look at now except the empty asphalt and a shadow patchwork on the grass in the park, Howser continued to stare out through the blinds. It was a feeling he had, an instinct about the town. Maybe his imagination was working overtime, yet he sensed something was different out there, that something had changed in the few hours since they'd brought Sarah Miller home from the river.

In the dark house now his sons are asleep. The lights in the hallway outside his room have been extinguished and the upstairs is quiet. He is standing at the dresser, studying his appearance in the silvered mirror. The Tiffany lamp on the nightstand bathes the room in a yellow half-light that flatters his badly sun-mottled skin. His eyes are bloodshot and the lower lids sag unflatteringly ("Hound Dog" is a nickname he has unknowingly acquired). He removes the bolo tie worn to town in the morning and places it on the dresser top. He picks up his father's old ivory-handled hairbrush and gives some attention to his sideburns, then sets the brush down beside the tie. Satisfied, he leaves his room, locking the door behind him as he goes. He walks down the darkened hall. The old floor creaks beneath his weight. If his sons wake and hear him, they might press their ears to the wood to listen as he passes but they will not open their doors. Her room is at the end of the hall. He can see the light under the door. She is still awake. She knows what night this is so she is expecting him. He enters her room without knocking. She lies in bed with her head propped up by three down pillows. Neither husband nor wife speaks. He disrobes at the foot of her bed. She rolls the covers back, allowing him to crawl on top of her. She lifts her night gown and pulls it up to her waist. His weight sinks her into the mattress where she remains near breathless while he ruts noiselessly on top of her. When he finishes, he rolls off the bed and picks up his clothes. She gets up and goes into the bathroom for a wet rag which she brings back to wash him off. Then he dresses quietly and leaves.

Years later, after his wife has abandoned him in favor of living with her sister in Glendale, Tom Danielson still makes his walk in the dark to her room. Now that she is gone, though, he masturbates into her toilet and rarely considers the absence of her warm body beneath him to be any great loss.

The driveway up to the Danielson ranch was dark. Yard lights were off and the long pastures flanking the road lay in shadow. Jamie parked out behind the barn so his father would not be able to see him from the house. He was late for evening feeding. Nightfall had caught him in town, hanging out with his friends. The Chevy Blazer was out front, but there didn't look to be any lights on inside the house. *Maybe the old man's off somewhere with his hunting buddies. Maybe he fell asleep in the bathtub. Maybe he's watching from the kitchen right now.* Jamie hustled into the barn where he switched on the light and took the ladder to the hayloft. He dragged loose a bale of hay and shoved it off the platform to the cement floor below, then climbed back down to the stalls, tore the broken bale into smaller sections and dumped them into the feeders one after another. He dipped an old Folger's coffee can into the barrel of grain in the tack room and distributed it equally into each horse's trough. Afterward, he took four buckets to the faucet out behind the barn, filled them up, and carried them back inside. When he put one of the buckets of water in with the sorrel, he noticed the repair done on the end stall. A couple of two-by-four patches had been nailed onto the inside gate. He supposed that during the night

115

the sorrel'd gotten spooked and had kicked at the boards until they broke. Jamie leaned over the gate and stroked the horse's mane, wondering what had spooked her. Then he grabbed the big push broom and swept out the barn floor. Finishing that, he straightened up the tack room and doused the light.

He left the barn and crossed the yard. The house was dark. He entered through the back door. The windows were closed and the constant odor of kitchen garbage and fried grease permeated the downstairs. He turned on the light switch by the pantry. The dishes he'd left in the kitchen sink after breakfast had been washed and put away. That meant Mercy had been by as she'd promised. He took a can of Stroh's beer out of the refrigerator and drank it where he stood. There was no sign of his father. It was late but maybe he'd gone out, after all. Jamie crushed the empty beer can and stuck it into the waste-basket with the rest of the trash. He decided to watch some TV. He came down the hallway guided by light from the kitchen and turned at the stairs. As he reached for the banister, a voice from the living room startled him.

"They dragged your girlfriend out of the river this afternoon."

He heard a wooden creak as his father leaned backward in Grandma's ancient oak rocker. Jamie paused for a moment on the threshold between light and dark, then moved inside and let the room swallow him up.

"She wasn't lookin' too good, neither."

Though Jamie was unable to see his father, he knew he was sitting there by the fireplace, not twenty feet away.

"We broke up yesterday," said Jamie. His own words echoed back at him.

His father coughed once and spoke again, a harsh disembodied voice rattling out of the dark. "The tramp killed her. Same one as raped her. Fuckin' chief doesn't know what the hell he's doing."

The living room windows were closed and the drapes drawn. In the stagnant air, that familiar smell of bourbon and Old Spice reached him where he stood.

"I saw the stall," said Jamie.

"The horse got spooked," the voice replied. "I nailed it up this morning. It'll do."

Taking another couple of steps forward, Jamie located the sofa and let his weight rest against it.

"She looked okay."

"Wasn't nothing there to hurt her. Just spooked herself." The rocker creaked again and Jamie thought for an instant that his father was getting up. He waited for footsteps on the carpet but heard none. The voice asked, "You been in town?"

He knows I was late but he doesn't give a shit. Why not? Jamie nodded. "Yeah."

"They talkin' about the girl?"

"Uh-huh."

"What were they sayin'?"

"I wasn't paying attention."

The darkness felt suffocating now. Jamie wanted to get out before his eyes adjusted to the shadows and made visible the figure in the rocking chair. He backed away from the sofa. His father spoke as he moved. "You knew that girl was no good, didn't you?"

"I don't know."

"Did you love her?"

"No."

"I don't believe you."

"Who cares?" he said and walked out of the living room.

His father's voice chased him as he went. "I never loved your mother, neither."

Jamie went up to his room and locked the door.

Clayton stirred the rice with his fork and tried not to look up. He knew she was watching him, scrutinizing him, trying to figure him out. He slid the rice onto his fork and took another bite and let the fork drop to the side of the plate.

"The question is," she finally said, "do you like it?"

"Not bad," he said, swallowing. "Not bad at all."

"That's a commercial, not a compliment."

"It's good," he said, trying again. "What's in it?"

"Garlic, ginger, green onions, broccoli, celery, carrots,

mushrooms, bean sprouts, zucchini, bell peppers, boiled chicken and bok choy. Among other things."

"That's all?"

"They were out of snow peas. I had to make do."

"Well, it's very good. I'm impressed."

"Thank you." She smiled.

"You're welcome."

"Do you want any more?"

"No, I'm finished. Thanks."

Jane stood and began clearing the table. She took her own plate first. "When I was a little girl, my mother told me that if I didn't eat all the food on my plate, I'd never get any bigger and eventually she and Dad'd have to sell me to a circus." She smiled as she picked up his. "I was a charter member of the Clean Plate Club for years."

"Let me help," offered Clayton, sliding his chair back.

"No, you sit there and relax. This'll only take a minute."

Jane carried the dishes over into the kitchen and stacked everything in the sink, rinsing the plates and glasses off but not bothering to soap them down yet. She could do that later when she was alone and bored. She filled the sink with water to let everything soak, then dried her hands off and came out of the kitchen. "Let's go outside."

He nodded and got up. She opened the back door and he followed her out into a small fenced-in yard that bordered on a dark empty field. The sky was black and clear. A wind had come up in the last hour. It swept through the long grass beyond the fence, freighting hay smells across the summer dark. Jane pulled two lawn chairs together and she and Clayton sat down beside each other. Brass wind chimes rang erratically next door in her neighbor's lot.

"Nice yard," Clayton commented, looking around. "Got your own fruit trees and everything."

"The pears and apricots are great. I don't care much for the persimmons. The sparrows enjoy them, though."

"How long have you lived here?"

"About four years."

"So this wasn't your parents' house?"

"No." The wind tossed in Jane's hair and she brushed it off her face. "You know where Thrifty's is, down there

118

on the south end of Slater and Main? That's where we lived. Our old house used to be right on that lot. The whole block was bulldozed about ten years ago. Made me sick."

"It happens. This is America, remember? 'They paved paradise, put up a parking lot.' "

"I know, but you never think of it happening to the house you grew up in. It seems sacrilegious."

The wind gusted and a car with a broken muffler clattered by on the road out front. When it had passed, Clayton said, "So you've lived here in town your whole life?"

Jane laughed. "Do I seem that provincial? Actually, I left the nest three weeks after my high school graduation. June 27, 1969, to be precise. I was accepted at Cal during my senior year and got a job on campus for the summer. They let my friend Cindy and me stay in the dorms while we looked for an apartment in Berkeley." She looked him in the eye. "Yes, I actually departed Rivertown for the big city. Local girl makes good."

"Did you find it tough leaving?"

"Well, my father died the first month I was away."

"Oh no."

"He'd had a stroke my junior year and just never really got any better. Then he developed pneumonia the week of my graduation and missed seeing me go through the ceremonies. My mom called me the morning they took him to the hospital. I tried to get home but I missed my bus connection in Stockton. He died before I even got there. I've always felt guilty that I wasn't with him when it happened. I still think about it from time to time. Makes me sick. After the funeral, my brother Frank and I helped my mom pack up all her things so she could move back to Ohio where she grew up. Her sister, my aunt Nancy, and the rest of my mom's family still live there. They wanted her back with them. They wanted me, too, except I'd spent two summers visiting Aunt Nancy when I was a kid and the Midwest and I never hit it off too well, you know what I mean? It was fine for Mom because she grew up there, but I missed California. We didn't have to sell the house for six months, so Frank and I stayed there and shared it. That worked out okay. We both cooked and took care of the cleaning. Frank kept the outside looking nice and he paid the utilities from the money he made working at the 76 station. He's such a good guy. I'd love him even if he wasn't my brother. He was really there for my mom and me when Dad died. And afterward, when it was just him and me, he made sure I was feeling all right about things and wanted to stay and everything, even when he pretty much knew I was going to be leaving again—which I finally did later that fall."

She stopped a moment and smiled at him. "What? You looked like you were going to say something."

"I was just trying to imagine what it must've been like living in your parents' house without either of them being there anymore."

"It felt terrible, of course. Very empty. That's why I left. It was just too sad staying. God, my whole life had been in that house and then all of sudden my parents were gone and my brother and I were living there by ourselves like orphans. It was depressing. I just had to get out."

"Does your brother still live here in town?"

"No, he got a job in Bakersfield while I was away at school and moved there when the house was sold. He's married now. They have two little girls—Kirstin and Jennifer. Frank and I still talk on the phone once a week. He's doing great. And Mom flies into Bakersfield from Ohio every year at Thanksgiving or Christmas and I drive down and we all get together then. We still have a good time. I love my family. They make me happy."

She shifted in the lawn chair to face Clayton. The wind fluttered in the white embroidered peasant blouse she was wearing. "Am I boring you, by the way? I always feel like I'm boring people when I tell them my life story."

"No, I'm enjoying it. It's a great life."

"I'm not making a fool of myself?"

"Just tell the story."

"How about something to drink? I was just going to get a glass of juice, but you can have whatever you want. How about a beer?"

"Juice is good."

"Okay." She got up. "I'll be back in a second."

He watched her cross the yard and reenter the house.

As the screen door banged closed, he got up from the lawn chair and walked over to the fence at the rear of the yard. There were homes in the small lots on both sides of Jane's property. The house with the wind chimes ringing was dark, but the one to the right of Jane's yard had the garage open and a light on inside and in the driveway a balding man dressed in tan trousers and an old white T-shirt tinkered with the engine of a vintage black-and-chrome hot rod. Between wind gusts, Clayton caught snatches of music from a pocket transistor radio tuned to an Oldies station playing '50s rock and roll, *I've been searching for you girl, bobby socks and a pony tail.*

Jane came back out on the porch. "Is apple juice okay?"

"Fine," Clayton answered from across the yard.

A few minutes later, Jane returned outdoors with two glasses and a bottle of apple juice. She spotted Clayton leaning on the fence and walked over and handed him a glass. She filled his, then her own, and set the bottle on the fencepost.

"Thanks," said Clayton. He took a drink and stared at the grass swaying in the empty field. Far off in the dark, heavy farm equipment left until morning, or perhaps until another season, sat silently in the wind. "Who owns all this?" Clayton asked, nodding at the field.

Jane set her glass on the fence. "A man named Tom Danielson. He owns most of Rivertown, in fact. Inherited it from his father. *He* got it through his wife from the man who built the hotel you're staying in."

"He's a rancher?"

"Not anymore. Doesn't need to be. He's the richest man in the county. An old-fashioned land baron."

"A Rivertown Rockefeller, huh?"

"Closer to Howard Hughes, to tell you the truth. Tom Danielson is a very strange man."

Clayton took another drink of apple juice. When he'd drained the glass, he said to Jane, "So, you were telling me the story of your life. You were on your way to school."

"Um, yeah, I went back to Berkeley just after Thanksgiving, I think, found a place to live, and in January I enrolled for winter quarter."

"What was your major?"

"Psychology."

"I should've guessed."

Jane laughed. "I was young, okay? I needed to study something relevant."

"Psychology?"

"I wanted to learn about relationships."

"Why women shop and guys watch football, right?"

"Exactly."

"Okay, go ahead."

"So, I am going to the university and living in Berkeley. Six of us, two guys and four women, shared the upstairs of a house near Telegraph Avenue. Cindy got us into the place with another girl she knew, Naomi, and Naomi's cousin Wanda from New York. We found the guys through an ad in the *Berkeley Barb*. What a mistake! The guys were crazy. And they made us crazy, just living there with them. For one thing, this was the spring Nixon got us into Cambodia, remember? And Kent State was about to happen, which would make things even weirder, if that was possible. So there was a lot going on in Berkeley and on campus, speeches and marches, people screaming at each other and worrying about Ronnie Ray-Guns and whether or not there'd even be a university the next year. It was a pretty wild time. I don't think anybody went to class. And these guys we were living with, Matt and Terry, were completely nuts. It wasn't enough that they were incredible pigs but they were lunatics, too, you know? Raiding grocery stores, pulling dine-and-dashes whenever we'd go out to eat somewhere, shoplifting stuff like party napkins and plastic coat hangers, useless stuff they'd take just to take and then give away on campus. The guys eventually got themselves banned from every store in Berkeley, which was pretty hard to do in those days. Well, that was bad enough, but then Terry convinced himself that he was in love with me. Drove me completely crazy."

"You fell in love with a shoplifter?"

"No, he fell in love with me."

"You sure it wasn't the other way around?"

"Yes I'm sure. See, I was in love with Matt."

"The other shoplifter."

"Yeah, and Cindy had a monstrous crush on Terry. Of

course, he wouldn't even look at her because of me, which created a little tension in the house, if you can understand."

"Sounds like college."

"It was," she said. "I mean, there was a lot more to it than that. We were all at one time in one political group or another at Berkeley and the personal things going on between us tended to get in the way of our part-time efforts to stop the War. You know, how can we possibly stop the War in Vietnam and Cambodia, and let this other one go on for months in our own house? It was ridiculous. So, I married Matt at the end of my junior year."

"You married a criminal?"

"He never got caught."

"Oh."

"He used to bring me Ding Dongs whenever they'd raid the markets on Telegraph."

"You married him because he brought you Ding Dongs?"

"No, I married him because he was a really neat guy, very smart, very together, great in bed, and the only one who ever let me have my own space when I needed it. He never told me what to do. So I married him."

"How long were you married?"

"Sixteen months. We drove up to Tahoe on a Friday evening, got married, and came back the same night. It was pretty romantic, really, when you think about it. We just did it. I didn't even tell my brother for a month. I was scared my mom would find out and call me up and yell for a day and a half."

"So what happened?"

"She got over it."

"No, to you and Matt."

"I'm not sure what happened, actually. Things were great at first. We moved out and got our own place across the bay in Sausalito where we lived during our senior year. That was fun. I loved being married, waking up every morning with the same person next to me in bed, someone I loved and *wanted* to have there beside me. It was wonderful. But when school ended, so did our marriage. We had *so* much fun that year. For graduation, all of us dressed up as corpses from Vietnam. We painted our faces in death's-head masks and walked up to take our diplomas. It was Matt's idea. A lot of the parents booed us, which, of course, made Matt ecstatic. In the summer, then, when Watergate was going down, we all got together and watched it on the tube in the afternoons. We made popcorn and drank wine and waited for Nixon to face the music. It made great theater but when Tricky Dick resigned, that was that. A week later, Matt moved out and went to India with Terry."

Jane reached to her left and took the bottle of apple juice off the fencepost. She opened it and refilled her glass. Clayton held out his own glass and she poured him the last of the juice then placed the empty bottle down in the grass.

"You didn't know he was leaving?"

"Oh sure, but what was I going to do? That was Matt. He even said one time that the only reason he married me was because marriage was one of the only things he hadn't tried yet and it seemed like something he ought to know about."

Clayton watched the wind blow in Jane's hair. "And after he got to know what marriage was all about he split, right?"

"I suppose that sounds a little cold, but it wasn't like that at all. He cried more than I did the morning he took off. It hurt him a lot, but it was something I guess he felt he had to do for his own sanity, or whatever."

"And you?"

"It wasn't as hard as I thought it would be, maybe because I always knew it would happen as soon as Matt got something new in mind. And he did, so he left. He and Terry hitchhiked across India and into Thailand after we broke up. About six months later, they came back to the States and moved onto a ranch in Oregon with some people Terry knew. They both stayed there and worked. I think it was about a year later Terry met a girl named Jannie Mae in Salem and moved in with her. But I didn't even know he and Matt'd come back from Thailand until I got a birthday card from Matt the following March. I was living in Santa Cruz then, taking some night classes and working on the boardwalk. Matt and I never did file for divorce. It wasn't any big deal. Maybe if one of us had met someone else and gotten serious we might have, but it never mattered that much. We weren't living together anymore so it seemed as though we weren't married. The papers were just something else. I always missed him though. Missed him a lot. I still miss him. Jeez, and it's been, what, more than ten years since I saw him last. A long time. A really long time."

"Do you ever hear from him?"

She waited for the wind to die down slightly, then shook her head. "He, Terry, and Terry's two-year-old daughter Shawna were killed in a car accident in Oregon almost seven years ago, driving up to Salem in a storm on Christmas Day. Terry's van got broadsided by a logging truck and went into a flooded ravine."

In the brief silence that followed, the radio in the next lot filtered music into the dark that evoked blue chiffon and white carnations and crepe-paper decorations in a half-lit gymnasium. *Will I see you in September, or lose you to a summer love?* Then the wind rose again in the fruit trees and the silence and the music in the small yard were displaced by Jane's voice. "After Matt died, I quit my job on the boardwalk and drove back up here, I think it was just after New Year's, and I remember driving past our old house and seeing some little kids playing out front in the yard. I wanted to stop and tell them who I was and how much I'd loved playing in that yard when I was their age. More than that, I think I wanted to tell them to keep playing as long as they could, to have absolutely as much fun as possible, because one day there wouldn't *be* any more yards to play in. I didn't stop, of course. I chickened out and went past. And when I finally did pull over, a couple of blocks away, I sat there and had a good cry."

She leaned against the fence, facing west like Clayton and staring out across the empty field, watching the windsweep in the long grass. "There's nothing worse in the world than regrets. You know that?"

Clayton nodded.

"You know, the ones you dwell on in bed at three o'clock in the morning. It's absolutely true. When Matt and I were married, he asked me over and over again to drive up here with him and show him where I grew up, show him the little corner of the world that produced his wife, but I was so embarrassed by Rivertown at the time, so ashamed of being thought of as Betty Jo from Hooterville, that I refused to do it. So we never did."

"And now you wish you had."

"It would be nice to have at least one memory of both Matt and my home together. Just one to show that my life has had some continuity." She sighed. "I suppose we all have our personal ghosts, don't we?"

"Yes, we do."

Jane turned her gaze north toward Rivertown's lights. "I do love this town, though. I really do. I couldn't say that when I was growing up here. There were too many other things, people, that I let get in the way of all this. You know how it is when you're young—anywhere's more appealing than the place you grew up in, everybody's more interesting than your own family. I don't know. When I was at Berkeley I always seemed to be apologizing to everyone, my roommates and friends, for coming from a hick town on the river, as though it made me somehow less a person than my friends who came from the city. Now I wouldn't apologize to anyone about Rivertown."

"You're just a rube at heart, huh?"

She smiled and reached out and rubbed his wrist. "You're a strange guy, Jack Clayton, but I like you. You listen well. That's a rare quality in a man, believe me."

"I appreciate the compliment," he replied. "Most women tell me I do nothing but talk about myself."

"Well, they're wrong."

Clayton stepped away from the fence. "How about giving me directions to the john."

"Sure. Just go in the back door, through the kitchen, turn right at the hallway. You'll find a light switch on the wall there. Bathroom's the second door down on the left. You can't miss it."

"Thanks."

"Don't get lost."

"I'll call if I do."

He left Jane at the fence and crossed the yard. At the

porch, he looked back through the fruit trees. She was still leaning on the fencepost, her chin resting now on her forearms, her eyes fixed somewhere out in the windy dark. Clayton opened the screen door and went inside.

He walked through the kitchen to the hallway where he found the light switch and flicked it on. Before going down the hall to the bathroom, though, he wandered into the front of the house, found a table lamp, switched it on and had a closer look at the home Jane had made for herself.

Her house was small and cluttered, but the busy look it had was not careless. Even the hundreds of little knick-knacks scattered about seemed to have some particular decorative place and purpose. The seashells and colored wooden candleholders, a sprig of dried and crumbling tumbleweed and a large glazed green jug full of smooth blue stones sifted with the miniature dolls and dozens of picture postcards for space in the front rooms. Houseplants (ferns and coleus, ivy, maidenhair, and wandering Jew) were on windowsills, redwood bookcases, antique stands, and descending from the ceiling in handwoven plantholders. She had also stuck little coffee cans of potpourri in the odd corners of each room, giving the house a distinctly sweet and peppery scent. Clayton moved to the photographs on the walls and mantel, each one framed in old wood or polished brass or blue porcelain. The people in the pictures were ones Jane Crockett had known in her life—father and mother, brother, grandparents, cousins. Friends, too. Those were the glossies in the porcelain frames, high school and college students smiling in beach sunsets or on backpacking trails, familiar faces given a place in her home for the special memories they inspired. Studying the photographs, he wondered which face belonged to her husband Matt. Or maybe his photograph was upstairs in her bedroom, occupying one corner of her nightstand or dresser or vanity. Everyone holds certain ghosts forever prisoner in the heart. Jane was no exception. Clayton turned off the table lamp and walked down the hall to the bathroom.

Outdoors, the music from the neighbor's driveway had stopped and the hot rod had been rolled back into the garage and the light extinguished. Only the wind sweeping out of the west disturbed the silence now. When Jane heard the toilet flush, she gathered up the glasses and the empty apple-juice bottle and headed for the back porch. As she reached the top step, Clayton opened the screen door and came out. He saw her and held the door open.

"It's getting a little cool out," she said. "I decided we should go in."

"Okay."

He maintained eye contact and she blushed.

"You didn't get lost."

"No, I didn't," he replied.

"That's good."

He leaned forward and kissed her once, lightly, and eased back again.

She smiled, and whispered, "I guess you liked my cooking."

"You're an excellent cook."

"It's nice to be appreciated."

"I'm always appreciative of home cooking."

She set the glasses and bottle on the railing and leaned inside the door and flicked off the back-porch light, putting them both in the dark. Then, sliding her arms up to rest on his hips, she said, softly, "How about showing me some more appreciation?"

10

Six miles east of town in a brushy wooded area, Jamie
Danielson kicked at the gravel and gazed down the dirt
road. Insects buzzed in the brush around him. The sticky
odor of tarweed hung in the hot dry air. It was a little
past noon. He'd been waiting half an hour now. Where the hell
was Danny? Jamie stepped back into the narrow sunshadow of Stuart's Mill where the grass grew tallest and gray
lizards hid in the weeds. The old mill leaned four stories
tall overhead, twice as wide and long as the town's high
school gymnasium. Larger than either of the bonded ware-
houses north of town or Coburn's old distillery on South
Main. Someone brave enough to climb the old iron ladder
on the west wall up to the roof could see clear across Green
River in one direction and down to the center of town in
the other. What had once been the largest stamp mill on
the river was now an abandoned warehouse, an indoor
junkyard, a refuge for small animals. Still, even aging and
run-down, there remained something vaguely attractive
about the old stamp mill, particularly in the middle of
summer when its dark interior provided shade and privacy.
Kids had been hanging out up there for as long as Jamie
could remember. Both of his older brothers had lost their
virginity in the mill. It was the place to be when you needed
some privacy. Nobody hassled you up there. Of course,
not everyone appreciated the isolation. Once on Halloween when they were kids, a bunch of them tied Ernie Long

up in a bed sheet and carried him out to the mill and left him there overnight. When they came back the next morning, they found him still bound up and shivering, soaked and whimpering in his own piss from fright. After that, Ernie'd do just about anything you wanted if threatened with another night alone in there.

Deciding to wait for Danny inside the mill, Jamie walked around to the east face and entered through an old fire door. It took a few moments for his eyes to adjust to the dark. Threads of light filtered in through cracks in the redwood walls. The interior was shrouded in shadows that draped over rusting industrial machinery and scores of packing crates and ten-foot loading pallets stacked almost to the low ceiling all over the ground floor. Jamie walked around taking care not to trip over anything. What a putrid place this is, he thought. It stunk, too, thanks to the million or so rat craps on the floor. If Danny didn't show up in the next five minutes, he was going to have to go back outside into the heat. Waiting never failed to piss Jamie off. He was always on time. Why couldn't everyone else be, too? The problem was that people never did anything except out of fear. What was the use in being nice? Smile at someone and they take advantage of you. Like Sarah. Yeah, just like Sarah, in fact. He'd given her enough chances. He'd given her plenty of chances. She abused them. She didn't know when she'd had a good thing. He thought about the first time they went out to the river together when they were sophomores: hide-and-seek in the bushes, clothes on the sandbar, sex in the water. Good times. And then the other night at the railyard. And her phone call three nights ago, *I have to see you, Jamie . . . Don't fucking come out here! . . . Please, babe, I gotta see you! . . . I'm telling you, don't come! . . .* And then the river again. She didn't listen to a goddamn thing he ever told her, so there was no reason to feel bad about her. It was her own fault. Her own goddamn fault. Where the hell was Danny?

Danny Williams leaned up against a fence railing to catch his breath. He'd been running for almost twenty minutes now up from the trees by the highway where he'd parked the pickup. His throat was parched and his eyes watered. The fact was, he was out of shape. He hadn't even run a mile yet and felt like he was about to die. And, shit, he used to do five every day on the track after school. Okay, okay. Slow now, take it easy. He felt a chill on his skin and saw how badly he had been sweating. Jeez, a heart attack. Great. He could just see himself croaking in the dust on his way to getting stoned. His father'd love hearing that. *It's all that dope the kid was smoking. That dope and that rock music all the time. My son's a goddamn fool. Long-haired hippie idiot. And a pussy.* Fuck you, too, Pop.

Jamie wandered into the dark, past the rusting machinery and the pallets loaded with crates of junk. The air smelled worse the farther in he went. It stunk like an old cat that had crawled off to die. Dead animals made him sick to his stomach. Just seeing one made him want to puke. He hoped he wouldn't accidentally find this one. Where the *fuck* was Danny? The walls shifted, creaked, and settled again. Support beams were caked with dust and bird droppings and the panels above showed cracks in the floor of the second level. The old building's chief attribute at this point was that it was still standing—no small miracle. It was bound to be knocked down in the near future. As soon as someone with a real estate development plan bought Stuart's Ranch, that'd be it for the old mill. It was a firetrap anyhow. Only the grace of God had kept it there all those years. Jamie thought, *Shit, maybe I'll do it myself sometime. Just go ahead and light the whole fucking place up*. He started to stretch, then stopped. Somewhere off in the dark near the fire door came a sound like footsteps on the cement floor. With all the boxes there stacked so high, it was hard to see but he was sure somebody was there. He watched for movement in the shadows. He held his breath and listened again. Danny? *That little asshole. He thinks he's going to scare me this time. Okay, that's cool. We'll see who gets the shit scared out of them*. Jamie dropped to his hands and knees and crept forward until he reached the spot where he imagined Danny sneaking up on him.

He took another look. No one was there. He crouched back down and waited. Then he heard the footsteps around behind him, not far from where he'd first been standing. It startled him. Maybe he'd underestimated Danny after all. The little guy was moving like a goddamned Indian. Jamie crouched down further and inched his way in behind a collection of old shipping crates. *Danny, you little faggot. You're going to get your face smashed for this.* Jamie let his breath out again. *Fucking Danny.* A noise from behind him made him jump. Then another, louder this time and closer, footsteps padding somewhere nearby.

Deciding to put an end to Danny's little game, Jamie shouted, "Danny, you asshole, I know it's you. You're not fooling anybody. Knock it off or I'm leaving." He waited for a response. None came. "All right then, go fuck yourself. I'm out of here."

As he started backward away from the crates, the entire stack flew apart above him, collapsing in one great avalanche in his direction. Jamie felt himself struck high up on one shoulder blade. The pain shot through his back. His face hit the pavement. Another crate glanced off his arm. A third landed on his right leg. Stunned, he tried crawling away on his stomach. Behind him, more crates tumbled free. Before Jamie got more than a few feet from the falling crates, a massive hand grabbed the back of his shirt, folded into it, and jerked upward, raising him from the concrete floor. Jamie struggled to break free. The shirt shredded and he fell back to the floor. Scrambling to his feet, he swung one of the crates into the path of his attacker. Then, ignoring the cry of pain behind him, he ran to the stairwell and up into the heart of the mill.

Danny Williams rolled his pantleg up to his kneecap and sat down in the dust. A thin line of blood trickled down from his shin into his sock, staining it a dark red. His knee was swelling already and it ached badly. He looked back at the rock he had tripped over. He would've gotten up and given it a kick except that he knew he'd just end up breaking a toe. Sweat was dripping down his forehead, burning in his eyes. The pain in his leg was getting worse.

It made his head swim. He patted his shirt pocket with his hand. The dope was okay. Score one for him. If he had lost any of that, he might just as well have broken his neck and died when he fell over that rock. He wondered if Jamie would appreciate the sacrifice he had just made. Probably not. Danny looked at his knee again. The bleeding was beginning to slow a little, but his kneecap was swollen like a pink balloon. He tried standing. He fell over onto his injured leg and cried out. Tears welled up in his eyes and mixed with the dust to blind him. He had to get up and get moving, had to get to the mill before Jamie got too pissed off. Things were out of control these days, lot of weird shit happening. Sarah was dead. Nobody understood that at all. Jamie wouldn't talk about it. He acted scared. They could all hear it in his voice on the phone. What did he have to be scared of? Sarah's the one who got killed. Maybe he thinks he's next.

Jamie stopped along a metal ramp that led into shadows ahead. The wooden floor under the ramp was cracked and he could hear footsteps on the concrete down below. Why hadn't the guy come up the stairs yet? What was he waiting for? Jamie listened to the footsteps. They'd slowed now, as if the guy wasn't sure where to look next. If he hadn't gotten away down there by the crates, he was sure the guy would've killed him. Who the hell was he? That's what Jamie wanted to know. Why the fuck was this happening? The footsteps stopped. Or at least he couldn't hear them anymore. Maybe it wasn't the guy at all down there. Maybe it was Danny. Sure, Danny and the fucking Lone Ranger. Right. Forget Danny. What he really needed was to find some way out of the mill, an exit to the outside. If he could make it into the woods, he'd be okay. So far he'd given a good run to whoever it was down there chasing him, but how long would he be able to keep it up? He was tired as hell already. If he got caught again, well, maybe he wouldn't be able to get free. Jamie slumped against the wall and tried to think of a way to avoid getting killed.

The mill creaked and settled. Outside the afternoon wind had risen. The draft it created in the splintered wood of the old walls cooled the dank air inside the mill. Leaning sideways with his ear pressed to the wall, listening to the wind outdoors, Jamie felt vibration in the metal ramp under his feet. It startled him and he trained his attention away from the wall. As he did, the sound became clearer— a tramping in the floorboards underneath the ramp. Footsteps. Heavy ones. Jamie crouched down against the wall. *The guy's on the stairs and he's coming up.* The vibration in the ramp quickened and Jamie thought about running. He glanced back along the dark wall in the direction of the stairs. Standing motionless in the shadows at the end of the ramp now was a large figure. Jamie froze. Now it was too late to run. *How'd he find me so fast? Who the hell is he?* His legs numbed by fear, all Jamie could do was gaze into the darkness at the tall figure poised not more than forty feet away. *What's he waiting for? Does he want me to beg? Is that it?* Staring at his pursuer, expecting any second to see him cross the short distance between them, Jamie blinked to clear his vision . . . and watched the figure dissolve before his eyes. He stared hard into the shadows. The figure was gone, the ramp empty. Nobody was there at all. Just the dark. Jamie got to his feet and took off quickly along the ramp, heading away from the stairs. He decided if there was an exit somewhere, it'd have to be farther up in the mill. No way was he going back down that ramp again.

He headed away from the wall, deeper into the center of the mill. Lining the ceiling overhead were wide metal conduits that looked like ventilation shafts of some sort for the old machinery. Climbing up into one of them might take him higher into the mill, maybe even to the roof. So far, though, he hadn't seen any openings or access ladders. The upper interior of Stuart's Mill was a maze of shadowy passages and blackened machinery. Maybe with a map or a floor plan he'd have an idea where he ought to be heading. Without one, he was rapidly becoming lost. Worse yet, the farther he moved from the outer wall, the darker it got. Just walking around felt unsafe. The floor seemed solid enough, but the location and design of the inner walls and machinery were confusing and he'd already banged his head once on a bent section of pipe hanging down from one of those ventilation shafts. Down another ramp now and onto some kind of catwalk. As quietly as he was trying to walk, his shoes still clanked softly on the iron planking. He considered removing them to go barefoot. What were the chances of stepping on a nail or something? In a place like this? Fuck it. He'd tiptoe before he'd take his shoes off. The catwalk ended at a large section of iron siding that ran floor to ceiling. Maybe it was a wall, maybe part of the machinery. He couldn't tell in the dark. He headed left again anyhow, supposedly increasing the distance between himself and the stairs while lessening the chances of getting surprised. He was playing it safe. Actually, he was playing it like a chickenshit and he knew it, but so what? Medals weren't handed out for stupidity and right now his nuts were just a little more important to him than his ego.

A couple of minutes later he discovered the office. Finding it would've been more of a thrill had he not come upon it like he did, making his way along in the dark by touch, one hand, his right, on the wall, the other held out in front of him. He hadn't even known the office was there until his left hand banged straight into the window. It was a miracle the glass didn't shatter on contact. All the fingers on that hand hyperextended and his wrist snapped back halfway to vertical. Although it hurt like hell, it could've been worse: an artery sheared open on the jagged glass, blood spewing all over the floor, a slow and messy death. The door to the office was just off to the side of the window. He tried the knob with his good hand. It was unlocked. Twisting it slowly until it opened, he let himself into the office, then quietly closed the door behind him and locked it.

There was a metal desk in the middle of the room. Right away, he crawled underneath it and sat there in the dark, rubbing his aching wrist and debating his next move. Goddammit, why did he have to be so stupid? And fuck Danny, too, wherever the hell he was. Jamie stuck his head out from under the desk for a quick look around the small room. The shell of a filing cabinet stood against one wall, drawers missing. A pile of discarded cardboard boxes sat in another, more junk, scraps of paper, shadowy little odds and ends scattered about on the cold floor. Not much of an office anymore. When the mill was abandoned, it had obviously been trashed like a fire sale—"Everything must go!" So why'd they leave the desk? It's got to be worth a few bucks, right? *Probably so you could hide your ass under it, dumbshit! What difference does it make?* Listening again, Jamie heard noises echoing in the mill. Somebody walking, running? Close? He wasn't sure. He stiffened and sat up, and banged his head loudly on the underside of the desk. The sound carried into the dark corridors outside the office. *Nice going, asshole! Why not just tell him where you're hiding?* Jamie slid out from under the desk and crawled to the door and pressed his ear to the wood and listened. What he thought he heard, was *sure* he heard, made his heart jump. Footsteps again. If he got caught in the office, his ass was history. The place was a deathtrap. The knob turned freely without opening. *What the fuck?* He remembered he'd locked it. *Okay, jeez what a jerk!* He unlocked it and tried it again. Same problem. It was either loose or broken on the inside. *Goddammit! Now what?* He locked it again and swung around for a closer look at the office. Keeping his head down below the level of the window, he duck-walked across the floor to the other side of the office where the cardboard boxes were piled. Even with his eyes fairly well adjusted to the dark now, it was still difficult to see clearly more than a few feet away. However, it appeared the door was the only way into and out of the office. The other three walls were blank, which meant it was the door, the window, or nothing. He crawled in behind the stack of boxes and sat up against the wall. Somewhere close by in the heart of the mill, maybe just down the ramp, he heard more noises, indistinct, arrhythmic, moving. He was dead. That was all there was to it. Like a dumb mouse chasing cheese in a maze, he'd trapped himself. *Shit!* He looked up at the ceiling . . . and saw the outline there in the corner. He blinked in surprise, and sat up. A square panel, maybe eighteen inches across. An access panel. For what? He leaned up just enough to steal a glance at the window. As if he could actually see anything in the dark out there. Then he stared again at the panel. Whatever it was, and wherever it led, it was a way out. The question was, would he fit? Fuck it, he'd make himself fit.

Pressing his back flat against the wall, Jamie eased himself to his feet. The panel was probably eight to ten feet overhead, obviously meant to be reached by ladder. Well, since there wasn't one handy, what were his alternatives? The desk? *Sure, no problem. Drag it over into the corner, jump up, open the panel and . . . and if the guy's anywhere nearby that's about how long it'll take him to find you in here and kick your ass. So forget that. Make any noise at all now and it's game over.* Okay, the desk was out. What else? Sounds again, nearby. Footsteps? Yes. *He's coming. Right now. You better do something fast.* Jamie's eyes darted from one corner of the office to the other. How the hell was he supposed to reach the goddamn panel without a ladder? Fly? The cardboard boxes! Maybe he could stack them like a staircase and climb right up to the panel. He bent down and grabbed one. It was light, which meant empty. In fact, it was too light. No way would it support his weight. If the boxes weren't full, they were useless. He looked at the door. Pretty soon, the guy'd just . . . The knob turned once and stuck. Jamie froze. The knob jiggled again. He shrank back to the wall and watched in horror as the doorknob rattled a third time. Too frightened now to glance at the window for fear of seeing that dark face at the glass, Jamie cowered beside the pile of cardboard boxes. If the door opened, he'd pretend he was dead. And if that didn't work, he'd jump up and throw himself through the window. The door thumped in its mounting and the knob rattled again. Then everything went silent. Doorknob, corridor, office, the mill. All quiet. Considering that this might be a trick, Jamie remained still. One thing he'd never gone for was having a trick played on him. The idea of being the butt of a joke offended him, particularly in a case like this when the punchline probably went "Ha ha, you're dead!"

The footsteps moved off. From his hiding place beside the boxes, Jamie heard the guy go. It wasn't a trick after all. Surprised at his luck, Jamie scuttled to the window and pressed an ear to the wall. The footsteps continued away, heading apparently off into another section of the mill. This didn't exactly solve Jamie's dilemma, but it did buy him a little time. He was afraid to try the door again, worried that fiddling with the doorknob would draw the guy back. On the other hand, he still had no other way out of the office besides the ceiling panel. If he smashed the window and climbed through, there might be time enough to run. But probably not. Maybe the best plan was to wait the guy out, sit still in the office until the guy got tired of looking for him. And how long would that take? Another hour? All night? He was already getting hungry and needed to take a piss; staying put was out of the question. That left one choice: the desk—sliding it over to the wall and using it to climb out of the office through the ceiling panel. The second he moved it the guy'd come running, except maybe if he did it fast enough he could still get up through the panel. All he needed was a head start, and if the guy'd gone off far enough, he might have it. If he went now.

Jamie crawled over to the side of the desk. It needed to be moved about six feet. He was sure he could manage that, regardless of how heavy the desk might be. Taking a final peek at the window, Jamie braced his palms flat against the desk, then took a deep breath . . . and shoved as hard as he could. The metal casters under the legs screeched as the desk slid across the concrete floor and slammed into the pile of cardboard boxes against the far wall. The instant it struck the boxes, Jamie leaped on top of it. He punched up at the ceiling with both fists, driving the access panel upward off its mounting. Then he grabbed hold of the frame and pulled himself up. He got as far as his chest when he heard the footsteps pounding down the ramp outside of the office. Something crashed into the door. Jamie squeezed himself higher into the opening. The door boomed again and the hinges popped in their mountings. Struggling to fit in the shaft above him, Jamie bent awkwardly to pull his legs up and discovered that his hips were stuck in the narrow opening, caught somehow on the belt loops of his blue jeans. The booming at the door stopped. Realizing what was coming next, Jamie twisted frantically to free himself. The office window exploded. Glass and dust blew inward, and something heavy tumbled in onto the floor. And stood up, glass crunching underfoot. Six feet above the desk, Jamie jerked his knees violently upward in the same instant he shoved downward with his hands against the floor of the shaft. His hips came free. As they did, he pulled his legs up in one quick motion into the ventilation shaft and rolled away from the opening. A hand came up through the panel; it flopped and waved, grabbing for him. Jamie crawled down the shaft another few feet, then stopped and looked back again. The hand was gone. He sat still and listened. The office below was quiet, too. Obviously the guy couldn't squeeze through the access panel. Did that mean he'd give up the chase? Not a chance. The guy was never going to give up, which meant the safest thing for Jamie to do was to get out of the shaft before the guy found another way in.

Jamie crawled hurriedly along to his right, less concerned now with what might be ahead than what he knew was behind. Each shuffling stride produced a metallic echo. But noise was irrelevant now. Forty feet along, the narrow tunnel veered off in a forty-five-degree angle and came to an abrupt end. Had it not been for several faint threads of sunlight passing into the mill from high above, Jamie might have crawled right out into mid-air and dropped forty feet onto the roof of the freight elevator that was stuck down on the ground floor. He peeked down into the shaft. Hell of a fall, no doubt about it. He leaned farther out and craned his neck to look up. What light there was in the shaft filtered down from the upper mill through a series of tiny cracks or holes in the roof. He rolled over onto his back for a steadier look and saw a maintenance ladder nailed onto the wall directly overhead, extending up the side of the shaft into the shadows. He looked down to see if it led in that direction as well. It did. Not that he had any intention at all of climbing down. He wasn't that stupid. The best chance he had of getting out of the mill was to keep climbing higher, right on up to the roof if necessary.

Jamie followed the course of the ladder upward with his eyes. Fifteen, maybe twenty feet above him was a dark square cavity in the wall, the freight elevator's third-floor stop. Climbing up there wouldn't be a problem if the wooden rungs were still sturdy. Of course, if dry rot or termites had set in, it'd be a quick trip down. Deciding he had no choice, Jamie reached up and curled his hands around the first rung. He gripped and pulled on it a couple of times, gauging its strength. It seemed okay. Satisfied, he slid out to the edge of the shaft and grabbed hold of the ladder with both hands. Then, trying to avoid looking down, he swung out over the shaft and began to climb.

Reaching the third floor, he crawled onto the loading platform and carefully made his way inside. He looked around. It was a small storage room whose walls were covered in a dark, musty layering of thick cobwebs and sawdust. Off to his left was a set of shelves built onto the wall. Parked on them were dozens of old jars, stained and clouded, filled with nails and other odds and ends. Lying on the floor beneath the shelves were sections of iron pipe in varying lengths. Beside him on the loading platform were more shipping crates, like the ones that had bounced off his head downstairs. Threads of sunlight sliding in through invisible cracks in the wall directly across from him divided the shadows and warmed the dry air. Before doing anything else, Jamie took a second to check the shaft behind him. *The guy's down there somewhere, probably trying to figure out where the hell I went. Keep looking, dickhead.*

He wished he had his father's 30.06. All this running and hiding made him feel like a coward. On the other hand, it was better than getting his neck crushed and winding up in the river like Sarah. So what was his plan now, huh? *Well, for starters* . . . he shoved one of the shipping crates off the loading platform and into the shaft. He watched it tumble down into the darkness and crash loudly onto the roof of the elevator. Then he did another, and a third, and a fourth. He looked down the shaft again. *Now we're getting somewhere! The guy'd have figured out where I went anyhow. This way he'll have to bust his ass to get me.* Dragging over more crates, he shoved one after another into the shaft until the entire roof of the freight elevator was buried under a pile of shattered wood.

Feeling confident that he'd bought himself more time, Jamie walked away from the shaft and had a look around.

What little sunlight there was felt warm on his face as he passed through the shadows, reminding him of how cool it was in the mill. Pressing his palms against the wood, he could feel the heat outdoors. Overhead, the ceiling was out of reach. That didn't matter because there weren't any access panels in this room anyhow. No doors either, other than the one leading out into the shaft. On the far end of the room were more crates and cardboard boxes filled with pipes and lumber, and a canvas tarpaulin covering a large table. When he tried removing the tarpaulin, it caught on something underneath and ripped. He pulled again and it tore in half, exposing a large electric table saw. The steel surface was pitted and rusting and several anchoring bolts were missing. It wasn't in working order but it looked nice and solid. That was okay. Jamie smiled. He had a use for it that didn't involve cutting up any damn two-by-fours. He looked back over at the loading ramp. *That fucker's never going to get up through the elevator with this thing parked on top of it.* Forgetting the dull ache in his wrist, Jamie shoved aside a small sawhorse and positioned himself behind the steel table and curled his fingers to get a good grip. Then, his shoes finding traction on the rough floor, he lifted and pushed in one smooth motion, heaving with all his strength. The table saw didn't even budge. He tried again, straining this time until his eyes watered. His fingers slipped, banging his injured wrist against the side of the table.

"Goddammit!" His voice echoed in the walls. "Fucking thing!" He rubbed his wrist. "Shit!"

Unless he could either lift or push it on his own, it wasn't getting across to the shaft. Jamie shoved at the table again in a vain attempt to budge it from the floor. *How the hell did they get this fucking thing up here in the first place?* He leaned down and worked his back under the edge of the table, then surged up with all his strength, raising it half an inch or so before the table saw fell back again, causing the entire floor surface to lurch and groan under the weight. He gave up. It was just too heavy for him.

He kicked the table. "Goddamn useless piece of shit!"

If he couldn't seal off the elevator, nothing would stop the guy from eventually coming up the shaft after him.

And if he couldn't keep the guy off his ass, he was going to die. Soon. The idea of it made him furious. Why him? What the hell did he do? Frustrated, he kicked the saw-horse and sent it flying across the room.

"Shit!"

He ran over, picked it up and slammed it into the wall. Then he kicked the wall himself.

"God-fucking-dammit! Let me out of here!"

Dirt and woodshavings flew off in every direction.

"Let me out of here!"

Jamie kicked the wall again as hard as he could. More dirt and shavings fell away. He kicked it a third time and the entire wall buckled, freeing more dirt. Jamie stepped back in surprise, his eyes fixed on a series of iron studs running in tandem eighteen inches apart from floor to ceiling. He was stunned. Of all the spots to kick the wall, he'd hit the one where the old iron roof ladder was attached to the outside of the mill. He hurried to the other side of the room and rooted through the stacks of piping until he found a piece that suited his needs. Bringing it back, he scratched a mark just left of the studs about four feet off the floor, then started bashing on the wall there with the end of the pipe. The wood was thick, almost two inches, but badly rotted, and in less than a minute the pipe broke through into sunlight. Jamie dropped the pipe and kicked at the edges of the hole, sending shards of rotted wood cascading off into the sunlight. When he'd widened it to a ragged oval of about three and a half feet in diameter, he crawled out and grabbed hold of the iron rungs with both hands and hurried down the ladder. Ten feet from the bottom, he jumped down into the dust and took off for the woods.

Crouching low now in the brush, Jamie held the long grass aside so that he could see back toward the mill. He felt like yelling out something taunting and crazy, something to prove he wasn't intimidated any longer. When he tried to speak though, a peculiar feeling of dread passed over him, swelling in his chest and throat, strangling the words at his vocal cords. It wasn't over yet. He might've gotten away, but that wasn't the end of it.

Then he heard the voice, a familiar one, shrill and plaintive, calling to him from somewhere inside the mill. "Jamie, where the hell are you?"

What the fuck?

"Sorry I'm late, man!"

Oh, shit! Danny. You little prick! You showed up after all.

"Jamie, come on. Give me a break. The truck broke down . . . Hey, I brought the shit . . . I got it right here . . . Where are you?"

Jamie choked hard and swallowed. He knew he should call out. He knew he should jump up and shout, *Danny, you stupid motherfucker, get the hell out of there!*

Instead, he turned and ran.

11

"You looked the place over?"

Howser took a biscuit out of the little red basket and buttered it with the back of his fork. The remains of the fried chicken dinner he'd eaten lay on the plate in front of him.

"Inside and out," replied Corey. "Didn't find anything, though. Place was empty. Boxes and birdshit. Junked hardware. That's about it. No tramps. No bodies. No nothing. Just a big hole in the wall that someone'll have to fix." The two police officers slid into the booth across from Howser. Early-evening sunlight tinted the big plate-glass window. The Grill was noisy with the supper crowd. A line for those waiting to be seated started off to the side of the cash register and reached backward to the door. Conversation was animated and constant.

"Nobody's hiding out in there, Chief," said Beef. "Let me talk to the kid. I'll find out what's going on." He grabbed one of the biscuits and crammed it into his mouth.

Howser opened the manila folder he'd been keeping on the seat beside him and slid it across the table. He tapped the top page with his fork. "You guys read this yet?"

"No," replied Corey. "What's it say?"

"Nothing on the prints."

"No record at all?"

"None. Maybe he's underage—no driver's license—or from out of town—"

144

Beef cut him off. "One of the tramps?"

"Possibly," said Howser, "but if so, he's never been picked up anywhere. Not even for vagrancy. It might also be the suspect's never been printed. Or he's just not in the computer. There could be any number of reasons those prints aren't on file."

Beef took another biscuit and reached for the butter. Noise levels in the diner grew as steaming dinner plates collected under the heat lamps on the kitchen counter and the line at the cash register lengthened. Howser took back the folder and closed it. He stared out the window to the street where orange sunlight streamed through the haze of road dust as traffic drifted by. "Anyone give a call out to the Williamses'?"

"Jane tried ringing 'em up an hour ago," said Corey. "Nobody home."

The chief nodded. "We'll keep trying."

"Want us to take a ride out there?"

"No," said Howser. "I'd rather have you both in town tonight. If Jane can't get hold of Williams by, say, nine o'clock, I'll drive out there myself."

"You don't believe the kid's story, do you?" asked Beef, a look of incredulity drawn on his face. "Killer tramp in the mill?"

Howser shrugged. "If Danny Williams shows up tonight either in town or at home, we can bring Jamie in and give him a lengthy reading of the trespassing statutes in this county. But if the kid doesn't show up, and we have to go looking for him tomorrow, well, we have a serious problem on our hands regardless of where we first heard about it."

"Reserves still out on the river looking for clothes?"

"Just Randy and Al," said Howser. "I sent the others home an hour ago. I'm still waiting on the autopsy from Doc."

The waitress for Howser's table came over. She was a nice-looking girl in her late teens, with straw-colored hair tied up in a short ponytail by a pink ribbon. Her blue eyes were a little glassy from taking supper orders for the past two hours but she maintained a pleasant smile. "Two for dinner?" she asked the officers.

"Not these two," said Howser. "They're on their way back to work."

"We are?" asked Beef.

"Yeah, we are," confirmed Corey, sliding out of the booth. "Come on, let's go."

Beef grabbed the last three biscuits and stuffed two into his pockets as he stood up. Cramming the third into his mouth, he followed Corey out the front door. After they were gone, Howser reopened the folder and went over it again. He wasn't all that surprised that the prints had come back unidentified. It was another one of Murphy's laws for police work: when the best hope you've got of identifying someone is by their fingerprints, you can be certain those prints won't be on file anywhere. So, whose were they?

His waitress brought the check and left it on the table. Howser closed the folder, took the tab to the register, paid it, and left the diner. Outside, the smell of hot asphalt and freshly cut grass mingled in the twilight air. He walked up the sidewalk toward the courthouse, the late sun in his eyes. A few people he passed nodded a greeting, but nobody spoke. He walked quickly. In Sutter Park, small children played with colored toys while their parents looked on. Were they safe out of doors? That was the question beneath the vague expressions they shared with Howser as he crossed the lawn. He had nothing to offer to them by way of assurance and so passed by without acknowledging their unspoken concerns. He entered the courthouse through the front door and took the old elevator up to his office.

After sticking the Stockton report back into the filing cabinet and opening the blinds to the street, he sat down at his desk and hit the intercom. "Jane?"

"Yes, Chief?"

"Anything on Danny Williams?"

"Not yet. No one's answering out there. Alfie says he thinks they're up in Stockton for the rest of the evening. Won't be back until late. I really doubt we're going to be able to get them until tomorrow."

"Well, did Alfie have any idea whether or not Danny went with them?"

"That's what we're trying to find out right now. No one seems to know for sure. Apparently they left pretty early this morning."

"And no one saw them on their way out of town?"

"I guess not. Alfie still has a couple of Danny's friends he's trying to run down, but right now it looks as if the whole family went."

"How do we know when they're coming back if no one talked to them?"

"Alfie says they have a boy come in to feed their animals when they go away and he says they called him last night to look after things today and tonight."

"So, we know Danny must have gone with his folks, right? Or he'd be there to feed the animals himself?"

"Not necessarily, Chief. Alfie says Danny doesn't do any of that kind of work around the Williams place. His father doesn't trust him with the feeding schedules. He'd rather hire another kid to do it even when Danny's going to be there."

Jim the cat poked his nose into the office, gave the air a couple of sniffs, then turned around and wandered off again down the hall.

"Okay. Look, Jane, maybe I'll take a run out there myself. Tell Alfie to patch right through to me if he turns anything up. Otherwise I'll just assume we're still drawing a blank on the family and I'll wait there until they get home."

"It might be pretty late."

"That's all right. I've got an empty slot in my social calendar this evening."

"No date, huh?"

"No date."

"You could've called me."

"I heard you've been seeing that Clayton fellow from the hotel."

"Who told you that?"

"This is a small town, remember?"

"I think you'd find him interesting. The two of you are a lot alike."

"Oh really? How's that?"

"You both ask a lot of personal questions."

Howser laughed. He glanced over at the clock. Getting late already. "Listen Jane, I got to go. Remind Alfie he's got east *and* west patrol this evening and if he complains about it, have him get me on the radio."

"Okay, Chief."

"Have fun tonight."

"Thank you."

He switched off the intercom and looked for his car keys.

Jack Clayton straddled a wooden chair at his hotel window (where the air was only marginally cooler than in the middle of the room) and stared outside at the street below. The whining of mosquitoes on the other side of the storm-screen reminded him how close the town was to the river. He'd just switched off the desk lamp, putting himself in the dark. He preferred it that way. There was nothing to look at anyhow and lately the room had begun to feel a little dreary, cramped and shabby, reminding him again that he was a long way from home. Why now, though? Homesickness was not something he'd been bothered much with the last few years. Yet listening to Jane talk about Rivertown, moving away and returning again, brought it out somehow in himself—those winter feelings of emptiness and nostalgia he'd been disregarding for so long now. Maybe he *had* been away too long. He thought about another July in a place where the skies blew pink above the ocean in the morning and the waves broke blue and warm under his window all summer long. The sand and the girls and the guys four-wheeling in Malibu after dusk. *The guys.* Where did they go? USC? UCLA? Baja? Vietnam? Wilshire Boulevard? What he remembered was a completely different kind of place, the other side of the world from Rivertown, another planet, and everyone there dark-skinned and blue-eyed and rich as hell. Zuma, Malibu, Topanga, Pacific Palisades. Pretty goddamn far from Rivertown. Did he even know the way back anymore?

A car pulled up outside. Clayton leaned forward at the window and watched Jane Crockett get out and close the door, not bothering to lock it. She walked to the bottom of the steps, stopped and looked up at him. She smiled and waved. Though he doubted she could see him behind the dark screen, he waved back. Then he got up from the window and went to meet her in the lobby downstairs. He closed his own door but, like Jane, left it unlocked. *Yes. Very far, indeed.*

Leaving Rivertown, Howser drove south along the county road. Far away to the west he could see the headlights on the interstate moving off to Stockton and Sacramento in one direction and down to Fresno, Bakersfield and Los Angeles in the other. Did they notice him? Probably not. Rivertown wasn't even on most of the maps you get at service stations or travel agencies. Few people going anywhere special deliberately passed through Rivertown. You stumbled into Rivertown. You got lost and wound up in Rivertown. Or else you lived there. It was not exactly the Twilight Zone but sometimes it seemed as though the two shared a common border.

He turned onto Mustang Road and headed out into the grassland on the trailing edge of the valley. Looking up through the windshield, he could see the stars sparkling in the night sky. On night watch in San Jose, he had rarely seen any stars. The city streetlights and the neon had washed them out of the evening sky. Having grown up outside of town where the night skies were always clear and filled with stars, he had grown to miss the sight. This was part of what his coming to Rivertown had been about: the stars and the summer wind, the quiet and the solitude. When it came time to retire, he'd buy himself an acre and a half of land and a trailer, rig up a chicken shed, and sling grain until he was ninety-nine. That's what was in his blood, being outdoors and working on his own time. Being a cop was only a job, one he was good at and did because once in a while he even felt needed. They needed him in Rivertown, he knew that much. When that wasn't true any longer, he'd return the badge. No one'd have to tell him, either. He'd know before they did.

Howser swung off the highway at the Williams property and drove slowly up the narrow gravel service road until he came into a large yard facing a round Quonset hut and an old white barn. The ranch house was off to the left on the high side of the yard. A porch light glowed over the back door, but it looked to be dark inside the house. Howser brought the car about in a three-point turn, put it in reverse, and backed into a narrow spot between the barn and the fence so that he was facing both the driveway and the yard. He shut the engine off and killed the lights. He had some waiting to do.

"Do you think they're going to get married?"

Standing in the lawn shadows below the veranda, Jane leaned over Clayton's shoulder and looked up into the hotel where Ellen was cuddling with Alfie in the chair at the front desk, kissing him first on the ear, then on the nose, and rubbing her own cheek softly against his. Most of the lights were off indoors and the lobby was dim.

"I hope so," whispered Clayton, his attention, too, on the cop and the girl. "It's pretty disgusting watching them rehearse."

Jane pinched him. "Haven't you ever been in love?"

"Of course."

"Don't you miss it?"

A window closed up on the second floor and the light behind it went out. Most of the tenants were in their rooms up above. Clayton lowered his voice. "There are times when I miss being in love, and other times when it doesn't seem as important."

"In other words, sometimes you're aware of your loneliness and the rest of the time you're repressing it?"

"No, it's just that I think I ought to be ready to have a relationship before I get into one."

Jane thumped him on the thigh with her fist. "But Jack, that just sounds so mechanical. So pragmatic. Love isn't like that. You can't say one day you're not going to fall in love and the next you are."

"Why not?"

"Because that's just not the way it works."

"Jane?"

"Yes?"

"Tell me something."

"What's that?"

A large delivery truck drove past down on the road. The roar of the diesel engine rattled the lobby windows. He waited for the noise to subside, then asked, "How come women are always lecturing me?"

She squeezed his arms. "Because you are so obviously in need of help and only women are capable of giving it to you. Can't you see that? It seems perfectly clear to me."

"You have beautiful eyes, do you know that?"

That caught her off guard. "See," she stammered, "I knew you liked me."

"Of course I like you, Jane. You're funny *and* beautiful."

"Wise and wonderful."

"Right. And sexy, too."

"So what are you going to do about it?"

Clayton took her arm and led her around back of the Walcott into the arbor under the drooping willow to a stone bench, sat her down and slid in beside her. Hidden in the darkness by the wild growth of honeysuckle and bougainvillea, he kissed her gently on the cheek and eyelids and lips, and caressed her breasts with his fingertips.

Her arms wrapped about his waist, she murmured, "Jack?"

The slightest breeze drifted through the yard, fanning in the willows and the dark blue shadows above. "Yes?"

Jane removed his right hand from her blouse and squeezed his fingers in her palm. She kissed him on the chin and whispered, "Let's go somewhere."

Howser turned on the car stereo, searching for a little music to keep him company in the dark. The radio in the black-and-white was only able to get the AM stations, but he didn't mind. As long as it wasn't elevator music or heavy metal it would be fine. Moving along the dial, he found Creedence Clearwater Revival. That was good. He'd always liked John Fogerty. The man's music reminded him of the country—gravel roads and small towns. *Wrote a song for everyone.* Yes, he did. Howser turned up the volume and kept rhythm on the steering wheel with a pencil. He settled back into the seat, trying to get as comfortable as possible. It was going to be a long evening.

He wished he'd sent Alfie out on this one. It would have been a good experience for him. Right now Alfie was probably indoors at the Walcott, necking with Ellen Kelleher while Howser was parked in the dust outside of a cow barn waiting for the owner to come home so that he could ask him whether or not his son had shown up for dinner.

He turned the stereo down and grabbed the mike.

"RP1 to base. Susan?"

He waited a few seconds. Then a voice came on.

"Yes, Chief?"

"Did Jane leave yet?"

"She'd just gone when I got here and that was, let me see, about an hour and a half ago. Do you want me to try and get hold of her for you? I think she was going out to the Walcott. I can ring the desk there for you if you'd like."

"No thanks, Susan. How about getting Corey for me."

"Yes sir. He's answering a complaint at the Starlite Drive-in. If you hold on, I'll patch him through."

"I'd appreciate it."

Howser set the mike down on the passenger seat and rolled down the window, letting some fresh air into the unit. The smell of manure from the back of the barn was ruining the effect for him, however. Maybe he ought to have parked somewhere else.

"Chief?"

Howser picked up the mike. "Go ahead, Susan."

"Corey's away from the unit. It'll probably be a few minutes."

"That's fine. I'm not going anywhere."

He laid the mike in his lap and turned the volume on the stereo back up again. Another song. *Empty lake, empty streets, the sun goes down alone, I'm driving by your house though I know you're not home. I can see you, your brown skin shining in the sun* . . . The song reminded him of—what else?—Kathy. What *didn't* remind him of Kathy? She was always there when he was alone. *Walking real slow and smiling at everyone* . . . She wouldn't be alone tonight.

He knew that. Did she ever think of him? *Those days are gone forever, I should just let 'em go, but . . .* He felt like she never thought about him except he knew there were probably times when maybe she even missed him a little. Not enough to call, though. *I can tell you my love for you will still be strong, after the boys of summer have gone . . .* What was the matter with him? He'd gotten what he wanted, hadn't he? He'd gotten out of the city. He had a new job, a good one, working with nice people, most of whom he actually liked as much as respected, and a few he counted now as friends. He'd gotten just what he had always told Kathy he'd wanted. There was only one problem: Why couldn't she have wanted it, too?

Corey's voice came on the radio. "Chief?"

"Here."

"Need something?"

"Well, I'd like to find out what happened to Danny Williams without having to park my butt out here all night. Seen any of his little buddies yet?"

"Funny you should ask, Chief. We're out here at the Starlite handling a disturbance complaint, and who do you suppose we've got in the back of the unit?"

"I'm not in a guessing mood. What'd the idiots do now?"

"Busted into the storage closet of the refreshment center and appropriated several boxes of melted ice cream bars which they used to smear the windshields of about two dozen parked vehicles. Seems Jamie couldn't handle the idea of some folks spending a nice quiet evening at the drive-in picture show."

"Anyone hurt?"

"Just the usual bloody noses. Nothing too ugly. We've seen worse. Movie wasn't even interrupted and Starlite's security's got a couple of kids washing the customers' cars off. Beef's taking statements from Bud's employees, so he ought to be out here for at least another half hour, forty-five minutes. I'm running mister big shot downtown right now. We've been asking about Danny. Looks like nobody except Jamie's seen him since yesterday morning. Talking to people out here, though, I expect if he shows up anywhere around town we'll know about it. Seems Jamie's tramp-in-the-mill story's made folks a little nervous. If

Danny shows up in one piece and still breathing, I guess everyone'll feel a whole lot better. Anything else we can do for you?"

"No, I suppose I'm stuck out here for a while."

"Well, if something new turns up, we'll give you a holler."

"Thanks."

Howser signed off and leaned back in the seat. He tried to imagine Jamie Danielson and his friends staging their own ice cream riot at the drive-in movie. It was ridiculous. Here was a bright, good-looking kid with lots of friends, lots of money, a nice car, who shot stray cats with a .22, picked fights in the late innings of city league softball games, shoplifted almost monthly at Thrifty's and treated school rules and city ordinances with equal disdain while bullying everyone around him into doing likewise. Jamie, who had every reason and opportunity in the world to be an overachiever, was instead a punk, a bona fide juvenile delinquent whose only saving grace was his last name. But no child of Tom Danielson would ever rot in a Rivertown jail. It seemed every night Jamie was into something new and his father treated it as a joke. He laughed about it, the old "boys will be boys" kind of crap. He bailed him out, paid his fines, got him off, let him loose. It was his town and Jamie was his boy. And in Tom's eyes, the kid couldn't do a damn thing wrong. There was a story, though, Howser had heard from Jane when he first came to Rivertown. It was a story about Danielson and his older sons, Nathan and Lucas, and a stunt they'd pulled at the Cal Expo back in the late sixties, something about knocking down exhibition stands and drawing knives on the security personnel and Danielson himself intervening to free his sons and then breaking young Nathan's jaw in the pickup truck on the way home. Jane said the story was interesting in that, so far as she knew, no Danielson had ever been involved in any kind of trouble outside of Rivertown since, despite all the turmoil they were used to causing at home. Apparently it had cost Tom more than money to get his boys off. Having to barter for his sons' freedom like that with strangers had not only humiliated him, it had damaged his reputation in that part of the state, something Danielson swore to his friends would never happen again. As it turned out, Lucas moved to Montana a year later on his twenty-first birthday and Nathan was killed in the air war over North Vietnam in 1973. Only Jamie was left to risk his father's good name. But the baby of the family stayed close to home, never causing anybody outside of Rivertown any trouble at all. He apparently recognized the boundaries of his playground and observed them with remarkable care. Inside of Rivertown, however, he never let up. Every Friday night (or any summer evening, for that matter), he'd drive into town with his friends and get himself arrested for everything from disturbing the peace to loitering to assault. By midnight, he and his buddies would be back on the street again courtesy of the old man. Why they acted like they did was fairly obvious—at eighteen, nineteen years old, you'll do whatever feels good so long as you think you can get away with it. Why the old man bailed them out was a little more difficult to understand, but Howser assumed it probably had something to do with demonstrating who ran Rivertown, whose property it was, whose playground. On the other hand, there was no way Howser could let Danielson's kid use other people's lives for his own amusement. The fact was, if he once stepped beyond that line where his father's influence protected him, the kid was going to take a long fall.

Downtown, the last necking teenagers had departed Sutter Park. Only the squirrels were left on the lawn. The streets had quieted considerably in the last half hour; traffic was sparse. A solitary police car pulled into the city parking lot beside the courthouse. The patrolman got out and went into the building. In the backseat, illuminated by the glare of passing headlights, his prisoner stared out through the side window. Across the street, sitting with Jane on a sidewalk bench in the shadows of a broad sycamore tree, Jack Clayton studied the face behind the glass. "Who's that in the car?"

"I don't know. I can't tell from here."

"Looks like a kid."

"That wouldn't be unusual. They tend to visit us with

alarming regularity during the summer. Disturbing the peace. Assault. Public drunkenness. Loitering. The usual for male adolescents."

The patrolman came out of the building, clipboard in hand. He opened the passenger side of the black-and-white and tossed it onto the seat. Closing the door, he looked up and saw Jane. She waved to him and he waved back. An old blue Dodge, radio blaring, drove down the street. The cop waited for it to pass, then came across.

"Out for a little stroll, huh? Decided to come downtown for some excitement?"

"Something like that," answered Jane. "Guess we're not the only ones."

The cop described the events out at the drive-in, then jerked his thumb in the direction of the car. "See, I think they get lonely every so often and miss our company. We're like family now. I don't know about anybody else, but I look forward to having them over."

"Sounds like you're a regular home away from home," said Clayton.

Corey smiled at him. "We try."

A warm breeze swept through the park. Overhead, the sycamore swayed. Dust blew in the street.

"Corey," said Jane. "This is my friend Jack."

The cop reached over and shook hands. "Glad to know you."

"He's staying at the Walcott," said Jane.

"And you're showing him the sights."

"Absolutely."

Four more cars passed by the courthouse. The last one, a red Chevy Blazer, slowed through the traffic light and pulled over at the curb just beyond the city parking lot. Tom Danielson climbed out. He went immediately to the cruiser and looked in the window. He tapped on the glass and Jamie slid over, raising his arms to show Danielson the handcuffs he had on. Tom nodded and walked back to his truck. He reached in and turned the engine off, leaving the parking lights on.

"He's looking for me," said Corey. "What do you bet he wants to write me a check for his kid's bail?"

"Tell him we only take American Express," said Jane.

The cop laughed. They watched Danielson glance repeatedly at his wristwatch. Jamie tapped at the window of the cruiser with his cuffs and Danielson motioned him to stay put.

"Where's Beef?" Jane asked.

"Still out at the Starlite, as far as I know. He had a lot of statements to take. There were seventy-five kids seeing the show out there tonight."

"He's not talking to all of them?" replied Jane.

"No, but quite a few. It's going to take him a while yet. Of course, it'd go a little quicker if I was out there helping but seeing as we have the prisoner right here, somebody's got to stay with the unit, you know. Rules."

Danielson tried the door to the courthouse. It was locked. He came back around to the curb and looked up the street in one direction and back down in the other.

"Tom's getting edgy now," said the cop, kneeling behind the park bench. "He hates to be kept waiting."

"Looks like he's in a nasty mood tonight," said Jane.

"Oh, he's always in a nasty mood."

They watched Danielson walk back to the Blazer and lean in through the open window. He gave the horn a long blast.

"Uh-oh," said Corey, getting up. "I guess I'm being paged."

"Good luck."

As he headed off across the street, the cop shouted back, "This is where the fun begins."

At midnight, Howser opened the car door and got out. He had been sitting now for almost three hours and he needed to stretch his legs. The older he got, the less time he was able to spend sitting in a police car without becoming uncomfortably restless. There was a time when he had been able to do a good nine hours, no problems at all. Now he was lucky to do a couple without going nuts. First his rear end went, then his back. After that, the pain drove him out.

Dust swirled about in the breeze as it swept the yard. Howser sneezed once violently. Being out in the country might be good for the soul, he thought, but it was hell on an allergy. It was dry on the Williams ranch. There was little hint of the river, five miles to the east. The hills, and the long fields in between, soaked up the humidity from Green River leaving nothing except a faint coolness that would otherwise be absent from the summer air. Howser walked around to the back of his car and looked out across the fields to the main road running across the front of the Williams property line. The quiet impressed him; all he could hear was the crunching of his shoes in the gravel. And if he stopped moving . . . only the wind pushing slowly through the grass in the long open field.

He stared back at the house. Just that forty-watt bulb burning over the back porch and another light on somewhere indoors. The kid *could* be home. He'd already knocked once, when he'd first arrived, and had gotten no answer. Still, the kid might've been inside with the TV or stereo on and a pair of headphones strapped to his ears. He might even've been sleeping. Of course, Jane had called earlier, so had Susan. Maybe Danny Williams just wasn't answering the phone. Howser decided to try knocking again. If the kid was asleep, he'd wake him up. If he was in there watching TV, maybe he'd find that out, too. In either case, he'd have his answer and be able to get back to town and into bed at a decent hour.

Howser crossed the yard and went straight for the back door and knocked. He waited a few seconds and knocked again. He leaned his ear to the door to see if there was any sound coming from inside. He knocked again, pounding harder this time. He left the porch and walked around to the front of the house where the doorbell was mounted almost flush with the frame. He rang fourteen times. He could hear it echo inside, but that was all. No footsteps, no voice. Either the kid was not home or he was inside and not planning to come out. Howser stepped down off the front porch and walked around to the north side of the house. The windows there were dark and empty. He realized that the light he thought he'd seen inside must have been a reflection from the back porch. It appeared as though no one was home after all. If he wanted to find out whether or not Danny was with his parents, he'd have to wait until Joe Williams returned. That's all there was to it. Disgusted with his luck, he headed back across the yard to his "office." The wind came up again lifting more dust into the warm dark air. As he reached the car door, Howser noticed a pair of headlights down on the county road approaching quickly from the west. A small pickup truck going like hell. If he hadn't been so far out of town, Howser would've jumped inside the unit and put out a call on it. As it was, trying to organize any sort of pursuit now would be a waste of time. Before he even got off the radio, the driver'd be twenty miles away. He leaned against the roof of his own vehicle and watched the pickup race past, running over the last rise into the darkness on the other side of the hill.

The black pickup truck ran quickly up the highway, negotiating the curves with ease, barely touching the weeds that bordered the roadside. The driver leaned out the window, feeling the wind in his face, grinning widely to the thrill of speed in the dark. On the passenger side, Calvin Arnold opened the glove compartment and stirred through several layers of road maps, gum wrappers, stained Burger King napkins, and Union 76 credit-card receipts until he found a stick of Doublemint gum which he unwrapped and popped in his mouth. He looked over at Ray Maddox and grinned. His cousin grinned back and jammed his foot even harder down on the gas. Calvin laughed and took the wet chewing gum from his mouth and stuck it on the back of Ray's right hand. He howled as his cousin flung the hand about, vainly trying to free the gum without taking his left hand off the steering wheel. The pickup swerved wildly, sliding down the road from one side to the other into the night.

Farther ahead, perhaps two miles in the distance, a single figure rose from up the slope of the deep ravine of manzanita brush and crossed into the middle of the road. He squatted over the black pavement and traced a circle six times in the dust with a forefinger whose skin was discolored and bro-

ken. His eyes rose to meet the horizon where the road swelled up at the knoll a hundred feet to the south. Nearby, the long shadow of the broken oak branch, ragged and thick, stretched across one lane a few feet below the rise. He traced an arc above the circle and another beneath. There was no reason to hurry now. There would be time enough to hide when the lights broke the horizon. Then he would see what might happen to the laughing boys with their truck upside down and no place to run.

Back in the cab of the pickup, Calvin chose another station and turned the radio volume up two notches until he could hear neither the engine nor the draft whistling through the quarter windows. He was feeling good. Ray was an excellent driver and Calvin loved nothing better than to head out of town with him racing the wind. Ray leaned over and yelled, "Turn the fuckin' radio down!"

Calvin just laughed and pointed to his ears. Ray yelled again. Calvin laughed again and shrugged, then shouted back at his cousin, "I can't hear you. Some asshole's got his fucking radio turned up too loud."

He reached under the seat and dragged out the Styrofoam cooler. In between bumps in the road, he opened it and took out another can of Stroh's. He shook it once and held it out the side window while jerking off the tab. The outside of the cab, from the door to the rear bumper, went white with beer foam. Calvin took a long gulp and passed it over. Ray took a swig and handed it back. He coughed and wiped his mouth with the back of his hand. Calvin dropped the beer can and it rolled under the seat. As he lurched forward after it, his cousin swore out loud and the truck swerved violently to the right. An instant later, as the pickup went airborne, Calvin wondered if the shots of tequila he'd had earlier that evening at Moss's Big Belly were somehow just then taking effect. Never before in his life had he felt so disoriented. The pickup truck flipped twice end over end before it made contact with the ground halfway down the ravine. It struck the manzanita nose first, dislodging Ray from his place behind the wheel and exploding him out through the windshield and onto the hood of the pickup. He did not remain there long. The small truck careened off the embankment and went into a long, slow, tumble down through the manzanita to the dark bottom of the ravine. In the middle of the last rollover, Ray was crushed and thrown clear, landing dead face-down in the brush with the final wrenching of smashed metal and glass. Calvin was trapped inside the pickup, caught by the sleeve of his shirt on the tapered end of the gear lever.

The pickup came to a rest deep in the manzanita right side up, windshield missing on the driver's side, roof crushed, radiator spewing a cloud of steaming antifreeze. A deep laceration above Calvin's eyebrow streamed blood over most of his face, blinding him and causing him to panic and fight wildly to extricate himself from the cab even though there was no reason to do so. The event was over. He had been in a bad accident. That was all. The truck had swerved to avoid something just beyond the top of that last knoll, at a speed too great to remain on the road. Calvin kicked at the passenger door until it opened, then crawled out of the cab into the darkness and lay there trying to think. His forehead was bleeding and his right shoulder ached, yet he was alive. He looked back at the cab and suddenly remembered his cousin. Where was Ray? As Calvin sat up to look back inside the cab, he passed out.

What's wrong with you, man? You scared of a chick? Scared she's going to bite? Get the fuck over there and tell her how good she's lookin'! Tell her this is her lucky night and Regaining consciousness, Calvin became sick to his stomach. He bent over and vomited into the dirt between his knees. Frightened, he called out for his cousin. His voice echoed into the blackness of the ravine. He tried again. Hearing no response, Calvin crawled slowly back over to the cab of the pickup and stuck his hand inside under the seat and fumbled about until he felt the flashlight Ray had always kept there for emergencies. *Ray, where are you?* Calvin drew the flashlight out and pointed it into the shadows and flicked the switch. It did not come on. He banged the flashlight softly into his palm and tried the switch again. Nope. He banged it harder and worked the switch again. Fucking thing! He shook it furiously and ran the switch back and forth, back and forth, then threw the light off into the manzanita. Goddammit anyhow. Suddenly it occurred to him that the pickup might explode. He'd seen it happen often enough on TV. Christ, he'd survived the wreck only to be burned alive. He crawled as quickly as he could away from the pickup and into the manzanita. How far was safe? He crawled at least sixty feet before he stopped. Was that far enough? Well, it didn't matter because he was too tired now to crawl any farther. He slumped to his side. Maybe it wouldn't blow up anyhow. *Yeah, if it hasn't blown by now, it probably won't.* Had he smelled any gasoline? Not that he could remember. Maybe he was okay. He rested his head on his left arm and did his best to fight off waves of nausea and pain. The immediate fear dimmed.

He lay there, listening for his cousin's voice, listening for sirens on the highway, people coming to help, anything. All he heard were strange rustling noises in the manzanita, stirrings like a night wind rising. The brush around him crackled and swayed, and another sound entered his consciousness, like a gusty wind . . . but not the wind. Something like . . . gunny sacks dragged across loose gravel? A scraping noise in the dirt and brush. It seemed to be coming from all around him. A shuffling of footsteps too careless or too heavy or too tired to be lifted, or maybe too many footsteps to be heard individually, yet moving together, almost in unison, around him. The wind, but not the wind. With his face pressed to the ground, Calvin sucked in his breath and listened. Then he heard a voice close by speak, saying . . . what? . . . His name? . . . Then an awful wrenching pain, beginning in his left ankle and fanning upward, took over his consciousness. Something had his ankle in its grip and was twisting and tugging him from the underbrush. He grabbed hold of the nearest manzanita bush and resisted momentarily, but his leg . . . *God!* Calvin screamed as his kneecap popped from its joint, tearing loose ligaments, tendons, muscle. His leg torqued violently and his lower torso spasmed in the severe jerking, twisting motion that pulled him out of the underbrush. Fainting at last from the agony of overstressed bones fracturing simultaneously from ankle to hip, Calvin Arnold watched a giant smiling face draw near.

Howser woke with the headlights of the Williams sedan shining in his eyes. He sat up in the seat as the white Buick swung past him and stopped in front of the house. He heard Joe shut off the engine and get out. The yard went dark again and two car doors slammed closed. Howser looked at his watch. It was a quarter after three. He'd been sleeping for over an hour and hadn't heard Williams coming up the drive. It had been a long night but Howser knew it was going to get even longer if the kid had not spent the last fourteen hours in Stockton with his parents. He yawned and climbed out of the cruiser as he heard Joe opening up the back door. He reached back into the car and honked the horn. Then he flicked the rack lights once on and off and started walking toward the house.

"That you, Alfie?" yelled Williams. His voice echoed off the barn and out across the field in the dark.

"Nope, you got the chief this time, Joe."

"Well, what in God's name are you doing in my yard in the middle of the night?"

As he drew closer, Howser could see Joe's wife, Kitty, waiting by the door under the porch light, her round face blank and stony. Howser thrust his hand out to Williams who took it weakly, shook once, and let go.

"What's this all about? Doc don't even make house calls this time of night."

Howser tried to smile but the look on Williams's face and the fuzzy state of his own brain just then told him he'd be better off getting things over with as quickly as possible.

"Is your boy with you there, Joe?" asked Howser, nodding in the direction of the house.

Williams cocked his head to one side and let his mouth fall slightly open. Kitty shifted her arms up under her breasts and lowered her eyes. The porch light was shining now directly in Howser's face and he moved half a step to his left into Williams's shadow. He decided that neither of them had understood the question. He tried again. "Is Danny here with you folks?"

Joe put his hand up to his lip and pulled on it. He opened his mouth even wider as though he were trying to draw in huge gulps of air. Kitty wiped her nose with the sleeve of her sweater and let her right arm fall to her thigh. Joe coughed and cleared his throat. Howser started to ask the same question a third time when Williams cut him off. "He didn't come along with us. We didn't ask him to neither."

"Is he inside?"

"In the house? Now?"

"Yeah. I see the lights are out but I thought he might be in there anyhow."

Joe turned to Kitty who smiled. He asked her, "Is Daniel in there, honey? Hiding in the dark?"

"No, I don't think so, Joe. Doors were still locked."

"Kitty doesn't think he's in there, Chief. I guess she'd know, too, since she locked things up before we left. Isn't that right, Kitty?"

She put her fingers to her lips and nodded. Howser stared at them both then shook his head, averting his eyes from theirs. He knew there was something going on here though he was at a complete loss to figure out what it was. The three of them stood motionless in the porch-light shadow. Joe broke what passed for a grin and glanced at his wife. She ran her left hand back through her hair and left it folded behind her neck. A faint breeze fanned Howser's face. He thought, *Christ, these two have been living out here by themselves too long. No wonder the kid spends all his time hanging around town.*

"Am I missing something here? What's the joke? All I want to know is where your boy is. Why does that seem funny to you people? Just tell me he's okay so I can go home and get some sleep."

Joe Williams turned his back on Howser and stepped under the porch light, waving his wife inside ahead of him. She disappeared into the kitchen without saying a word. Williams stopped on the door sill and switched the porch light off, throwing the yard, and Howser, into darkness. Before going inside he said, quietly, "Kitty and me are going to bed, Chief. If you see the boy, how about sending him home? We'd sure appreciate it."

A moment later, Howser found himself standing alone

again in the empty yard. He watched the lamps go out one by one inside the house until the only light anywhere came from the stars overhead. He scratched his head and walked back over to the unit and got in and leaned back in the seat, stretching his arms out across the seatbacks. He closed his eyes. Then he opened them again and looked at his watch. Almost a quarter to four. He yawned and started the engine. Then he switched on the headlights and drove slowly out of the yard and back down the driveway.

Less than a minute after he'd rolled out onto the county road, the dispatch came on the radio. "RP base to RP1."

Howser grabbed the mike off the dash and responded. "Chief here. Go ahead."

"Chief, we have a TA out on Mustang Road."

"How bad?"

"One fatality. However, the officers on the scene believe there were two passengers in the vehicle."

Howser felt the breath sucked out of his chest. Incredible. He didn't need this tonight. "IDs?"

"One so far. Raymond Maddox."

God, that's even worse, thought Howser. Rivertown boy. A local. Danielson crowd. He slowed to swing the car around and head back in the opposite direction.

"Who's out there right now?"

"Officers Harris and MacAlister. Officer Cox and Dr. Sawyer are both en route. Dr. Sawyer called the ambulance. Officer Harris has requested a winch to raise the vehicle from the ravine; we've called Redmon's Garage. He should be there, too, sometime in the next half hour."

"Turn Alfie around and send him back to town. We don't need a circus out there. Radio Doc. Tell him I'll meet him there in ten minutes."

"Yes sir."

"RP1 out."

Howser stuck the mike back on the console and flicked on the light bar.

Corey guided the black-and-white up to the very edge of the ravine and directed the spotlight down into the manzanita where the pickup had left the road. They were going

165

to need the additional light to see anything in the brush. Corey edged the car forward until the front end angled slightly downward. Then he set the parking brake and jumped out.

"Is that close enough?" he asked, walking forward to take a look for himself. The front tires were in the gravel on the slope of the ravine.

"Put it this way," said Beef. "Any closer and you'll be buying the city a new black-and-white."

"Maggie'd love that. She's been on my ass to get her one of those new Toyotas. I can just see myself telling her, 'Darling, I just bought a new car . . . not for you, though!' "

"I'm lucky as hell Connie's scared of driving."

"Yeah," Corey agreed. "Insurance is a bitch." He pointed at the unit. "Does this help much?"

Beef nodded. "I think we're going to be able to get a better idea where Cal got off to."

"How far do you think he could've crawled?"

"I expect we're going to find him pretty close by."

"Redmon coming?"

"Susie got his wife. She wasn't too happy with the phone ringing in her ear at three in the morning, but Mike'll have his winch out here within the hour. We'll get the kid's truck out then. Both Chief and Doc ought to be showing up any time now."

Satisfied that the lights over the ravine were positioned well enough, Corey gave Beef the thumbs up. "Okay, let's go find the kid. I don't want to be stomping around down there any longer than I have to."

Howser saw the flares first, burning bright red in the distance. Closing, he saw the flashing ambers on Corey's unit parked at a crazy angle on the road. He slowed as he approached the top of the hill. The beams of light from Corey's headlamps pointed down into the darkness below the edge of the road. Pulling up alongside the other patrol car, Howser parked, turned the engine off and got out, leaving his own hazard lights flashing. Out on the roadside, the silence was amazing. No wind, no traffic. *Like the world holding its breath*. He didn't see his officers anywhere but assumed they were down below in the ravine with the pickup. He stepped to the slope and called out. "Corey!"

A flashlight beam shot up out of the dark a dozen yards to Howser's right and the patrolman's voice echoed back at him from far below. "Down here, Chief!"

Howser went back to the unit and got his own flashlight, returning to the edge of the ravine and fanning the roadside with the light until he spotted the tire marks on the slope and the route the truck had taken crashing downward through the manzanita. He followed it into the black ravine, bracing himself with one hand while using the flashlight to light his way down to where Ray Maddox's pickup lay smashed in the dark. He aimed the light at the vehicle and saw the passenger door bent open on its hinges, beer spilled out into the dirt from a Styrofoam cooler lying open in the footwell.

"Ray came out through here, headfirst," said Corey, coming out from the brush. He pointed his own light at the windshield whose safety glass was badly splintered. Howser stared at the gaping hole, trying his best not to imagine Ray passing through it on impact.

"Where is he?" asked Howser.

"You didn't see him?"

"No."

"Over here."

The patrolman led Howser around the pickup to the driver's side and flashed his light up the slope of the ravine until the beam came to rest on a white sheet covering a body only a dozen yards from the roadside. "Up there."

"Oh, jeez. How'd you spot him?"

"Just got lucky," said Beef, coming out of the brush. He directed his own flashlight onto the body. "Missed him like you did the first time. Spotted him on the way back up to call in."

"What about the other one?"

"Well, we think he's around here somewhere. It's hard to see how he'd be in any shape to go very far. We've been searching the brush right in this area."

Howser knelt down and peered inside, flicking his light about the interior of the pickup. Fragments of broken glass were scattered throughout and the seats and dashboard

167

dripped beer from the cooler. It was a mess. The entire pickup was a mess, damaged beyond hope of repair—not that it would matter to its owner any longer. Howser shook his head in disgust. He'd seen dozens of wrecks in the Valley, nineteen along the stretch known as Blood Alley alone, three bad ones in the rain one winter weekend. One in particular, the Alvarez family, he'd never forget as long as he lived. He hated traffic accidents because, more often than not, they involved kids. He especially hated the part that required him to call up the parents in the middle of the night and try to explain to them why their son or daughter wasn't going to be coming home that night. He straightened up again and swept the brush with the flashlight.

"It looks to me like the kid drove pretty near straight off the road into the ravine," said Corey. "We got some real short skid marks up there. Now, they could've been screwing around and lost control, except the road's pretty straight and Raymond was a damn fine driver, for a kid. I don't know."

Howser ran the flashlight over the undercarriage. "Tires are fine. They didn't have a blowout. Maybe they swerved to avoid an animal in the road or something. A deer, maybe."

"No deer 'round here," said Beef.

"Well, the cause of the accident isn't our concern just yet." Howser flashed the light at the manzanita. "You say Calvin's in there somewhere, right?"

"We think so."

"Well then, we've got to find him. We assume he's hurt, maybe unconscious, and can't hear us or can't respond. When Mike gets here he'll drag the truck out and if we still haven't found anything we'll bring the chainsaws and spotlamps down in here and see if we can't clear things out for a better look. I'd rather not go home wondering whether or not Calvin fell out of the cab on his way down here from the highway. All right?"

Another pair of headlights flashed overhead from the road. A car door slammed and a voice called out from above.

"That's Doc," said Corey. He pointed his flashlight up

168

into the dark and waved it in a circle, same as he'd done for the chief.

"I'll go up," said Howser. "You guys keep looking for Calvin."

"You want to give us any hints where to start?"

"Use your imagination."

He left his men by the wreck and climbed back up to the roadside. He was exhausted by the time he reached the top and had to pause to catch his breath. Now he knew just how badly he'd let himself get out of shape. Doc was waiting beside the black station wagon. Howser walked over and they shook hands.

"Hell of a thing to get dragged out of bed for, huh?"

"Where's Raymond?" asked Doc.

"I'll show you."

Howser led the coroner to the edge of the road and shined the flashlight on the white sheet spread at an angle in the brush on the slope of the ravine. Doc started down the slope. Howser handed him the flashlight and followed. When they reached the body, Doc lifted the sheet off to begin his initial examination. Howser looked away into the dark. He knew that if he looked under that sheet, he'd see the kid's face in his dreams for a week. *It doesn't matter how often you see them, the latest one is always the first.* He took a deep breath and waited for Doc to cover the body again.

"Did you know the boy?" asked Doc, folding the sheet back over the body and standing up. Even in the dark, the coroner's face was visibly ashen and grim.

"No," replied the chief. "Not beyond booking him for disturbing the peace on a couple of Saturday nights."

"His mother and I were in grade school together. Sent each other red paper hearts every Valentine's Day till the sixth grade when her father moved the family to Rancho Cordova. She didn't come back again until she was in her twenties. Then, of course, she'd been married to Earle a couple years already and had a kid, a skinny little boy named Sammy. Cute little guy, too. She said he looked like me. I thought he did, too. Never told Earle that, though. He'd have made her switch doctors. Anyway, they lost Sam in the Feather River on a camping trip in 1966.

I'll never forget it. Seemed like the whole town went into shock. Everything closed up for the funeral. Terrible thing for people who knew the Maddoxes, especially those of us who grew up with Jean. A year later, she was pregnant with Raymond. He was a good boy, too. Mirror image of his dad. Bad-tempered and feisty sometimes, but a sweet kid under the skin if you took a little time to know him. He doesn't mean half the things he says to people. I know everyone says this, Chief, but with Raymond it was true. Things he does are just his way of letting you know he's around. He runs his flag up the pole on weekends so we won't forget he's alive." Sawyer stared down at the white sheet. "How can I tell Jean? How's she supposed to understand this?"

Up on the road, the ambulance arrived. Flashing emergency lights reddened the night sky above the ravine. Howser listened to the attendants unloading a gurney. Doc Sawyer lifted the white sheet and repositioned the boy's limbs for transport. He shouted up the slope to the attendants, "You boys get down here and give me some help!"

Howser clapped a hand on Doc's shoulder and said, "I ought to go see if my guys've turned up the other boy."

Sawyer nodded. "I've got care of Ray now." He handed the flashlight back to Howser. "You go ahead."

A horn sounded from up above as another vehicle arrived at the accident site. Looking up to the road, Howser saw the flashing amber from Mike Redmon's tow truck. A door slammed closed and a loud voice echoed from above. "Chief, you down there?"

"Over here!" Howser aimed the flashlight straight up toward the road and held it until Redmon came into view atop the ravine carrying a six-volt Eveready lantern in his hand. Mike switched on the lantern and directed it toward Howser and Doc, balanced on the slope.

"Is the wreck there?" asked Redmon.

"No," said Howser. "Over that way." He pointed with the flashlight. "Come on down, I'll show you."

The two ambulance attendants appeared with the gurney beside Redmon on the edge of the road. They lifted the stretcher off and Redmon helped them steady it as they started carefully into the ravine. Their shoes kicked dirt loose that slid clear down to Doc and Howser. Redmon stumbled and fell backward onto his butt a few yards up the ravine from the body, then regained his balance and made it the rest of the way down without falling again. Dragging the cable and hook from the electric winch, he shuffled sideways across the slope. He looked sleepy and worn. Howser thrust a hand out. Redmon ignored it and instead asked, "You catch the kids that wrecked my place yet, Chief?"

"We're still working on it, Mike."

"I'll bet you are." He bent down and peeked under the white sheet. "Maybe we got one of them right here tonight, huh? What do you think?"

"Mike," said Doc Sawyer, "what makes you so god-damned ornery?"

"You should've seen what those little fuckers did to my shop." Redmon turned to Howser. "Tell him, Chief. Tell him what a goddamned mess it was."

"It was a mess, Doc. A goddamned mess."

"Okay, go ahead and have your little joke, but when I catch the little bastards that trashed my shop I'll bust their fuckin' faces up so bad you'll have to teach 'em sign language to take their statements."

"Okay, Mike, why don't you just get your winch hooked up to Ray's pickup and drag the thing out of the ravine for me. I'd like to get the hell out of here before sunup."

"Just show me where the kid parked it."

"Follow me."

"Hold on a minute. Let me run out some slack in the cable."

Redmon headed back up the slope to the tow truck to switch on the electric winch. Howser turned to Doc Sawyer. "When you finish with this one, you might as well come on down, too. We may need your help locating the other boy."

Sawyer nodded. The two ambulance attendants were just then preparing Raymond Maddox for transport. They had his body on the stretcher and were fastening the straps

171

as Redmon, cable and hook in tow, followed Howser down into the brush.

Thirty or forty yards away from the pickup now, out into the thickest portion of the manzanita, Corey could no longer hear Beef thrashing around in the darkness behind him. With only the flashlight as a guide, he crawled on hands and knees through the dense brush. Moving through it was claustrophobic: twice he had tried to stand up only to feel the branches around him catch and tangle in his hair. He was sure that when he got home his clothes would be full of ticks. He'd only chosen the direction he was moving in because of a number of broken manzanita branches he had spotted in the brushline after Howser had gone back up to the roadside. The more he had found scattered about, the deeper he'd been led into the brush. However, if Calvin had managed to crawl in this far, thought Corey, they'd never get him out. Not in the dark, anyway. Even in the daylight, they'd need chainsaws to cut a pathway large enough to use a stretcher. He swept the flashlight beam across the manzanita in his path and called out, "Cal? You in there, kid?" He paused a moment to listen, then tried again. "Cal?"

Nobody could crawl out of a car wreck and wind up this far away.

"Cal?"

There's nobody in here but us squirrels.

Corey worked himself around to start back in the opposite direction. Manzanita snared and tore at his shirt. Both his knees were scraped raw under the fabric of his pants. His legs were numb from the pain. Slowing for a second to shift the light from his right hand to his left, he heard movement in the underbrush to his left. He stopped crawling and aimed the light in that direction. The manzanita was too thick. He couldn't see more than a few feet into the brush. His flashlight wavered in his hand. The brush rustled again. He tried calling out.

"Cal? Are you in there?"

He waited, poised on his haunches until the aching in

his thighs forced him back down onto his already skinned and battered knees.

"Cal!" he yelled. "Goddammit, are you in there or not?"

He whipped the light around and heard a harsh rustling in the manzanita just beyond the perimeter of his light, then the unmistakable grating of hardheeled shoes or boots in the dirt hurrying away. Corey tried rising in hope of getting a better look but the branches were too thick above him. He yelled out and flashed the light back and forth across the underbrush. "Cal!"

Ten, maybe twenty yards away, the manzanita rustled as if by a harsh wind rushing through, but farther off now and diminishing second to second. Corey sat there motionless, listening. He covered the light with the palm of one hand until the rustling faded away and the ravine was quiet again. Then he let out his breath and realized he'd been so intimidated by the underbrush and darkness he hadn't even given thought to drawing his revolver. Somebody had been out there, but who? Calvin? After an accident like that? And running away? Not a chance. That wasn't Calvin. Unless he'd been hearing things, somebody else was in the ravine.

Then Corey's own name echoed in the brush. Beef was shouting for him from the direction of the wreck. The patrolman aimed the light forward until he located the broken path in the manzanita that led back the way he'd come, then stuck the flashlight in his belt and began crawling as quickly as he could. As he emerged on all fours from the underbrush, Corey called out and a trio of flashlights swung in his direction, blinding him until he put a hand up and waved them off. He stumbled out of the brush and into the clearing, struggling momentarily to regain his balance.

Beef laughed out loud. "Where the hell you been, buddy? You didn't get lost in there, did you?"

Corey smiled weakly and straightened up for the first time in half an hour. When the flashlights dropped away from his face, Doc and Redmon and the chief were staring at him.

"I think I might've found the kid," he said, brushing himself off.

"No shit," said Beef. "Where?"

"Back in there about fifty yards or so. I'm not sure exactly."

"You saw him?"

"No, but I heard him."

"Calvin?"

"Yeah," said Corey. "But we're going to need chainsaws to get him out."

"Well, let me tell you, partner, it'd take more than chainsaws to get Cal out of the predicament he's in now." Then Beef directed his flashlight to the ground in front of the pickup where Calvin Arnold's body lay stretched out on a dark blanket.

Corey walked past Beef and the other three men and shined his own flashlight on the body. The boy's clothes were torn and dusty and both shoes were missing. One leg, the left, was grotesquely swollen and deformed; a jagged splinter of bone poked through the jeans just above the knee, the faded denim stained black about the wound. His face was caked with blood and dirt, too, from his forehead to his chin. His nose was smashed flat, his mouth a toothless cavity above the jaw. The boy was barely recognizable. Horrified, Corey switched off his light.

"Makes you want to puke, huh?" muttered Beef, behind him. "I found him in the brush over there." He motioned with the light to the underbrush on the driver's side of the pickup. "Almost stuck my foot in his face before I saw him."

"Evidently, he tried crawling back up to the road," said Howser, "but died before he got more than a few yards."

"Excuse me," said Doc, and walked off to the slope of the ravine to call for the ambulance attendants.

Howser addressed his officers. "Beef, go make sure Doc's boys find their way down here all right. Corey, you can radio in and get things squared away at the hospital for Doc. I'll finish here with Mike and meet you guys up top."

Redmon was busy inspecting the damage inside the cab

of Maddox's pickup. He'd already fastened the winch hook to the frame rail and readied the cable.

"Mike, what do you say we get the pickup out of here? I think we're all a little tired."

"That's fine with me, Chief." Redmon climbed out of the wreck. "Just give me the word and I'll drag this thing out of here."

"Do you need any help?"

"Nope. She's ready to go when you are."

"All right then. Let's do it."

Redmon checked the security of the cable hookup once more, then followed the two patrol officers up into the dark to start the winch. A few minutes later, the two ambulance attendants came down into the ravine. Howser watched them wrap the boy in the same blanket he'd been lying on, transfer him to the stretcher and strap him down for transport back up to the roadside. They did this and carried him off without uttering a word. After they'd gone, Howser picked up the broken flashlight Beef had found in the brush and tossed it into the cab of the pickup along with an empty Stroh's beer can. He stayed behind long enough to see the winch pick up the slack in the cable and begin hauling the wreck up through the manzanita.

12

Jack Clayton threw off the sheets and squinted his eyes. The sunlight passing through the tinted window shades colored everything in the room a bright yellow. He put his hand up to block the glare until his eyes adjusted. He was alone. What time was it? He rolled over and reached under the bed, searching until he found the clock. Ten thirty. No wonder Jane was gone. But this is Saturday, he thought. Who gets up before ten on a Saturday morning unless they're watching cartoons? For some reason he couldn't picture Jane watching *Scooby-Doo*, so where did she go? Clayton rubbed his eyes and tried to wake up. He hung his legs over the edge of the bed and forced himself onto his feet. He looked around for his pants. He couldn't see them. Nor his shirt and socks. Okay then, he was just going to have to start the day in his boxer shorts. He walked across the room and opened the bedroom door and called out down the hall, "Jane?"

No answer. She was gone, all right. Well, now he remembered her leaving though it seemed to him she'd said something about coming right back. Apparently not, since she had left several hours ago. He walked down the hallway and into the kitchen. It was empty and the curtains were drawn open to the sunlight. He looked through the glass. Nice day out. Something for breakfast, maybe? He went to the refrigerator and poked about inside for a little food. He didn't want anything he had to cook.

"An orange sounds good. May I have one of your oranges, Jane? Thank you."

Clayton peeled the rind away and ate from the center, wiping the juice from his chin as it dribbled out of the corners of his mouth. Before he could finish, the phone rang. Should he answer or not? It rang two, then three, then four times. He set the orange down on the counter and picked up the receiver.

"Hello?"

"You're up finally, huh?" Jane's voice.

"I thought you were at work."

"I am now."

"Didn't you leave here three hours ago?" asked Clayton.

"Yes, but I had a couple of places to go first. Why?"

"No reason. You woke me up."

"Yes, I did. Where are you?"

"In your kitchen."

"Jack, I hope you're not going through my cupboards."

"Nope, just your refrigerator. Don't you ever go to the market? There's nothing here to eat except a couple of oranges and an old head of lettuce."

"You didn't find the carrots then, I assume."

"No."

"Good. I'm saving them for myself."

"You called to make sure I didn't eat your carrots?"

"No, I just wanted to see if you were up yet."

"I'm not only up, Jane, but I'm standing here in my underwear in the middle of your kitchen."

"Well Christ, Jack, go put your clothes on. What if my neighbors see you?"

"You told me last night your neighbors never pay any attention to you at all."

"I lied. They spy on me with telescopes and video cameras and I don't want them seeing a half-naked man in my kitchen on a Saturday morning, especially when I'm not home."

"What does it matter if you're home or not?"

"Go put your clothes on."

"I can't find them. Maybe you took them to work with you by accident."

"Did you look in the closet?"

"No, not yet."

"They're in the closet. I threw them in there this morning while you were asleep."

"I'll bet you never tossed Howser's pants in the closet."

"No, I didn't. But then he didn't throw them all over like you did."

"You're sweet, Jane."

"Get dressed, Jack. The slumber party's over."

"Mind if I use your shower?"

"Please do."

"Thanks."

"Want to have lunch with me?" asked Jane.

"Sure."

"Meet me at the courthouse at noon."

"All right."

"Get dressed!"

She hung up. Clayton put the receiver back on the wall. Why Howser had let Jane get away, he'd never understand. They'd made love in this kitchen last night. A fond memory if ever there was one. They'd both laughed hysterically at the awkwardness of coupling on the countertop, but sex was supposed to be fun and Jane's enthusiasm was infectious. They'd had a great time. He finished the orange and stuffed the rind down the disposal. Then he ran water into the sink while looking out the window again. It was a beautiful day outside, deep blue skies, windless and warm. Jane had opened the screens before she left and the fresh air passing indoors from the garden on the side of her house smelled wonderful. He looked across Jane's yard to her neighbor's. Was there really someone inside gazing back at him through a pair of high-powered binoculars? Doubtful. And even if there was, so what? Jane shouldn't care what anyone thought. Truth was, they were lucky to have her in town.

He walked back to the bedroom and opened the closet and retrieved his pants from the floor beside Jane's stock of shoes. After dressing, he searched for a pen and a scrap of paper. Using an eyebrow pencil and the back of a canceled envelope, he wrote a note for her to find when she got home: "Thanks for ironing the shirt, honey."

Howser flipped Corey's accident report onto the desk. Two boys involved in a traffic accident, one killed instantly and the other sometime after impact. Two teenagers DOA at City Memorial Hospital, two local kids whose families were in shock. By morning, it was a feeling shared throughout Rivertown. Walking up Main after eating breakfast at the Grill, Howser had heard the names Raymond and Calvin at least two dozen times. The boys' pictures were on the front page of the morning *Courier*. They might not have been loved by everyone in Rivertown, but they'd still been native sons. Losing them less than a week after the railyard shooting and only days after the discovery of Sarah Miller's body in Green River only increased the incredulity people were already feeling. There'd never been a summer like this in local memory—and Danny Williams was still missing.

Howser went out into the corridor to the stairwell and listened as he looked down. Then he walked back into the office and punched up the intercom. "Jane?"

"Yes, Chief."

"Danielson here yet?"

"Haven't seen him."

"He was supposed to stop by at eleven." Howser looked up at the clock. "It's almost quarter after now. Can you buzz me when he arrives?"

"You want a warning?"

"I want to be sure my makeup's right."

"I'll call before sending him up."

"Heard anything from Doc?"

"He's been in the basement all morning, working on the two boys. Sarah's body was just released to her family a little while ago. The Millers are shipping it east to Pennsylvania tomorrow. I guess they have an old family plot there. Doc signed off on it when he came in after breakfast. Told me he'd have the report for you by lunchtime. He

179

also said he was going to take a run over to Stockton this afternoon."

"Did he say why?"

"No."

"I'll give him a call myself later on."

"Okay."

Howser switched off the intercom. Paperwork was piling up. The investigation of Sarah Miller's death had drawn so much attention from his officers and himself that the day-to-day stuff was beginning to backlog. Someone had broken into the janitor's closet at the high school. Corey and Beef had been working on that case the night of the railyard shooting. Howser had given the paperwork on that and Redmon's Garage to Randy and Al. It wasn't really the sort of thing the reserves were supposed to get involved with, but there was no other real choice. He needed his regular officers for Sarah Miller's case. Routine patrols were now tied into the ongoing investigations and overtime had become prime time. People were feeling a little skittish, so it was important that the department raise its visibility factor even if doing so meant cutting into time needed to pursue the very investigations that had everyone nervous in the first place. It made for a sort of catch-22, of course, but one not all that uncommon with police work. They'd just juggle patrol routes and work schedules, and make do the best they could.

Howser picked up Corey's report and read through it once again, trying to imagine how his patrolman might have been mistaken about what he heard there in the dark. *Somebody was down there with me in the brush. I couldn't see him but I swear he was there. I don't know who the hell it was, Chief, but it was somebody.* Was the wind blowing out there last night? Sure, gusting off and on. So what? Is that what he heard? The wind? Or could Corey have confused the sounds he heard with the ones the rest of them were making in bringing Calvin's body out of the brush?

The intercom buzzed.

"Yeah, Jane."

"Company's arrived. Want me to send them up?"

"I suppose so."

"Something wrong?"

"Nothing a couple days' fishing wouldn't cure."

"No rest for the weary, huh?"

"Nope."

"I'll tell Tom to go easy on you."

"Thanks, Jane. You're a pal."

"I knew you appreciated me."

"You're the only reliable person I've met since I took this job."

"That's me, old reliable."

"You know what I mean."

"I'll send them up."

"Thanks."

Howser took the accident reports off the top of the desk and stuffed them into the right-hand drawer. Then he got up and went to the window and opened the shades. He didn't want Danielson to think he was hiding in the dark. A couple of minutes later he heard footsteps in the stairwell outside his office and returned to the desk. The door opened and Tom Danielson strode in without knocking. Three men—Horace Long, Nate Arnold, Earle Maddox—filed in behind him and squeezed together shoulder-to-shoulder against the cabinet. Five others Howser knew only by face waited out in the corridor. Ordinarily, Howser would have felt strange not standing and greeting each man with a handshake but in this case he found it easy not to.

"You find the Williams boy yet, Chief?" asked Danielson, stopping in front of the desk. His checkered work shirt was stained dark with sweat, and a stale milky odor filled the small office. Howser noticed that Joe Williams was not among his visitors. That figured.

He ignored Danielson's question and addressed the men behind him instead. "Nate, Earle, I'm really sorry about your boys. I know we had a little trouble with them from time to time but I never felt it was anything serious. I just want you to know that."

Both men nodded without looking up. They were sweating profusely, clearly uncomfortable in the office of the chief of police. Maybe they were feeling a little used by Danielson this morning. Not that they'd ever admit it aloud. Nobody could afford to fall that far from the man's good graces. Cops could be hired and fired, but Tom Danielson would be in their lives as long as they were in Rivertown.

"I hear that might not have been an accident out there last night," said Danielson, his stare fixed on Howser. "Word has it those two boys might've been killed deliberately by somebody hiding out there on Mustang Road, waiting for them to come along when they did."

"Really? Who's saying all that?"

"Doesn't matter who's saying it. What we want to know from you is what you're doing about it."

"Well, that would probably depend on whether what you hear is true or not, now doesn't it? Anyhow, what the hell does this have to do with you? Didn't we have this conversation out on Green River? And didn't I tell you then that these investigations are none of your business? What is it with you?"

Danielson leaned forward and placed both hands in the middle of Howser's desk. "I'll tell you what's with me, mister. *You* are. You and the way you're running things from this office. What the hell did we hire you for? You don't do a goddamn thing all day except sit at this desk and diddle on the radio with the ladies. Is that how they do things in the big city? Or is that the reason you're working here now?" Danielson bent closer until his huge red face blocked the other men from view. "You're looking as useful as tits on a bull, Howser. You hear me? Show us something to let us know we're getting our money's worth from you or get the hell out. We might be country people, Howser, but we know when we're getting jerked off."

Then he straightened up and motioned for the men at the back of the room to leave the office. When the last one had gone, Danielson walked to the door, looked back at Howser, and winked. "Think of this as a pep talk, Chief. It's late in the game and we're down by a couple of touchdowns. We don't want to bring in your backup, but time's running short and you either got to perform or sit. It's up to you."

He turned his back on Howser and walked out into the corridor, closing the door behind him. As the echoing of voices moved down into the stairwell, Howser opened the intercom to downstairs. "Jane?"

"Yes, Chief?"

"I'm going out. I'll probably be gone for a few hours. If anything on the Williams boy comes in, go ahead and patch it through. Otherwise I'll call in later on, all right?"

"Sure."

"Listen, while I'm gone, there's something I'd like you to do for me, if you could. Got a pen handy? There are some files I want you to dig up for me." After telling her what he had in mind, Howser took out his keys and locked the desktop. Then he stood up and went to the window, parting the blinds. Through the slats he could see Danielson and his circle of admirers getting into their trucks out front. Howser let the blinds close. A couple of minutes later he was heading down the back stairs on his way to the parking lot. Once out into the sunlight, he climbed into the unit and hit the ignition. He was going to take a drive. If he was lucky, he'd cool off enough by midafternoon to come back and work on an idea that had been nagging him since he watched Sarah Miller's body dragged out of Green River forty-eight hours ago.

In an empty field a mile and a half from town, four teenage boys stood apart in the dry grass shouting at each other in the bright sunlight. Two of them were young towheads dressed in identical white T-shirts and Sears blue jeans. A third had black shoulder-length hair, a purple tie-dyed shirt and a red bandanna hanging from the rear pocket of a pair of brown corduroy trousers. The fourth boy, dark-haired too, wore only a pair of faded jeans; his bare upper body was tanned to a smooth brown. Their voices carried across the sunburnt field to the treeline where three off-road vehicles were parked on the edge of a shallow creekbed gone to dust in the heat of the season.

One of the towheads left the group and wandered off toward the shade. He went to the blue Nissan four-by-four and sat up against the front bumper, head hung to his chin, eyes closed. Then he began undressing. The three boys still in the field stopped shouting and stared at him, eyes squinting hard into the white light. The rattlesnake grass rippled in the breeze. The other towhead drew a Scout knife from his back pocket and pried open the blade, then flung it into the dirt where it stuck inches from his right foot. He bent down to retrieve it, then pitched it into the grass again an inch closer to his big toe. The two older boys paid no attention. They were still watching the one by the four-by-four who by now had stripped off the last of his clothes and was climbing naked into the cab of the truck. The towhead pulled the door closed and hung his forearms over the steering wheel. He stared blankly through the dust-clouded glass. The noon wind gusted through the trees, littering the air with thousands of dried strands of Spanish moss from the oak branches. The older boys left the towhead with the pocketknife alone in the middle of the field and headed for the shade.

Jerry Hardisty strolled up to the four-by-four and knocked on the windshield. Inside the cab, Howie Long refused to answer; he closed his eyes and gripped the steering wheel with both hands. Jerry took the bandanna from his back pocket and used it to wipe off a section of glass. Roy Lee, standing by the front bumper, pounded on the hood with his fist. The noise reverberated through the small truck. Howie, looking hangdog, butted his head against the dashboard. Jerry and Roy shook their heads and wandered off down into the shady creekbed to smoke a cigarette. A cry went up from the field where Ernie Long bent over, grabbing at his foot. A tennis shoe lay in the grass a few feet away, the pocketknife stuck in the toe. Ernie struggled to remove the white sock from his wounded foot. Before he got it off, the sock was stained a dark red. He tied it like a tourniquet around the wound and then sat spraddle-legged in the dry grass waiting for the pain to ease. The hot sun beat down on his head and the wind rose and fell and the shadows expanded beneath the treeline.

Another pickup truck crossed the field from the highway, intruding upon the quiet chatter of the birds. The Chevy half-ton drove in under the live oaks with a blast of dust and leaves, and the sparrows flew skyward. Jamie Danielson threw open the door of the pickup and bounced out, leaving the key in the ignition and the stereo booming. The two boys came up from the creekbed to meet him. One had a deck of playing cards in his hand. The other smoked a cigarette. Both looked drowsy and bored. Jamie greeted them with a grin. "Hey guys."

Jerry Hardisty sat down on the bumper of the pickup and flicked ash off the cigarette into the dirt. "So what's the word?"

"My old man's downtown finding out. He's talking to the chief right now. Said if he had to, he'd shove some firecrackers up Howser's ass. Everybody's pissed off."

Roy reshuffled the deck of cards and spread them out face-down on the hood of the truck. "That was no fuckin' accident last night."

Jamie stared at him. "I was down at the salvage yard this morning checking it out. You guys should've seen the—"

"What about Danny?" interrupted Jerry. He took another drag off the cigarette and blew a soft smoke ring into the air.

"Abbott and Costello didn't find anything out at the mill, so nobody's looking anymore. Lazy fucks. They think he ran away. Danny's own folks don't even give a shit. I tried calling him this morning and his mother hung up on me. The bitch."

Roy scooped up the cards and dealt himself five off the top of the deck. "So they're just waiting until some square-head finds him floating in the river, is that it?"

"How the fuck should I know?" replied Jamie. "Do I look like the chief?"

Jerry dropped the cigarette and snuffed it out with the toe of his boot. "What about Sarah? They find her clothes yet?"

Jamie answered without hesitation. "I didn't hear anything about that."

"Nothing at all? Nobody said anything?"

"I said no, didn't I?" shouted Jamie. "No one asked anything. No one said anything. Okay?" Jamie walked out into the sunlight. "Where's Goober and Gomer?"

Jerry looked out across the grass to where Ernie had been sitting. The towhead was gone. The field was empty.

"Howie's in the truck," said Jerry. "I don't know where Ernie went. He had his knife."

Jamie walked over to the Longs' four-by-four and looked in. Howie was lying nude on the front seat with his eyes closed, pretending to be asleep. They all knew Howie took his clothes off when something was bothering him. Jamie rapped on the glass, then tried to open the door and found it locked. Jerry wandered up and leaned on the hood. Jamie banged hard on the driver's door with his fist, denting the panel. Howie Long's eyelids fluttered but stayed shut.

"What's Gomer's problem?" asked Jamie, watching the towhead go fetal on them.

"He's scared."

"Of what?"

"Dying."

Twenty feet away, Roy pitched his cards one after another into a circle he'd drawn in the dirt by the front wheel of Jamie's truck. Across the empty field, Ernie Long came hobbling toward them through the dry grass with a white sock tied around his foot. The grass swayed about him in the wind, like waves at sea.

Jerry lit up another cigarette and flicked the spent match toward the creekbed. "What're we going to do?"

"Not a fucking thing," said Jamie. "As long as everyone keeps their mouths shut, it'll be cool. I'm not worried." He reached for Jerry's cigarette. "How about a smoke?"

Clayton sat on the wooden bench with his back to the green wall waiting for Jane to come down from the ladies' washroom on the second floor. It was cool inside the courthouse, though stuffy, and it smelled to him like that old church in Anaheim his mother used to take him to when he was a kid. He watched the sunlight coming in from the windows up above, slanting downward to the checkered tile floor below. Old buildings fascinated him. There was something about the way the slightest noises echoed throughout, as though the rooms and the walls absorbed and mimicked human presence. Libraries were like that, the ones without noise-suppressing carpets and soundproof wall paneling. Some old schoolhouses were, too. And a few churches. Places where people worked quietly and moved about on tiptoes and spoke with each other in low voices or careful whispers. Whispers echoed in those walls, sometimes more so than shouts. They stuck to the wallpaper and paint and whispered back as you passed.

Clayton heard footsteps on the staircase, heels clacking on the polished granite steps.

"Jack?"

"Down here."

"You waited for me!"

"You asked me to, remember?"

"I know."

"So you took your time just to see how long I'd wait, huh? What if I'd taken off?"

"I would've had to go to lunch with someone else, I suppose."

"It might've been tough finding someone around here. This place is like a morgue."

"It *is* a morgue, Jack. Right below our feet on the basement floor."

"You know what I mean."

"It's a Saturday. No one works on Saturday except morons like me."

They walked across the lobby to the front door. Sunlight glared on the brass handles.

"This really is a great building," said Clayton.

"When I was a little girl, Frank and I used to sneak in here on Sundays while everyone else was in church and play hide-and-seek. It was wonderful."

They stepped out into the sunlight. Clayton shielded his eyes with the back of his hand.

"Where do you want to go?" he asked.

"Well, I have to be back in thirty minutes. Is the Grill okay?"

"Fine."

Clayton closed the menu and took a drink of water. The smell of deep-fried potatoes and hamburgers filled the diner with a hazy smoke dissipated only slightly by the electric ceiling fans rotating slowly overhead. Jane closed her own menu and tucked it with Clayton's between the sugar bowl and the napkin holder.

"What are you going to have?" asked Clayton, taking another sip from the water glass.

"I guess a salad. Nothing else sounds good."

"Don't eat anything then. No sense forcing yourself."

"I'm not forcing myself. I'm hungry," said Jane. "I just can't think of anything I want to eat, so I'm going to have a salad. Is that okay with you?"

Clayton laughed. "Sure. It's fine. Eat what you want."

"Well, what are you going to have?"

Clayton shrugged. "Hamburger. Fries. Coke. What else is there?"

"That's what I mean."

The waitress brought Clayton his Coke and set a straw down with it. Then she came back and refilled his and Jane's water glasses, took their orders and walked off again. Clayton took the straw and stuck it in the Coke. Steam rose in the kitchen, billowing out across the lunch counter.

"So, did you hear what happened last night? About the accident?" asked Jane. She lifted her eyes to meet his.

Clayton took a sip of his Coke. "Ellen told me at the hotel this morning."

"Well, it's a pretty big deal, let me tell you. Those boys might've been juvenile delinquents, but they had families in town and we're not big enough to lose any kids without feeling it."

Clayton dragged a napkin from the holder and wiped off the table in front of him. "How's this any worse than that girl last week or the tramp who got killed?"

"It's not a class thing, Jack, if that's what you're implying. Everyone felt just as bad about Sarah, maybe even worse. And the tramp thing was sad, but you can't expect people to feel the same way about someone nobody even knew. It's impossible to hurt as much for a stranger as you do for a friend. You know that as well as I do."

"Oh really? Ask a tramp about that."

"Huh?"

"Affection doesn't have as much to do with familiarity as you think it does. Trust me."

The waitress brought Jane's salad and Clayton's hamburger. She asked if there was anything else she could get them and they both shook their heads. She walked back to the lunch counter and disappeared into the kitchen. The ceiling fans were rotating faster now and the steam from the kitchen began to dissipate. Three men in work overalls came into the diner and sat down at the counter next to a couple of kids eating ice cream sundaes and vanilla wafers.

"Did that other kid turn up yet?" asked Clayton, between bites.

"No."

"Well, do you have any idea at all where he might've gone off to?"

"I doubt anyone really believes he ran away, if that's what you mean."

"So, they think some tramp killed him, don't they? Some revenge-thirsty criminal from the great railyard shoot-out tracked the kid down and killed him in revenge for the old guy you people shot down last week."

"That's Jamie Danielson's story. I don't know too many people who believe it. The chief sent a couple of officers up to the mill to look around and they didn't find anything. And what do you mean by *you people*? *I* didn't shoot anyone. The chief didn't shoot anyone. Why are you holding everyone in Rivertown responsible for something only a few people had anything to do with? Do you think the chief just let Danielson and his friends blast away at those tramps? Do you think he didn't try to stop it? What was he supposed to do, stand in the line of fire and knock the buckshot down with his badge? That's expecting an awful lot from him, Jack. Don't you think?"

Jane stirred angrily through the salad with her fork. Clayton watched her. He realized he'd made a mistake bringing the tramp thing up again and wondered if there was any way he could change the subject without being too obvious. He took the straw out of the glass, crushed it, and stuck it in the ashtray. Then he picked up the Coke, looked at Jane who continued to pick through her salad, and drank half of the soda in one gulp then set the glass back down again.

"Don't take it so personally," he said. "I wasn't implying that you or Howser had anything to do with shooting that old man. You know what I meant."

"We're not a bunch of gun-crazy rednecks, Jack. That's the first time anything like that's ever happened at the railyard and everyone feels pretty bad about it."

"Are you talking about the rape or the shooting?"

"Both."

"And which do you suppose the good folks of Rivertown feel worse about?"

Jane put her fork down and leaned forward. "Jack, how do you know one of those tramps *didn't* have something to do with Sarah's death or the accident last night? Huh? What makes you the expert?"

"Experience."

"What kind of experience?"

He was going to have to tell her now. Maybe he even wanted to tell her. Besides, he was afraid sooner or later she'd find out on her own, which would be considerably worse all around. Clayton lowered his voice and told her, "I spent sixteen months with them."

"With who?"

"Tramps."

"The ones out at the yard?"

"Not specifically, but others just like them."

"When was this?"

"About nine years ago."

"Why?"

"I don't know. Just to do something different, bizarre, adventurous, I suppose. I'm not sure why. Put it this way: The rails are one of the few places where you're only defined by who you are at any given moment, by what you do and how closely that connects with what you say you're going to do or what you've done in the past half hour. Personal histories and phony appearances don't mean much in a boxcar in the middle of the night. You are who you are, as they say, and at the time that was the most satisfying way for me to deal with the people around me."

190

"Did you tell the chief you've had this . . . experience?"

"Should I have?"

"What do you think?"

"I think he's probably handling things just fine on his own. I'm not a cop. What do I know about his job?"

Jane put down her fork. "You know, Jack, it wouldn't take much on your part to fit in here in Rivertown, you know what I mean? No one's asking you to buy a pair of overalls and a cowboy hat, but you're living with us, sharing our food, breathing our air, and I would think you'd feel that helping us is next to helping yourself."

Clayton drained the Coke in one last gulp and stared out the window. Did Jane really think Howser cared what a drifter had to say about a bunch of railyard vagrants? He'd already decided this woman was one of those dangerous optimists who were at their deadliest when locked into a cause, because they'd never let go until it was resolved in their favor. People like that were worse than obsessive; they were fiends. Jane must've made a marvelous radical back in college. If they'd turned her loose, she'd have gotten the War stopped inside a week.

"So you think I should talk to your boss, huh?"

"Yes."

"And what would I say?"

"Just what you told me."

"That I lived in dirty boxcars for a year and half, so if he wants to solve the case of the murderous tramp, he'd better listen to me?"

"Don't be facetious."

"I'm just trying to get a handle on what you think I ought to say to the guy. See, I'm not as convinced as you are that he's going to be interested at all."

"You don't even know him."

"I know cops. I've met hundreds of them. Most of them are pretty much alike. They're all clones of Joe Friday."

The waitress came by with the check. She put it down next to Clayton's plate and walked off again. Jane watched her go, then said, "You're right. All cops are the same. And you're no different from the guys drinking Ripple out of bottles in brown paper bags."

"Maybe I'm not."

"Come on, Jack. Give the guy a chance, okay? For me? Talk to him. Tell him what you know. You don't have to say any more than you want to, but be a sport and help us out."

"I'll think about it. How's that?"

"Is that the best I'm going to get?"

"For now."

"All right then, I'll take it. Just don't think about it too long." She looked up at the wall clock. "Oh, great. I have to get back. Listen, Jack. Really! Talk to the chief. Please? We'd both appreciate it."

She leaned forward and kissed him. Then she took a five-dollar bill out of her pocketbook and put it on the table. "I've got to go. Give me a call later, okay?"

Clayton nodded and she got up and walked out of the diner, waving back over her shoulder as she left. He left a tip on the table and took the check, along with Jane's money, up to the cash register, wondering as he paid how exactly he was going to explain himself to Jane's chief. No matter what he said, it was certain to make for some interesting conversation.

Howser pulled on the hand brake, locking it into place. Then he opened the car door and swung his left leg out, hanging it over the door sill into the grass. He slumped back into the seat and brushed his hat back on his forehead. Christ, it was hot! He drew a handkerchief from his breast pocket and blew his nose. This was one of his favorite spots in the county, twenty minutes from town to the north, down a back road a mile and a half from the highway. It was a quiet, shady little clearing overlooking the river where the green water flowed by and flocks of blackbirds chattered in the willow trees on the opposite bank.

He'd had to get away from town and do some thinking. Danielson's brief visit had seen to that. But that wasn't the only reason. What the hell was going on? It was as though someone were deliberately trying to screw him up, make him look bad in front of these people. And this time there wasn't likely to be any rookie traffic cop riding in on a white horse to bail him out. All those assholes who had wanted him to fail since he left San Jose would have a field day with this one when they found out. *Big fish drowns in small pond. Howser, that idiot. Who the hell hired the guy in the first place?*

Then there was Danielson. The guy reminded him of the desk jockeys back in the valley, always looking over his shoulder, yelling in his ear. What the hell did he want? It wasn't his kid lying in the morgue. Not yet anyhow. And his interest in the welfare of others didn't exactly fit his personality. If he didn't like how the town was taken care of, why didn't he just slap on a badge and run things himself? Because guys like Tom Danielson don't work that way. They delegate jobs while retaining authority. That way when the screw-ups occur, they can blame the hired help.

Howser stuck his head out into the air, trying to catch a little breeze, some cool air, anything. He was feeling tired. He knew he needed some sleep. In fact, he needed several nights' sleep. He had a lot to make up, and no time for it. Maybe he'd made a mistake coming to Rivertown. Maybe he shouldn't have left the valley. At least there he'd kept relatively reasonable hours. Kathy might not have thought so, but compared to where he was now?

No, he'd been right to leave. He had to. The 7-Eleven fiasco had seen to that. And Kathy? Would she have stayed if he had? Would it have made that much difference to her? She always claimed to be adventurous, the one who loved going places and discovering new things. Yet, when it came to finding something truly fresh and original, she bailed out. Why? Because Kathy never wanted a real change. No, all she really wanted was something to distract her from the boredom of everyday life. Well, she was probably getting it now. A new toy to play with every goddamn Friday and Saturday night. Christmas, all year round. An unending succession of Santa Clauses, all, and only, for her.

A voice came on the radio.

"RP base to RP1."

Howser ignored it. *You're calling the wrong guy, Jane. I'm out to lunch. Ask anyone in town. They'll tell you.*

"RP base to RP1."

Didn't you hear what I said? I'm just tits on a bull. Call someone else.

"RP base to RP1. Chief, are you there?"

He stared at the radio another few moments then picked up the mike. "What do you need?"

"We have a call from out near Pendergast Ranch. Two girls on horseback found Danny Williams. Alfie's on it already with Doc Sawyer. Over."

Howser let the mike drop to his lap. He watched the heat ripple on the hood of the unit and wondered what he was supposed to say when they asked him for the thousandth time what the hell he was going to do.

"Tell Alfie I'll be there in about ten minutes. I'm up on North County Road 18 and leaving now."

"Chief?" There was a pause. "What are you doing up there?"

"Investigating."

"Investigating what?"

"Never mind. Is anyone else there now besides the two girls?"

"Not yet."

"Good. Have Alfie seal off the access road."

"Will do."

"I'm leaving right now."

"Chief?"

"RP1 out."

The boy was lying half in and half out of the long grass at the base of a scrawny oak. He was wearing only an old wash-faded pair of Levis and a yellow sock on his left foot, no shirt, bruising clearly visible on his upper torso, ribs to neck. His hands and forearms were covered with dust, his face swollen and pale. Dried blood clotted in his nostrils.

Howser glanced over at Sawyer. "Well, Doc?"

"He's been dead since, maybe, yesterday afternoon sometime, maybe even later. I can't tell for certain out here, obviously. But if I had to make a guess, that'd be it. At least sundown yesterday."

Howser tried not to stare at the boy. He'd managed to avoid it with the Maddox kid in the dark the night before but now out in the open in broad daylight, well, who liked looking at dead people anyhow, much less dead children? Yet, for some reason, he couldn't take his eyes away this time. None of them could. As Howser watched, a large bluebottle fly landed on the boy's fractured nose, then walked slowly across to his eyelid. Nobody moved. They all saw it but no one had the nerve to step forward and brush it away, almost as if they were waiting for the boy to do it himself. Howser squinted in the bright sunlight. Sweat trickled off his forehead into his eyes and made him blink. That broke his gaze. He glanced around at Sawyer and his two boys, then Alfie nearer the squad car and, waiting a little farther back, the two girls whose picnic on horseback had been ruined by their grisly find. They all seemed to be swaying slowly in the heat. Maybe not. Maybe it was just his eyes and his own footing that had become unsure in the last few minutes. He looked back down at the boy. The fly had gone.

Howser finally cleared his throat. "Get him out of here."

For a few seconds, they all just stood as they had been, swaying evenly in an invisible wind. Howser stared at their faces, drained of color in the white light, their eyes dull and blank. The attendants stirred first, then Alfie and the two young girls, each seemingly following the other.

Doc Sawyer walked off toward the station wagon without looking back. Over his shoulder he said to his boys, "You get that child covered up and taken care of. Then meet me downtown."

The girls freed their horses, tied by bridle and rein to one of the larger oaks, and climbed back up into the saddles. As they turned to go, Howser walked over and whispered to them, "Sometime this evening, maybe a little after dinner, I'd appreciate it if you and your parents would meet me down at the courthouse. Okay?" The girls nodded, then put their heels lightly into the horses, urging them off.

"You know what I think, Chief?" said Alfie. He walked

out from under the tree, rewinding the camera he'd used to photograph the body.

"What's that?" said Howser, his words forced out in a hoarse whisper. Watching Sawyer's assistants cover the boy up made his throat feel suddenly tight and dry.

Alfie said: "There's a monster hiding in this town."

Independence Day

13

The Fourth of July came to Rivertown in the hottest week of the summer. The skies were drawn in a blue so clear it hurt the eyes. In the week of the Fourth, the entire town was bleached of color and nothing moved above the dust on Main Street. The water table fell in every well and the tall dry grass in a dozen vacant lots looked incendiary through the noon hour and beyond. Even the surface of Green River warmed and lightened. In the middle of town, the oldest widows and widowers on Rose Avenue, and the youngest children from Elm over to Tenth Street, all stayed indoors between nine and four, content to eat crackers and suck on stale lemon drops while watching television game shows in shade-drawn parlors until evening when the sky yellowed and the dogs and cats all over Rivertown made their way out into the light again.

The largest funeral in fourteen years was held in Rivertown the week of the Fourth—thirty-five cars in dark procession stretching up along County Road 9 from Christ Church to the old Gold Hill cemetery on a long knoll west of town. Gold Hill held six generations of citizenry, a thousand faces under the dust and the murmuring grass and the carved granite headstones and plain redwood markers sun-faded and dulled over a hundred and forty warm blue delta summers. And then, less than a week before Independence Day, it had three more.

The boys were buried in a common ceremony interrupted once by a swirling wind and twice by the shrieking cries of a restless female child somewhere near the back of the crowd gathered on the stony southwest slope of the cemetery. Friends and acquaintances drove out together early that afternoon for something more subtle and mysterious than simple family ties. Few people standing there solemnly in the grass and sunlight even knew the boys by more than name and face, fewer still by reputation and personality. They were last names in the Rivertown phone directory, nicknames in a high school roll call, loud voices on the corner of Main and Lawrence on a Friday evening. But not strangers. No one born in Rivertown was ever really a stranger to anyone else born there. The borders of the town were too confining for that. There was no place in Rivertown to hide, no hope of remaining unnoticed for long, no chance of being ignored or undiscovered. It was an unspoken truth that nobody born in Rivertown would ever be buried anonymously on Gold Hill.

Howser drove out with Alfie and Ellen and stood alongside them in the southeast corner of the crowd where their presence would be more acknowledged than felt. Clayton hung back with the car under the oaks away from everyone else, but Jane went directly to the side of the caskets where she stood shoulder-to-shoulder with Tom Danielson and the families of those men who had crowded so sheepishly into Howser's office the week before.

. . . O God, whose most dear Son did take little children into his arms and bless them; give us grace, we beseech thee, to entrust the souls of these children to thy never-failing care and love . . .

When it was over, and the last words echoed away in the grass, everyone drifted back almost aimlessly to their cars, their quiet communion broken with the lowering of the caskets into the ground. Clayton slid off the hood of Jane's car and climbed back into the driver's seat. Howser walked slowly to his black-and-white behind Alfie and Ellen, whose tears were as much for the moment as for the occasion. Jane Crockett whispered condolence into the ear of Kitty Williams and kissed her on the cheek and squeezed her hand briefly before letting go and joining the rest of the town filing down the grassy slope to the narrow road.

An hour later, the surface of Gold Hill was empty again, and the wind moving in the long grass made the only sound on earth under the soft blue skies.

Cars began pulling into the dusty fairgrounds parking lot just after eight o'clock the morning of the Fourth. It was cooler than it would be in a couple of hours and early was the best time to get tablecloths nailed down and plastic cutlery laid out. This processional rolling out from the middle of town was of a sort entirely different from that dark one earlier in the week, but the town's involvement with it was no less considered and special. And this year, with all that the summer had brought already, the picnic was something the town needed.

By ten-thirty, most of Rivertown's populace was either milling about the fairgrounds or on their way there. Unlike the carnival atmosphere that pervaded the county fairs and the gargantuan Cal Expo in Sacramento, Rivertown's Fourth of July picnic had neither the glitter nor the trashy midway elements. There were no mechanical arms swinging metal seats about in midair, no wooden floors spinning above the crowds to the excited screams of thrill-ride enthusiasts. The Rivertown picnic was barbecued chicken and potato salad, baked beans, hot dogs, fruit salad, soda pop, apple pie, biscuits and beer. Live music and dancing. Flags, color, conversation and laughter under canvas tents and shady oaks.

Jack Clayton drove the VW bus in at eleven and found it difficult to find a place to park. Most of the spaces were already occupied by station wagons and pickup trucks. He located a spot under the oaks near the picnic grounds and inched his van as close to a tree as he could without scratching the bark with his fender. The branches and the Spanish moss hung down on his roof and made opening his door a little difficult. He set the parking brake and crawled out on his hands and knees. As he rolled out onto the grass, he heard a laugh coming from behind the van.

"Trying to hide from someone, Jack Clayton?"

Clayton got to his feet and smiled, brushing dirt and

stickers from his hands. "I didn't know this many people even had driver's licenses in Rivertown."

"They don't." Jane stepped up and gave him a quick kiss on the nose. "They just snuck in while our guys were out arresting jaywalkers downtown." She took him by the arm. "Come on, make yourself useful. I need some help setting up."

"They put you to work, huh?"

"I'm the biscuit lady this afternoon. Wait until you see the food. I've gained ten pounds this morning just watching it all carted in."

"I'm starving," said Clayton.

"We'll take care of you."

"Thanks."

"By the way, I thought you promised to dress up today." She nodded at the same faded jeans and denim work shirt he had on every time she saw him.

"Take a look," he said, folding the waistband back. "I changed underwear before I came over."

"That's wonderful, Jack. I guess I underestimated you again. Your commitment to fashion is commendable."

"Just trying to fit in."

"We're flattered."

She led him up the empty fairgrounds midway toward the picnic tables under the trees in front of Murphy's Red Barn. The big doors of the barn were swung open and Clayton could hear guitars inside jamming and tuning and sliding bottleneck riffs, playing a loose and funky version of "Long Tall Sally."

"Isn't this a little early in the morning for you, Jack?" she asked, taking his hand and wrapping her fingers into his. "I didn't think you ever got up before noon."

"I try not to, but this time I just couldn't sleep. Guess I was just too anxious to come down here and see you." He winked at her.

"What an uncharacteristically sweet thing for you to say, Jack. Thank you."

"You're welcome."

They came to a set of benches pushed together under the trees and sat down on one of them. Nearby, dozens of baskets, tins, and buckets of food lined the tables as the women from the Rivertown Independence Day Committee worked frantically to get everything set up by lunchtime.

"Jack, I want you to put on your happy face for at least a couple of hours, all right? You're going to have a good time today."

"Now you sound like Pollyanna," said Clayton, "playing the glad game to a room full of cripples and idiots."

She laughed. "Which are you? An idiot or a cripple?"

"Both."

"Sometimes I think you like feeling miserable."

"Sometimes I do."

"Well, not today, all right? You're going to have fun and smile and be cheery to everyone you meet. You got that?"

"Sure."

"All right, then," she said, grabbing Clayton by the wrist and pulling him along. "Come with me. I've got plenty of things for you to do while you're cheering up."

Howser rinsed the glass off under the cold water and stuck it with the rest of the dishes in the green plastic basin on the edge of the sink. He told himself that he had to wash the dishes more than once a week. He glanced around at the kitchen, garbage bags stuffed and tearing, open envelopes scattered about, dish rags on the table and the counter, three cupboards open, an old milk carton horizontal on the chair by the phone, dishes piled up under the window. It made him feel like a pig and he wondered what Kathy would think if she saw the way he was living these days. No, he didn't wonder. He knew exactly how she'd feel—damned fortunate that she got out when she did.

Howser tossed the dish towel onto the counter and walked into the bedroom. He put on a shirt and closed the screens he'd opened during the night. His bedroom was a worse mess than the kitchen. Clothes were piled everywhere. He picked up a heap and dropped it into the middle of the bed. It was hopeless. He'd have to do it another time when he had both the energy and the desire to play housekeeper. Then again, maybe he'd just go ahead and hire one of the girls downtown to come in once a week and do it for him.

Hearing a knock at the kitchen door, he buttoned up his shirt, pushed his old socks under the bed with his foot and walked up to the front of the house. Through the window over the kitchen sink he saw Alfie's black-and-white parked out in the driveway. He opened the door to let him in.

"Morning, Chief."

"Come on in. I'm just straightening up a few things. Get yourself something to drink from the refrigerator if you like."

"That's all right, Chief. I'm fine. Ellie fixed me up a pitcher of pink lemonade last night and I drank half of it for breakfast this morning."

"Who's working the river today?"

"Craig and Dennis. Corey sent them to the old landing. They're supposed to cover a mile and a half down to Hadley Road and come back in for the picnic."

"Archie's got patrol?"

"Yeah, and Randy and Al are working the fairgrounds."

"Okay," said Howser. "Let me get cleaned up and we'll go."

He walked to the bathroom at the rear of the house. Closing the door, he heard Alfie yell, "Ellen'll meet us there. She's bringing a ham and some corn stuffing and a grape–Jell-O–and–fruit mold we made last night. I promised her you'd try some."

Howser flushed the toilet and buckled up his pants. Then he washed his hands, took the tube of toothpaste out of the medicine cabinet and quickly brushed his teeth. He could hear Alfie puttering about in the front room, restless and anxious to get out to the fairgrounds. He rinsed off the toothbrush and stuck it in its brass holder, then opened the bathroom door. Alfie was staring out into the yard, whistling tunelessly under his breath.

Howser went back into the bedroom and picked up the folder lying on the floor beside the bed. He'd brought it home from the courthouse the night before and had stayed up past three a.m. reading and re-reading it. *Fatalities in the River District*. He'd taken Charlotte Burkie's advice and had Jane pull the file on deaths out by the railyard and the river. Over the last twelve years alone there'd been twenty-three. All transients. No prosecutions. A few of the deaths had been dismissed by Doc as accidental—six drownings, three falls from the bluff up near the old riverboat landing. The remaining fourteen involved beatings of one sort or another, either in the woods adjacent to the railyard or in some proximity (half a mile or so) to Green River. No witnesses, no arrests. The most recent one had occurred eight months before Howser's arrival in Rivertown. Funny thing was that nobody seemed overly concerned about any of the deaths. Seeing the folder on Howser's desk, Alfie had offered the observation that "a drunk tramp's meaner than a junkyard dog." None of the investigations had gone any further than questioning a few tramps and photographing the spot where the body had been found. Each fatality had been dismissed as "misadventure." Police Chief Lou Hudson had retired and moved to Sarasota, Florida, only a couple of weeks after the last killing. The timing of his retirement was particularly interesting since the guy was only fifty-eight and supposedly in good health.

Howser stuck the folder into his nightstand and shut the drawer. He returned to the kitchen where Alfie stood gazing out at the front yard.

"You ready?" asked Howser. Alfie grinned that same old smile at Howser, the faithful-golden-retriever smile, saying, sure, just give me an order.

"If you are," he answered. "Don't worry about me. I'm not in a hurry. Take your time, Chief. We got all day today."

"Let me see if I have my keys." He patted his pocket. "Okay, let's go."

Alfie led the way through the kitchen and out the back door. Howser followed, closing and locking the door behind him. The heat hit him instantly. It would be brutal later on.

His patrolman said, "You're going to enjoy this a lot."

"Alfie, I'll tell you. I'm looking forward to enjoying something around here for a change."

By noon the fairgrounds were draped with state Bear flags and Old Glory hanging from poles and booths and tree branches in a kaleidoscope of patriotic color that shoved away the memory of black suits and pallor from the week before. The Rivertown Hornets high school marching band played at the entrance to the picnic grounds and an informal barbershop quartet sung a cappella. Pennants from the high school, green and yellow, dangled from ropes pulled tight and tied between trees and car bumpers. Ribbons were stretched and arched and bowed in a hundred bright rainbows over and around the fairgrounds and across the picnic area and down from the rafters inside Murphy's Red Barn to the straw-covered floor beneath. Colored balloons in red, white and blue floated in tightly bound groups on strings wrapped around car antennae and tall steel and redwood lampposts, while single ones dangled and lurched from the wrists of the smallest running children hurrying everywhere at once.

Music spilled out of the Red Barn, reaching clear to the lunch lines winding through the oaks beside the picnic tables. Behind the barn, up on one of the knolls surrounding the fairgrounds, a firecracker went off, then another, then two Roman candles and a cherry bomb. Smoke from the detonations drifted down lazily and hung over the trees. A boy's laughter echoed, mixing with the nervous tittering of people made jumpy by the unexpected noise. Two reserve officers rushed up the slope looking for the perpetrator of the joke, though by the time they got there only shredded paper and the bitter odor of cordite remained. They returned shaking their heads and smiling together at some private joke and held their hands up in mock despair. But no one cared all that much anyhow. It happened every year at the picnic. Firecrackers, even illegal ones, were an expected tradition and the smells of chicken frying on outdoor skillets and hickory-barbecued beef turning on an open spit quickly pushed away what faint lingering traces of gunpowder were left in the summer air.

Inside the Red Barn, a soft country ballad whined on steel guitar and electric mandolins. Howser sat on a bale of hay just outdoors, listening. Though he'd never been an especially big fan of country-and-western, he liked live music—particularly guitars and fiddles. Scores of people wandered by, ones Howser had met only in passing with a handshake or a nod and a promise to talk at a later date when things were a little quieter. These were basically nice, well-meaning people who, like anyone else, wanted only a good life for themselves and their loved ones, whether friends or family. Independence Day for them meant a break from the small-town routines that so consumed their lives.

Up above him, some boys were swinging out of the hayloft on a heavy iron chain. Howser shaded his eyes with the back of his hand and craned his neck to look. They were whooping and whistling as the chain carried them out into midair in a half arc, reaching as high as twenty feet over the yard below. Howser watched their feet kicking furiously in an effort to gain more distance. Few people wandering in and out of the barn paid attention to the kids circling in the air overhead, and those that did only paused briefly to smile and nod, perhaps remembering when they, too, swung out on an old chain or rope from Murphy's hayloft on the Fourth of July.

Deciding he needed a walk, Howser got up and ambled off toward the rear of the barn. A six-foot-wide path crammed with rusting ranch equipment led between the barn walls and the oaks that grew beside it. Taking care to avoid catching his clothing in the rusting bales of barbed wire and a partially disassembled cultivator, he followed a row of old stacked fencing two-by-fours as a makeshift pathway through the elongated junk pile to the dry grass beyond. Behind the barn, two high school kids were sitting side by side in the bed of an old hay wagon sharing a cigarette. The girl, a short freckle-faced redhead, wore a lime-green halter top that displayed the message *Stop Staring at My Tits!* She'd just taken a drag off the cigarette when Howser came around the corner. Seeing him, she tried hiding the cigarette down by her thigh. The long-haired boy sitting beside her fidgeted in embarrassment. Howser knew they were just killing time until nightfall when they'd go out, maybe with friends, and do their more serious celebrating. He winked at the girl and walked past without saying a word. What did he care whether they were smoking or not? They weren't his kids.

Walking on past the back of the barn, Howser came out onto the edge of the grassy field that bordered the fairgrounds. A few tables and benches had been set up in the grass beneath the oaks, though nobody was using them just now. Most of the picnic crowd still milled about the front of the Red Barn, eating from paper plates and listening to the music from inside. Adults chattered. Children shrieked. Smiles and laughter ruled the day. A Piccolo Pete went off somewhere, then a string of firecrackers. Howser headed off toward the empty benches. Even in a small town there could be such a thing as overcrowding and noise saturation and an overwhelming desire for some solitude. Besides, he wasn't in the celebrating mood. Sitting by himself on the bench, Howser unbuttoned his shirt, loosened his belt, and opened his cuffs. He took his shoes and socks off and let his toes sink into the dust. He was going to sit there for a while, at least until his stomach let him know he had to eat. Back in the fairgrounds, the dance crowd swelled out into the trees shading the picnic tables. The volume of laughter nearly matched the music in the midsummer heat. He knew that he ought to be back there in the picnic grounds socializing and stumping politically to ease the panic that was beginning to grab hold of Rivertown. This afternoon, however, more than community support, he needed a little nap. When he was tired he didn't think clearly. He'd been drowsy that night in the 7-Eleven. Drowsy and stupid. He wouldn't allow himself to make the same mistake again. So he closed his eyes and sat back.

A light breeze fluttered under the trailing edges of the tablecloths and tipped over a few paper cups. Clayton reached into a small wicker basket and drew out another biscuit, putting it on his plate between the fruit salad and four barbecued chicken wings. Without bothering to ask, Jane Crockett handed him the honey. He took it and began twisting the lid from the jar.

"You knew, huh?" he asked.

"Woman's intuition."

Clayton opened the biscuit and poured honey onto it and took a bite. "What does your intuition tell you I'd like for dessert?"

"What my intuition tells me you'd like and what you're going to get here are two entirely different things, so . . ." She leaned over to her right and cut into one of the strawberry pies, drawing out a neat slice. "Here." She slipped it onto his plate.

"Good guess. That's just what I'd have asked for." He winked.

"Uh-huh. I'll bet." Then she gave him a handful of tickets.

"Take these over to Mrs. Bundy."

Clayton looked around at the women passing among the checker-clothed tables. There were so many of them it was almost impossible to tell who was serving and who was waiting to be served. "Which one's Mrs. Bundy?"

Jane put her hand on Clayton's cheek, turning his head until it pointed toward a table off on the right. "See, over there? The woman in the blue smock?"

Clayton located a short, stocky woman wearing a white dress and a blue gingham smock. The bright sunlight directly overhead made her gray hair shine silvery and white.

"You mean the lady who looks like Aunt Bea?"

Jane punched him lightly on the forearm. "Be nice, Jack. She's a sweet lady."

"Okay."

"Did you talk to the chief yet?"

"No."

"You promised you would, remember?"

"I know."

"So, are you going to talk to him today?"

"Is he around somewhere?"

"I'm sure he is."

"Okay, I'll look for him after I finish eating."

"Just so long as you do it."

"Scout's honor."

Clayton left Jane at the food tables and gave Caroline Bundy his wad of tickets and strolled off under the live oaks with the rest of the lunch crowd. He found an empty place at one of the picnic tables and sat down to eat. Children ran by with colored streamers in hand while fire-department personnel sitting in lawn chairs beside one of their engines gleefully detonated confiscated firecrackers. Under the shade trees by the barbecue pits, Rivertown's answer to the Osmonds, the Dobson family singers, finished tuning their banjos. Nine musical wizards on the five-string box: Eleanor and Pete, their kids Marla, David and Stuart, and Marla's children, Tammy, Susan, Arnold and Carl. While eating, Clayton watched them entertain. All cheery faces and goodwill, holiday in their eyes. To these people, Rivertown was just a place they lived, one they'd known all their lives, somewhere they'd been born into and could not easily leave, a subtle trap that closed tighter each passing season. It was hard to come into Rivertown from the outside, to even begin to belong. Yet it was probably harder still to get out for those whose belonging was a birthright. They might never be allowed to leave. Then again, maybe they shouldn't. What was out there anyhow? The real world? If they thought life was claustrophobic in small-town America, they ought to try forty-eight hours in urban America. They had no idea.

On Main Street, the sidewalks were empty except for a blond teenage girl walking a black Labrador near the curb downtown. Heat waves rippled in the street and the sunlight glared a blinding white from the whitewash on the storefronts at the Rexall drugstore, the Wells Fargo Bank and the J. C. Penney's next to the old Roxy theater. Red metal flags stood straight up in three dozen parking meters along Main abandoned by the cars that had seemingly gone away on the long morning. Shades were drawn and green CLOSED PLEASE CALL AGAIN signs were visible in every storefront window. Sprinklers watered an empty Sutter Square Park. Summer pollen settled on the awnings up and down the empty street. Before reaching Marshall Avenue, just past the Roxy theater, the girl with the dog entered an alley and disappeared from view. A gust of wind came up and blew a cloud of dust halfway up the block. The state and federal flags above the Wells Fargo flapped loudly. Inside the alley, a car door slammed and an engine roared to life. Tire rubber shrieked and the pickup lurched from the alley, vaulting beyond the sidewalk into the middle of Main Street. Grabbing frantically at the wheel, the driver barely controlled the pickup before it slammed sideways into the curb on the far side of the street. The tail end swung around, rear wheels spinning violently, blue smoke rising in the air. The pickup raced out of town to the south, receding quickly into the distance. As the cloud of tire smoke and exhaust dissipated in the draft, the black Labrador came bounding out into the street barking and barking at a mirage that refused to disappear.

Clayton gnawed the last chunk of meat off a barbecued chicken wing and dropped it on the paper plate. Then he got up and dumped everything—chicken bones, corn cob, napkins and beer can—into a garbage can buzzing with hungry yellowjackets. It had amused him to see the number of people increase in the last half hour, particularly the kids. When he was in high school, all he and his friends ever used to do on holidays was hang out and get wasted. What else was there to do? You stopped burning firecrackers when you turned fifteen and discovered what girls were for. After that, days like the Fourth had no genuine significance other than the fact that they occupied everybody else's attention, leaving you alone to do what you wanted. And, of course, what you wanted, if you had any real character at all, was to cause a little trouble and do the things that everyone told you *not* to do the rest of the time—like smoking a little dope, getting laid, running around. All the good times you could have before responsibility set in. Maybe the kids in Rivertown were already responsible members of the community. Sure they were.

Dipping into an ice chest for another can of beer, Clayton headed toward the Red Barn. It was time to make good on his promise to Jane. Winding his way through the picnic tables under the trees, Clayton searched the barn crowd. Jane had told him Howser would be in uniform, so that's what he looked for. It didn't take him much more than ten minutes. After confirming that the town's chief of police was neither kicking his feet up in the sawdust with the swing-dancing set, nor parked on a bale of hay inside the barn, Clayton simply shifted his attention out across the grassy field beyond the fairgrounds. There he spotted Howser sitting alone at a table a hundred yards away in the shade beneath the oaks. Clayton drained the can of beer and dumped it into a trash can. He strolled out across the field. Reaching the trees, he took a seat opposite Howser at the picnic table. The chief was dozing. Should he wake him? *Yeah, but take it easy. You don't startle a guy wearing a gun.*

"Warm today, huh?"

The chief's eyes opened to a squint. He didn't appear all that surprised to see someone sitting there. He grunted, "Too goddamned hot for me."

"Too hot for everyone," said Clayton. He stuck his hand out. "My name's Jack Clayton."

The police chief leaned across the table and they shook hands. "Glad to know you, Jack." He yawned, his face sweaty and flushed from the heat. "What can I do for you?"

"Jane sent me over here," said Clayton. "It seems we're supposed to have a talk."

"About what?"

"A problem you've been having."

"Which one? It's been a busy week." A pair of yellowjackets buzzed the table and Howser swatted them away, then refocused on his guest.

"Chief, this wasn't my idea," said Clayton, ducking as one of the yellowjackets returned. "I'm just here as a favor to Jane."

"That's okay," said Howser. He smiled. "It seems she likes you, too."

"Oh yeah? Did she tell you that?"

"Jane Crockett wears her heart on her sleeve. When she meets somebody she likes, twenty-four hours later everyone knows about it. You've been the talk of the town for a week now."

"That's nice to know."

"You ought to feel flattered. Jane's not easily impressed."

Across the field, the band at the Red Barn had taken a break and the crowd was drifting off from the dance area into the outskirts of the fairgrounds, several people headed now in Howser's direction. He rapped on the table with his knuckles and stood up. "Let's take a walk."

They followed a narrow old cattle trail to the top of the low hills above the fairgrounds and stopped on a grassy ridge beneath a stand of live oaks. The sun felt hotter. A dry hay smell replaced the barbecue smoke in the air. Laughter and music were gone. The sky overhead was white.

Clayton parked himself under one of the oaks with his back resting against the bark. Before he could get comfortable, though, Howser said to him, "Why don't you tell me what you're doing here in Rivertown?"

"Huh?"

"What'd you come here for?"

Clayton shrugged. "I heard it was a swell place to visit. A friend of mine used to live here. He told me I ought to come up and have a look around. Stay for a few weeks. See the sights. Why? Did I miss a No Vacancy sign or something?"

"I'm just curious, that's all."

"There's no mystery here, Chief. I'm just bumming around, you know?"

"Just bumming around."

"Yeah."

Howser laughed. "So that's why every time I see you, you're wearing the same old clothes—those shoes, that pair of worn-out jeans, the shirt?"

"Huh?"

"Or is this just an attempt to fit in while you're here?

Trying to pass for one of the locals? Come on, Clayton. You're staying in a hotel that charges forty bucks a night. That's a lot of money for a guy who can't seem to afford a decent change of clothes. And that beat-up old van of yours? I took a look at it last week. It's got a new set of tires. Michelins. Not the cheap ones, either. You're not some bum. Why're you trying to make yourself out to look like one?"

"Fuck you," said Clayton, getting to his feet. He swatted a yellowjacket away from his face and walked out into the sunlight.

"We've been watching you all week. Did you know that?"

Clayton jerked around, surprise etched on his face. "What for?"

"New face in town. Questionable behavior. The usual reasons."

"That's bullshit."

"I heard you made an unauthorized visit to the railyard a few days ago. Is that true?"

"Who told you that?"

"Never mind who told me. Just answer the question."

"See you later," said Clayton, starting away toward the trail that led back down into the fairgrounds.

"What were you looking for out there?"

"Have a nice day, Chief."

"Come on, Jack. Talk to me!"

Thirty yards away, Clayton stopped and stared back at the police chief, still waiting in the shade of the live oak. Even at that distance, he was sure he detected a slight grin on Howser's face. *Is the guy playing a game or what? Jane didn't say it'd go like this.*

"Did you know the old guy who got shot?" asked Howser. He walked out into the sunlight toward Clayton. "Is that it?"

"I didn't know any of them," replied Clayton. A cheer rose from the fairgrounds around the Red Barn where a Roman candle shot up over the trees and exploded in a shower of sparks. Two more followed in tandem, the detonations echoing out across the field.

Howser wiped the sweat from his forehead with the back

214

of his sleeve. He looked fatigued from the heat. "Look, Clayton. Jane and I talked about this yesterday. I know what you came out here to tell me."

"Oh yeah?"

"You wanted to say that wearing secondhand clothes doesn't make a person stupid. That those tramps had a good thing out at the railyard—running water, shade, quiet, privacy. Both the river and the junction within reasonable walking distance. And why would they throw all that away just to attack some kids? Doesn't make any sense. Well, I've thought about that. But you see my problem—the one Jane sent you out here to help me with—is that either the tramps attacked the girl or all nine kids, including Sarah Miller, lied to us."

"What'd the tramps have to say?" asked Clayton, shading his eyes with the back of his hand. Above the fairgrounds, a flock of small birds flew east in the direction of the river.

"Not a word. Ignored all our questions for four days, then thanked us for the hospitality and left town."

"Well, maybe they didn't feel you were interested in their side of the story. This isn't the friendliest place in the world, you know. Even if it was the tramps who raped the girl, not everyone out at the railyard could've been involved, right? But the probability that only a few might've been guilty didn't prevent the rest from getting shot at, did it? And you wonder why they weren't being helpful? Well, take a guess."

"I forgot that you're the expert here."

"I didn't say that."

"Come on, Jane told me all about you. Did you do it just for kicks? Or was there some 'personal statement' you were trying to make?"

"What're you talking about?"

"Playing tramp."

Clayton marched back up toward the chief of police. "Look, if you think something I did a long time ago has any connection to what's been happening around here, you're wrong. That's just more bullshit."

Howser wiped his brow again with the back of his sleeve. "Hey, there's no reason to get all bent out of shape, Clayton. I'm only trying to do my job. You said you came out here to talk. Okay, I'm listening. So go ahead. Talk."

Clayton walked back under the oak and sat down again where the shade made the ground marginally cooler. Howser remained in the sunlight, staring at him.

"Jane forgot to tell me you were an asshole," said Clayton.

"You probably didn't ask her. Listen, Clayton, I'm just interested in how the hell you got involved with the tramp thing. Seriously. That's all I want to know. Okay? You talk. I'll listen."

Clayton stared out into the sunlight. The heat had dried the ridge so fiercely there was almost a glare in the summer noon light. After a pause, he said, "Did you go to your high school reunion?"

"No, I had patrol that night. Couldn't get off. Why?"

"Well, I went to mine, and it freaked me out. Ten years flashing before my eyes, ten fucking years of getting old, seeing my buddies getting old, watching things change, slipping away. I grew up three blocks from the ocean in Redondo Beach, probably the biggest sandbox and swimming hole in the world. Great playground for a kid. Probably *the* greatest place in the world to be when you're young, especially if your family's got some bucks, and not a bad place to grow up even if they don't. Southern California's the biggest goddamn supermarket of self-indulgence this planet's ever seen. Whatever you want to do, it's there. Day or night. Surfing, sex, parties. You name it, they got it. I'm sure we spent more time hanging out at the beach than we ever did in class but, big surprise, it didn't last forever and when it went, it was gone so fast we hardly knew what had happened."

Clayton's grin had gone, replaced by a vacant gaze that suggested too much careless thought just then had begun to work overtime in a decidedly uncomfortable corner of his memory. A breeze swept up and stirred again in the grass beneath the oak.

"Out of nine of us who hung out together in high school, two were dead before graduation—Chris playing Mario Andretti two miles above Malibu on Rambla Pacifico in a Chevy Nova with bad brakes, and Bobby thinking he's

Superman in a bar fight in Tijuana—and another, Willie, less than three months afterward, walking into a trip wire in Vietnam. Of the six of us lucky enough to make it into the real world, two were alcoholics by the time they'd made their first six-figure promotions on Wilshire Boulevard and another's working on his fourth marriage living above a beauty parlor in North Hollywood while Roger, his best friend from USC, is busy banging Rod's first wife and living off the alimony Rod had to shell out for playing high school sweethearts one year too many. By the night of the reunion only one of us was anywhere close to having his shit together, and it wasn't me."

Clayton looked over in the direction of the fairgrounds. Far beyond the live oaks and the picnic tables, left of the parking lot, was a softball field he hadn't noticed earlier. The infield was red baked clay but the outfield grass was a beautiful green with players in T-shirts and caps wandering around waiting for the game to begin.

"The day after the reunion, I gave notice at work. Two weeks later I took off and started moving around, New Mexico, Colorado, Oregon, Arizona. I'd decided there was more I wanted to do with my life than digging a grave and parking myself in it with a station wagon, a backyard barbecue and a pair of screaming kids. The girl I'd been going out with at the time didn't appreciate that, of course. The last time we talked on the phone, she told me I was a coward. Said I was scared of growing up, scared of responsibility."

"Maybe she was right."

"Hey, I'm sure she was. But I didn't care. It was over. I dumped my old life and drove around the West for about a year, staying in KOA campgrounds and national parks until the engine in the Corvair I was driving blew up on me outside of Grant's Pass. Then I hitched a ride up to Portland where I hopped the rails with a couple of guys I'd met in Albuquerque. We were just going to do a freebie down to the Bay Area and out to Denver except when they got off in Salt Lake, I decided to stay on."

Clayton scratched in the dirt by the base of the oak with his fingers, then looked up at Howser and said, "I remember calling home that night and getting my little sister on the line and making the mistake of telling her where I was and what I was about to do. She was only sixteen at the time, and she started crying right there on the phone. She said I was scaring her. I didn't know how to handle that, so I put the phone down and walked away. An hour later I climbed into a boxcar with a bunch of strangers and rode off without the faintest idea what the hell I was doing."

A mile away to the east, a vintage biplane flew in lazy circles above the valley trailing a long silk banner behind the tail that read HAPPY BIRTHDAY, U.S.A. Sunlight glinted off its wings as it banked over Rivertown.

"I guess that still doesn't answer your question, does it? Well, let's put it this way: I think everybody finds a time in their lives when they just get fed up and want to start over. Most of them do it by quitting their jobs or changing addresses. Some people get divorced. Others get married. What matters is that they're trying to kick-start a life that's gone dead on them. That's how it was for me, at least. I really didn't care where the hell I went as long as it wasn't back to my apartment in Long Beach. And once I was out, that was that. There was no going back. I committed myself to something I knew nothing about, figuring if I stayed with it long enough maybe I'd learn, whether I wanted to or not. And it's true. You do get to know your way around pretty quickly—who to hang out with, who to avoid, where to get your next meal, what things cost and, more importantly, what's for free. But this is a big country, too, and it's easy as hell to get yourself lost. One rainy morning just two months in, I woke up under a trestle in Knoxville to find the guys I'd been traveling with had disappeared, along with most of my stuff. All they'd left me were my clothes and the blanket I'd been sleeping on. I didn't even have enough change in my pockets to make a phone call. It was cold as shit out and I had to walk six miles that morning in the rain to get breakfast at the rescue mission downtown. They gave me a chocolate doughnut and a bowl of tomato soup just for showing up. One of the best meals I ever ate. I was going to call the cops to see if there was any hope of rescuing my stuff when a tramp there at the mission talked me out of it. Said not only wouldn't it do me any good, but that once I told them

218

where it'd happened they'd probably try to run me in for trespass. This guy, he called himself Jughead Jimmy, told me to forget what I'd lost and to get on with what I had. 'And don't trust nobody,' he said, 'unless you need something. Then grin and kiss ass.' "

"That's always good advice," said Howser.

Clayton nodded. "Kept me healthy, no doubt about that. I don't know how the guys who stay on the rails for years handle it. There was always something new to watch out for. One night up in Olympia I saw a guy get stabbed in the neck over an old pair of shoes. The tramp who did it never even checked to see if the shoes fit or not. He just knifed the guy and walked away. Didn't even bother to take the shoes. Then the ambulance and the cops showed up and nobody would admit they knew the guy who'd been cut. That's something else you learn. Everybody's a stranger. The biggest mistake you can make is to think you've got real friends on the rails. Raiding dumpsters with a guy and sharing the food you turned up together doesn't make the two of you friends for life. Won't necessarily even make you friends for the evening. Surviving is all that counts, and it's not about teamwork. You learn that real quick. Look out for number one. Do what it takes to get yourself by. It's a tough way to live and some people are better at it than others. Maybe it's an instinct. I don't know, but I sure didn't have it. The sixteen months I spent on the rails nearly broke me for good."

The droning of the biplane increased as it neared the fairgrounds. Down by the Red Barn, helium balloons in red, white and blue were freed into the clear blue sky. Raucous cheers accompanying their release drowned out both the plane engine and the wind in the oaks.

Watching the plane bank slowly over the trees, Clayton said, "The thing is, though, I didn't have to be on the rails. It was my choice. And when I decided I'd had enough, I just walked into a Greyhound bus station in Omaha and bought a one-way ticket back to California. See, the whole experience was just a big adventure for me. I knew it wasn't permanent. I had other plans for my life. But I met guys out there who'd been on the rails for maybe ten, twenty years. What kind of plans did *they* have? Work is always easy to find, but maybe a job isn't. And maybe the same is true of a place to live. The truth is, rescue missions and railyard jungles are where you go when there isn't anywhere else.

"Do you understand what I'm saying? Tramp life's about as shitty as it gets. Anyone who's ever been there'll tell you that. And attacking a bunch of teenage kids would only make it worse. Tramps don't need to go looking for trouble. Every day, just being who they are'll get them enough of it. I'm telling you, there's no way those tramps would've attacked either the girl or her friends. They're just not that masochistic."

Howser rubbed the toe of his boot in the scrub grass and flies buzzed up exposing the decomposed carcass of a tiny rodent half-hidden there in the dust. Wiping sweat from his face, he said, "Okay, so maybe the kids started it. Maybe they went up and hassled the tramps. Maybe one of them picked a fight and the girl ended up getting raped as a result."

Clayton shook his head. "You're still not listening to me. Even if there was a fight, none of the tramps would've stayed around waiting for the law to arrive. By the time you and that vigilante party got there, the yard would've been empty. You wouldn't have found a soul, I promise you. I've seen it happen. I've been there when a jungle cleared out and I'll tell you, tramps are easily spooked, especially by the law, and especially in towns like this one."

The biplane circled the fairgrounds as the colored balloons filled the sky. More firecrackers were detonated. Children shrieked with delight. The rising balloons slowly separated on the wind as the small red biplane with the long trailing banner performed a snap-roll for the crowd below. Rivertown's celebration of Independence Day had begun in earnest.

"Look, Chief," said Clayton. "I have no idea what's going on in your town, but I can promise you this much: Those kids lied to you, and an old man got killed last week for nothing."

14

Howie Long removed his white T-shirt, draped it over the century plant at the curved edge of the concrete and un-buckled his belt. Beside him, the water barely rippled in the breeze. He peeled off his jeans and underwear and laid them on the cement and stood naked in the sunlight. In his opinion, this was the best swimming spot in the entire county. Bailey's Reservoir had been abandoned for years, lying unused since a new facility three times its size had been built on the west side of town. The paint around the concrete edges of the reservoir was sun-faded and chipped in a thousand places and the sidewalls were covered with a thin patina of slime. The tank itself was filthy and dank. Thousands of insects flicked across the surface of the water; the bottom was nearly buried in algae and mud. On warm days, the reservoir smelled horrible. But so what? Those were the things that preserved the reservoir as Howie's private pool. What really mattered was that it was not crowded like the municipal swimming pool downtown and there were no rules telling him what he could and could not do.

Howie dangled his feet in the green water. The surface hardly shifted. He wriggled his toes trying to break up a layering of surface algae near his shins. The water began to bubble and churn until a small whirlpool formed in the scum, ripping it into a dozen tiny green swirling islands. Howie raised his leg from beneath the water with a great kick, exploding through the algae, creating a sluggish wave that petered out after traveling only a few yards across the reservoir. He leaned back on his hands and looked up past the trees to the blue sky above. God, he would've liked to have a girl sitting next to him just then. Maybe Phoebe Cates. Howie'd gone to see *Fast Times at Ridgemont High* nine times just for her pool scene. Now he pictured her lying naked next to him, her breasts shiny and wet. He had never had a real girlfriend, never even a date. Most of his sexual fantasies were filled with women he had no chance of seeing in the flesh. Sarah Miller was the one exception. She and Annie Connor'd had a secret place down by the river where they had lain out in the sun totally naked. Only it hadn't been a secret to Howie. One day he'd spied on them for five and a half hours. He'd even taken off his own clothes while doing so. Now Howie remembered how Sarah looked in the woods that night by the railyard. She was lying on her back and her jeans were off and she was crying and he was lying on top of her with his zipper open. Just behind him, Jamie was yelling *Come on Howie, she won't hurt you. You won't hurt the little guy now will you, babe? See, Howie, she's promised not to hurt you. Come on, you got guys waiting so hurry up, there you go, that's right, hey, Howie you're really getting the hang of it now. Okay, Goober you're on deck. Howie's on Sarah and you're on deck, yeah!* It was nothing like the fantasies he'd had. Sarah's eyes were nearly swollen shut and her face was dirty and her upper lip bleeding where Jamie had slugged her. After squirting inside of her, he'd gotten up and walked off into the woods, ashamed of what he'd done. It hadn't even felt that good.

Howie dove into the water. The sunlight vanished in the deepest part of the reservoir as he opened his eyes underwater. The murkiness always made swimming to the bottom interesting. Fighting downward through the algae, he searched with his fingers for the slimy cement floor. When he found it, he quickly reversed himself and shoved off hard from the cement, propelling himself up again through the green darkness until he broke the surface of the tank. Long beads of water flew off his face as he shook his head. He wiped his eyes clear with the side of his hand

and smiled. Only in the dark green water of the tank could he not be dirtied by what he had done to Sarah Miller.

The sun burned down on him from above as he floated a while in the dank water. Then he sucked in his breath and dove again, down to where the algae was thick as seaweed. He tore through it with his hands, touching again the slippery bottom of the tank, counting through double digits the length of time he could remain underwater. He wiped the soggy slime from his face and opened his eyes and released a few bubbles through his nose and counted down to the last moments he could hold . . . ninety-six, ninety-seven, ninety-eight, ninety-nine, one hundred . . . then, his toes barely slipping, kicked off the bottom of the reservoir with a furious push upward.

He clutched the warm cement, panting heavily for a minute or two, then relaxed and laid his head in his arms. When his breathing finally slowed, he pulled himself up out of the water and sat on the edge letting the sunlight and the heat of the concrete dry his skin. The breeze riffled the hair on his arms as they dried. He let his mind go blank and after a while he could no longer tell whether his feet were still in the green water or out. He lay back on the concrete. The water lapped quietly at his ankles as he slept.

Twenty minutes later his sun-trance was disturbed by a rustling in the blackberry bushes at the north end of the reservoir. At first, he thought it was only the late afternoon wind blowing through the brush. The skin on the back of his neck tightened and he shivered. He rolled over onto his side. If somebody was watching, were they hiding because he was naked? His penis stiffened at the thought of somebody spying on him. For some reason, he liked the idea of being watched. What was there to be nervous about? Still, he kept his eyes fixed on the bushes. The breeze died away. The bushes rustled again. Howie crawled forward and slipped quietly into the water. He sunk himself up to his chin and pressed his back flat against the cold concrete wall. Treading water to stay afloat, he tried to be patient and wait until whoever was there either showed themselves or grew tired of spying and left. Five minutes passed, then ten, and the tank water began to grow uncomfortably cold. He searched the perimeter of the reservoir. The bushes on the north end bowed and swayed as the breeze came up again. Was somebody there or not? He had to know. Howie took a deep breath and let himself slide beneath the surface. Sinking down through the thick algae, he kicked out and swam toward the north. His plan was to sneak up on them by approaching from underwater. At the north end of the tank he'd surface and have a peek from just above the edge of the cement. He held his breath and crossed the dark underwater of the reservoir keeping both hands out in front of him as a precaution against swimming headfirst into the wall. As his outstretched fingers made contact, Howie pushed upward along the slimy concrete wall toward the sunlight diffused in green algae above him. Less than a yard below the surface he released the last of his air and so was unable to dive again in the instant he saw the shadow appear above him. The large hand that plunged down through the water seized the hair on top of Howie's head, twisted it into a fist, and slammed Howie's cold face against the green cement again and again while Howie tried desperately to free himself from its grip. His nose shattered first, then his cheekbone, then his jaw. He flung his hands out, scratching frantically at the slimy walls of the tank. Blood from his head wounds spewed out in a cloud. His chest convulsed violently and he inhaled the filthy water of the reservoir directly into his lungs. The instant he died, a fistful of hair tore away from his scalp and Howie Long's body broke free of that monstrous grip, sliding alone again back down into darker water.

15

In the evening of the Fourth, the heat settled and shadows fell across lawns and asphalt. A breeze moved from the river across town, fanning the elms and willows and blowing dried and fallen petals from the sidewalks, fluttering in the yellow canvas window shades covering open windows. It filled the air with the sweet scent of summer flowers. On the Walcott veranda, Alfie Cox and Ellen Kelleher sat shoulder-to-shoulder in the rocking swing whispering stories and promises and affections to one another away from the curious ears of the tenants. Lawn sprinklers hissed in the arbor behind them, pelting with cool water droplets the nightblooming jasmine on the white trellis and the sweet gardenia and rose beds beneath the fence line and the aluminum siding on the toolshed where the lawn mowers and edgers and garden shovels and rakes and hand tools were stored in the dark.

In a lighted corner room three flights above them, Jack Clayton flipped the *Reader's Digest* onto the bed and went to the window. He wondered what Jane was up to. After he had returned from his walk with Howser, Jane and he had taken a bottle of wine over to the all-city softball tournament and had lain there in the grass until twilight. Clayton'd expected to spend the night with her, but after the city fireworks display at nine she'd made some excuse about being too tired to entertain and he'd been forced to come back to the hotel alone. Not much fun in that. Feeling bored a little later, he'd tried phoning her house but nobody answered. Maybe she was in the bathtub. More likely she was out somewhere enjoying herself while he was stuck alone in the hotel reading phony human-interest stories and sweating to death. He'd try phoning her again later. If she still wasn't home . . . well, he'd think of something.

Clayton leaned closer to the stormscreen where the dust moths fluttered, beating against the wire, flailing themselves half to death for a spin around the desk lamp, a chance to circle the electric flame. He flicked at them with his forefinger and they fell away. He thought of something that made him smile. An interesting metaphor: tramps as dust moths, beating their heads against society, closed off and shut away, outcasts in another dark. The moths returned, their tiny wings making the softest patting against the screen. Clayton reached over and switched off the desk lamp, putting the room into darkness. The pattering at the screen quieted. He swung around in the chair and faced back into the room. The fragrance from the window did not follow. Instead, his room smelled stale and stuffy from old furniture and papers and his own sweat and dirty clothes. He needed a shower yet didn't have the energy to undress and walk down the hall to the bathroom. Maybe in the morning. Tonight, without Jane around, he was the only one having to smell himself anyhow and he'd gotten more or less used to it. He listened to the moths fluttering patiently outside the screen. *The tramps'll come back to Rivertown eventually. There's no doubt about that. Where else do they have to go? Rivertown's railyard is ideal. They'll be back as soon as something is settled. They have all the time in the world. What else do they have to do except wait? A tramp wears patience like a middle name; it's a fixed part of his identity, like his clothes, the food he eats, the places he sleeps. They'll return like summer's dust moths, lingering now off in the dark, watching for the lamplight glow to return.*

Fifteen blocks to the south, Jane Crockett followed the darkened sidewalks between Cantwell and Ash streets. The old gray tennis shoes she was wearing barely padded

226

on the concrete and neither ears nor eyes were distracted from the noisy chatter of television sets and radios tuned to network sitcoms and Top Forty countdowns from local affiliates in the state capital and the Bay Area. Jane breathed quickly through her mouth as she walked, drawing on the dry air and trying consciously to keep the summer dust and pollen from her sinuses. Summer had been her worst season as a child; she'd been forced on several occasions to stay indoors for days in succession ruining the bluest mornings and clearest star-flung evenings of the year. But now, without her mother there to lock her in a steamy kitchen, Jane ventured into the warm dark, risking her allergy for a chance to see the night sky and breathe in the intoxicating fragrance of summer gardens.

She heard a dog barking somewhere back behind the lots at Derry Street. It was joined by another, then a third, yapping out some frustrated and anxious cry against a ghostly cat, or perhaps a dozen cats, crossing unclaimed territory. Jane walked with her arms folded under her breasts, eyes focused on the hazy shapes coming into view a block at a time ahead of her. She was not afraid of the dark, never had been; the night air and the distance she'd walked so far had made her feel drunk somehow, hyperventilating jasmine and honeysuckle until her thoughts became scrambled and confused. A girl's voice rang out and echoed across the way behind the trees to the south, calling out a name Jane could not make out in the busy air. A breeze pushed through the willow above her and drowned the female voice in a soft sweep of tattering leaves.

Hurrying now, she crossed the road and passed under the last streetlamp in this section of town. Ragged stems of bougainvillea brushed at her face from the entrance to a driveway. She tossed them off with the back of her hand and wondered what the hell she was doing out there on her own in the middle of the night. *Am I crazy or what? Am I doing this for him or for me?* She listened to the light echoing her footsteps made on the sidewalk as she hurried to the west. Up ahead, shadows fluttered in the breeze, creating a kaleidoscopic effect through the willow-lined corridor, lights and darks falling to the sidewalk and rising back up again. *Step on a crack, break your mother's back*. Still being superstitious in that way after all these years, she tried avoiding the cracks in the concrete but it was dark and she knew she'd already stepped on several. Jane conjured up a vision of her mother hunched over in agony from an excruciating and incomprehensible pain in her back. Maybe the curse would be unable to cross state lines to Ohio. When she was a child, Frank and she used to run along the sidestreets of Rivertown almost every Saturday night, crossing in and out of the summer moonlight, chasing cats down the dusty alleyways with bricks and tin cans and marbles and old oily rags wrapped around softballs and dirt clods, staying out in the dark past midnight, playing deaf to shouted threats from all directions, hiding in storage sheds and unlocked garages and making prank calls from pay phones behind the old Roxy theater to the sour pasty-faced widows and snot-nosed drunks on Elm and Eleventh. She couldn't do that any longer. Frank was gone now, and she was grown up and responsible. So the games were finished. Or were they? Did growing up really make that much difference? One thing was certain: as an adult, there would never be as many places for her to hide, no garbage cans or cardboard shipping cartons to slither into, no blackberry bushes to curl up in. But Jane had known that already. Because even her own bed, and the warm darkness beneath her flowered pillow and pink cotton sheets, provided little or no refuge from anything any longer. That was, unfortunately, something she'd had to leave behind a long, long time ago.

The radio sitting in the open window across the yard from Howser's back door spilled music out into the lazy dark. Lying on his side in bed, Howser listened to the melody and the drumming rhythm as it made its way through the night air from his neighbor's house into his own. *"Is this the train to Desert Moon?" was all she said*. Overhead, the spiderwebs crisscrossed his bedroom ceiling. He'd given up fighting with them. The daddy longlegs had more time than he did and probably even a greater stake in the outcome of this little struggle. Fine. He'd let them be. At least until he settled a few other things in his life. *Those summer nights when we were young, we bragged of things we'd never done. We were dreamers, only dreamers.* Howser rolled over onto his back. The sheets felt cool and he shifted again to let as much of his skin touch the fabric as possible. His eyes closed and the room seemed to shrink. Every part of his world had, in fact, been reduced to dark and claustrophobic interiors—his office in the Rivertown courthouse, the black-and-white, that 7-Eleven store in San Jose—all places of his waking hours, folding up in his mind, closing in on him day after day. He rolled back over onto his stomach. *The night we stood and waited for the desert train, all the words we meant to say, all the chances swept away.* Kathy's leaving should have made his world larger, since two always occupy more space than one, yet it had not worked out that way. Not at all. Instead, even her name swelled that feeling of claustrophobia, wrapping about him and threatening suffocation.

There was no reason for him to feel that way. She was gone two years now. Why couldn't he shake her from his brain? Or, for that matter, from his heart? Because he'd found no one yet to take her place. Nature abhors a vacuum. He'd learned that in high school, though it was only in the last eighteen months that he'd seen vivid evidence of its truth. Since he lacked someone new to love, Kathy remained, perched on high in his memory, refusing to depart until displaced by another. And when would that be? Could he live alone for the rest of his life, Kathy's ghost floating in his mind year after year like a fragment of a dream?

He opened his eyes and got up off the bed and crossed the room and swung open the closet. In a corner behind an old pair of cowboy boots was a small Kinney's shoebox bound closed with string and yellowing strands of Scotch tape. He picked it up and carried it back to the bed with him. He undid the string and tore at the tape until it gave way and the top of the box came off. Inside were perhaps thirty to forty pink and white envelopes and other assorted scraps of paper written on in a neat and curving script— Kathy's handwriting. He took them out and laid them on the sheets and began fanning through them. They were letters Kathy had written to him nearly twenty years earlier. He searched through the envelopes looking for something unique and identifiable among them, something to remember that Kathy by. Did they carry her fragrance? He sniffed at the corner of one, where she'd printed "Smell here!" Maybe there was still a faint scent; he wasn't certain. He opened one envelope and the dried petal of a red rose fell out onto the sheet. Inside a note read: *"Thanks so much for the flowers, honey. They were so beautiful I thought I'd share them with you."* He'd sent her a dozen roses on her birthday in January. The twelfth. See? He remembered. She'd always said he would be the kind of husband who would forget birthdays and anniversaries. He never forgot either, even now. He turned the dried petal over between his fingers and rubbed it until it began to flake. He put it back inside with the note and opened the rest at random, and one after another drew out the old sheets of stationery and sifted through the handwritten lines. What did they make him think about love now—that it was really after all nothing more than a word tossed off when the need for either sex or companionship was at its strongest? How could anyone tell? After Kathy, Howser wondered. Then again, maybe somehow he was missing the point—that love was just like everything else: it comes, and then it goes, unnoticed on approach and swift on departure. How else could he resolve the voice in Kathy's letters with the person who had walked out on him two years ago? *I hope we always love each other like this, Carroll. I know I will.*

Howser sorted through the box, reading the letters and notes, stacking the envelopes, dating them, putting them aside for another night, another time. Down near the bottom he found a little envelope with a flamingo etched onto the outside of it. Unlike the envelope he had found earlier, this one still carried a distinct scent of a young girl's perfume, sweet and fragrant, preserved somehow on the fabric of the paper all those years. He held it to his nose and breathed in deeply. There was a tiny card inside the envelope which he pulled out, opened and read. In a careful scrawl was written, "Words can't express what I'm feeling tonight—I love you. So glad you're here!" There was no signature but he knew whose words they were. And he replaced the card inside the envelope and gathered up the rest of the letters and notes and dried petals of old rose blossoms and jammed them again into the Kinney's shoe-box and put it back in the closet behind the old cowboy boots where he'd deliberately hidden it twenty-two months before.

He fell asleep half an hour later and dreamed a restless dream of noisy, unfamiliar faces and indistinct highways running off toward a dark and windy horizon in another sweltering summer night. It was a dream he had been having frequently since that night at the railyard and this time only a distant hammering sound in his head shook free and dissolved the image of hundreds of contradictory road signs storming over him. Waking flat on his back, he opened his eyes to the dark ceiling and an insistent knock-ing at his kitchen door. He got up and searched for his pants in the shadows. He found them draped over the back of his chair and pulled them on. Then he walked through the dark house, feeling his way to the kitchen, and switched on the back-porch light. When he opened the door he saw Jane Crockett standing there, arms folded under her breasts, a smile on her face.

"Did I wake you?" Jane asked in a half whisper. She glanced up at him. He looked drowsy, half-asleep, and suddenly she wondered if maybe she'd misjudged things. In the silence of his driveway, she felt uneasy. She'd walked three miles for this and was now beginning to imag-ine herself a fool. *Maybe that's exactly what I am. Oh, jeez, why couldn't I have stayed at home and watched the news or something*. Then she heard his voice and he was talking to her.

"Are you going to come in or just stand out on my porch all night?"

A breakthrough. It was okay, after all.

She whispered, "I'm coming in," and stepped over a large potato bug on the doormat, easing her way past him into the kitchen. He leaned out after her and looked down the driveway to the road. Then he ducked back inside and closed the kitchen door behind him, switching off the porch light. Jane was standing by the sink, feeling a little tired now and flushed.

"Where'd you park your car?" he asked. "I didn't hear you drive up."

"It's at home in the garage. I walked."

"You walked? In the middle of the night? That's two miles."

"Three," she replied, "but who's counting?" Jane reached up by the cupboard and drew down a hand towel. "It wasn't that bad. I needed some fresh air."

Jane turned to the sink and opened the tap, running cold water on her hands, washing them and letting the water flow onto her forearms as well, cooling her skin.

"Want something to drink?" asked Howser.

Jane closed the tap and dried her hands on the blue towel. She nodded. "I'd love something to drink."

"Beer, milk, bottled water, orange juice, soda."

"How about orange juice?"

He drew the carton out of the refrigerator and opened it. Jane reached over to the cupboard to the left of the sink and brought down a glass with daisies painted on the sides. Howser filled the glass for her and left the carton open in case she wanted more. Jane drank slowly while looking at Howser. She was trying to see how he was taking all this. It had been a long time since she'd just showed up on him and she was not entirely sure it was the right thing to do anymore. Maybe he was seeing someone else. That was a possibility, though a fairly unlikely one. Rivertown was small enough that any kind of affair was pretty much impossible to hide, and Jane was certain that she knew him better than that. He didn't have a woman hiding in the closet or under his bed. No, he was alone tonight. Jane drained the glass and set it in the sink and ran water into it.

"I know what you're wondering," she said, turning back around to face Howser who was still standing by the open refrigerator. "You're wondering what I'm doing here drinking your orange juice in the middle of the night when I ought to be home, or at least out somewhere entertaining another man on a nice warm summer night, huh?"

Howser closed the carton and put it back in the refrigerator and nudged the door closed with his elbow. "Something like that. I don't get that many visitors out here past midnight." He reached over and switched off the kitchen light. "Come on, let's go into the back. It's cooler there."

Jane nodded and followed Howser down the hallway to his bedroom at the rear of the house. In the dark, he looked larger than he did in the light. His shoulders looked wider and his legs longer and he appeared to move more heavily on the hardwood floor even though he made little or no sound as he walked. A light came on in his bedroom as Jane entered. Howser stepped away from the desk lamp and motioned for her to take the old swivel chair she'd found for him at a flea market in Stockton the summer before. Jane spun around once in the chair and giggled. Howser sat on the bed and smiled. Jane reached back over her shoulder and switched off the lamp, letting the room pass once more into a silvery-blue darkness.

"What'd you do that for?" he asked.

"I like the dark," said Jane. "Especially in this room. Makes me feel more relaxed. Please don't make me turn it back on."

Jane could hear the bedsprings squeak as Howser leaned back on one of his pillows. Her eyes had not quite adjusted to the dark and she could only just make out his face in the shadows, though he was no more than a few feet away.

"So, I guess you're wondering what I'm doing out here tonight."

Howser twisted on one elbow and smiled, knowing Jane could not see his face. He shook his head. She hadn't changed at all. Even after all the time they'd worked together, there was still one Jane for the day and another at night, and they were as different as two sisters, one cool and subdued, the other brilliant and funny, both warm, both very attractive, both good to him. He had no preference. He rolled onto his back then pulled his legs up and sat against the headboard, waiting until his eyes adjusted to the shadowlight and he could see her expression across the room. She was smiling for him, a half-grin tucked around her lips.

"I wasn't wondering at all, Jane. I know why you're here."

"You do?" she asked, feigning incredulity.

"Sure."

"Were you expecting me or something? Did someone call ahead and warn you that I was on my way?"

"I didn't say I knew you were coming. I just said that I wasn't wondering about the reason you're here, because I know why you are."

"And why's that?"

"Clayton. You want to know what we talked about. What he told me."

"You think I walked three miles to find out what you and Jack Clayton spent the afternoon talking about?"

"If you're going to tell me you came out here to crawl into bed with me, Jane, I'm not buying it."

She smiled. "It's true, though."

He strained to see her face in the half-light from the open window, but he could only make out the curve from her nose and cheek down to her chin. Her lips and eyes remained in shadow.

"If you remember, I used to come over here all the time."

"That's right. You used to. Not anymore."

"You know as well as I do why I stopped coming."

"I know."

"Then don't be upset about it."

"Do I sound upset?"

"A little."

"Why did you send Clayton to talk to me today? Did you really think there was anything he could tell me that I didn't already know? Anything I hadn't already thought of? I've been a cop for a long time, Jane. I've listened to a lot of stories."

She tried to find his face now in the dark wash that fell from the ceiling down across his bed. He was leaning back again, though, and unless she was prepared to climb onto the sheets with him she was not going to be able to see him clearly enough to make out any expression at all on his face.

"I was just trying to help. Jack's a smart guy—"

"He knows a few things," said Howser, cutting her off.

234

"Okay, he knows a few things. But maybe some of what he knows can help you."

"The tramp thing, right?"

"Exactly. He said he lived with them for over a year—"

"And there was no way they would've raped that girl."

"I believe him," she said. "Don't you?"

"It's not my job to believe him."

"No, but somebody's killing people here in Rivertown, and if Jack can help you figure out who it is then maybe it *is* your job to at least listen to him."

"You think so, huh?"

"Yes, I do."

A breeze gusted through the window on the street side of the room, pushing against the pull-down shade and drawing light in behind it where Howser sat on the bed facing Jane in the warm darkness. His eyes were open and wet. She could see that much in the instant before the shade fell closed again. It might just have been the sweat from his brow beading up and running off into his eyes that gave them that soft shine she'd seen a moment ago. Her own skin felt salty now and wet; the breeze fanning over it made her realize that as the sweat was cooled in the circling air. Yet she also knew there was something else, a pressure forcing that look onto the curvature of his eyes, the moisture welling up from somewhere behind the eyelids rather than trickling in from outside. And now, that pressure was coming from her and she did not like the feeling. That was not why she was in this room with him now.

He whispered, "We're not making progress with any of the investigations. People are getting scared. Losing confidence in us."

"No, they're not."

"Yes, they are. I could see it on their faces out at the fairgrounds today. They're nervous as hell. They don't feel safe anymore, and I don't blame them. Why should they? Two weeks ago a pretty sixteen-year-old girl went out to the railyard with her friends and came back raped and beaten. Five days later her body's floating in the river. Then her boyfriend comes to us with this crazy story about getting chased through an abandoned mill by some wild transient. We go out there to have a look around and of course we don't find a thing, except now it turns out a friend of his who was supposed to meet him at the mill is missing. The same night two of his other buddies get killed in a mysterious truck wreck and twelve hours later we find our missing kid lying under a tree with his neck broken. Jane, in two weeks we've had a rape, two homicides, a somewhat suspicious fatal traffic accident and a near-riot at the railyard. Not to mention the midnight trashing of a local garage. These people have all the right and reason in the world to be scared and upset. Let's face it, we haven't done a goddamn thing to make them feel any differently."

Jane watched him get up off the bed and stop at the window, parting the shade and staring out at the road and the arc light burning in his neighbor's yard in the next lot.

"Carroll?"

Howser let the shade fall back against the screen. Only his silhouette against the windowframe made him visible in the dark. Jane shifted on the chair and let her legs drop to the floor.

"Do they think I like seeing people killed?" said Howser. "Do they think it doesn't bother me, like I'm used to it or something? What kind of clown do they think I am anyway?"

"I'm sorry."

"What for?"

"Just the way everything's gone. It's not your fault. You can't let it get you down."

"It's not the investigation. I can handle that. Fuck-ups on the job I'm used to. That's not it."

"I'm listening."

"Are you sure? It's about another woman."

"I don't think of Kathy as being another woman, Carroll."

"She'd appreciate hearing that."

"You know what I mean."

"Yeah."

"So?"

"I can't get rid of her, Jane. She follows me everywhere. Everything I see and do reminds me of her and it's killing me. You know, I came up here thinking I'd get away from it, that time would just wash it away, let me start over. But that hasn't happened at all. In fact, it's gotten worse."

"Well, this job hasn't exactly given you any peace of mind. That's half the trouble right there. And then you haven't worked that hard to find someone else, either. And really, that's all that's going to set you free from her."

"I know that. When I'm not downtown, I'm just sitting here alone staring at these walls. So, you're right there. It's my own fault, I guess. Living like this, I'm just hurting myself. On the other hand, I don't know what else to do. I have the job I came here for, and whether it's going great or shitty, it's still the job I chose. And I choose to live alone, so I've sort of stuck myself in this situation. That's why I say, I know I've only got myself to blame. Maybe I just don't belong here. Maybe I made a mistake coming here in the first place."

She watched him cross the room and return to the bed, where he sat down and leaned back against the headboard. Jane continued to search for his eyes in the blue shadowlight, straining somehow to find something in their expression that was absent from his voice. When he didn't speak, she filled the vacuum herself.

"The quiet," she whispered. "I love the quiet out here so much." She drew another soft breath and held it. "Listen." The shade flapped lazily at the screen, but made no sound. A breeze passed in and out of the room. Across the yard the light over his neighbor's garage went out. Four birds circling to the south swept noiselessly into the willows then off and away again. The stars swelled and glimmered in the night sky. "Nothing. See? Silence. So quiet."

Howser coughed once and shifted his feet on the bed.

Jane leaned forward in the chair and it creaked. "When I was a little girl, I used to have a dream about wandering through empty rooms in a big old house looking for something, although I wasn't sure what. Everywhere I went I'd hear voices and music nearby, in the next room or the one above on the next floor but I'd never see anybody—not my brother or parents or friends or anyone—just this long curtain lace in the windows and doorways passing light through the sheerest fabric and pushing at my face as I walked from room to room, calling after my own echo. I'd wake up afterward feeling so lonely I'd be in tears all morning."

Jane could see his face now, brow wrinkled and concerned, and in the pale silver light he looked either worried or disturbed. Was it for himself or for her? Maybe for both of them.

"Do you know what I think it means, Carroll?"

"That you were asleep?" he said, with a sudden grin.

"I'm serious."

"Sorry, I just have a hard time with other people's dreams."

"This isn't only about me."

"It isn't?"

"No, it's about you, too."

"Me?"

"Do you want to hear?"

"Yes."

"Well, it's just that wandering through that house made me think that I was trying to find someone or something to give me the sort of direction or answers that I wouldn't be able to find on my own—when what I really needed to realize was that wherever I went, whichever room I wandered into, would be the right one, no matter what. Do you understand?"

"No."

"Okay, look: all that time I was in one place I was always wanting to be somewhere else because I thought that I needed to be somewhere different, in a certain place with certain people listening to certain things in order to discover what I needed to know about myself and my life. But what I realized finally was that where I was didn't matter, because the voices I was following belonged to people who were just wandering, too, people who weren't any closer than I was to discovering just the right things to carry them through. That's when I thought to myself, 'Look around, Jane. Who knows any more about all of this than you do? No one, that's who. Those empty rooms are just other places, no single one more important or right than another. And those voices might just as well be echoes of your own because you can do as well wandering and looking by yourself as you can chasing after something or somebody else that probably isn't important anyhow.' See what I mean? The dream was telling me to start living *my* life, not somebody else's. So I did. And now I'm happy. This is *my* life now, Carroll. *My* home. And it's yours now, too. This house and this town. It's where you belong."

She paused and waited for a response. None came. She peered through the shadows, searching for his eyes again, but either he or the light had shifted. His face was in black now and his body only a form there before her like the rest of his furniture, shapeless and silent. She whispered, "Carroll?"

"Yeah?"

She could see him nod. The movement from his head made the dark around him ripple and flutter. Jane reached forward and squeezed Howser's foot. She felt herself flush. It was the first time she'd touched him in this room in almost a year. Something came back and she held on to it and whispered, "Carroll, you have to let Kathy go."

She felt him stir slightly. Those were the same words she'd spoken to him dozens of times in other ways yet this time in the dark somehow they carried a different weight.

"I mean, we've all been rejected one time or another. But usually after the first forty-eight hours we stop kicking and screaming and start looking around for someone new. I don't think you've gotten past the yelling yet. Carroll, if this is the only time you ever have this happen to you, you're going to be lucky. Really."

She searched for the expression on his face somewhere beyond her touch. When she located it in the twisting shadowlight she saw a smile and moved over to the bed and slid in beside him. Then she put her arm around his shoulder and kissed him on the cheek. "You know, my mother still sends me baskets of fruit at Easter."

"Huh?"

"She thinks I'm lonely and she sends me baskets of fruit and flowers to cheer me up. It's her way of letting me know someone out there loves me even though I haven't given her any grandchildren yet."

"Are you lonely, Jane?"

"You mean with all the men I have chasing me around, am I still lonely enough to walk all the way out here in the middle of the night to climb into bed and commiserate with you?"

"Yes."

She slipped her hand under his chin and pulled his face toward her and kissed him first softly, then again deeply and open-mouthed. A few seconds later she pulled away and opened her eyes. He was still there in front of her, looking surprised. She thought to herself, *Maybe I've done the right thing for once*. And there was a look on his face that verified it.

"What about Clayton?" he asked. "I thought the two of you—"

She let her arms fall around his neck. "Not tonight."

Then she kissed him lightly on the nose and pulled back for a reaction. The yellow shade rose and fell again quietly at the open window and the bedsprings squeaked as Howser shifted his weight to face her directly. With the heat off her dark skin rising into him, he showed her the barest smile in the fading shadow.

An hour before dawn the telephone in the front of the house rang and Howser turned over in bed, soaked with sweat, moving off Jane Crockett's shoulder to his own side where the sheets were cooler and dry. He was dreaming again—a dry wind hammering at the clapboard siding on his house, flipping the bedroom window shade up off its rollers, kicking that stack of old newspapers off the back porch, sweeping gravel and dust high on the night sky, obscuring in a dark haze ten billion stars passing east to west and out over Green River again. He tossed in his sleep, shaking the bed. Jane rolled toward him, blinking once into the dark, then slumping back into a lacy white dream of her own. The kitchen phone was ringing now four, five, six times, echoing into the hallway. Howser heard it as ornamental bells clanging on tall gray telephone poles rocking violently in a dust wind on a long highway a lifetime from the Rivertown city limits. Unable to stop the ringing inaccessible to him in the air above, Howser ignored it and stretched his cramping arms and legs out again over the white sheets, stained and wet still from the anxious and heaving movement of his body and Jane's only an hour earlier. The phone sounded in her dream, too, as piano scales played somewhere nearby in a large empty sunroom. The notes at the upper end of the scale danced in the walls and mimicked the shrill and hysterical voices she'd been chasing through a hundred tall doorways now, but since she could locate neither the piano nor the music room in which it sat, there was little she could do about the disturbing ringing in her ears. Lying now in the moonshadow of the upper windowframe, Jane edged her face next to Howser's, woke briefly, kissed his ear, and whispered something she would not remember later. She fell back into a white light that was changing just then into the sheerest curtain lace.

16

Feeling almost narcoleptic the next morning, Howser needed everything he had just to pry himself out of bed and get downtown. His eyes burned and his brain winked on and off as he went over the reports that had been piling up on his desk for five days now. He picked up the newspaper. Charlotte Burkie's column had the feature headline on the front page again. More originality, too. RAPE SUSPECT STILL AT LARGE. Where'd he read that before? Charlotte hadn't even bothered to call the courthouse for information. In fact, she rarely called in about anything. Preferring the direct approach, over the past two weeks she'd telephoned the Millers, Williamses, Maddoxes and Arnolds in favor of speaking with anyone on the professional side of the investigation. Small-town journalism, Charlotte Burkie–style. She called her column "Personals" when the fact remained that she appeared daily on the front page, not back in the "Family" section with the traditional gossip and gardening. In Howser's mind, Charlotte's articles on Rivertown were little more than advice-to-the-lovelorn pieces without the accompanying questions. He read them as rarely as possible.

He closed the paper and shoved it away. He had a headache and didn't have time to read the paper anyhow. Taking care of the reports on his desk was what he was getting paid for. He opened each folder and scanned the top sheets. It was tedious work, filling out forms and making recommendations. He needed a secretary. However, since the town couldn't afford to pay one, most of the clerical work connected to the job he did himself.

There was a knock at the door and Howser yelled, "Come in!"

The door opened slowly and Alfie peeked his head around the edge and smiled. "Morning, Chief."

Howser looked up at the clock. It was eleven thirty, and counting. He looked back at Alfie who was still standing there with his neck crooked around the door.

Alfie smiled again and waved. "Remember me?"

Howser cracked a slight grin. "That's right. Didn't you used to work here?"

Alfie came in and closed the door behind him. "Now, Chief, I can explain—"

The phone rang. Howser winced and motioned for Alfie to answer it. He'd had enough of the phone already that day and swore he wouldn't talk to another person. Besides, Jane had prepped him for this one, so he knew who it was already. Alfie picked up the receiver and said, "Chief's office."

"Yeah, he's right here, hold on."

Alfie cupped his hand over the receiver and thrust it in Howser's direction. Howser just shook his head and said, "I'm not here, Alfie. I'm out. Tell them I'm out on a call."

Alfie waited a few seconds then said in a half-whisper, "Chief?"

"You heard me. I'm not in."

Alfie waited another moment or two, then became frustrated and said, "It's Don Long. Says it's important."

Howser scowled and grabbed the phone. "Yes sir, Mr. Long. What can I do you for today?"

Then Howser knew he had made a mistake in taking the phone from Alfie. He heard the phone change hands and Tom Danielson's voice echo back at him through the line.

"Long's boy Howie didn't come home last night, Howser. He's missing just like the Williams kid. I want you to find out where the hell he's gone off to."

"Why don't you ask your own boy? Seems to me if anyone ought to know, it'd be Jamie, don't you think?"

"You know damn well if the boys knew where Howie'd got off to I wouldn't be taking time to talk to you. Now listen to me and listen good . . ."

Howser whispered over to Alfie who was edging toward the door, "I'm going to get you for this."

". . . I won't call again. I want that boy found and I want him found by Monday. That gives you a day and a half. Rivertown's not so big. An experienced lawman like yourself shouldn't have any problem. You got me, mister?"

"Sure, Tom. We'll pick him up and deliver him right to your doorstep. No problem. Sorry for the delay." Howser heard a loud click on the other end of the phone, then a dial tone. "Thank you, too." He hung up.

Alfie smiled and said, "Well, at least it was short."

"Yeah. Thank God for small blessings, huh?" said Howser. "This is getting to be like a bad movie."

"You said that last week."

"It was true then, and it's true now. What does Danielson think we're doing down here, running a day-care center for his kid's pals? Apparently Howie Long didn't make it home last night."

Alfie pulled a chair up to the desk. He straddled it and sat facing Howser. "So, what're we going to do about it?"

"What do you want to do? Do you have any idea where he is?"

"No."

"Well, neither do I. And I'm not going to start worrying about it for at least another hour."

Howser pushed the stack of papers over to the right and drew out a note Jane had left on his desk earlier. He handed it to Alfie. "Here, check this out if you want something to do."

Alfie took the note and read it. Then he looked back at Howser with a frown. "Let me guess: you want me to go out there and make sure she's taking her vitamins, right?"

"We got a call in from her brother and sister. They're in San Francisco for the week and just asked if someone could go out and look in on her once before they get back."

"Why don't they just call her up?"

"No phone, apparently. Just her and a TV set. Listen,

go ahead and take a little drive out there this afternoon and have a look around. Make sure everything's okay. Then, after dinner, you can come back here and help me go over some of these statements Corey took at the Starlite."

"I thought you wanted me to check out Bailey's Reservoir today?"

"I do, *after* you run out to the Johnson place."

Alfie frowned. "Just tell me one thing, Chief: Why do I get all the shit jobs?"

"Because you're the shit patrolman," said Beef, strolling into the office. He knocked on the door as he passed it. Corey followed him in, carrying another folder stuffed with more reports.

"You gave Alfie the Johnson house stake-out, Chief?" asked Corey.

"I asked him to go up there and have a look-see then come back," said Howser. "We're in public service, remember? Someone calls, we respond."

"Don't forget to water the roses while you're there, Alf," said Beef. "I know she'd appreciate it." He laughed.

"Thanks, guys," said Alfie. "I'll remember you at Christmas."

"Are those things done?" asked Howser, grabbing the reports from Corey.

"Naturally," said Beef. "We're professional pencil-pushers now. We always get our homework done and in on time. You know that."

Beef took off his hat and sat on the corner of the desk. "Chief, when are you going to let us have some serious conversation with Jamie and his little buddies?"

"Soon as you give me a reason, other than your desire to kick some butt."

"Us, kick butt? You must be mistaken, Chief," said Corey. "That's not our style."

"Chief, I don't know what you might've been hearing," said Beef, "but in all my life I have never touched another human being in anger."

Beef winked at Alfie. Howser walked back over to the window and peeked out through the shades. Traffic was moving slowly down Main in the bright light, people drifting along in the heat. A small group of children crossed the park lawn and headed up the street to the east. One of them tripped and fell to the pavement. The others ran on ahead laughing. The traffic light in front of Sears changed to red. Howser turned back toward his officers. "Did you guys get out to the garbage dump this morning?"

"Yep," said Corey, "and the hatchery and the dredge and the old Linwood Cannery. No luck."

"All right," replied Howser. "Then get me the list and let's see what we've got left."

At the Walcott, Clayton closed the door to his room and walked down the hall to the stairs. Insulation inside the Walcott was so poor that the summer heat seemed to slide in through the cracks in the redwood windowframe. The wallpaper had even begun to peel, neo-Victorian floral patterns rippling along the top of the enameled wainscoting. Ellen had gone out to the hardware store and bought him a small metal desk fan and mounted it on the nightstand beside his bed. The draft it created kept the room temperature more tolerable, at least in the evening.

Clayton passed Ed Morton's room at the top of the stairs and looked in on the old man watching major league baseball and eating a honeydew melon. Though sweat was visible on his face, he was still wearing his bathrobe. The set was on so loud he didn't hear Clayton walk by to the elevator. Downstairs, the lobby was empty. Ellen was folding laundry out back and the phone in the office was off the hook. The front doors were wide open. In Clayton's box at the desk was a note. It was from Jane: "Sorry, no can do lunch today. Much work. Maybe supper?" He folded the note and stuffed it into his shirt pocket and headed outside. Fifteen minutes later, he was driving east out toward Green River where the air was somewhat cooler. He made a right off the highway onto a one-lane road that led down a short grade through a thick hedge of blackberry bushes and ended at an embankment overlooking a nice shady stretch of the river. Jane had given him directions to this spot where she and her first boyfriend

246

Bobby Dupree had come one August evening for a picnic that wound up being her first sexual experience.

Clayton climbed down out of the van, leaving the doors open on both the driver's and passenger's sides. It needed airing out. Walking around to the back, he took out a bedroll and a jug of water and stepped over to the dirt embankment. Below, the river flowed slowly by in the shade of willows and blackberry bushes along the bluff. Clayton slid down to the sandbar. He brushed the sand from his jeans and looked up. No clouds and no haze. Perfect blue sky. He opened the jug of water and drank a third of it. Then he opened the bedroll and laid it out on the sand. After another drink from the jug, he took his clothes off and put on a pair of old cutoffs.

He waded out a few feet into the river. The water rippling around his legs gave him a slight chill but felt good. He bent over and dunked his head. The current swept up on his thighs and brushed past heading south. Skeeter-eaters flicked across the surface of the water, lighting down and dancing off again. Sparrows in the cottonwoods along the shore chattered on and off. Clayton eased farther into the river and stretched out into a soft dive, sliding headfirst into the cool green water. When he surfaced again he was flowing with the current. It carried him along a dozen yards or so until he paddled his way across to the shallow sandbar just off the opposite shore and submerged himself there up to his waist, digging his heels into the sand against the swirling eddies. He leaned back, closing his eyes and taking a deep breath, letting his body sink again into the river. After a few minutes, his eyelids grew numb from the cold and he crawled out to dry off in the sun. He lay on his stomach on the sandbar and let the sun color his upper body. He stretched out until the muscles in his legs and arms strained to a soft ache. The sand felt warm on his skin.

He wished Jane had come out with him. He'd been thinking about her all day. He suspected she'd gone to see Howser last night. That didn't really bother him. She had her own life. How long was he going to stay in Rivertown anyhow? Until the end of the summer? Even then he'd be gone by September, just a few weeks away now. Though that was not what he'd told Jane, it was true nonetheless. And if it was just about sex, then no big deal. He'd take off and only think about her until he was in bed with somebody else. But if it wasn't just sex, then what? Half of the problem turned on the question of what he had actually come here for in the first place. Back in Tucson, Mick Norman had told him Rivertown was a quiet place where he'd be able to kick back, do some sunning on the river and maybe, with any luck, get laid. He'd been mostly right. Clayton turned over onto his back and put his hand up to block the sun. Mostly right because Mick hadn't counted on him taking to Jane like he had, feeling special about her. An hour after meeting her, Clayton knew Jane was the kind of woman he'd been wanting to meet for a long time, more than just a face and a smile. Someone sweet enough to give him a reason to stop all the running around. That was the problem. Jane was great, no doubt about it. The question was, was he ready to spend the rest of his life in small-town America? Well, nobody was that great.

He yawned and closed his eyes. The sound of the swirling current made him drowsy. A fly landed on his back and he twisted to swat it away. A splash came from the river, probably a fish breaking the surface of the water. He ignored it, and a few minutes later fell asleep. The river slid by easily without him, sunlight coming from the west still sparkling brightly on the surface as it went. A breeze crossed the water and fanned the dust up the side of the embankment. The leaves rippled in the cottonwoods overhead. Sleeping, Clayton dreamed a sunset dream of blue mountains and pink seas under an expressionless sky. Wading in a warm, white surf, his legs lost in the swirling tide, he heard a voice calling to him out of the surf. But the sea was urging him forward and away so he could not turn to see who it was he was hearing. Then the calling ceased and the sea went flat, and the sunset pink and blue dimmed and darkened, falling into twilight, leaving him alone, sloshing uselessly about in an empty tide. He was awakened by the sound of voices on the bluff across the river.

Two boys. Teenagers. One talking louder than the other.

"Yup, life's a bitch, then you die."

"She's pretty pissed off."

"Good for her. Annie's got the biggest fucking mouth in the county. She's just going to have to stay put until we get things under control. When's Jerry getting back?"

A lighted match flew out in a soft arc over the river and vanished into the swirling current. Clayton crept along the sandbar toward the shade of the willows whose branches extended to the water's edge. He couldn't see much more than the outline of the two boys up on the embankment across the river; they couldn't see him at all.

"About an hour or so. He had to go to the feed store for his old man."

"I don't trust Goober." Another burning match sailed out over the water. "I don't want you guys leaving him out there by himself."

"Maybe she'll rape him."

"If she gets away, we're in deep shit."

"We're already in deep shit."

A rock came hurtling out over the river and crashed into the trees less than thirty feet above Clayton's head.

"I'm taking care of it. Don't go paranoid on me."

"I don't want to go to jail for something I didn't do."

"Fuck you! You were there, just like the rest of us. That makes you as guilty as anyone else."

"Bullshit. I didn't do anything and you know it."

"Prove it. It's your word against ours and the twerps'll say whatever I tell them to. Don't even *think* about fucking with this. We got a plan and we're sticking to it. That means *all* of us."

Another burning match was sent airborne above the river. Then there was a period of silence. Clayton watched one of the boys take a cigarette out of his jeans and light it. He took a long hit and blew the smoke into the breeze. He offered it to the other boy who shook his head.

"Come on," he said, offering again. He passed the joint to the other boy who sucked on it, coughed harshly, and passed it back. "Good shit, huh?" He took another hit himself and held the smoke longer in his lungs. Crouching in the shadows by the river's edge, Clayton watched the two boys pass the joint back and forth until it burned down to the nub. The first boy flicked the spent roach off into the water, then said, "Let's go. I got to get back. The old man's been on my case all week and I told him I'd be home by four."

The boys left the bluff, their voices fading in the distance. A few minutes later, two car doors slammed shut and an engine started up. The vehicle that drove off kicked up a cloud of dust that caught in the breeze and cascaded out over the river.

Clayton waited until the air was quiet again before stepping back out into the sunlight. The last dust from the spinning tires settled onto the river. Exhausted from the heat, he waded back into the river, ladling water in his hands as he went, splashing it up onto his legs and waist, trying to cool off. He lowered himself completely into the current and slipped under the surface. The water chilled his skin; swimming felt nice. Coming out of Green River on the far shoreline, he shook the water from his hair and sat down on the bedroll, got out of the wet cutoffs and began putting his street clothes back on.

A long gravel road led up a rise to the Johnson house in the old orchard. Alfie drove slowly, taking care not to raise too much dust. He parked the unit along the west side of the house and shut off the engine and climbed out. The place was quiet. The roses out front were still blooming a bright red and yellow in the sunlight even though the ground beneath them was cracked and gray. He walked around to the back of the house and found the garden hose coiled up under the crawlway next to the fruit cellar. The cellar door was open. It gave off a smell of rotting apples. As a kid, he used to believe the bogey-man lived down there in the dark waiting for bold and foolish children to pass by unescorted. The Witch Lady's bogey-man. All the kids used to sneak up there in the middle of the night to steal apricot and raspberry preserves from the Witch Lady's cellar. One night he accidentally dropped a case of glass jars filled with peaches. When he tried to escape,

250

Nathan Danielson and three of his friends shoved him back down the stairs and closed the cellar door, sealing him in. That was probably thirty years ago, yet Alfie could still remember how he felt stuck there in the stinking dark, bawling his eyes out and kicking at the floorboards, trying to escape. The others ran, leaving him there to face the Witch Lady alone. She came down from upstairs and dragged him by the ear into her kitchen and made him take a mop and sponge back to the cellar where he remained the rest of the night swabbing the concrete and searching on his hands and knees for the tiniest shards of broken glass. He had a lot of memories tied up in this house, not many of them very pleasant.

He connected the hose to a faucet half-hidden behind a trellis of bougainvillea and dragged it out around to the rosebushes beside the front porch and laid the nozzle down flat in the dirt. Then he walked back to the faucet, turned on the water, and returned to the roses to make sure the water was flowing out evenly. As the hose undulated with a change in water pressure, he straightened it out. When the soil began to flood, he walked back to the faucet and turned the water pressure down slightly. He didn't want to drown anything. Inside, he would remind the old woman that her water was on so she'd know to come out and turn it off before dark. He checked the hose once more, then went up to the front door.

There was the barest breeze fanning the porch in the pale blue light as Alfie stepped up under the eave and peeked through the curtains riffling inward from the parlor window screens. His boots caused the floorboards to creak slightly. The sound they made, coming in the quiet like that, startled him. *Ten years old again and scared to death of the Witch Lady and her haunted house in the white orchard.* He glanced back across the yard to the road beyond. The air was clear and cool and he imagined how nice it would be down on Green River, lying there in the boat taking the sun and listening to the catfish tapping the underside of the hull. He leaned forward and rapped softly at the screen door and waited for sounds of movement from inside. It would have been just fine with him if she tottered over and told him to get the hell out of there, she didn't want any goddamn visitors. Maybe she was lying inside somewhere, stiff and smelly, like old people get when they die by themselves in the middle of summer. He pictured himself finding her keeled over next to the rocker or in the kitchen with the cookie cutters. He rapped at the front door.

"Miss Amy?"

This was all standard procedure. Not particularly relishing the idea of the chief getting on his back for unlawful entry, he sure as hell wasn't going to just walk right in.

"Miss Amy, you in there?"

The faintest whisper of weight shifting on old hardwood floorboards came from inside. Alfie did not hear it, not consciously at least. Instead, he glanced around, beginning at that moment to feel somehow very vulnerable on the old woman's porch, though he wasn't sure why. His spine tingled briefly and he took hold of his holstered gun butt to steady himself. The curtains fluttered. He tried the door knob. It was not locked. Somehow, he hadn't thought it would be. Alfie opened the screen door and slipped inside.

The hallway from the entry followed the blue strip carpet ahead to the kitchen where the sunlight shone brightly through a back window. On his left was an empty sewing room. The mantel clock was ticking slowly in the parlor to his right. He took three steps and listened again. Nothing but the clock. He moved toward the parlor, failing to notice the light in the kitchen broken for a fraction of a second by something passing the window.

In the parlor, slants of pink sunlight from the stained glass in the bay window on the east side of the room glided across the love seat and the potted ferns. The air was so still that Alfie was amazed the movement of the pendulum in the open clockwork failed to cause a disturbance. The room smelled of camphor and stale perfume—and something else, too. An odor almost like spent tobacco or dried hay smoldering in a slow burn under heavy canvas, yet so faint as to border on the imagined. There was a small white porcelain teapot and a china cup on a marble stand next to an empty oak rocker on the north side of the room beside the clock. Alfie resisted the temptation to taste for freshness what little liquid could still be seen in the pot.

He leaned over and touched the seat of the rocker. It was warm. He touched it again. The clock chimed three times to mark the hour. Alfie reached higher on the seat back and pressed his palm flat against the burgundy fabric just up to the left of the outline Miss Amy's body had apparently been making in that chair for the last sixty years or so. It was not as warm as the seat. He looked around. On the south side of the room, a string of crystal prisms stretched limply across the upper face of the window clearly beyond the reach of the sun. Beneath them a black iron stand held the drooping remains of four coleus plants, their red leaves folded and dead, given over to the heat and the relentless summer light. Alfie looked out through the lace toward the porch he had been standing on minutes earlier. He walked over to the fern and thrust his fingers into the soil in the center of the plant and pulled them out again, dry. He craned his neck forward and looked into the clay pot. The soil was cracked and crumbling. He pushed the back of the rocker. It swung into a creaking rhythm, drowning out the clock. He grabbed the rocker and stopped it, then held his breath for a beat. He hadn't counted on any of this and it was making him feel a little edgy. This was supposed to be a simple case of watering some flowers and checking up on an old lady. So, where was she?

He reentered the hallway. Ahead on his left was the open door leading to the dining room. Farther on to the right was an alcove and the staircase that led upstairs. Beyond that were the swinging doors to the kitchen and pantry. Alfie straightened his badge, then placed his left hand on the wall and his right on the pistol butt, inching his way toward the dining room. He stopped there and looked inside. It was empty like the parlor, but there were dirty plates and silverware on the rumpled tablecloth and a chair knocked over. Either the old woman hadn't done any dishes in a few days or she'd had some real slobs as dinner guests last night. He ducked back into the hallway and continued toward the kitchen. Reaching the dark alcove to the staircase he noticed for the first time a faint buzzing coming from the kitchen. Flies. Lots of flies. Was the door to the backyard open? He took one quick glance up the staircase and walked forward to the kitchen.

Alfie was barely through the swinging doors when shock stopped him in his tracks. Cupboards were thrown open and their contents scattered and spread about on the floor. Sacks of sugar and flour, little spice tins and India tea bags lay with the usual garbage, torn open and emptied everywhere in open drawers and strewn across counters. And the entire kitchen—floor, walls, and enameled tile countertops—was stained and soaked in huge reddish-brown splotches of sticky blood. He'd seen cattle slaughtered when he was a kid, yet it was nothing like this. More than anything, it just looked like quarts and quarts of terracotta enamel splashed from nickel water balloons. The thing was, of course, there weren't any balloon fragments soaking with the rest of the crap, nor were there any cattle carcasses lying about. Only the blood. And it had already attracted hundreds of flies through the open window screen above the sink. The buzzing of the flies and the stifling heat in the kitchen and the sight of so much filth and disarray, and the smell of it, warm and rotten, made him queasy. He staggered backward out of the kitchen to huddle in the alcove at the bottom of the staircase.

"Jesus, sweet Jesus!"

His stomach flipflopped and his vision went black and he pitched forward grabbing the sides of his head. As he tried to steady himself, he heard a groaning in the ceiling above him, like somebody's weight shifting on a weak section of floor upstairs. Alfie got to his feet, hands shaking. His voice echoed loudly in the walls, "Who's there? Who's up there, you son of a bitch?"

Then, horrified at the realization that he'd just given away his own location, he cringed and ducked down beneath the stairway overhang, cursing his own fear. He dug the fingernails of his right hand into his thigh and listened. The faint buzzing of the swarm of flies wild in the kitchen seemed to grow louder, matched only by the pounding of his heart. Jesus, what was he going to do? He leaned out of the alcove and twisted his neck to look as far up the stairs as he could. Just shadows above the railing atop the second-floor landing. He'd have to go all the way up if he wanted to see anything more. Down the hall in the parlor, the curtains washed backward through the string of prisms, causing them to clink together in the silent air.

Alfie found some life returning to his limbs. He counted to twenty forward and backward and took a deep breath. If he wanted to, he could get the hell out of the house now and call for a backup. That would be proper procedure. Chief'd appreciate it. The guys, though, they'd say he was chickenshit, especially if it turned out the old lady was only upstairs taking a nap. But the kitchen. Jesus! Another problem: What if the old woman *was* upstairs and not napping; what if she was in trouble that very instant? What if she got hurt while he was cowering outside? Hands trembling, he fought his own instincts and pulled the .38 from his holster. Then he rose to his feet and slowly entered the dark staircase, following the curve of the banister as it ascended into the brown shadows of the second floor.

There were two bedrooms upstairs, one at each end of the hallway, both facing north over the front driveway. Amy Johnson's bedroom was on the west end of the house. The east room was kept for guests, family most often. It had been vacant since her brother and sister moved to Stockton; neither of them stayed the night any longer. An octagonal stained-glass window mounted in the wall backing the rectangular stairwell might have brought light into the hallway but the stained glass hadn't been washed in years and the caked-on grime made the window virtually opaque. Alfie stepped up into the dim hallway and looked quickly in both directions. The door to the old woman's bedroom was cracked partway open. The one to the guest room was closed. Directly in front of Alfie was a small linen closet. It, too, was shut. The upstairs smelled of dust and mildew. Keeping an eye on the guest room door at the east end of the hallway, Alfie moved sideways down the hall toward the old woman's bedroom, brushing the old velvet wallpaper with his fingers as he went. When he got there, he stopped again and listened. A window shade inside the room was flapping on and off in an irregular breeze. He shifted his weight. The floor creaked beneath his boots. A bird squawked somewhere outdoors and a moment later the clock down in the parlor began chiming the quarter hour. Waiting until it finished, he nudged the door open with his toe.

It could have been the wind blowing for three days through that open window that had caused what he found in her bedroom. Or, perhaps, in the shameless privacy of her own room, the old woman had found it neither necessary nor desirable to keep up the appearance of order present elsewhere in the house. A breeze was indeed passing through the silk curtain lace that very moment, but it was obviously not the wind that was responsible for what he was looking at. He stared at the room in disbelief. Clothes and blankets and bedsheets were strewn everywhere. A marble-topped vanity and nightstand and two wicker chairs were knocked over. One of the chairs was broken. The mahogany four-poster bed was listing badly to port and the boxspring had collapsed. The lampshade next to the tipped-over nightstand was ripped and a crystal clock lay shattered beside it on the powder blue carpet. Stationery dumped from a rolltop desk on the far side of the room littered the floor, mixing with the greasy trash from a dozen or more crushed and scattered grocery bags. The TV set had been kicked in. A pane of glass was missing in the window nearest the bed and the canvas shade there flapped in the draft. A thin veil of dust, drawn in through the open window, had settled on everything. The room had been trashed deliberately, just like Redmon's Garage.

Moving inside, Alfie became aware of a rancid odor he hadn't noticed from the doorway, something like rotting old fruit baskets or week-old garbage soaked in rosewater. He covered his nose and mouth with a handkerchief and tried to locate the source. The door to the old woman's bathroom was closed but there was a light on inside and he heard water dripping softly into an empty sink. Reasonably certain now of what he was about to discover, Alfie opened the door and leaned into the bathroom. There he found the old woman lying face-up in a bathtub barely half-filled with water. Her eyes were closed. *She's just napping, soaking herself into a soapy dreamland. No, she isn't. Any idiot can see she's dead. Even a shit patrolman.* If the fact that the cloudy water was dyed a hideous shade of pink was not convincing, then the dozens of slash and puncture wounds covering her pale, almost translucent upper torso would surely do the trick. Alfie clamped a hand over his mouth and backed out of the bathroom. Turning, he hurried from the bedroom into the hallway and ran for the staircase. He had to call for a backup now. He had to get out of the house.

It was too late. Though the Witch Lady was dead, her house was still haunted. If Alfie heard the tiny linen closet opening behind him as his hand grabbed the banister, it did not register at all in his brain. He did not turn to meet the hands that shoved him into, and over, the railing; nor did he even cry out during his brief fall to the first floor.

The Road and the End

17

Howser reached down and closed the spigot to the outdoor faucet, shutting off water to the hose before the rosebushes flooded any worse. He hadn't even realized the pressure to the hose was still on until Corey's tires splashed through a narrow conduit of water streaming down into the driveway from the flower beds beside the house. At twilight, the driveway and the orchard surrounding the Johnson house had faded to gray shadows and a windless quiet. Taking care to avoid stepping in the water (things were bad enough indoors without having people track mud across the old carpets), Howser walked back around front and leaned inside Corey's unit to switch off the light bar. The swirling amber strobe was not only running the battery down in the black-and-white, it was also annoying him. He stepped up onto the porch and looked down at the bottom of the long driveway where two more cars had just arrived. A third, Randy's, with the light bar flashing, was still half a mile away but coming on quickly. Howser opened the screen door and went inside again.

Indoors, the house was even quieter than it had been earlier: the flies had gone from the kitchen and the clock had stopped finally, the weights suspended on brass chains inside the casing having run down at last from lack of attention. Corey worked on opening the fusebox behind the house where the white linen and a few bath towels still hung on the clothesline in the backyard. His hammer and screwdriver barely disturbed the silence inside the house. Howser wandered into the parlor where the quiet was the most overwhelming and watched the light from the head-lamps splinter in the curtain lace hanging motionless against the beveled glass in the bay window. Had Alfie been through here already earlier in the day? What had he found?

Car doors were opening outside now and Howser could hear footsteps in the gravel. At the rear of the house, Corey was removing the casing from the fusebox. Maybe they'd even get some lights on in the house, not that it mattered much now. What they'd needed to see, they had, and once was enough. Two bodies: a police officer and an old woman. A disaster. Howser watched Randy swing up into the driveway, light bar swirling in the dusk, and he stepped away from the bay window, back into the shadow at the side of the room. He walked out of the parlor and down the hallway toward the kitchen and went up the stairs into the dark.

Nobody'd even noticed Alfie hadn't returned from the orchard house until Ellen had called in asking for him at six-thirty. Susan, sitting in at dispatch for Jane, had for-gotten to write him in as active for the afternoon and the other officers had just assumed he was either off for the day or taking a long lunch with Ellen at the Walcott. Howser himself had not given a second thought to Alfie failing to come back, figuring like everyone else that he'd just taken the day off again. Who could've imagined some-thing like this had happened? Yet that was no excuse and Howser knew it. Someone—the dispatch, the other men, himself—should have noticed, and asked, and checked up on Alfie's whereabouts simply as a matter of procedure. They were supposed to be professionals, and forgetting about one of their own out alone in the field was a disgrace. It was the 7-Eleven all over again, only this time the cavalry hadn't arrived in time.

Howser stood by an upstairs window in the guest bed-room on the east side of the house looking out over the driveway, watching Doc Sawyer's boys unloading two stretchers from the rear of the station wagon. It was be-coming a ritual. *We have to stop meeting like this, Doc.*

Howser heard them open the front door and enter the house. Had Alfie come in that way, or had he played it safe and gone around to the back? The door there was wide open. Anyone could have walked right in. But no, that would not have been Alfie. He'd have knocked first, then entered gently through the front, pausing a moment to wipe his feet on the mat before stepping inside. He would not have surprised anybody. In fact, he might just as well have telephoned ahead.

Twilight was ending, fading its shadows into the dark blue air. Howser could not see anyone outside any longer. He did hear someone coming up to the second floor, someone looking for him, calling him to settle something he'd rather have taken a little while longer to work out on his own.

"Chief?"

Dennis's voice.

"Chief? You up here?"

Howser heard the reserve officer step up onto the carpet and begin walking away down the hallway to the west, still calling.

"Chief? Doc's downstairs. You in here somewhere?"

The door to the old woman's bedroom opened and Dennis's voice became muffled in the walls. Howser reached up into the windowframe and pulled the shade down, tying it closed. Then he crossed the room and went back out into the dark hallway. Below, on the ground floor at the foot of the stairs, Doc Sawyer was having a look at Alfie's body before moving it to the morgue for the autopsy. Dennis came back out into the hall from Amy Johnson's bedroom. The lights came on downstairs in the kitchen.

"Chief?"

He stepped lightly on the carpet as though trying not to wake anyone in the upstairs of the old house and tiptoed over to where Howser was standing.

"Chief," whispered Dennis. "Doc wants to know if he can go ahead and take care of Alfie. You know, wrap him up and all and bring him and the old lady back to town."

Howser swiveled his head and looked back into the tiny closet, standing open and empty behind him. Why was it open? It was a linen closet. Had Alfie opened it? Howser turned his back to the stairs and peered down over the railing to the landing where he'd found Alfie's body, broken and bloodied, dead, on the hardwood floor. It was clear he'd fallen from the top of the stairs. How, though? Had he been pushed? By whom? Either way, they'd take the whole house apart to come up with a definitive answer as to what had happened there earlier in the afternoon. It was more than two bodies this time. It was more than two kids. This time, thought Howser, it was family. And if he'd had trouble feeling something about death in Rivertown before this evening, that was no longer the case. What had happened was suddenly very personal. Alfie might not have been the greatest cop around, but he was Howser's, and he was a friend. Regardless of what the official line might be about the identity of a victim being beside the point, in real life it mattered. It mattered a lot.

The telephone ringing shook Clayton from his bed where he'd been sleeping since late in the afternoon. Tangled up in the sheets, he fell off the mattress reaching for the receiver. On the fifth ring he finally got to his feet and picked up the phone and heard Jane's voice.

"Jack?"

"Yeah? What's going on?" Clayton glanced at the window. It was dark out. He'd slept off the last half of the day. He grabbed the clock and tilted the face up so that he could see the hands. Eight thirty. He'd slept almost five hours since returning from the river. Maybe he was coming down with something.

"Jack? Are you there?"

"Yeah," he said, trying to sit up and clear his head. "I was just taking a nap. I'm here. What's up?"

"Did you hear about Alfie?"

Clayton ran her question over once in his thoughts. The wave of adrenaline surging just then in his chest gave him a clue as to what she was talking about. The way she'd phrased her question and the tone of voice she'd used in delivery had just told him everything. He was no longer drowsy.

"He's dead, Jack. Somebody killed him this afternoon. They just found his body a little while ago."

The adrenaline rush swelled up into Clayton's head and fogged his thoughts. *Killed?*

"We're stunned. Absolutely stunned. It's a nightmare, Jack. This whole thing is a nightmare, and instead of waking up, we just seem to be sinking deeper into it. I don't know what we're going to do."

Clayton got to his feet, dragging the phone with him.

"Jane?"

"Yeah?"

"Can you hold a minute?"

"Sure."

Clayton set the phone down on the bed and leaned over to switch on the lamp. Sitting in the dark, listening to a disembodied voice telling him somebody he'd just met a week ago had been found murdered that afternoon, was a little too strange.

"Sorry," he said, picking the phone back up again. "I had to turn a light on."

"Jack?"

"Yeah, Jane?"

"I need a favor."

"Anything."

"No one's been able to get through to Ellen since she found out about Alfie a little earlier. We're not exactly worried, but we don't think she should be left completely alone tonight. You're there already and you know her. Do you think you could look in on her? Maybe see if there's anything you can do? I'd really appreciate it. I'm sure she would, too. She likes you. I think it'd help a lot."

"No problem at all."

He heard a sigh at the other end of the line. She was trying to find a smile somewhere inside. That was good.

He heard her say, "Thanks, Jack."

"I'll get dressed and go down right away. You're sure she's here in the hotel?"

"I don't know where else she'd go. She doesn't have any family in Rivertown. The Walcott's her home. I'm sure she's there, but if she's not, give me a call back right away. I'm at the office."

"Okay. Well, I'll do what I can."

"I really appreciate this, Jack."

"Don't worry about it."

"I'll talk to you later on then. Bye-bye."

She hung up. Clayton put the phone down and sat back on the bed. He was almost fully awake now with Jane's words still ringing in his head: *Someone killed Alfie this afternoon.* The town had gone crazy, and now he was supposed to go downstairs and sit with a woman who'd be feeling something nobody could really ease for her, not tonight at least, something no human being ever deserves to feel. And there'd be nothing Clayton could do or say that would make her feel the least bit better about it. All he would be able to do was to sit there and watch her cry, hold her hand if she wanted it held, nod if she spoke and offer something in the way of condolence for politeness' sake, eventually leaving her alone to suffer something for which few people are ever prepared. He finished buttoning up his shirt and headed for the door.

With the ambulance gone, the old orchard house was just about empty. The only lights still on were above the back porch and inside the kitchen where Howser watched Corey scrape dried blood and flecks of gristle from the tiles on the countertop into small plastic lab bags for Doc Sawyer. The rest of the house was dark and silent again. Just as they'd found it at sundown.

"You ready to hear my theory, Chief?" Corey sealed another baggie and set it on the counter next to the sink with the others. The back door was propped open to let some fresh air into the kitchen; Howser stood just inside.

"Sure, go ahead."

Corey put down the razor blade he'd been using on the tile and took a cigarette and a Bic lighter from his vest pocket. He slid open the window above the sink and lighted the cigarette.

"There's more than one of them, Chief." The patrolman slipped the yellow Bic back into his pocket. "Whether they came back sometime after the shooting or they've been here all along, I don't know. But there's more than one of them here and they're pissed off.''

Howser looked out the back door at the orchard where moonlight cast strange anthropomorphic shadows from the scraggly branches of the apple trees.

Corey said, "They're out there, Chief. I swear it. Maybe it's only a handful. Maybe it's a whole fucking army of hobos. Who knows? But unless we flush them out, well, it scares the living shit out of me just thinking how easy it'd be for them to keep on killing. Hell, we barely got enough men to watch over downtown."

"What's their motive?" asked Howser.

"Revenge. What else?"

"We kill one of their people so they kill six of ours, including an old woman?"

The patrolman held the cigarette up to the screen. "You got it. The oldest motive in the world."

"Doesn't make sense to me."

"Why not?"

"Well, for starters, how are they getting around? Tramps don't own cars and we don't have much of a public-transportation system out here. And where are they hiding? We've already checked all the empty structures in the area, right? Houses, barns, fruit driers, sheds, grain silos. The old feed mills."

"Lot of wooded acreage to cover. Lot of river, too."

"Fine, but it's one hell of a hike from the river over to here, farther still to Mike's garage or the location of the wreck out on Mustang Road. And if there's really more than one of them like you say, then why haven't they been spotted anywhere?"

The patrolman took a long drag on the cigarette and exhaled the smoke through his nostrils. "Maybe they have."

"Where?"

"Mustang Road." He tapped the cigarette on the washboard, depositing hot ashes into the sink. "Maybe they were crossing when the pickup came along. Maybe that's how Raymond ended up driving into the ravine. He caught 'em in his headlights and tried to swerve and ran right off the road. Maybe they followed him down into the brush.

That'd explain a few things, don't you think? Like Calvin's injuries."

"And the sounds you heard."

"Exactly."

"I have a question of my own."

"Shoot."

In the backyard, clean linen draped from the clothesline flapped loudly as the breeze picked up. Howser felt a slight chill now and closed the door with his foot. Then he asked, "Why didn't you tell me about the fatality file on the rail-yard and the river?"

Corey dropped the cigarette butt into the sink and ran the tap, washing the cigarette down the drain. "Mostly accidents, Chief. Drownings, falls." He turned off the water. "Lot of drunks stumbling around in the woods and along the riverbank, getting themselves into trouble."

"Not all accidents, though."

"No, sir, we had a couple of clear cases of homicide. Voluntary manslaughter, at the very least."

"There were more than a couple, Corey. I counted four-teen deaths listed as homicides and I didn't see any arrests in the file. No warrants sworn out. No complaints drawn up. Why not?"

"You'd have to ask Lou Hudson that question. Those were his decisions, not mine."

"You had suspects."

"No, sir, we didn't. Just bodies."

"Witnesses?"

"Nope."

"Who reported the location of the bodies?"

"Look, Chief, I'm the wrong person to talk to. Lou handled everything himself. I never even saw one of the stiffs."

With the back door closed, the odor of dried blood filled the kitchen air again. The stench rose by the second. The lateness of the hour combining with the smell in the kitchen made nausea inevitable. Still, certain questions needed answering now and Howser decided he'd stay long enough to puke all over himself before letting this conversation go unresolved.

"Are you trying to tell me your Chief Hudson went out

alone to each of the crime scenes, marked the location of the bodies, took pictures, searched the area, tagged and bagged evidence and transported the victims back to town all by himself?"

"No, I guess Tom helped some."

"Danielson? How the hell did *he* get involved?"

"Lou called him in, I suppose, because Tom owns the land where most of the bodies were found. Again, you'd have to ask Lou. He ran the whole show, except for the autopsies, of course, which Doc took care of."

"All of the victims were transients and all were beaten to death."

"Yeah, Lou figured in each case somebody got drunk, picked a fight and kept on swinging until he realized he was just pounding on dead meat."

"And nobody around to break it up either, huh?"

"It's pretty isolated out there. Even if you yelled for help, it's not too likely anyone'd hear you."

"And if anybody *did* hear something, they never said."

"Not that I know of."

Howser reached over to the brass wall plate next to the door and flicked off the porch light, darkening the rear of the house. He faced his officer. "What do you say we call it a night? You can come back and finish up here in the morning. Doc'll be coming out early with the SID people from Stockton. You can meet them here."

"Sure."

Howser left the kitchen. The patrolman ran the tap once more to wash the remaining cigarette ashes down the drain, then turned off the light above the sink and walked out into the hallway. Howser was waiting for him at the bottom of the stairs just beside the spot where Alfie's body had been discovered earlier in the evening. He told Corey, "You go ahead and take off. I'll lock up."

The patrolman nodded and headed for the front door. Howser switched on the flashlight and went back upstairs. In the dark, the hallway seemed even narrower than it had at sundown. Hearing the front door close, Howser directed the light down the hall and walked to the woman's bedroom. Inside, a window was still open to the right of the bed. The curtain lace billowed inward like a ghost floating in the windowframe, yet it flew noiselessly, too, and Howser could hear his own breathing above the fabric flapping in the draft. In a way, he was glad the lightbulbs had been broken. He'd seen plenty of the woman's room earlier, trashed and emptied out onto the floor. A horrifying mess. It made him shiver. He pointed the light into the bathroom. His own reflection shone back at him in the mirror hanging there on the wall above the sink. The glass was smudged and dirty. They'd lift prints from it in the morning, dust the medicine cabinet, the sink, the toilet, and, of course, the tub. Maybe they'd get a break and find something interesting. They were overdue for one, even if they had to spend a week inside the place looking for it.

Outdoors, Corey drove off, spinning gravel under the tires clear down to the highway. A quarter mile away, he hit the siren to wake the roosters on the next property. When the noise died away, Howser switched the flashlight off and listened in the dark. As he shifted his weight, the floorboards creaked. Now the orchard was still. And he thought, *She must've loved the quiet out here very much. To be this far from town, alone and isolated each night from family and friends, she'd have had to love the quiet. Maybe it was only after her TV set ran its test pattern at two in the morning that the old woman became aware of it, but there was no doubt that she did. And since she did, she must also have loved it for what it was—her own private and personal rhythm, the sound of what it was like to be her. Gone now, though. Why?*

Four miles southeast of the orchard house, Jamie Danielson wandered up to the fence separating the old railyard from the woods and stared through the tall wire into the darkness where the tramp jungle had been only two weeks before. Behind him, Ernie Long sat in the dust Indian-style worrying about his brother Howie. Plenty of times Howie had run away, but always he'd told Ernie where he was going and when he'd be coming back again.

"Well?"

Jamie answered Ernie's latest plea the same way he had

all the earlier ones. "How the hell should I know where your fucking brother is? What do you think I do, follow him around all day?"

Jamie hacked at the chain-link fence with a metal pipe he'd picked up down by the gate. The railyard had been empty since the night of the shooting and it was too dark to see anything, especially since Ernie had lost the flashlight running out of the old lady's house.

"Listen, Goob," said Jamie, bouncing a pebble off Ernie's shoulder. "Howie's probably dead anyway, the dumb shit, and there's nothing you can do about it, so stop whining."

Ernie felt sick to his stomach. He missed his brother and didn't care for Jamie saying he was already dead. No way was Howie dead. Sarah was dead. And Danny and Calvin and Ray. But Howie was just off hiding somewhere, maybe hurt, and Ernie needed to find him more than ever now.

"Goober? Do you hear me?" said Jamie, leaning over Ernie now. "We got more important things to worry about than your stupid-ass brother. Do you understand what I'm saying?"

Ernie flew up off his feet and hurled himself into Jamie, driving him backward into the fence. He crawled on top of Jamie, swinging his fists at Jamie's head and screaming, "Fuck you! Fuck you! Fuck you!"

Jamie tried to push him off. When he couldn't, he yelled for Jerry and Roy, lurking back in the woods by the pickup. "Get him off me, goddamm it! Get him off!"

Ernie kept screaming and punching furiously at Jamie's face, covered up now by elbows and forearms. Jerry and Roy hurried up out of the woods, amazed at what they saw. Ernie had gone completely nuts. Not only that, he was kicking Jamie's ass. Jamie tried vainly to get hold of Ernie's wrists to stop the blows raining in on his upper body. "Fucking maniac! Get off me! Get off!"

"Fuck you! Fuck you! Fuck you!"

Jamie worked his way out from under Ernie, taking two more hard slugs to the back of his head in the bargain as he rolled away. He crawled to the base of the fence off to his right and slumped in the dust. Ernie, his face wet with tears, stayed put and wiped the saliva from the sides of his mouth. Jamie got up and ran to the pickup and jumped inside. He slammed the door shut and flicked on the key, bringing the stereo to life. Roy followed and tried talking to him through the window.

"This is crazy, Jamie. We got to figure out what we're going to do. We got to have a plan or we're all going to end up in jail. Do you hear me?"

Jamie turned the stereo up louder, pounding rhythm with his fists on the dash.

Roy turned to Jerry and shouted, "He's crazy."

Jamie turned the radio up louder still, and began bouncing on the seat and shaking the pickup up and down on the suspension.

Roy looked at Jamie bouncing around like an idiot inside the pickup. They were all going to go to jail and he knew it. He picked up a rock and slammed it into the fence. "This is out of control. Totally out of control!"

"No shit," said Jerry.

"We're out of here. Fuck them."

"Right."

They walked up along the fence until the radio was lost in the night air. They found an opening in the wire and crawled under the fence into the railyard. There was nothing but dust and dry matted grass in every direction; the boxcars themselves were hidden in the distance by the dark. The boys had been inside the yard hundreds of times before and instinctively knew in which direction to walk from the fenceline and in a few minutes found themselves sitting up on the edge of a rusting Southern Pacific flatcar.

Jerry lit a cigarette and passed it over to Roy who took a short drag off it and passed it back, blowing smoke out into the dark.

"Jamie's losing it," said Roy.

"Don't worry about him," said Jerry. "We're getting the hell away from here. Fuck those guys. We're not going to go to jail. Fuck that."

Across the yard the lights from the pickup came on. From where he was sitting, Jerry could just make out the broken pattern the headlamps were throwing into the woods. The horn sounded once and echoed away in the distance. The lights went out.

"He's going to take the truck," said Jerry.

"He can't," said Roy. "Steering wheel's chained."

"Oh, yeah."

The headlights came on again, then started dimming and flashing rapidly, high beam and low, like a giant strobe flickering out into the shadows. And the horn blared, and again, sending a flight of dark birds rising up from the woods into the sky over the railyard. Roy jumped down from the flatcar and walked out into the weeds. A breeze was beginning to come up out of the west and it fanned the air in the yard and swirled the dust at Roy's feet. He said, "You think Howie's dead?"

"I have no idea," said Jerry, "and I don't care. I just don't want to be next."

"My dad says the cops think the tramps are back in town somewhere, getting even with us for shooting at them that night. Says there's going to be a lot more people killed before it's over."

"It's fuckin' Jamie's fault. This whole thing. The guys got wasted because of him. And he doesn't even give a shit. That's why we got to split. Just being near the guy is dangerous."

The lights had gone out again in the pickup and the yard was quiet. Jerry took out a joint and they both smoked it. Twenty minutes passed. The wind blew stronger in the trees and suddenly the railyard felt bleak and cold.

"Come on," said Jerry, sliding down from the flatcar. "Time to hit the road."

"Now?"

"Yup. We're out of here tonight. This town's history."

They walked back across the railyard to the opening in the fence and crawled back under the barbed wire. Back at the clearing, Ernie was still sitting in the dust where they'd left him. The radio was turned off inside the pickup but Jamie was perched high up on the roof, grinning like the Cheshire cat.

"Hey, dudes," he said. "Where'd you go? Me and Goober thought maybe you were out there getting killed or something. Didn't you hear us honking?"

Ernie was quietly carving his brother's name in the dirt with his Scout knife. Jamie beat his fists against his chest in a miserable Tarzan imitation. He had hoped for a laugh from his audience. Getting none, he quit and put on a serious look. He said, "We got to do something about that tramp, you know."

Ernie rolled back over to face Jamie. He held the dirty knife up in his fist. "I'll take care of him. I'll cut him."

"Like you took care of Annie?" asked Jamie.

"That wasn't my fault. She took off when Alfie got there. What was I supposed to do?"

Jamie jumped down off the pickup. "You were supposed to be watching her! When push came to shove, you let her get away! I should've known we couldn't count on you."

Ernie hung his head again and stuck the knife in the dirt. He looked from Jamie to Roy to Jerry. They were all staring at him, blaming him for the mess they were in. And if they had to go to jail because of him? What was he supposed to do?

"I'm sorry," he said, hoping maybe they'd forget about Annie and help him find Howie, wherever he was. He was wrong.

"That's not good enough, Goober. Thanks to you, we're dead meat."

"Leave him alone, Jamie," said Jerry. "It's not his fault."

"It *is* his fault. Soon as she talks, we're fucked."

"No, *you're* fucked. Roy and me are getting the hell out of here while we still can."

"What do you mean, *getting out of here*?"

"We're gone. Splitting. Now. Tonight. Out of the county. And we're not coming back either. Fuck jail. Nobody's locking us up."

He and Roy started walking toward the pickup. Jamie stepped in their way. "Hold on there, Tonto. You mean you little chickenshits are running? Is that what you're telling me?"

"You got it."

They walked around him and climbed into the pickup. Roy started the engine and rolled up the window.

Jamie yelled out, "You're going to leave me here with this dickhead?"

Jerry leaned up and out the window on the passenger side. "Be nice to him, Jamie. Maybe he'll give you a lift back to town, huh? Later, guys!"

Roy put the truck in gear and headed down through the dark to the gravel road leading out to the county highway and Interstate 99, five miles farther to the west. By sunrise, they'd be six counties away. Maybe if they were lucky, that'd be far enough.

18

It was the oddest kind of déjà vu. The city morgue, with its old cement walls painted a pale shade of lime green, reminded Howser somehow of the bus he took to elementary school in Santa Clara when he was only eight years old. The cold green metal walls and dark vinyl seats and that constant smell of mildew and disinfectant permeating even the window glass and the dirty sheet metal floors. The school bus and the morgue. He looked back at Doc Sawyer, sitting across from him with his feet kicked up on the big rosewood desk. Whatever the connections were, he was not in a Santa Clara County school bus; he was downstairs in Rivertown's morgue. Nor, unfortunately, was he eight years old with only a weekly arithmetic quiz to worry about.

"Okay, Doc, make it quick. The basics."

"Just the basics, huh? The old bottom line?"

"That's right."

"Okay, Chief. First of all, you know that blood you found in the kitchen?"

"Yeah?"

"Chicken blood."

Sawyer smiled when he saw Howser's expression. He'd obviously been waiting all morning for this and Howser had not let him down.

"Let me have that again."

"Just like I said. That mess in the kitchen, all that blood

276

your officers scraped off the walls for me belonged to chickens, I'd guess about a dozen or so. Don't ask me how it got there. I'm just telling you what it is."

"Chickens?"

"Chickens."

"Jesus Christ."

"Same with the tub upstairs where you found Amy Johnson. It was her body, of course, but not her blood. It was chicken blood dumped into the water. Most whacked-out thing I've ever seen."

"I don't understand."

Sawyer got up from the desk and opened the door to the lab. Then he crooked his forefinger at Howser, who was obviously going over in his brain what he'd just been told, and said, "Well, maybe you will when you see what I have over here. There's something you're going to find interesting."

Howser jumped up and followed him over to one of the examining slabs. Sawyer pulled the sheet back revealing the old woman's corpse. He smiled as Howser choked once and covered his mouth with a handkerchief drawn from his shirt pocket.

"Don't worry about it, Chief. No matter how many of these you see, you never quite get used to it."

"Yeah." Howser grunted, feeling a little embarrassed.

"You all right?" asked Sawyer.

"Just get on with it."

"Okay. Chief, look at this here. See these wounds? They're new, fairly fresh in fact."

"Sure they're fresh. We just brought her in last night."

"Of course you did. But you're not following me."

"That's because I don't see what you're getting at."

"These wounds, look at them. Shallow. Scratchy. Ragged. Look at them. Closely."

Howser leaned forward and ran over each mark on the woman's chest with his eyes. The problem was that he didn't have the faintest idea what he was supposed to be noticing about them other than that they were everywhere.

"Do you see what I mean?"

"No."

"Well then, I'll tell you, Chief. They were made with a

penknife. How do you like that? A small penknife. The kind you probably used as a kid to scratch graffiti into a school desk."

"Look, Doc. I'm not as smart as this badge says I am. You're going to have to explain what you're trying to tell me. I'm not so sure I'm following you."

"She wasn't killed in the bathtub, mister. None of these cuts were deep enough or severe enough to have been life-threatening. Christ, not a single one of them would have made a fatal wound. In fact, they had nothing at all to do with her dying. She was dead, Chief, before any of this was done. Now don't ask me why all that chicken blood was there. I don't have the faintest idea. But that blood in the bathtub couldn't have belonged to her anyway because she was dead long before whoever it was cut her up. She didn't bleed a drop. The woman died of pneumonia almost a week ago."

"Pneumonia? In the middle of summer? In this heat?"

"It happens. Amy was an old woman. I saw her myself only a couple of months back and I told her then she'd better get someone out there to look after her."

"All right then, Doc. Tell me this: Why all the butchery, why cut her up if she was already dead?"

Sawyer folded the sheet back over the old woman and looked over at Howser.

"That one," he said, "is yours, fortunately. Not mine." He set down the sheet. "You're becoming a popular man in Rivertown, Chief."

"Yeah, I'm the new star at the snack bar," said Howser, walking to the service door. "I appreciate you rushing this stuff through for me, Doc. I owe you one."

"Don't send me any more business for a while and I'll call us even."

"I'll do my best. Thanks."

Howser left Sawyer there in the morgue and ran up the back stairs to his office. He had one more phone call to make before lunch. Stockton SID was out now at the Johnson house. They'd be there all afternoon. It was a lot of work. Everybody was busy today, himself included. The reports on the bodies lay scattered across the desk in front of him: The old tramp, Sarah Miller, Danny Williams,

278

Calvin Arnold and Ray Maddox, Alfie, and Amy Johnson. Reading any one of them was like reading them all. He pushed the reports away. Seven bodies now, and another kid, Howie Long, out there somewhere, missing. He didn't want to read any more. It was enough already. In fact, the first one, that old tramp, had been enough. They finally had a name for him, courtesy of the FBI computer in Stockton—Frederick Mock, aka Frederick Anthony, aka Ferdie Sloan. Mr. Mock had been a well-traveled individual; his rap sheet showed a pattern of vagrancy and trespassing busts from coast to coast covering four decades. He'd probably come here expecting a nice, friendly respite from the rails but it hadn't turned out that way. Rivertown wasn't such a friendly place after all, was it? No, it wasn't. In fact, starting with Mr. Mock's death, it was becoming a kind of mausoleum with trees.

He picked up the message on his desk and rang the dispatch. "Jane?"

A moment later, Susan's voice came on the intercom. "Jane went out for the afternoon."

"I've got a note here on my desk."

"Yes, the mayor called while you were out. He'd like you to get down to City Hall tonight a little early if possible."

The city council was convening a town meeting of sorts to discuss the rising mortality rate in Rivertown over the past couple of weeks. Howser wanted nothing to do with standing up at a microphone fielding questions and advice from the public. However, the mayor thought it was a great idea. More politics.

"I'll put it under consideration. How about ringing Jack Clayton for me at the Walcott?"

"Yes, sir."

"I'd also like you to try and get hold of Lou Hudson for me."

"In Florida?"

"Sarasota. That's right."

"Who should I call first?"

"Clayton."

"Yes, sir."

A few moments later Howser heard Clayton's voice at the other end of the line.

"Hello?"

"Jack? It's Howser."

"Yeah, Chief. I was just on my way out the door."

"Okay, I'll make it quick. How about taking a ride out of town with me tomorrow?"

"Where to?"

"A town called Curry. It's about two hundred miles southeast of here."

"I know where it is. That's three hours down the road. What do you want to go there for?"

"Turns out some of the people we chased out of here last month wound up in a tramp jungle at the old Curry junction. I'd like to have another talk with them and I'd like you there listening to what they have to say."

"You got to be kidding."

"Look, only a few days ago you were telling me how ignorant I've been about tramps. Okay, I'm no expert. I admit it. I need your help. I just want to talk to a couple of the guys we had in the jail up here and I thought that having you there might help cut through a lot of the crap, you know what I mean?"

"I suppose."

"So, are you going to help me or not?"

"We're just going to talk, huh? That's it? No warrants or anything? No bullshit?"

"We're just going to ask some questions, that's all. We talk, you listen."

"What time do you want to go?"

"Can you get out of bed by noon?"

"No, but I'll make an exception for you. How does eleven sound?"

"I'll pick you up at the hotel."

"Fine," said Clayton. "Tomorrow."

Howser hung up. Maybe his luck was changing. He grabbed the file on Stiles and Robinson and stuck it inside the desk. Finding even two of the tramps they'd had in the lockup after the shooting was a small miracle. The threads of this case ran all over the place. That they should be able to follow one that had run beyond the county was a damn good sign. It meant that figuring it all out wasn't necessarily hopeless. The trail of killings led somewhere. There had to be a pattern, a reason; it only needed exposing. A break here or there could do just that, whether it came from a mistake by the killer or a stroke of luck for the good guys.

Five minutes later Susan called upstairs to inform him Lou Hudson had already left on a fishing trip into the Gulf of Mexico and wasn't expected back until the end of the month. So much for luck. Any answers Rivertown's former chief of police might've been able to provide would have to wait now. Howser locked up the office and went downstairs. The courthouse was empty today, the civil service offices closed for the Sabbath. He walked outside. The street was quiet. There was a breeze circulating in Sutter Park. The shady lawn was filled with people enjoying lunch. As he started down the steps, a frail middle-aged woman called to him from up the sidewalk. She intercepted him halfway to the street. Her face was flushed and sweaty and she was nearly out of breath from having hurried the four blocks to the courthouse from her home on Cedar Street. He steadied her, putting his hands on her shoulders.

She said, "It's about my daughter Annie."

Late in the afternoon, a van drove along a sleepy country lane nine miles east of town. Here, the flat plain of the valley began its slow rise into the rounded foothills where modern agricultural engineering gave way to the old sheep- and cattle-grazing land. Today the hills were empty, wildflowers proliferated in the hot sun.

"Make a left up there," said Jane.

There was a break in the old wire fence at a shallow ditch and Clayton swung the van sharply into it, spinning the front tires in the gravel. The van lurched out of the ditch and onto a dirt road running straight up toward an oak windbreak at the crest of the hill. Through the splattered insects sun-dried on the windshield, Clayton saw a slim white building sticking up into the blue air. The structure had a steeple stuck on its roof and a bell mounted in the steeple. Up ahead on the building's facade was a sign

281

hand-lettered flat and bold in black beneath the steeple, reading: PARKER SCHOOL.

The old schoolhouse stood on top of the hill looking east toward the foothills and west out over the wide valley. It had been more than twenty years since regular classes were given within its walls, yet no one in Rivertown seriously considered tearing it down. It was used only for occasional historical tours now and special club day meetings on state holidays when the town's other meeting halls were booked. The property it stood upon was not all that valuable any longer, not since serious cattle grazing had ended in the last century. There was nothing up there on the knoll with the old building now except scrub grass, tarweed and a stand of live oaks giving shade to the dust and wildflowers growing in the erratic reach of its branches.

The van came to a rolling stop a dozen yards from the front porch of the schoolhouse. When Clayton set the parking brake and got out, he found Jane already waiting for him, her blouse open at the collar, hands jammed nervously into the front pockets of her jeans. She was staring up at the schoolhouse where it rose above her, tall and white, its western windows reflecting the colors of the end of the day. As Clayton moved forward beside her, she drew her left hand from the pocket and knotted her fingers with his. She tugged on him and they walked across the yard to the old building.

The cloudy glass panes in the small windowframe to the side of the porch were scratched and cracked and the wooden steps themselves were weathered and warped. Clayton let go of Jane's hand and scraped the toe of his boot on the flaking paint. He craned his neck and shaded his eyes with his hand to see high up to the steepletop. Sparrows sailed and darted in and out of the square bell housing. Clayton climbed the ten steps to the front door and turned around. To the north an air force jet disturbed the empty blue, angling a slender white line onto a silent corner of the sky. Clayton watched the contrail until it began to billow and swell, unraveling and fading again back into blue. He leaned up against the porch railing and waited for Jane to join him. She was still taking it all in: her old school, the yard, many memories.

"Feeling a little nostalgic?" he asked.

She approached the bottom step and closed her eyes with a smile. Her eyes were watering now in the yellow light; the sun was warm on her face. She hummed a private note to herself and shook the knotted brown hair loose from the back of her neck. Never to be nine years old again. No more blue gingham and saddle shoes. School was out now and her friends were all gone home. But it was okay, and she was not alone.

Clayton asked, "Are we going to go in or just daydream out here all afternoon?"

"We're going in," she said, and climbed the stairs. She depressed the latch and tugged at the door, pulling it open. Then, grabbing Clayton by the wrist, she led him inside.

The redwood paneling on the inside of Parker School, stained and unpainted, gave the interior of the schoolhouse a shadowy look in the late afternoon. The small windows on the front of the building brought light only into two small alcoves used as coat closets. Clayton leaned into one to look at the dozens of brass hooks, lacking the shine of their original patina, mounted low on the narrow walls. Jane moved past him through the archway into the middle of the classroom where four flat shafts of yellow light from the ceiling-level windows were passing above thirteen rows of wooden desks and cascading onto the opposite walls. The desks themselves had flat drawing surfaces and curved seats mounted on black wrought-iron supports. They faced a large blackboard nailed to the front wall. A heavy oak teacher's desk and chair sat beneath it, a few feet from the wall. The blackboard slate was clean now, but chalk-dust was still evident in the metal tray running the full length of its bottom. The flag to which Jane had pledged allegiance every morning of her childhood schooldays was missing from the long staff to the left of the front desk, as was the color-coded "Map of the Modern World" she had finally come to memorize in the fifth grade. Their absence gave the entire room a singular emptiness she had not counted on. Clayton entered the classroom behind her. He stopped at one of the desks near the back and tried to read the graffiti cut into the wood. It said: *Gina is a woman*. He licked his forefinger and rubbed it over the letters. The ink had dried into the wood a long while ago. It was not going to smudge now. He left it alone and ambled forward up the aisle to a spot a few feet behind Jane, who was lost in some sort of reverie gazing at the blank slate blackboard.

"You really went to school up here?"

Jane nodded with a smile. He made a full circle, trying to take it all in at once.

"A genuine one-room schoolhouse, huh?" Clayton squeezed into one of the tiny desk seats and stretched out his legs. "How old were you?"

Jane slipped into a desk across the aisle and up two rows from Clayton. She fit a little more easily into her desk than he did in his. She didn't find it all that uncomfortable. It still felt somehow familiar.

"Twelve," she replied. "My last year here. That was sixth grade."

"A long time ago, huh?"

She straightened her legs out, too, pushing her feet through to the desk in front of her and resting her heels on the seat back. "A long time."

"It's a big room," said Clayton. "Bigger than I would've thought." He glanced around, counting the desks with his forefinger.

"Seventy-eight," she said, before he could finish. "Six grades of kids went here. Seventy-eight in all."

"Not all that small, really."

"No, not that small."

He looked around at the walls rising up to an arched ceiling, then took a deep breath through his nostrils and smiled. "Smells like an old school. The polished wood or something."

Jane breathed in, too. "Nice, isn't it?"

"I like it. Kind of musty, but good. My old school in Redondo always smelled like Lysol and paint."

"This used to be a church."

Clayton looked up at the windows and wondered whether there had ever been stained glass in the frames, drawn and colored with religious portraits.

Jane said, "That's where we get the steeple and the Gothic look. The Methodists put it up in the 1860s and used it until sometime in the nineties. Then Carl Parker, who owned all this land back then and had leased it to the Methodists for their church, took it over and had it converted into a school so his daughter Faye could take classes without having to ride all the way into town every morning."

"That was decent of him."

"He had a philanthropic streak in him somewhere, I suppose."

"I'm sure it made his little girl happy."

Jane wriggled her feet free and slid out of the desk. So did Clayton. He stood up and walked over to the big desk and opened one of the drawers. It was empty. He tried the one beneath it.

"Looking for something?" asked Jane.

"Just snooping."

There was a stack of papers shoved up against the back of the drawer. He drew them out and leafed through them with his thumb. They were activities assignments and records for one of the local Boy Scout troops, hopelessly out of date now and obsolete. On the bottom was a folder with a cartoon rendering of several boys and their scoutmaster putting up tents in the wild.

"What did you find?" asked Jane. She walked up to the desk.

"Oh, just some old scouting things from the sixties. Reminds me of the artwork in the old *Boys' Life* magazine I used to read as a kid."

"Let me see," said Jane, reaching across Clayton's arm for the folder.

He flipped the folder onto the desk. Jane picked it up and skimmed over the scouting materials while Clayton returned to rifling the rest of the drawers, releasing from each a sweet musty scent as though the old desk had not been opened in years, which was probably true. Listening to him search, Jane hid a grin with the back of her hand. He was crazy, she thought, but a lot of fun. They'd spent a wonderful afternoon on the river, swimming, eating French bread and cheese, making love in the shade by the water's edge. Maybe the picnic wasn't over yet. She smiled to herself, imagining them making love on the teacher's desk. That might be interesting.

As the hour drew late, the angle of sunlight slanting in ran closer to horizontal, leaving the classroom further in shadow. Finished with the drawers, Clayton wandered over to the door at the front wall to the right of the desk.

"Where does this lead?" he asked, reaching for the brass knob.

"There's a kitchen back there, and I think some storage closets."

Clayton opened the door and went through.

"Wait!" she yelled. "Jack!"

Though she was pretty sure they were alone in the schoolhouse, being this far from town still made her nervous. If Alfie could be killed going out to water an old woman's roses, maybe nobody was safe anywhere. The last way she wanted their picnic to end was with the two of them getting murdered by some maniac. Clenching her fists, she followed Clayton through a cramped hallway lined with dark cedar shelves to the back of the schoolhouse.

The kitchen was just a narrow rectangular room looking out through three windows onto the playgrounds behind the school. Beneath the windows was a long hardwood counter running from the west wall to a locked door on the east. It had a flat, unpainted surface, cut now and pitted, and drawers like in an industrial cabinet, each with an identical odor of stain and mildew. Opposite the windows was a sink and an old ivory-and-black woodburning stove and another small wall-mounted cupboard. The windows were almost opaque with dirt. The walls and ceiling were painted a glossy shade of green that gave the room a little more light than it might have had unpainted.

Jane tried the faucets over the sink and got only a grinding sound from the pipes below the floor. Clayton ran his fingers lightly over the countertop while trying to see out through the filthy glass.

"What did they have a kitchen in here for?"

Jane got down on both knees to have a look in the stove. She answered, "Lunch."

"Kids didn't brown-bag it out here?"

"Some did."

Clayton nodded absently. He was still trying to imagine

286

what it must have been like in a school with six grades of kids jammed into a single room, each learning a different lesson at the same time. Jane squeezed past him to the back door and unlocked it and opened it up, letting in some fresh air. The sharp odor of acetone and mildew escaping into the yard was even stronger than she had noticed when coming in. It had obviously been a while since anyone had been up to the school. She walked out onto the porch. It was warmer outside than in, even though a breeze had come up from the west. Stepping down into her old playground, Jane was drawn immediately to the old wood and chain swing set sagging in the sawdust sixty feet from the back stairs. Seeing it again made her grin. She walked up to it and touched the old slatted seat, unable now to support the weight of a first grader, much less that of an adult. What would she have given to take just one more ride? She could see herself as a child roaring up into the air, shrieking and thrilled with the exhilaration of flying above her friends lost in play beneath her and oblivious to the excitement that held her in thrall with each reeling pass under the bar and out again over the sawdust and upward. There she was, kicking her legs furiously, urging more speed and height before the morning bell could ring, calling her away to second-grade arithmetic and spelling.

Jane knelt down and brushed her fingers over the seat. The aging slats were bowed, paintless now, gray and splintering, and the chain links supporting it were rusty, but a relic like her old swing was precious and irreplaceable. She would have liked to have taken the seat and given it a soft push, just to see it swing free once more way up into the air. Fearful, however, of having it fall apart at her touch, she did not. Instead, she dragged herself slowly away from it, leaving the swing set still and solitary again in the sunlight, preserved and intact.

She listened to Clayton fumbling through the kitchen cupboards, a curious pack rat seeking out the exceptional to scrutinize. It was funny, she thought, how everything about Rivertown seemed to fascinate him. Things she took for granted, had grown up with, and no longer even saw consciously, he fixated on and scrutinized endlessly. How did he see her? Was she one of the novelties, too? She listened to him banging about the innards of the cast-iron stove, familiarizing himself with it, just as he had with her. Was it fair? She wasn't all that different from him. She laughed at the same bad jokes, wept during the same movies on the late show. Maybe fairness wasn't the point. She looked over the yard again, letting her gaze come to rest on her old swing, hanging there, suspended by chain and hook in the yellow light. It looked like an old turn-of-the-century postcard, *"After Children at Play."* She'd left this place once. Now she'd returned and it was a homecoming of the same kind returning from Berkeley had been, because finding herself at Parker School reminded her once again of what and who she had been once in an early summer morning twenty-one years before. And in doing so, it restored to her something she had obviously left behind when she first drove west out of Rivertown on her way to the big city. That was why fairness in the way she was treated by Clayton and the people she'd known in Berkeley never mattered all that much. She'd always known that in Rivertown were people who would know what she was worth whenever she chose to seek them out. They would always be there, waiting for her return.

Inside, Clayton leaned up for a tiny engraved metal dish balanced on the top shelf and knocked the cupboard off the wall with an errant elbow. It slammed down across the stove and fell broken in two large sections to the paneled floor. The sound reverberated in the walls of Parker School.

"Jack!"

Hurrying back indoors, she found Clayton bent over the results of his carelessness. He looked up at her and winced. She knelt down beside him and tried to piece the cupboard together. The back mounting had split free from the four shelves nailed to its sides and there did not appear to be any way to refasten it, aside from a liberal dosage of Krazy Glue and staples. Clayton lifted one of the broken slats serving as a shelf and tossed it over his shoulder onto the stove, shaking his head in disgust at himself.

"Goddammit."

"We can't fix it?"

"I doubt it," he said. "Sorry."

"Oh well," said Jane, getting up and moving back against the counter. She let him pick up the pieces of the small cupboard and stack them neatly on the stove. Like a reckless kid caught red-handed among the shattered remains of a priceless family heirloom, he was still trying hopelessly to fit the broken cupboard parts together.

"Jack?"

"Yeah?"

"Can I ask you a question?"

"Sure, go ahead."

"If you could have one wish, what would it be?"

He set the shelf down and faced Jane. When his eyes met hers he could see she was truly interested in his response.

"I don't know. What would you wish for?"

"To spend my life here in Rivertown, fixing my house up, having children, maybe teaching, growing, being happy."

"Everyone wants to be happy, Jane."

"Even you, Jack?"

"Even me."

"Then why aren't you?"

"What do you mean?"

"Don't you think that if you were satisfied with your life, truly satisfied, you wouldn't spend so much time wandering around?"

He sat back against the stove and said, "I'm not unhappy, Jane. And I don't know what makes you say I am just because I'm not ready to sit down in one spot and calcify like everyone else around here."

Her eyes flashed. "You think just because someone lives in a small town they're ready for Social Security when they turn eighteen, huh?"

"I didn't say that."

"Well, then, what are you saying?"

"I'm saying that I am not unhappy, despite the fact that I do not own any real estate. What's your point here?"

She pushed off from the counter and wandered back down the hall toward the classroom. Clayton scowled, irritated now. He listened to her footsteps echoing away on

289

the hardwood floor. He gave her a few seconds on her own, then followed.

It was almost dark now in the classroom; the afternoon shadows were replacing the slants of light in the upper half of the room, and Clayton felt as though he'd been shut inside a large cedar closet. Jane was sitting in one of the desks again, her feet propped up on the chair in front of her. Clayton walked up to the desk directly across the aisle from hers, straddled the chair, and eased himself down into it. Then he folded his hands on the desktop and looked over at her.

He asked, "What do you want to know, Jane?"

She stared at him unblinking, her expression impassive and empty. The school fell silent; the sparrows, gliding now in and out of the bell steeple, crossed noiselessly from one end of the sunset sky into the other. Clayton decided she had not heard the question. He started to ask it again when she said, "How much longer are you planning to stay?"

"In Rivertown?"

"Yes."

"I don't know."

"Give me some idea. I mean, are we talking days, weeks, months—what? I need to know."

Clayton shifted in his seat. He knew what this was coming down to; he'd been expecting it all week despite her side trip to Howser's. He just wasn't sure he was ready for it. What could he say? She went on before he had the chance to say anything.

"I'm not a child, Jack," she whispered, giving him a few more moments to put his answer together.

"No, you're not."

"Well?"

"Next week."

"You're leaving next week?"

He got up out of his desk and walked to the west wall. She stayed in hers and drew circles on the wood with her forefinger.

"Is this what you brought me up here for today, Jane? To ask that question?"

290

Her eyes were lowered. "I just wanted you to see something that's a part of me. Something very special."

"So I'd understand why you live here, right?"

"Something like that. Yes."

"You didn't have to bring me up here to find that out, Jane. And that's not the point here, anyway."

"What is, then? Tell me."

"You want to know why your Rivertown can't be mine," said Clayton, crossing the room to the front desk. "You want to know why I haven't discovered it like you did or adopted it like Howser has."

"I know why you haven't."

"And why's that?"

"Because you haven't tried."

"No, Jane," he snapped. "I just haven't wanted to, that's why. There's nothing for me here." Clayton cringed as that last sentence came out. He hadn't wanted to put it that way. One glance at Jane's face and he knew he'd hurt her. Wonderful. She twisted away in her seat, putting him behind her left shoulder, out of view. And, thought Clayton, this was supposed to have been a nice little drive into the country. It was ruined now. He sat up on the teacher's desk, and resolved to try and keep his mouth shut.

Jane held her back to him and a minute passed in an uneasy quiet. The shadows thrown in the fading light fused with the stained redwood in the one-room schoolhouse and disappeared altogether as a purple twilight moved steadily into the west. The birds from the bell housing fluttered and tapped in passing at the glass high above in the windowframes. Another minute went by. Clayton decided to say something. To explain. When he spoke, his voice sounded oddly out of place, disturbing as it did the silence in the room.

"You're right, Jane. There's just been too much looking, too much riding around." His words echoed briefly and fell away again. "I feel like I should be settling down, too. You know what I mean? Parking the van and sleeping in my own bed. Stopping somewhere longer than a summer."

"But not in this town," whispered Jane, from her seat

in the dark. Clayton drew another long breath and held it before answering.

"No. Not here. Not now at least."

He saw her slip out of the desk and get up. He felt the floorboards vibrate faintly under his feet. She was moving off down the aisle toward the front door. He heard the latch click as it opened and then closed again.

"Jane?"

He called again and got only another echo in response. She was gone. He slid off the desktop and stood there a moment. The walls of the classroom seemed suddenly tall and black, claustrophobic and blank. He gave his eyes a chance to focus on the floor in front of him, then he walked carefully down the aisle toward the door.

Jane was standing away from the schoolhouse by the van in the last rays of daylight. She was stirring the ground with the side of her foot, raking the dust in a scribbling pattern, waiting for him to come out of the building. Her arms were folded and her head was down. She heard him step onto the porch. She didn't know why she'd run out of the school like that. He'd only said what she knew he was going to say: He wasn't going to set up housekeeping in Rivertown. There wasn't anything for him to do there. She knew that, too. He didn't have a home automatically waiting for him as she had, or even a job like Howser's. He was a drifter who had always said he'd be moving on, sooner or later. So why was she taking it like this? Maybe because he was leaving in the middle of everything—their relationship, the murder investigation, his own small-town summer. She'd known him less than a month, slept with him a dozen times, cooked for him, talked for hours with him in the dark, yet for some reason knew hardly anything about him besides the fact that he'd done some traveling here and there and had only uncomfortable memories to show for it.

She heard him on the stairs now, coming down to the yard. Her stomach tightened. There was a warm breeze circling the school, and the dust at her feet was rising on its own. She spoke before he did.

"I just wanted you to like this place as much as I do."

He sighed and stopped and sat down at the bottom of

the steps. "I do like it, Jane. I like the whole town, everything and everybody. I'm easy."

"Then why are you leaving?"

"Because Rivertown isn't my home. Not like it is yours. I'm just another tourist hanging around for the summer. You know that as well as I do. Just passing through on a blue day in June. I never meant to stay even this long, to tell you the truth. I really didn't. It was only your smile keeping me here, Jane. Nothing else."

She felt his words, physically. They thumped in her chest. She looked across the yard at him and saw the expression on his face, a tight grin drawn on his lips. He was doing it again, but this time it wouldn't be enough.

"Jack," she said, staring into his eyes. "I've been trying since that first night not to fall in love with you." She hesitated half a second, and continued, "I'm not going to tell you how successful I've been. You don't need to know."

She let her eyes fall back to the ground. If she was about to cry, she didn't want him to see it.

"Fair enough," he said.

The breeze gusted through the heavy oaks, churning transparent dust devils in the shadows and long grass at the sides of the yard. It gusted again and Jane imagined she could hear the old chains on her swing wrapping and chinking lazily at the rear of Parker School, the slatted seat rising and falling now, shoved gradually into motion by an insistent and invisible hand. Would the breeze be strong enough to ring the cast-iron bell? She looked up at the steeple, empty now in the sunset, the birds gone elsewhere for the evening. She hadn't heard the bell sound since she was twelve. A long time ago. The rope that ordinarily hung down from the bell housing had broken and nobody had bothered to rehang it. Dust blew across her eyes and she closed them as they stung. She heard Clayton stand up on the stairs. Another gusting and still the bell did not ring. She couldn't wait any longer. There was no frenzy in the summer wind.

So she said, "We should go back."

And she slipped away from the side of Clayton's van and walked around to the passenger door. It was becoming too dark to see anything and the picnic was over. She climbed inside and waited for him, her fingers folded under her thighs. His own eyes irritated now in the rising air, Clayton stepped off the bottom step and followed Jane's path to the van. He took the ignition key from his shirt pocket and got in. The engine turned over on the second try and Clayton put it in gear. Then they drove back down through the gravel and ruts to the bottom of the hill. It was almost an hour beyond twilight before they made it back to town.

19

*The boy stood in the radiance of sun rays between shadow
and shadow, exploring his father's bedroom with his eyes.
Dust motes traveled down the shaft of light and settled on
tiny stocking feet. He peered into the mirror atop the dark
oak dresser and saw that he was alone. He climbed up onto
the quilted mattress and sat with an arm and a leg hooked
around a bedpost and stuck his toes out toward the sunlight
until they glowed. His feet grew warm. He left the bed and
tiptoed across to the dresser and opened the drawers, one
by one. He ran his hands under piles of socks and underwear, long pants, handkerchieves, shirts. The boy sifted
through his father's clothes with his fingers, mussed them
and played. When he withdrew, his hands smelled of laundry and fathers. He pressed his fingers to his nose as he
went into the closet. There he knelt among his discoveries,
sampling each before choosing a favorite. When he came
out again, he paraded about the room in a pair of black
patent leather shoes pretending he was his father. Clop,
clop, clop, clop. His feet slid back and forth inside the shoes
as he walked to the bedroom door then back again into the
closet. He dragged his father's summer coat off a hanger
and wore it, despite the fit. He crawled back up onto the
bed where his father slept alone at night and lay on his side,
looking for birds in the afternoon sky. He dreamed awake.
Dusk drew down its shade in the window. The wood floor
creaked behind the boy. In the mirror, he saw his father*

watching from the threshold. The boy cried. Crying made no difference. Twice that night he was beaten, but did not die.

The old silvered mirror was smudged. He took the handkerchief from his vest pocket and wiped it off. Then he straightened his tie and combed his hair. In the top dresser drawer were the cufflinks, monogrammed H.D., left him by his father. He took them out, fastened them to his shirtcuffs, and put on his coat. He checked the mirror once more, picked up the small satchel containing his work clothes, and walked out into the hallway. Locking the bedroom door behind him, he descended the staircase. Downstairs, the house was dark. In the kitchen sink were the leftovers from the supper he'd hardly touched. His appetite wasn't half of what it had been even a month ago. He hadn't time to eat anymore. Too much needed to be done. He left through the back door and strode out into the middle of the yard. His son wasn't home yet. The animals needed feeding. He looked at his watch. It was seven thirty. Had to be in town by eight, done by half past ten. Then he could run his errands. Tom Danielson climbed into the red Blazer. He had a long night ahead of him.

At nine o'clock, Howser took the elevator up to the second floor, then walked across the County Services lobby to the rear hall and up the walnut staircase to the city council chamber. The tall double doors were closed when Howser got there but he could already hear the shouting inside. He imagined it had been going on since the mayor's gavel struck. They're chewing on each other in there, he thought, like sharks. And the biggest one, Rivertown's Great White, Tom Danielson, was undoubtedly showing the greatest appetite. Howser searched in his pants pockets for some loose change. There was a Coke machine down at the end of the hall. Feeling badly dehydrated, he put off making his entrance for at least a couple of more minutes and walked down to get a drink. He put two quarters in the big red machine, punched a button, and drew out a can of orange soda. He opened it up and drained most of it in one swallow. Just feeling the cold soda in his mouth and throat felt good. His eyes watered and he wiped them clear with the back of his hand. Was the heat ever going to break? It'd never been this bad in Santa Clara County. Day after day, since the tramp got killed, the heat wave simply refused to let up. Some mornings he'd get into the office at nine and it'd be so hot he couldn't think straight, even with the fan on. Either Jane or Susan would bring up a pitcher of ice water for him, yet it hardly seemed to help. The heat put everyone on edge, himself included, making the situation seem that much worse, that much more desperate and hopeless. By midday, he'd peel the blinds back to look out the window, and Rivertown would shimmer there in the heat like some peculiar mirage inhabited by people he hardly recognized, strangers in a brick-and-asphalt oasis.

More to the point, the heat made him wonder just what the hell he was doing in Rivertown in the first place. It wasn't his home. Forget what Jane told him about belonging. Unless you happened to have been born in Rivertown you were an outsider and always would be. So what that they'd hired him to police the place? That didn't mean they had to accept him as one of their own. And if he walked into that meeting and handed the killer over to them? Then what? He'd be their friend for a while. They might give him a scout troop to lead and a parking place at City Hall with his name painted on it. And maybe a few of them'd go out of their way to buy him a beer at O'Shaughnessy's after bowling on Tuesdays. Lots of good things like that. Yes, he would become a popular guy. Until the next crisis. Until the next time they needed bailing out of an impossible situation and he didn't have the answers for them printed up nicely on Rivertown stationery. He smiled. It was okay, though. It came with the job and he was used to it. He'd survive as long as they did. He could wait. There were enough fringe benefits to keep him going for at least another couple of months. It was going to be fine. Probably.

Howser tossed the empty soda can into the trash beside the Coke machine and walked back up the hall to the council chamber. The shouting was still going on inside and he took advantage of it by easing open the door and slipping unnoticed into the rear of the room. He stood back in a corner against the wood and watched. It was just as he'd thought it was going to be: Danielson up at the podium running the show by yelling a little louder than everyone around him.

". . . We're going to find the people responsible for the brutalism that has turned our town into a butcher shop and they're going to pay, believe you me. When we catch them, they're going to pay . . ."

Howser found it difficult to avoid smirking at the call for another vigilante group—particularly a vigilante party from a group of high school washouts, small businessmen and Elks club members whose closest association to law enforcement had been a few parking tickets and syndicated reruns of *Dragnet* on television. It was a ridiculous notion. Predictable, but ridiculous. They might pile into their pick-ups and go running around the county like whores on a holiday, but the odds were that they wouldn't catch anyone and they'd be damned fortunate to get back in one piece. Rivertown was not exactly gun-crazy, but there were just enough loonies on Main Street to make Howser shiver over the prospect of these people poking their way into a few dark corners, rifles locked and loaded. It'd been bad enough that night at the railyard and up there the nuts had been confined geographically to a tramp jungle bounded on three sides by chain-link fence and by targets stationary and surprised. That wouldn't be the case this time. Which was why he wasn't going to let it happen. Vigilante days in Rivertown were over. They'd fooled him once by doing something he hadn't expected. He wasn't stupid enough to let them do it again.

". . . You all know me and you know what I stand for in this town and what it means to me and my family . . ."

Howser watched Danielson working almost frantically to drum up support for whatever it was he had in mind. Sweat was dripping down the sides of his face, and his shirt was wet and stained. Danielson looked crazy, yet was still commanding an audience, evangelizing for his own cause. And they were listening intently. Why? Were they all really that frightened, or was this just some elaborately disguised game they were playing with themselves?

". . . Why should we be scared to walk our own streets at night . . . ?"

Howser looked around at the men hanging on Danielson's every word. Most were in T-shirts or open-necked collars because of the heat. A few held handkerchiefs in their laps. Several looked drowsy. None were smiling. Someone had opened the metal-rimmed pane to the skylight, hoping perhaps that a draft would be created; the air in the room was hot and stale. Nobody was very comfortable, but neither had anyone left.

". . . If we let this go on any longer, by God, we deserve everything we get from . . ."

What Howser could not get straight in his own mind was the motivation behind it all. He'd been a cop so long he found it hard to remember life before the badge. And yet still he could not picture himself running off to hunt somebody down, particularly since that kind of thing had no real connection whatsoever with the law as he knew it. That was comic-book, bounty-hunter stuff—risky business for danger junkies and children too dumb to see what it was all about.

". . . What we need here is some of you to make a commitment . . ."

Watching Danielson foaming at the mouth, Howser wondered just which group Tom belonged to. He was too old to be considered a kid, yet he didn't seem the kind of guy who got off on the adventurous stuff. No, not him. He was too smart for that. He'd let others take the risks for him.

". . . Nobody's going to intimidate us in our own town . . ."

Howser realized now that Danielson should've been arrested that first night at the tramp jungle, particularly after the shots had been fired. Failing to do so had been a huge mistake. It had given him the wrong message about the way the law operated, as though in Rivertown somehow the words "badge" and "authority" were not necessarily synonymous.

". . . How about we get a show of hands here, take a vote and make a decision, what do you say? Mayor? . . ."

Howser did not even bother to raise his hand to vote

against Danielson's vigilante measure. He didn't care how many yeas or nays they came up with, because the game they were playing was not going to last much longer. A vote like that should never be taken. The fact that it was demonstrated where the real power sat in this town. Dick Millward got up from his seat and took over the microphone. He looked around the room, then said, "Well, Tom, it looks as though you got the vote you wanted, so I think it's time we hear from our chief of police."

Danielson leaned forward so that his voice would be picked up on the mike. "Sure thing, Mayor. Why not?"

"Are you in here somewhere, Chief?"

Howser pushed himself off the wall and swung into the aisle, making his way now through the crowd to the front of the room. He pushed past two men flanking the first row of benches and stepped toward the podium, catching Danielson's eye.

"Chief! There you are!"

Howser ignored him and reached forward to grab the microphone. He did not want what he was about to say to be missed by anyone in the room. The noise level was rising now and most of it was directed at him, but Howser kept his eyes focused forward and spoke evenly to the men shouting out at him.

"Anyone joining any unauthorized armed search party within five miles of Rivertown, or caught carrying firearms within five miles of this town, or found to be interfering with Rivertown police business inside or outside of these city limits, can plan to spend at least one solid week in their own private cell right downstairs. Thank you for your cooperation."

He stepped down from the podium and walked through the center of the crowd and out of the room without looking back.

20

The sign read BAILEY'S RESERVOIR, and the gate it was hung onto was locked. Ernie Long threw himself against it and shook the cyclone fencing until it howled and rang in the windy dark. His head felt light and dizzy and his face hurt. He'd been running for almost an hour, up from the county road where he'd left the truck, seven miles to Bailey's Reservoir, looking for his brother Howie who'd been missing now since the Fourth. If Howie was not at the reservoir, then Ernie had no idea where he might be. He'd looked everywhere else.

The wind blew through his hair and across his face. He could hardly see anything in the dark around him. Even the stars seemed swept loose, gone from the summer sky. He stood in front of the fence, wishing he'd brought Howie's flashlight. The sign hanging there on the wire banged against the fencing and the lock shook on the chain that held the gate closed. Ernie curled his fingers into the wire and pulled the two sections of gate as far apart as they'd go. Then he slipped between them. Sometimes it was good being skinny. The reservoir was only a hundred yards or so away now. The wind roared through the underbrush and shoved him sideways. The dark was disorienting and the wind hammered in his ears. His first step sent him sprawling into the brush. He scrambled out onto the path again, lowered his head, and ran forward up the slant of the hill, directing himself between the flailing bushes on either side of the path.

The waters of Bailey's Reservoir were hidden beneath a surface film of dust and leaves and broken twigs scattered across the brackish scum. Ernie arrived at the cement border and tried to catch his breath. All around him things skittered by, blown upward in raging circles and down again. He peered out over the water. Why did Howie come up here? The reservoir frightened Ernie. He had never known its waters to be anything but greasy and dark. Whatever it was that attracted his twin brother to this place eluded him completely. He backed away from the water. If only he'd brought the flashlight. The trees hovering overhead roared. He turned his back into the wind and squeezed his eyes until tears ran. The banging of the sign down on the gate echoed above the wind. Ernie took a couple steps to his right and stumbled over a small pile of clothes lying on the cement. A T-shirt and a pair of pants. He bent down to pick them up. Socks and tennis shoes. Underwear. He drew them close and recognized them. Howie's. They were dirty but dry, covered in the same dingy grit that floated motionless on the water of the reservoir. Ernie stuffed the T-shirt up against his nose. As he smelled it he looked around slowly, flicking his eyes about. Just the lifeless water and the dark. No Howie. Nobody at all.

Ernie folded the clothes into a manageable bundle and pressed them close against his waist and walked along the edge of the reservoir, hoping to find something else of his brother. He took care not to step too near the water. The wind tore loose one of Howie's socks, flinging it to the cement. Ernie worked a hand free and knelt down and picked it up again, jamming it this time inside Howie's underwear. Behind him, the brush kicked and swayed. The entrance to the frontage road was lost now, back there in the dark. He shivered as the wind gusted black across the water. Halfway around to the far side of the reservoir, he noticed something floating motionless in the scum, a sort of hump in the green water twenty feet from the lip of the cement. Seeing it gave Ernie a start. He dropped Howie's clothes. The hump faded to black and disappeared. Ernie stared at the spot where it had been. What had happened? His head buzzed and a sour taste rose in his throat. Then his belly cramped and he fell down onto the cement and puked into the water. He vomited until his gut emptied, then retched dry heaves until the sweat congealed on his face and steam rose from the pale skin on the back of his neck. He felt the cement under his body ripple in swells like waves on a summer sea. His eyelids burned and he had to squint to see. Had he been able to, he would have cried out for help, even knowing there was nobody to offer it. Tears ran off his nose and lips. His face flushed and he retched one last time then gagged and coughed and spat into the water. The wind turned his sweat into a chill.

He lay there a long while listening to his heart thumping. Jamie had refused to help him look for Howie. Jamie's dad swore he'd given Jamie the message about searching at the reservoir but Jamie never called back. And now he wouldn't even answer his phone. He pulled the shades down in his room and played his Van Halen records alone in the dark. Roy and Jerry were already gone two days now out of the county, driving away to the south where they hoped no one would find them. They didn't care, either. So who was going to help him? Chief Howser? He would not understand why Howie had gone off in the first place, not after Annie talked. Nobody would. That was why Jamie had closed and locked his bedroom door, and why Jerry and Roy were never coming back to Rivertown.

Ernie rolled back onto his stomach and looked out over the water, focusing where the hump had been before he'd gotten sick. Now it was there again, black and motionless. Ernie caught his breath and sat up and wiped the tears from his face. He stared at the hump, trying to figure out what it was, afraid of what it might be. He stood and began backing up, fixing his gaze on the shape in the reservoir. He took the Scout knife from his Levis and opened the blade. He bent down and picked up one of the longer tree limbs fractured by the wind on the west side of the reservoir and cut off the ragged branches and fashioned a pole of sorts. Then he carried the long stick back to the water and stuck it out toward the hump, hoping to use it as a hook to drag the hump back to shore. The stick broke and fell into the water, making faint ripples in the algae. Ernie tossed the stick away into the brush and sat down on the cement and removed his shoes and socks. Dust blew around him in the air and the brush shook noisily. A few feet away, the pool looked dark and cold.

Ernie slipped his shirt and pants off, and folded both over his shoes and socks. In his underwear, he squatted on the rounded edge of the reservoir, trying to summon up enough nerve to slide down into the water. A warm gust ruffled his hair. He slid forward and let his toes break the surface of the pool. It was cold. His ankles went next, then his calves and knees. Balancing on his hips, he lowered himself into the reservoir up to the middle of his thighs. He could feel the green spume foaming up his legs. No longer considering what he was doing, Ernie pushed off from the cement toward the dark hump suspended in the water a few yards away. He swam slowly, holding his mouth up and open above the surface of the pool while paddling dog-fashion with his hands. His legs hung cold beneath, dangling in the dark water as he struggled close to the hump ahead of him.

Then he was near it and he saw the hump was not black after all but a pallid white, and larger than it had appeared from the cement. And more of it floated sunken below the surface of Bailey's Reservoir than showed above. And gliding into it and touching it with his fingers, Ernie discovered that it was not just a hump but a body, skinny and nude, and a boy, like himself. He did not have to turn it over in the black water to see whose swollen face it wore. Only Howie ever swam in this place.

Ernie shut his eyes and reached down through the algae and took his brother by the wrist and tugged him back toward the cement. Pumping his feet furiously and paddling with his free hand, Ernie swept the water clean before him, stirring a deep current into the reservoir. He lunged for the concrete as it came within reach and dug in his fingernails, straining for a hold. Howie's body, floating in filthy and hard behind him, shoved at his back. Ernie pressed his eyelids even more tightly closed, squeezing his first tears loose into the reservoir. Gripping Howie high up on the arm now, refusing to release his drowned brother, Ernie struggled out of the water, scraping his chest and legs raw as he went, until he flopped over onto his stomach and shook with the effort and the cold. Tiny waves from his splashing lapped high on the concrete wall and off again. Ernie could not hear the wind passing over him any longer. His brain was buzzing with furious and distracted thoughts. He jerked on his brother's arm, trying vainly to lift him in one clean motion from Bailey's Reservoir. He scrambled forward to slide another hand under Howie's armpits and heave him up out of the black water. He screamed and collapsed backward, pulling Howie's bruised head and upper arms out onto the cement. His brother's body was cold yet Ernie rubbed the bloodless skin, working life less back into Howie's than into his own. He tugged again, gripping this time from his brother's biceps, bringing shoulders and rib cage from the water and throwing the last of his tears back in return.

Then a voice spoke behind him.

"Need a little help there?"

And a large piece of dry wood bashed into his face.

21

The Styrofoam cup balanced precariously on the dash-board in the sunlight, caught in a speed draft from the open windows where it fluttered slightly and threatened to fall. Clayton reached up and wedged the empty cup in against the windshield. Howser switched lanes, crossing over to the oleander-shrouded aluminum railing on the left, swinging the unit past an old white Ford flatbed they had been following for the last few miles. Interstate 99 opened up as far as they could see, vacant to the horizon, a bright shimmering mirage on the black pavement in the heat. Clayton stuck his arm out into the wind. The air-conditioning unit on Howser's black-and-white had been broken now for more than a month and the vents seemed to be sucking heat directly off the engine. Hurtling south on the highway, they passed cottonfields and grain silos and fruit stands selling cherries and peaches and pears. Traffic was light in the midafternoon and the air was blue and clear up to the roof of the summer sky. Clayton leaned back in the seat and tried to stretch his legs again. Howser slipped his right hand down to the bottom of the steering wheel and settled back into his own seat with a yawn. He was already tired of driving and they were still an hour away. The heat and the drafting air made him drowsy. Only the constant thumping of the tires running over the tar strips kept him somewhat alert. Howser shifted again in the driver's seat and dropped all but one finger from the wheel. He brought the speedometer up to sixty and held it there.

An eighteen-wheeler packing produce in a refrigeration unit for Safeway supermarkets thundered past, shaking the highway under the cruiser and shoving it off its track in a blast of wind. Howser checked the side mirror then maneuvered over to the slow lane as a Ford Bronco glided past, chasing the Safeway truck. A cloud of dust rose in the Bronco's wake, disturbing the silvery mirage in the distance.

Clayton had been sitting in silence most of the way, content to watch the landscape go by, but now he said, "You know, there's something I haven't been able to figure out."

"What's that?" Howser took his hand off the wheel to scratch his nose.

"Well, there's been, what," Clayton started counting on his fingers. "Seven deaths in Rivertown now, maybe eight with the kid who's missing, right?"

"Yeah."

"And Rivertown's not a big place, you know, small population. Yet, with the exception of what's been written in the *Courier,* there hasn't been any real publicity about this whole thing anywhere. I mean, I read the Sacramento paper every day and there hasn't been anything in there at all on any of this. Somebody's been managing this beautifully."

"You just noticed this recently?"

"It finally struck me this morning. I'd just like to know how you do it."

"I don't. Doesn't have anything to do with me at all. It's the city council and the people down at the *Rivertown Courier* writing what they want people to hear. Even Charlotte Burkie's crap is pretty innocent when it comes right down to it. She's on the team here. She's doesn't say all that much. Just 'kid missing' or 'local boys die in car accident,' you know."

"No one's saying 'murder' on the wire, in other words."

"You got it. What we've had here are a series of unconnected misfortunes. A rape, a drowning, a fatal car accident, a justifiable homicide involving a transient, and

307

the death by pneumonia of an elderly woman. A string of coincidental deaths. Nothing more."

"No serial killer, huh?"

"Definitely not."

"What about Alfie's death and the Williams kid?"

"Both still under investigation. Details presently unavailable. And because we're a small town, it's fairly easy to pull off. This isn't going to make *USA Today* as long as the council has anything to say about it. They don't want that kind of publicity and they'll do whatever's necessary to avoid it."

"And it's okay with you?"

"Put it this way: in San Jose, sometimes it felt as though we had a *Mercury-News* reporter riding along with us there in the unit. Every little thing they picked up on. They didn't miss a beat. Eyes burning holes in the back of your neck whenever you wrote a traffic citation. Take your gun out of the holster and you could almost guarantee your name in the paper the next day. A different world entirely."

"And not one you miss all that much, huh?"

"No, not much."

A silver Porsche 944 came up from behind and Howser watched it run past. The license plate was Nevadan and read HOT2GO. The woman driving did not even glance over as she eased by and moved away into the heat. Clayton counted his twenty-third fruit stand off the roadside to the west. A sign painted yellow and red on the wooden roof read: DON'T PASS US BY!!! There were half a dozen cars parked under a shade tree in front.

"How much farther?"

Howser eased back into the passing lane. "The tramp jungle's near a junction of the Southern Pacific about five miles from Curry so we're talking maybe another hour, hour and a half, I suppose. Don't worry. We're making good time."

"So how did you find these guys?"

Howser looked over at Clayton and grinned. "We have our ways. This one was hard but not impossible. Let's just say it took a while because they've moved around a fair amount since their stay in Rivertown, but we found them anyhow."

"Sounds kind of spooky."

"Like Big Brother's looking right over your shoulder, huh?"

"That's it."

"Well, in this case we just ran a few prints and descriptions out to all the towns holding railyards and asked the law enforcement people if they'd mind running out to take a look for us. We got lucky and found them down there in the Curry yard. If they'd stayed off the rails or left the state, I doubt we'd have ever seen them again."

"That makes me feel a little better."

"I take it your prints are on file," said Howser.

"About eleven years ago I got booked for vagrancy up in Siskiyou County. Place called Cecilville. They only kept me a couple of hours but that was long enough to get printed and have my picture taken. Wonderful experience."

"So you're a criminal?"

"No, it was a mistake."

"It won't look that way on the computer. Maybe you ought to be sitting in the backseat. In fact"—the chief reached for the radio—"why don't I just call in and run a check on you. How do you spell your name?" Howser started laughing when he saw Clayton's smile beginning to fade. "Just kidding."

Another twenty minutes went by. The farther south they drove, the more oppressive the heat became, bleaching the color out of everything along the way and making near mirages of the grain elevators in the distant fields. A horn honked. Looking to his right, Clayton saw a black Chevelle 396 on the frontage road across the fence running even with the cruiser. Its driver, a pimply-faced redhead, grinned at Clayton and waved. The kid gunned the engine and spun the oversized rear wheels. The Chevelle lurched forward and the tires chirped and smoked. The kid waved again. Clayton waved back. The kid raced the engine to a roar and a hand thrust out from behind the rear three-quarter window. It was slender and female, wearing cherry-red fingernail polish and carrying an obscene gesture. The kid pumped his foot into the throttle and sped away, spinning the tires furiously and blowing blue smoke from a set of chrome and black-crackle exhaust pipes. Clayton watched the black Chevelle rocket ahead. A mile up the road, the kid braked hard and swung onto another road heading west. As the Rivertown black-and-white reached the point where the kid had turned off, Clayton saw the Chevelle disappearing quickly into the distance, just a dot now on the white horizon.

"That kid's flying."

"Yeah."

"You're not calling it in on the radio?"

"Nope."

"Why not?"

"Well, for one thing, just us being here sent him running for cover. So we got him off the road for a while. And anyhow, by the time I did call it in, he'd already have backed it down again or parked it somewhere. All we could do is report him to the CHP and we don't have time for that. Besides, if he keeps driving like that, he'll get caught sooner or later."

"I suppose," said Clayton. "Nervy kid, though."

Howser frowned. "He's stupid and dangerous. One day he'll stack it up and take a whole family with him."

A blue Datsun pickup passed in the slow lane, the sunlight glinting off the flat rear window behind the cab.

"It pisses you off, huh?"

"You could say that."

"So you *do* take this stuff personally."

"Sometimes I do, sometimes I don't. Wearing a badge doesn't make a person less human."

"I didn't mean that."

"Look, the only way to slow a kid like that down is to have someone read him the riot act, and if that's not enough, pull his license. In either case, the people in the station wagon get to make it home for dinner. That's what matters. If the kid goes away thinking we're hard-asses, well, we can live with that. You got to make your priorities fit the situation. We want you to love us, nobody *enjoys* being disliked, but you people do a lot of strange things and the badge forces us to wade in the shit right alongside you—whether we want to or not."

"I suppose."

An Allied Van Lines truck roared by, its draft creating waves in the oleander. Howser rolled the window up a notch as a dust cloud billowed in the truck's wake.

"You want to know about taking things personally? Let me tell you a little story. About eight years ago—you might remember seeing this in the papers—there was a guy who snatched a nine-year-old girl from the sidewalk outside of her school in Mountain View. He drove her up into the Santa Cruz mountains near Los Gatos, beat her, sodomized her, locked her in the dunghole of an outhouse for fifteen hours, then cut off all the fingers on her left hand and pushed her out of his car on the Nimitz freeway at four o'clock in the morning. Didn't kill her, though. The little girl, her name was Laura Anne Steele, made it, she survived, and inside of seventy-two hours, somehow the detectives ID'd her attacker as a nearsighted, fifty-three-year-old TV repairman named Art Fowler. No priors, no record, nothing. Just one of those guys bouncing off the wall. Clean, so far as we knew, until he kidnapped the little girl. Anyhow, about a week later, just after dinner, I ended up being the hero who pulled him over for an illegal left turn a couple of blocks from the Winchester Mystery House. It was just dumb luck, of course, because it's not all that often you nail one of these guys when they're getting started. Usually they don't make mistakes until later on when, for one reason or another, they begin losing their enthusiasm for the game. Anyhow, the coincidence was that I had a picture of the guy right there beside me on the seat, so I knew who I had the moment I saw his face. He didn't run or anything. Just sat there behind the wheel grinning like a clown. I had my flashlight out and ran it over the inside of the guy's car, a late model LTD. And, Christ, he had a six-year-old black girl lying face down and naked in the backseat, scared out of her mind. I jerked the guy out of the car, cuffed him, and dragged him onto the pavement and over to the trunk. Before I could read him his rights, he said to me, 'You're never going to find them.' And I said, 'Find what?' And he said, 'Her fingers. You're never going to find Shirley Temple's fingers. I put 'em down the garbage disposal this morning.' Then he started laughing. Like what he said was so funny. Laughing and laughing. I went nuts and pulled my gun and jammed it against his forehead and held it there until my backup arrived. I didn't shoot the guy, but I swear I wanted to."

"He didn't have a gun himself, then, huh? No weapon or anything?"

"Nope, nothing but a roll of duct tape in his parka. I'll never forget the way he laughed. He'd maimed a little girl for life and treated it like a joke. Still makes me want to puke. I'll never forget it. I had nightmares for a month. Bad ones. The department finally made me take some time off. It wasn't until maybe three or four years ago that I stopped hearing his laughter in my sleep."

"You put him away, though."

"Yeah, we took him off the streets and dropped him in the nuthouse at Atascadero where the court says he belongs."

"He's still there?"

"As far as I know. Christ, I hope so. Art Fowler. A guy like that should never get out. Of course, if he does and ends up killing somebody, I'll probably wish I'd shot him that night."

"But you didn't," said Clayton. "That's what makes you different from the assholes of the world."

"Maybe, maybe not. I don't know. Sometimes I doubt if it had anything to do with police ethics or morality or anything like that. At the time, I can honestly say I felt like putting a large hole in the guy's head. I truly did. I just couldn't pull the trigger. Maybe I was just afraid to do it. I'm still not sure."

A station wagon driven by two women and filled with kindergartners sped by. Several of the kids waved as they passed. The back window on the station wagon was open and two of them had their legs hanging out into the hot draft. A piece of paper flew out of the window, onto the highway. Clayton watched it toss in the roiling wake of the station wagon then up over the oleander in the center divider and across into the north-bound lanes. He looked over at Howser who was holding the wheel steady, steering them between two broken white lines pointing straight away to a white horizon in the south. Clayton started to ask him something else about Art Fowler, then changed his mind and stared out the window instead. To the west, the big Rainbird sprinklers fanned water over a parched earth and kept the soil alive and the weeds at bay for another afternoon. The patches abandoned or ignored by the sprinklers had been bleached already to impoverished white half-acres given back to the wild grass. The land baked under the midsummer sun and there was no relief. In the cruiser, they accommodated themselves to the heat in the only way they could, trying to ignore it, while continuing to speed south, riding the last thirty miles to Curry in silence.

They parked in the empty lot of an old train depot and got out. Milkweed filled the cracks in the broken pavement and added color to the concrete and reduced the glare. There was no one around: a perfect stillness—no voices, no engines, no breeze. A sign, nailed to the south wall of the depot, read: CURRY STATION. The depot itself was only a long cement platform, four or five feet high, beside the rusting railroad tracks, backed by a flat and elongated structure in redwood. Wild rye had grown a foot high in some places between the ties and the dust buried the rails completely in others. Clayton walked over to the platform while Howser kicked at the gravel with the side of his shoe and looked down the tracks. They ran off into the distance a quarter of a mile past the platform and out through a corridor of willow and oak. Clayton climbed up onto the cement and walked over to a door under the overhang of the red roof. It was locked. He shook it but it refused to open. He called down to Howser, "Where are these guys we're supposed to meet?"

Howser squinted in the sun as he looked up at Clayton. "They'll be here. We're still a few minutes early. They're coming out from town."

Clayton nodded and turned back to the depot. There was a large sliding door in the center of the building bolted shut and a couple of other smaller doors farther down the platform. He walked down to have a look. His shoes clacked softly on the cement. Behind him, Howser was muttering something about the heat. It was cooler in the shade of Curry Station, yet Howser preferred to slide back into the front seat of the cruiser and sit there with the doors open, hanging one foot out into the dust. Clayton found one of the two doors unlocked on the north end of the depot. He opened it and walked into a small storage room. There was nothing inside except a few cardboard shipping boxes marked CURRY STATION, CALIFORNIA, and an old cap with the words *John Deere* sewn onto the bill. Shards of glass from a broken bottle of Budweiser littered the dusty floor. The room had a musty odor. Clayton opened a couple of the boxes, found them empty, then picked the cap up and put it on. Discovering it fit reasonably well, he wore it out the door.

He walked to the end of the platform and stood there a minute watching two chicken hawks wheeling through the blue sky in a lazy arc to the west. They were passing over something on the ground directly beneath them, banking slowly downward in tandem on the warm currents, slanting to earth and around again, holding intransigently to separate points on the same descending circle. He watched until the light hurt his eyes, then climbed back down to the pavement and the milkweed and walked around to the rear of the depot where it fronted an embankment shrouded in the same purple wildflowers and live oaks farther down the line. A loading dock jutted out from the middle of the building and several wooden crates were piled up on it. Thirty yards away a flatcar sat rusting in the tall grass and beyond that an old 1958 nile-green Dodge sedan, parked in the sun, tires and windshield missing. Making a complete loop now around the station, Clayton walked past the loading platform and the empty crates marked FRESNO and BAKERSFIELD and VISALIA and up to the flatcar and the wreck of the Dodge. There was a hole in the heavy bed of the flatcar and grass was growing up through the center of it, tips of wild oats poking a few inches above the wood. Clayton went over to the Dodge and looked inside. The instrument panel was gone along with most of the electrical wiring behind the dash, and the seat coverings were worn away exposing sponge and springs beneath. He opened the driver's door and got inside. The steering wheel was so hot from the sun that he could only touch it with the tips of his fingers. It wouldn't turn anyway. He tried pulling the gear lever into first and found that was jammed, too. The car was a junker. Even the glove-compartment door had fallen off, leaving a gaping hole on that end of the dashboard to match the one in front of the driver. His father had always gotten a kick out of fixing up old cars, though Clayton imagined even he would admit this one was beyond restoration.

He walked out from behind the depot just as Howser whistled for him. Two other law-enforcement officers were waiting there alongside Howser. He gave a casual wave. When he reached the cars, Howser did the introductions.

"Jack, this is Sheriff Ed Donnelly and his deputy, Bob Snider. Guys, Jack Clayton."

They shook hands all around and stood there a few minutes commenting on the heat, which Snider said had reached 110 degrees in downtown Curry only an hour earlier. Finally Clayton asked, "So, where's the jungle?"

"Right on down the tracks from here through those trees," said Donnelly, pointing to the north where the treeline formed shade and the tracks seemed to disappear into the dust. "We'll walk."

"Fine," said Howser.

As they started down the tracks, Howser looked back at Clayton strolling a few feet behind the others, his new John Deere cap pulled tightly down onto his fore-head.

"Nice hat."

"Think it's me?" asked Clayton, adjusting the bill.

"Yeah." Howser grinned. "It's you."

They followed the tracks away from the depot out into the flats, between the hillside to the east and the brushline on the west, where the sun blazed clear in the white dust and the midafternoon temperatures burned dry on the skin of their faces. They walked toward the willows hanging a green shade over the tracks a quarter of a mile away. Nobody spoke. They made their way down the line in silence—the heat having stilled any desire for conversation—and the only sound in the air at Curry Station was the rhythmic crunching of western boots on gravel and the casual chirping of small birds somewhere off in the leafy brush.

When the four of them reached the shade they stopped and Sheriff Donnelly removed his sunglasses and drew a small white pad from his back pocket. He leafed through it until he found what he was looking for and handed it over to Howser.

"I think these are the guys you're going to want to see today."

Howser read the names and descriptions and the notes Donnelly had made from his own interviews earlier in the week and written up for Howser's benefit on the way over from Curry. Then he pulled a slip of paper from his shirt pocket and placed it on the pad. His lips moved as he read through his own scribbled notes.

Donnelly asked, "How long did you have these two?"

"Four days," said Howser, skimming as quickly as he could. "We couldn't think of any reason to keep them longer than that."

Howser finished reading and nodded at Donnelly. "Yeah, this is right. Like I said on the phone, these sound like the same guys." He handed Donnelly back his pad. "Okay, so where do we find them?"

Donnelly put his sunglasses back on, gave a half-smile to Snider, and jerked his thumb over his shoulder. "Follow me."

He led them another fifty yards through the shade to where the treeline bordered a large open yard lying between the railroad tracks and an old two-story warehouse. The jungle wasn't much more than a few canvas tents and several dozen sleeping bags and bedrolls thrown down in the empty spaces between the tents and the side of the old building. The tramps were sitting around in small groups or leaning solitarily against the walls of the warehouse, smoking cigarettes and staring blankly into space. Most were either naked from the waist up or stripped to T-shirts and long pants, but one raggedy-looking tramp on the far end of the yard was busy doing cartwheels fully nude through a narrow line of shade, while several others sat drenched in sweat at the entrance to their tents, fully clothed in flannel shirts, overalls and parkas, waiting, it appeared, for the imminent onset of some dark and unseasonal storm.

Two faucets near the warehouse door, one near the ground at the base of the building and the other mounted on the top of a long iron pipe, leaked rusty water into the dirt. Donnelly walked across the yard, bent down, opened the tap on the long one and ran water onto his hands and forearms, then splashed a little onto his face and down the back of his neck. The tramps sitting near the faucet watched with a practiced indifference, waiting to find out which one of them the three cops and the guy with the John Deere cap had come down to see. Donnelly soaked his hands and ran them through his hair once before closing the tap. Then he straightened up and looked about, searching with his eyes from one tramp to another, catching their attention one by one, then moving on. He shot a quick glance back at Snider, waiting patiently with Howser and Clayton in the shade of the last big willow. Donnelly said something to the tramp sitting closest to the water faucet, listened to the response, nodded, and walked over to the warehouse door. It was open and he leaned in for a look, then stepped inside out of the light. Back under the trees, Clayton could hear Donnelly's voice echoing in the interior of the warehouse. He was calling loudly to somebody in there. A moment later he reappeared at the door and motioned to Snider with the fingers of his left hand.

"All right, let's go," said the deputy, and he led Howser and Clayton in a circuitous path across the yard through the grassy dust and the bedrolls, past the tramps murmuring wordlessly in their tents, to the brown warehouse entrance and inside.

It took Clayton a few seconds to get his eyes adjusted to the dark. Initially he was aware only of movement and voices in the large open space before him. Then the walls and the high iron-beamed ceiling of the warehouse came into focus and after that another smaller milling of tramps drifting slowly elsewhere in the lightless atmosphere. There was a smell to the old warehouse that had nothing to do with the deteriorating structure. Clayton knew it immediately as the stench of negligent and disinterested men remaining too long in one place. It was an odor he'd needed six weeks away from the railyards to even notice on himself and eight sessions at a cheap Laundromat in Vallejo to scrub from the fabric of the clothes he'd worn traveling. It wasn't something evident in the open air at Rivertown's Green River yard, nor even outside of the warehouse now. Indoors though, where the ventilation was as feeble and stagnant as that inside a closed boxcar late on a humid evening, the smell was as obvious and identifiable as the men who carried it.

As Clayton moved into the brown shadows, he noticed Donnelly standing over a tramp sitting with his back up against the east wall and his butt on the cool concrete floor. Both Donnelly and the tramp were looking at him. Or maybe it was not him but Howser and Snider coming in behind him on whom they were fixing their attention.

The tramp broke into a wide grin when Howser came closer. "How're you doing, Chief? Welcome to the Hilton."

The tramp bared a dark-toothed grin and stuck out an open hand. When it was ignored, he withdrew it again and sat there, still grinning but eyeing the four men surrounding him with a slightly wary gaze.

"Lenny here used to visit us downtown every Friday night," said Donnelly, nudging the tramp with the toe of his boot. "Didn't you, Lenny?"

"I sure did. Couldn't keep myself away."

"We'd find him raiding the dumpsters at Kentucky Fried Chicken and Denny's. Loved that garbage."

Lenny continued grinning. He didn't mind being the center of attention so long as nobody was arresting him.

"So why'd you leave us, Lenny?" asked Donnelly. "Go all that way up to Rivertown just to get yourself dumped in the slam?"

"I don't know, Sheriff. Guess I was just born to be adventurous, what do you say?"

"Where's your friend, Lenny?" asked Howser, stepping in beside Donnelly and looking down at the tramp. He could make out the lettering on Lenny's worn T-shirt now that he was closer. It read in shadowed Gothic print, red and black: *Take a Walk on the Wild Side.* The last two words were carved into the forehead of a death's-head skull.

"We talking 'bout Robinson?" asked the tramp.

"The tall skinny one you shared the cell with up in our town."

"That's Robinson, all right."

"Where is he?"

"You guys bustin' him?"

"Just want to talk," said Howser.

"Where is he?" yelled Donnelly.

Lenny glanced around. Twenty feet away a heavy black man sat on a gray packing crate reading a comic book. Lenny looked over at him, thought a moment, then glanced back at Donnelly and Howser, and called out, "Hey, chocolate bar, you see where Robinson got off to?"

Not even bothering to lift his eyes from the comic book, the black tramp said, "Fuck off, Lenny," and shifted his attention back to Batman and Robin cruising the sordid underworld of Gotham City.

Lenny stared at him, as though he'd change his mind any second, then gave up, shrugged, and said to the uniforms towering over him, "Guess he don't know."

Donnelly reached down and grabbed Lenny at the collar, wrapping the tramp's T-shirt into a ball at the neck with his fist and raising him up from the warehouse floor.

"How do you happen to be so popular, Lenny?"

The tramp choked once and spittle drooled out of the corner of his mouth. Donnelly relaxed his grip just enough for Lenny to answer.

"Guess I'm just a lucky guy, huh, Sheriff?"

"Yeah, real lucky. Where's your buddy?"

Lenny cringed as Donnelly maneuvered his boot heel onto the tramp's instep and pressed down hard. Clayton looked over at Howser, watching impassively with eyes wet and blank. Donnelly leaned harder on Lenny's foot until the tramp made a weak noise in his throat.

"Huh?" whispered Donnelly. "What was that?"

Lenny forced the words out before Curry's sheriff could squeeze him any harder. "I said he's out back, goddammit, taking a shit."

Donnelly backed off and released his grip, letting the tramp slump backward to the floor. Then he asked Howser, "You want Snider to go get him for you?"

"No, that's okay," said Howser, trying to avoid Donnelly's eyes. He felt his face flush. Donnelly's handling of the tramp embarrassed him and he felt like getting out of there. "We'll go find Mr. Robinson, have ourselves a little talk, then come back and finish up with this one."

"Suit yourself. Snider and I'll be out front if you need us. Just give a holler."

"Sure thing."

Howser and Clayton walked through the shadows across the cold warehouse floor to the rear exit, a metal door in the northwest corner of the building. Behind them, Clayton could hear Lenny moaning about his crushed larynx and a recent loss of personal dignity.

There was only one toilet serving as a latrine for the entire yard—an old plywood outhouse set under a leafy sprig tree in a flurry of dandelions half a dozen yards from the warehouse. Clayton and Howser smelled it before they saw it, the fierce stench carrying down either side of the building and rising in the heat. They could see the inevitable black flies racing in concentric circles about the outhouse, buzzing furiously round and round as though speed

320

itself would extend by whole minutes their brief lives. On the outhouse door someone had scrawled in charcoal *The shit stops here!* They waited a minute or so for the door to open. When it did, a tall, lanky, balding figure emerged, squinting uncomfortably through a pair of wire-rimmed glasses into the light. As his eyes focused he saw Howser's uniform and immediately turned back to the toilet.

"Mr. Robinson!"

The tramp stopped. Howser strode quickly up and dropped a hand on the tramp's shoulder. The tramp swung around and Howser said, "I'd like to talk to you."

A horsefly buzzed in the tramp's hair and he brushed at it with the back of his hand. A smaller one swung onto his cheek. He swatted at it, driving it off for the moment.

"Okay."

"Know what we're here for?" asked Howser.

More flies buzzed about them in the blue air.

The tramp said, "You going to tell me if I guess wrong?"

Howser looked around. There were more shade trees farther down the tracks beyond the warehouse.

"Let's go somewhere else. It stinks here."

They headed away from the flies and the outhouse, north from the big warehouse and the sweating tramps, down under an immense willow throwing green shade on a broad patch of earth. The tramp headed for the base of the tree and sat down, stretching out his long legs. Clayton sat down, too, nearby. Howser remained on his feet, shuffling in the dirt.

The tramp spoke first. "You want to know about the Kid."

"What kid?" asked Howser.

"He got away the night you killed Freddy."

"What're you talking about?"

The tramp looked over at Clayton, who was sitting quietly sketching stick figures in the dust with his fingers. "You a cop, too?"

Clayton shook his head.

"Just along for the ride, huh? That's nice. It's a good day for a drive. Man, if I had a car I'd probably . . ." His voice trailed off. A breeze rippled through the willow up above, tittering in the slender leaves. The breeze died away and the heat rose again from the ground. The day was getting on, reeling in the midafternoon shadows, slowing down.

Howser said, "Tell me about this kid."

The tramp coughed and a thin layer of dust shook free from his clothes. He straightened his glasses and blinked. "He's not with us anymore."

"Where is he?"

"Don't you know?"

"I will when you tell me," said Howser.

"I'm not sure."

"When did you see him last?"

The tramp met Howser's eyes. "Same as you."

Howser stared back up the tracks to the warehouse, tilting in the sunlight. Donnelly and Snider were camped out in the middle of the yard. They were the only ones standing. The tramps were all down now, massacred by the heat. Keeping his eyes fixed on the empty china-blue sky to the south, Howser tried again. "Tell me about him."

"It's kind of an involved story."

"I'm listening."

The tramp stirred beneath the tree. He coughed again and wiped his mouth with his shirtsleeve. When he spoke this time, it was in a flat, empty tone.

"We were at a junction town outside of Albuquerque, end of the summer: me, Lenny, Freddy, Woodpecker, Mister Clean, Dudley, and a lady tramp we called Birdtits. Everyone else had already packed up and gone west, chasing better weather, but we wanted to hang on a while longer, leastwise until the water dried up or we got run off. Well, one night we were all sleeping in the tent when Lenny woke us up saying he heard somebody outside collecting up the things we'd left by the fire after supper. We all sat there listening. Lenny was right. Sounded like pots banging together. Our pots. We would've gone out right then except, of course, we were scared shitless. After the noise stopped and we were sure whoever it was had gone, we went out and found that somebody had indeed snuck in and stolen everything we'd been dumb enough to leave out: jugs, cups, pans, steamers. Not to take with him, though. Just to carry down the tracks a quarter mile or so into the desert and scatter there on both sides of the tracks. It took us almost an hour to get everything picked up. Then when we came back, we found this kid parked in the middle of our tent, holding Freddy by the neck and warning us out. Lenny wanted to go find some two-by-fours and crack the kid's skull open, but the rest of us voted to leave him alone because the kid sitting in that tent with his hands around Freddy was, I swear to God, the biggest human being I'd ever seen in my whole life. At least a foot taller than me, and wider than Lenny and Mr. Clean put together. Big old head, too. Like a pumpkin. Poor old Freddy looked like a ventriloquist's dummy sitting there beside him. I could see right away the kid wasn't going anywhere he didn't want to go. Birdtits tried talking him out but that didn't do any good. The kid was either deaf or stubborn, maybe both, and Birdtits wasn't sexy enough anymore to make him forget about Freddy and the tent.

"It looked for a while like we were going to have to sleep out in the dirt again which really pissed us off considering all the work we'd done putting that tent up. Then the strangest thing happened: just as Lenny started in yelling for the fiftieth time, old Freddy poked the kid in the ribs and said right out loud, 'Son, let's get out of here. We know when we're not wanted.' And just like that the kid slipped his fingers under Freddy's belt and picked him up like an old suitcase and carted him right out of there and off down the tracks and gone, Freddy waving at us and laughing as he disappeared. We just stood there dumbfounded. Didn't know what to do. We couldn't call the cops. They'd have come in and kicked us all out into the desert. And nobody wanted to go chasing after that kid. Not in the middle of the night. There was nothing we *could* do except go back to bed and look for Freddy in the morning.

"Well, we never did find him. After looking up and down the tracks for a day and a half we decided poor old Freddy was a goner, which was sad because we'd all liked him. Freddy was a good guy. He taught Lenny and me everything we know about trampin'. He was our friend. But we went on without him for a month, sharing the tent with six instead of seven and that worked out to more

323

room for everyone—though none of us ever said we were glad Freddy had disappeared. Then it started getting colder at night and pretty soon we were packing up and getting ready to move on to warmer places. A couple hours before sunrise, on the morning we'd decided to catch the freight going west, we walked down the line, the six of us in the cold, planning on sneaking into one of the empties before the brakemen could finish their coffee. When we got there, we saw two characters sitting on the tracks next to a pig-gyback, their faces covered up to the wind. It was so dark out there at first we couldn't tell who it was, but when we walked a little closer we heard one of them laughing and that gave it away. It was old Freddy and the kid, sitting there in the cold waiting for us to show up. We said, 'Freddy, where the hell you been?' All he did was give us this big grin and start laughing. Wouldn't tell us anything about the kid carrying him off that night or what he'd been up to since nor even how he knew we'd be leaving when we did. Only thing he had to say after disappearing from us a month was, 'Me and the kid here, we're goin' with ya!' "

The tramp pulled his knees up and grinned. He had his audience where he wanted them. Howser hadn't looked away in minutes and Clayton had stopped drawing stick figures in the dirt.

"After that, Freddy and the kid traveled together. They shared a car all the time, usually by themselves. Freddy told us that the kid talked a lot, told him things, but we didn't hear any of it ourselves. The kid never said a word to the rest of us. Most of the time we avoided him anyhow, and Freddy told us the kid said we smelled bad. We didn't even know if he had a name since Freddy was the only one really talking to him and all he ever called him was 'the Kid.' I asked Freddy once where the Kid came from, and he just shrugged and said, 'Somewhere down the line, son. Just like you and me.' "

The tramp laid back against the tree trunk. He smiled and adjusted the fit of his glasses. Clayton's attention had shifted from the tramp back to the two chicken hawks, joined now by a third, sailing the circular air currents in the blue sky a hundred yards away above the warehouse and the yard.

"Well, Freddy and the Kid came with us after the junction town, west into Arizona and California, then back up around to Utah and Nevada and into the Northwest. By now it's maybe January or February and we're in a jungle outside of Portland, Oregon, and we're sharing a boxcar together, the eight of us, and passing around a bottle of Jack Daniel's to warm ourselves up when Mr. Clean says, 'Hey, boy, come here and have a drink.' At first the Kid just shakes his head. I told you, he never did a thing with anybody except old Freddy. But then Freddy tells him it's okay and he surprises us by coming over and letting Clean and Lenny pour liquor down his throat until he can't stand up anymore. It was pretty funny watching him reeling around stomping on people and making noises through his nose. Finally though, Lenny and Freddy and me have to carry him back to his corner where Freddy covers him up and puts him to bed. By then the rest of us were pretty much out of it, too—Clean'd stopped telling war stories and Birdtits'd quit flirting with me—and we all went to bed, except the Woodpecker, who wasn't done drinking yet.

"I never knew exactly what happened after that because I was asleep, but Lenny says Woodpecker set himself on fire lighting up a Lucky Strike and before anyone knew it the whole car was going up in smoke and flames, and we're all grabbing our packs and escaping while we still could. By the time we were all cleared out, and Woodpecker'd been rolled in the dirt by Lenny and Dudley, there was nothing left of the boxcar but frame and fire. And we're just standing there watching her burn, when we heard this awful sound starting up from inside where the fire was the hottest. It sounded something like an animal crying out. We looked around to see who didn't make it out with the rest of us and old Freddy went crazy, screaming that it was the Kid in there, and that we had to go in after him.

"Well, fuck that. Those flames were roaring now and the heat was so bad all of us including Freddy were having to back up and he was yelling for the Kid to come out.

325

And the crying just got louder and louder; worst thing you ever heard, Birdtits finally plugged her ears so she wouldn't have to listen anymore. And then it stopped, just like that. And, God, we all thought it was over; the Kid was dead. When all of a sudden the side of the car, about three feet from the door, exploded, just blew apart like a bomb going off and the Kid sailing out after it. He'd smashed a hole right through the damn car to get out of there. It was unbelievable. And we still thought he was dead because he was nothing but black all over and his clothes were all burned away and smoke was rising from his skin. But amazingly enough, the Kid was alive, though hurt real bad, burned over his whole body; his skin was just runny and wet. And he would've died for sure except for Freddy and Birdtits covering him up and ladling water onto his face and talking to him until the cops and the firetrucks finally showed up.

"Freddy went with him in the ambulance while the cops were telling us to pack up and move on, which we did, and it was almost four months before we saw them again. That was late in the spring, I think maybe around the middle of May, and they caught up to us on the Burlington, railriding piggybacks north into the Plains. They came through the rear of our camp just after twilight, I can still see it, with that poor Kid walking in behind Freddy wearing a big old grocery sack on his head that Freddy made him take off to show us what the fire had done. And it was awful. Made us sick to our stomachs.

"The fire'd burned him all away. There wasn't hardly anything left that still looked human. He had no nose or mouth or ears or anything. Just holes in the middle of his face, dark ones with no color, either. Freddy said he couldn't talk at all anymore, just sort of wave at you and stare. Creepy, you know what I mean? Only Freddy could stand to be with him any longer than a couple of minutes at a time. It was too much for anyone else. We'd have never let the Kid hang around at all if it wasn't for Freddy. Sometimes I'd see him walking alone out by the tracks at night and wonder how the hell he could've survived that fire. But he's strong. Real strong. One time, on a bet, I saw Freddy get him to shake a boxcar almost loose from the tracks. Couldn't tip it over, of course, but he made it move a little. I've never seen anything like him in my whole life, Chief, and I've been around some, too."

Howser looked over at Clayton whose eyes were still fixed on the sky to the south. The air was quiet now except for an indistinct singsong chittering of small birds somewhere. The quiet lingered while Howser worked a question over in his mind. The air moved just enough to raise the dust and let it settle again. Howser's throat had dried out, so when he finally spoke it was in a hoarse whisper.

"You're telling me this Kid is the tramp who broke through the wire that night up in Rivertown? The one who got away into the woods?"

"Yup."

"And his pal Freddy's—"

"The guy you people killed. That's right."

"And you haven't seen this Kid since Rivertown?"

"Nope."

"Has anyone else?"

"Not that I know of. Haven't heard a word about him. We'd all know if he was around somewhere. And he's not."

"So, you think he's still in Rivertown?"

"Unless he's humping it cross-country on foot. But I don't know where he'd go. We're the only people he knows and we had to leave your town without him."

Clayton got to his feet and brushed the dust off the rear of his pants. He yawned and stretched his arms. He felt like taking a nap, which was why he stood up, so he wouldn't fall asleep right there under the tree. He'd wait until they were back in the cruiser, then he'd be out like a light.

The tramp said, "You having some kind of trouble up there, Chief?"

"Trouble?"

"You got rid of all us losers, right? You made Rivertown safe for affluence. Must be something pretty bad going on up there to bring you down here."

Howser walked out into the sunlight, putting his back

to both Clayton and the tramp. Donnelly and Snider had retreated to the shade beyond the edge of the warehouse, but the naked tramp was up again doing his ragged cartwheels in the dust. His skin was tanned a dirty brown. Maybe it was all dirt and no tan. The heat didn't seem to slow him up at all. He rotated inexhaustibly across a narrow patch of ground, pausing only to adjust his line, then over and over again, through the widening sunshadow.

"Six people are dead," said Howser. He could hear his own voice echo in the air. "Three teenage boys, an old woman, one of my officers, and the girl you people were accused of attacking."

"Nobody from the jungle touched that girl."

"That's what you said up in Rivertown."

"And I'm saying it again, right now."

"Another boy's been missing since the Fourth."

"Those kids had no right saying what they said about us. They lied and got a friend of ours killed."

"The officer who died was a friend of mine."

"Nobody from the jungle ever touched that girl."

Howser turned back toward the willow. He knew what he wanted to ask now. Something was finally coming together.

"What about the Kid?"

"What about him?" said the tramp, shouting now. "He wasn't interested in girls. Ask Birdtits about that."

"I'm not asking whether he liked girls or not."

"He never left Freddy's tent."

"The tent's gone now."

"What the hell do you want from me?" yelled the tramp.

"The truth," said Howser. "About the Kid."

The tramp shook his head and scowled. "You're trying to get me to give you something on the Kid that you'd never find out on your own, something that's got nothing to do with your people up in Rivertown."

"Is he dangerous?" asked Howser.

"He and Freddy took care of each other, man, when nobody else was volunteering."

"Tell me about the Kid."

The tramp got up and jammed his hands into his pockets

and kicked the dirt at the base of the willow. "Freddy was the oldest tramp I ever knew. The oldest any of us knew still railriding. He told us he'd been everywhere. He told us a lot of things. He was always flapping his mouth. He said he owned the railroad, the whole thing: UP, Santa Fe, ARCO, Amtrak, Burlington, N&W, Southern Pacific, whatever you want, every line and track coast to coast, all of it. Said it was a gift from his great-grandaddy but nobody knew it because the will got lost somewhere back in Pennsylvania. He told this story to everyone he ran into, even brakemen and cops who weren't too fond of hearing tramps mouthing off in the first place. Freddy used to get the crap beaten out of him regularly for telling people to keep away from his railroad. We were sure he was going to get himself killed one day. But then he met the Kid and things changed. The Kid loved Freddy. And why not? The old guy had sat with him for three months in that burn unit holding his hand and keeping him alive. He protected the Kid. And after they got back on the rails, the Kid protected him."

The tramp looked straight at Howser and said, "He killed a brakeman in Yuma who tried dragging Freddy off a moving piggyback. He did a couple of bulls in Elko for the same thing and a third in Spokane. Broke their necks. Last March he crushed two Mormon kids' skulls in Salt Lake for beating on Freddy in back of a Burger King. A month later he did a fat rent-a-cop in a big yard outside of Santa Fe. We tried to talk Freddy into dumping the Kid but he wouldn't do it. He felt the same way about the Kid as the Kid did about him. He called every killing an accident, as though the Kid was just clumsy and hadn't meant to snap those people's necks like that. Freddy didn't want to hear anything else. He kept trying to tell us nothing was going to happen, as if nobody paid any attention to people getting killed anymore. But that night when all those guys drove into the jungle up in your town, even Freddy thought they'd come for the Kid. We could hear him inside his tent, telling the Kid to get out of there and go hide somewhere in the woods. That's why the Kid ran out like he did."

"Do you think he saw Freddy get shot?"

"I don't know."

Howser wondered now if maybe Jamie had told the truth after all about the monster in Stuart's Mill. If so, what were they going to do?

The tramp, as if reading Howser's mind, said, "I suppose you're going to go out and shoot him now, huh?"

Howser stared at him half a second, then rubbed his eyes and turned to Clayton and said, "It's getting late. Why don't you go and tell Donnelly he can take off. Tell him we're leaving in a few minutes ourselves. We won't need to talk with the other guy. Tell Donnelly we've heard enough. I'll meet you back at the car."

Clayton nodded and walked over to the tramp. He stuck his hand out and the tramp shook it and Clayton said good-by and headed off across the yard in the direction of the warehouse. Howser watched him go, then turned his attention back to the tramp standing under the willow.

"Nobody's going to shoot anybody," said Howser. "I'm sorry about what happened to the old man. But it's not going to go down that way with the Kid."

The tramp didn't say a word. He had both his hands wrapped around one of the willow branches and was leaning his weight backward beneath it.

"Look, I got to take off. If there's anything else you remember about the Kid that you haven't told me, anything at all," said Howser, "get in touch with Donnelly."

The tramp sighed and looked away to the warehouse, where a late sun was reddening the dark walls. "I told you, only Freddy ever talked to him. He was the only one who knew him."

Howser nodded. "Yeah, that's what you said. Okay. Well, thanks."

He gave the tramp half a wave and started off toward the warehouse and Curry Station, following Clayton's path along the tracks. It was going to be dark in Rivertown by the time he got home.

The tramp closed his eyes to the daylight and let his legs go limp so that he hung at an angle from the branch like a drunk or a corpse pushed sideways in the air. He listened to Howser's footsteps moving away in the dirt. Just before

330

Howser walked beyond earshot, the tramp called out, "Chief!"

As Howser stopped and looked back, the tramp shouted, "The only thing Freddy told us about the Kid, the only thing he ever said about him that I remember, was that he liked trains!"

22

The evening flowers bloomed in the summer dark at the Walcott where Jane Crockett sat in the porch swing with her back to the trellis listening to the grass crickets chirping in the heat. The front doors were open to a draft in the night air and light from the desk lamp in the entry hall poured out over the steps. Ellen Kelleher was walking inside, her shoes echoing on the hardwood floor. Jane smiled at her as she came out onto the porch carrying two glasses of iced tea on an aluminum tray. Ellen set the tray down on the table and pulled up a chair. She wiped the perspiration from her brow and took one of the glasses and had a drink. Jane stirred the ice in her own glass with her finger then took a drink, too. She sighed and leaned back in the swing.

"That's so good."

Ellen smiled and drank again, longer this time. The air shifted in the arbor. In the next yard, a lawn sprinkler, tipped slightly askew, was showering the ivy on the fence-line, causing black rivulets of steaming water to run out onto the sidewalk and into the gutter.

"It must be unbearable inside," said Jane, lifting the cold glass to her cheek, rubbing the condensation onto her skin. She had already stripped down to a blue halter top and a pair of cutoffs and still felt too warm.

"My bedroom's a furnace," said Ellen, blinking perspiration from her eyes. The ice chinked in her glass. Moths fluttered and fell in the lamplight at the open door. They made a faint tittering sound under the eaves of the porch, barely audible above the crickets in the arbor.

Jane drank again and set the glass back on the table. She looked at Ellen and wondered how well she really was. Jack Clayton had sat up with her the night Alfie's body was found and hadn't left until almost sunset the following day. It had taken that long for Ellen to fall asleep. Even afterward, she'd remained in her room another day and a half, desolate and mute, speaking only when addressed and limiting that to the tenants at the Walcott. This was the first Jane had really seen of her since Alfie's death. She seemed to Jane to be as well as anyone could expect so soon after suffering something that horrible. Her eyes were still clear. That was what Jane had noticed in particular. Ellen's eyes were still clear and bright. It had obviously been many hours since they'd seen tears and that was a good sign.

"I think this is the nicest place in the evening," said Jane, nudging the swing into motion with her foot. "So peaceful. I could sit here all night long, I think. The flowers smell so nice."

"It's been impossible trying to keep everything alive in this heat," said Ellen. "Even Mrs. Stamos's yellow roses have been wilting on me. I've been out every night spraying them by hand."

Jane glanced at the manicured flowerbeds along the latticed borders of the arbor and the bougainvillea blooming red under the jasmine and honeysuckle on the white trellis. She shook her head in amazement. "I don't know how you do it."

"Well, it would be nice if the weather cooled down some," said Ellen, reaching for her glass. She picked it up and took a long sip. Upstairs, in the south wing over the arbor, a light came on at the near window. There was a cough and a wordless muttering coming from above. Somebody was shuffling about and fumbling at the window-frame. Another minute passed and the screen slammed shut. The light went out again. Jane drank down to half a glass then drew out an ice cube with her fingers and rubbed it over her neck and upper chest until it melted away.

"Jack gave us his notice last night," said Ellen, looking down at her fingers, entwined on the tabletop.

"I know," replied Jane. "He told me."

A dog began barking somewhere down at the far end of the street. Another dog joined the first and the noise they made together echoed throughout the trees in the dark.

"I'm sorry he's leaving," said Ellen. "He's nice. I like him."

Jane patted her cheeks with palms wet from the melted ice. "So do I."

The barking stopped and the echo faded through the street. Ellen smiled and looked across at Jane. She said, wryly, "Maybe you and the chief'll get back together again, huh? He still doesn't have anybody, you know."

Jane held a tight smile on her lips, unsure of what to say. Ellen's suggestion reminded her of slumber parties she went to when she was a little girl: comic books and training bras and Beatle albums strewn over canvas sleeping bags, giggling debates on the meaning and risks of love—*You feel it in your stomach first of all, right here!*— and sex—*God, if a boy kissed me there I don't know what I'd do!*—and boys—*Ronnie's a boy and he's a friend, but he's not my boyfriend*—the first few struggles with innocent hearts secretly broken. Somehow everyone she'd known then had grown out of that necessary silliness and into a considered appreciation for what it was they were supposed to make of themselves as they grew out of colored pajamas and Archie Andrews, yet nobody she'd met since seemed to understand anything more about the topics of their debates, and the subtleties of that confusion, than they had themselves through all those long and lovely nights. *Carroll's a boy and he's a friend, and I love him dearly, Ellen, but he's not my boyfriend.*

"We're just friends," said Jane. "That seems to work out better for both of us. Sometimes you need someone as a friend more than you need them as a lover. I think that's probably the case with Carroll and me."

"Does that mean it's mutual?"

"No," said Jane, thinking about Howser tossing beside her the other night in a bed barely large enough to accommodate two children. "Just necessary."

"I suppose I was lucky to find Alfie," said Ellen. She tightened her fingers and looked at Jane, who smiled back.

"It was your turn to be lucky."

"I waited so long to find someone like him," whispered Ellen, leaning slowly forward in her chair. Her eyes glistened in the artificial light. "And then, one day, there he was."

Jane nodded. Behind her the incessant buzzing of the arbor crickets seemed somehow louder than it had earlier.

"Remember last spring when Halley's comet came around?" asked Ellen.

"How could I forget? Carroll and I got up at three in the morning to drive out to Swan's ranch and see it from the roof of the old windmill. I was a wreck the next day."

"My grandmother saw it in 1910 when she was seven years old. And when I was a little girl, she made me promise that if I was still on earth when it visited us again I'd be sure and see it, too. So when it finally came back, and Mrs. Vincent at the *Courier* told me which night it would be the brightest, Alfie and I went out into the valley after dark to wait for it. We stayed up all night, eating gingerbread cookies and strolling around in the fields. We took our shoes off and went barefoot and played tag and lay on our backs with our toes pointing up to the stars. The grass felt wonderful. And when we decided it was the right time, we got up and started looking for the comet. Alfie thought it was lower in the sky than it turned out to be and in another direction, but we finally saw it down in the southeast straight over Wheeler's field. It was just a fuzzy little thing with the plain eye, you know, but seeing it through my father's old army binoculars made it look especially beautiful and big, streaking there in the sky. Just like it had for my grandmother.

"Alfie kept saying, 'That's Halley's comet, Ellie! That's

Halley's comet!' and 'Ellie, look at the tail, look at the tail!' He was just like a little kid, jumping up and down. It was so funny. Then he put down the binoculars and kissed me and told me how much he loved me. He said that I was as rare a sight as Halley's comet because a girl like me only came around once in a lifetime."

She noticed the grin forming on Jane's lips and she blushed. "I know it was corny," said Ellen. "But I still cried."

Jane smiled and shook her head. "Love only seems corny when you're not lucky enough to be involved."

"You know, every afternoon since Alfie and I began dating, between the time I finished with the laundry and before I had to get out into the garden, I used to bake cookies for him to take out on patrol at night. I have a cookie cutter he liked that my mother gave me. It's shaped like a star. He liked it because it looked like the badge he wore. I must've baked ten thousand gingerbread and peanut butter and chocolate chip badges for him."

Ellen lowered her eyes. "You know what I've been doing since he got killed? Baking gingerbread badges, that's what. Dozens of them. Every afternoon at the same time. I don't know what else to do." She looked up at Jane and whispered, "What's wrong with me?"

"My God, Ellen—"

The phone rang inside the lobby. Ellen put her glass down on the table and looked away. The phone rang again. She said, "I better get it," and got up and walked back across the porch into the hotel. Jane leaned back in the swing. A honey fragrance rising gently behind her on a faint breeze drifted by the open porch and off into the dark. Jane pushed the swing into motion with her foot. She watched a skinny white cat make a hurried crossing of the fence above the rose beds, giving chase to something in the green shadows beyond. A few moments later, Ellen came back out onto the porch.

"It's for you, Jane."

"For me?" she said, getting up. "That's funny."

"I think it's downtown. It sounded like one of your policemen."

Jane walked past Ellen to the front desk and ducked

inside the office and picked up the receiver. Ellen waited just outside the front door, looking down the drive into the empty street.

"Hello?"

"Jane?"

"Yeah."

"It's Craig, Jane. Chief back yet?"

"No, not that I know of. He said he'd call in as soon as he could. Why?"

"Corey told me to tell you to get down here as soon as possible."

"What's going on?"

"I'm not supposed to say over the phone."

"Why not?"

"He told me not to."

"Well . . . oh, all right, I'll be down in a few minutes."

"Thanks."

Jane hung up and walked back out onto the porch where Ellen sat on the railing staring out into the night. "Something's happening downtown. I guess I have to go."

Ellen smiled and whispered, almost disinterestedly, "That's okay, I was getting a little drowsy anyhow."

"Are you going to be all right? I hate leaving like this."

"I'm fine. Really."

"You're sure?"

"Yes."

"Okay. But please, if you need anything call me, all right? Carroll and Jack ought to be back pretty soon now."

"Really, I'm fine. I'll probably just go to bed. Thanks for coming over. I appreciate it."

Jane looked at Ellen, trying to gauge how closely her expression matched her words. She noticed that her eyes had already lost some of the clarity they'd had only a quarter of an hour earlier.

"I'll stop by tomorrow, okay?"

"That'd be nice," said Ellen, beginning a slow retreat toward the front door. "Thank you."

"All right, well, bye then."

"Bye-bye."

Jane wandered to the bottom of the steps while fumbling in her purse for her car keys. By the time she found them

337

and turned around to wave good-bye, Ellen had already gone.

Forty-five minutes south of Rivertown, Howser swung the unit into the parking lot of a roadside diner to put a call in to the station. He'd told both Jane and Corey that he planned to be back by eight. Since it was already half past, he decided he'd better let them know he was going to be late. While Howser went to the pay phones, Clayton found a waitress and bought a large slice of cherry pie and took it with him to a booth by the window. The neon flickering from the large sign outside by the highway filled the interior of the diner with a pale green light reflecting smooth as oil on the polished Formica tabletops. The electric sign could be seen for miles, but traffic was sparse on the road and the diner was almost empty. Clayton ate his pie slowly with a spoon while waiting for Howser to get off the phone.

Howser dialed the station.

"Police department."

"Jane? It's me."

"Chief, where are you? You were supposed to be back here half an hour ago. Is anything wrong?"

"No, we're fine," said Howser. "We just ended up staying longer in Curry than we expected. What're you doing there? I thought you got off at five."

"I'll let Corey explain that. Hold on, he's right here."

There was a pause and Howser leaned out from the phone stall, looking for Clayton. He located him sitting at a window booth in the middle of the diner. Clayton had slept most of the way up the highway from Curry and still looked drowsy. Howser grinned to himself. *Clayton'd make a lousy cop. He'd never stay awake long enough to catch any crooks. He'd believed the tramp's story, though, about the Kid. Said so the moment they got in the car back at the depot. Said every tramp's got a story to tell and this one sounded crazier than any he'd ever heard but even so he believed it. He didn't know why, but he did.*

Corey came on the line.

"Chief?"

"Yeah, Corey, what's up?"

338

"Uh, Chief. We got someone down here I think you are going to want to talk to."

"Oh, yeah? Who's that?"

"Annie Connor. She just came in about an hour ago."

"No kidding? Did she say anything?"

"Just that she was glad to see us. Wouldn't say why."

"Don't let her walk, all right? I'm still about thirty minutes away."

"She'll be here. She said she came to talk. Says there's something she needs to tell you."

"All right. Well, put her in my office then and keep her comfortable until I get back."

"Will do."

Howser hung up and walked over to the booth where Clayton was sitting and slid in across from him.

"We have to go."

Clayton looked up at him, balancing a bite of pie on his spoon.

"Do I have time to finish this? It cost me two dollars."

"How come you didn't buy me any?"

"You said you were in a hurry."

"I am. We got to get back to town."

"What happened on the phone? Did you line yourself up a date?" Clayton glanced at the clock on the wall over the grill. "You still got time."

"Don't be a wise guy."

Clayton slipped the pie into his mouth and chewed it slowly. Outside on the highway a tanker truck hauling gasoline for Standard Oil rolled by heading south. The windows in the diner rattled in their frames as it passed. Clayton swallowed the pie and wiped his mouth with a paper napkin. Seeing Howser fidget in the booth, Clayton put the napkin down and said, "So, what did you hear on the phone that put this rocket up your ass?"

Howser looked out at the highway. A thin dust haze hung over the road in the wake of the tanker.

"A girl we've been looking for just wandered into the courthouse an hour ago."

"Her name wouldn't happen to be Annie, would it?"

Howser frowned. "How did you know?"

"When I was out at the river the day Alfie got killed, I

overheard two of your juvenile delinquents talking about a girl by that name. It sounded like they were holding her somewhere or something. I don't know."

"And you didn't tell anybody?"

"It slipped my mind when I heard about Alfie. Then, after sitting up with Ellen for two days, I guess I forgot completely about it. Sorry."

Howser got up and motioned Clayton out of the booth. "Come on, we got to hit the road."

"You don't want to hear about the girl?"

"You can tell me in the car."

"What about my pie?" asked Clayton, sliding out of the seat.

Howser reached down, lifted the last bite of pie off Clayton's plate and stuffed it in his own mouth. Then he pointed Clayton toward the door, dropped some change on the table, and followed him back out toward the car.

When they reached Rivertown, Howser dropped Clayton off at the Walcott and drove downtown to the courthouse. He parked his unit next to Corey's and took the back stairs up to the office. With the day-shift multitudes absent from the building, the place felt hollow as a tomb, particularly in the dark. It wasn't until he climbed to the fourth floor that Howser even heard voices above the echoing of his own footsteps on the cold cement. He walked down the corridor to his office and opened the door. Inside, he found Corey and Beef waiting with a blond teenage girl, frazzle-haired and freckled, seated in the swivel chair with her feet up on the big desk. She was wearing a sleeveless blue-striped blouse and a sun-faded pair of blue jeans. She was barefoot and her hair was filthy. She had a bruise above her left eye and her chin looked swollen.

Howser hung his hat on the halltree, looked at her and nodded, "Evening, Annie."

The girl stared at him. He walked to the cabinet and opened the top drawer and drew out a file. He flipped quickly through it then shut the drawer and handed the file to Corey. He turned back to the girl.

340

"By the way," said Howser. "I'd appreciate it if you'd take your feet off the desk."

She slid her feet to the floor.

"Thanks."

Howser grabbed a chair and pushed it up to the desk. "Here," he said. "Try this one."

The girl hesitated. Howser crooked his finger at her then pointed it to the chair.

"Come on. Have a seat."

The girl spun Howser's chair to the side and got up and edged past him to the other chair and sat down again. Then Howser took his place behind the desk and opened a side drawer and took out a pad of paper and an old blue pencil. Beef sat down on the bench along the far wall and Corey pulled up a chair beside the cabinet.

"Did either of you guys bring a tape recorder?" asked Howser, glancing at his two officers. They looked at each other and both shook their heads. Howser put the pencil down. "I didn't think so. Well, the last one I had wandered off. Maybe we can get a steno up here, what do you think?"

"We can ask Jane," said Corey, looking a little embarrassed.

"Let's do that."

Howser buzzed Jane's line and a moment later she came on.

"What do you need?"

"Can you get us a steno, Jane?"

"Didn't Corey bring the tape recorder up from the front desk?"

Howser looked at Corey for an answer to Jane's question. Corey shook his head and said, "I haven't seen it in weeks."

"Did you hear that, Jane?"

"No, what did he say?"

"He said we don't have one down there anymore."

"Is he sure about that?"

"Jane?"

Howser was feeling more impatient by the second. Six hours on the road had worn him down.

"Yes, Chief?"

"Can you get us a steno?"

"I don't think so," said Jane. "It's kind of late for that. Lorraine left at four. She's probably in bed by now. I can't believe we don't have a tape recorder around here anywhere."

Howser glanced at the girl again and noticed that her knuckles were bruised and raw. Where'd she been all this time?

"Well, look . . ."

"Hold on a minute," said Jane. "Craig just came in. Let me ask him."

Corey got up and went to the blinds. He split them in the middle and looked down into the empty street. Howser drummed his fingers on the desktop. Jane came back on the intercom.

"Craig's got one. He's on his way up."

"Good."

"Need anything else?"

"Nope, that'll do it."

He switched off the intercom and picked the pencil back up and scribbled a note to himself: "Get a tape recorder."

"I have to go to the bathroom," said the girl, looking Howser straight in the eye.

"All right," he said. "Do you know where it is?"

"No."

"Down the hall to the left. Last door on the right. You can't miss it."

"Thanks."

She got up quickly and slipped out the door.

"Beef, go with her," said Howser. "Make sure she doesn't get lost."

Beef pushed himself up off the bench and followed the girl out into the hallway, closing the door behind him as he went. Howser leaned back in the chair and shook his head. "What a day."

"Did you find those tramps?" asked Corey.

"Yeah."

"Well?"

Howser rubbed his eyes. "Well what?"

"What'd they say?"

Straightening the reports in front of him into a nice neat pile, he said, "You guys might've been right, after all. It

342

looks like there was a tramp. Something like Jamie described out at Stuart's Mill. A big kid."

There was a knock at the door.

"Yeah, come in!"

Craig opened the door and poked his head inside. He held a small Sony tape recorder in his hand. "You were looking for this?"

Corey walked over and took it from him.

"Where'd you find it?" asked Corey. "I looked all over for this thing last week. Couldn't find it anywhere."

"It was in the bottom of Alfie's desk."

"Oh, okay," nodded Corey. He laughed, "Yeah, that's right. I remember now. He was making tapes off the AM in the unit."

"Thanks, Craig," said Howser.

Corey pushed the rewind button and ran the tape back twenty seconds or so. Then he pushed play and got part of a song Alfie had taken off the radio one night a few weeks earlier . . . *a poem with no rhyme, a dancer out of time, but now there's you. Nobody loves me like you do.* Annie Connor walked quietly back into the room, followed by Beef. She slipped her way past Craig and sat down in the chair, facing Howser. . . . *Funny how life just falls in place somehow. You touched my heart in places that I never even knew. Nobody loves me, nobody loves me, nobody loves me like*—Corey switched it off. He rewound to the beginning of the tape and set it to record. Craig left and closed the door. Howser looked at the girl, then at his officers, and motioned for Corey to start the tape. He scribbled her name on the pad of paper in front of him.

"All right, Annie. You're on. What do you want to tell us?"

She looked right at him and said, unhesitatingly, "Jamie killed Sarah. He raped her, him and his friends, then he beat her up and dumped her body in the river. He started everything, not those tramps. They didn't have nothing to do with it."

The tape recorder ran with a faint whirring on the desktop. Howser scribbled a dark line under Annie's name. Without looking up at her, he asked, simply, "How do you know this?"

" 'Cause Sarah told me, that's how. We've been friends since we were babies. She's practically a sister. There's nothing I don't know about her. When her mom called mine and said Sarah was all beat up and raped by those tramps out at the railyard, I went to the hospital and asked her what happened. At first she wouldn't tell me. She was too scared. But the night she got out of the hospital, I snuck over to her house after her folks went to bed and woke her up and dragged her outside and made her tell me what happened. She wasn't even mad, not like I was. She still wanted to see him again, like it was her fault or something she got raped by his friends. She was in love with Jamie Danielson, but he didn't care about her at all. He just used her. Mr. Stud."

"Did she say who it was that actually raped her?"

"Yeah, those two geeks, Ernie and Howie. Both of them raped her because Jamie told them to. Then Jamie beat her up and when it looked like she was too messed up to pass it off as an accident, he blamed it on those old tramps. Well, they didn't have nothing to do with it. It was all Jamie. Sarah told me he said that if she loved him she had to prove it in front of his buddies, as in, do it with him right there in the dirt with everyone watching. She tried to leave, but he wouldn't let her go. Then, when she tried to run, he freaked out and told Howie and Ernie to go ahead and have a good time. He told them to screw her. And they did, too. They're such chickenshits, they'd do anything he told them to. And afterward Jamie told her that if she said it was anyone except the tramps who'd done that to her, he'd take her out some night and drown her in the river. That's why she was too scared to tell anyone the truth. A lot of good lying did, huh? He killed her anyway."

The tape spools squeaked as the recorder continued to run in the dark office. The girl's eyes were watering now and her face had reddened, too.

"I knew she went out there to see Jamie that night she got killed. I was at her house when she called him. I told her not to go out there. I knew he didn't love her. It was all just a joke, more of the same shit he pulled on her every time they went out. God, I hate him so much. He started all of this. It was his fault."

"Annie, why didn't you tell anyone about this earlier?"

"I couldn't. Sarah made me swear not to tell anyone and I was afraid that if I did, Jamie'd go ahead and kill her and it'd be all my fault."

"But you're telling us now. Why?"

"Because she's dead and they can't kill her twice."

"Annie."

Howser got up and walked around to the front of the desk. He shoved the tape recorder to one side and sat in its place, facing the girl.

"You're leaving something important out of this story, Annie."

"What's that?"

He looked over at his two officers, now obviously sharing Howser's thought.

"How can you be so sure it was Jamie who killed Sarah? That's *not* something she could've told you herself, am I right?"

She rolled her eyes. "Don't you guys listen? Who else could've done it? She went out to his house to tell him he'd dirted her for the last time. It was over and she was going to tell you guys who it really was that raped her. Get it? She was telling him to go fuck himself, so he killed her. He's an asshole. He deserves to piss his pants in the gas chamber."

The girl looked away. She had her hands on the sides of the chair now, digging her fingers in tightly against the wood.

Looking at the faint bruises on her hands and wrists, Howser asked, "Where've you been, Annie?"

She raised her eyes, surprised at the question she'd just been asked. "Huh?"

Howser thought about what he'd learned in the unit on the last leg into Rivertown, the part of the story provided by Clayton from what he'd overheard out on Green River that afternoon. Now he wanted Annie's part. He knew what she was going to say. He just wanted it on tape.

He asked, "Where'd they keep you, Annie?"

She was silent for a moment, as if uncertain whether to answer or not. Then she said, "In the orchard."

"Johnson house?" asked Howser.

She nodded.

"For how long?"

"One night, I guess. Not that long. I got away."

"Where'd they grab you?"

"Downtown. I was out walking Minnie while everyone was at the fairgrounds. Jamie drove his truck right onto the curb and jumped out and grabbed me and threw me in the truck and drove me out to the orchard."

"Was anyone else out there?"

"Roy and Jerry and Ernie Long. They were all waiting at the house."

"What about Howie Long?" asked Corey.

"I didn't see him."

"Why do you think they grabbed you?" asked Howser.

She shrugged. "I guess it's because Jamie was afraid that I knew he killed Sarah and he couldn't figure out what to do about it."

"Did you think he was going to kill you, too?"

"I don't know. I wasn't sure."

"But he told you he killed Sarah."

"He didn't have to, because I already knew he did it. And he knew that I knew he did."

Beef interrupted, asking, "What about the old woman? Did you see her there, too?"

The girl looked over at him. "Yeah, in the bathtub."

"She was in the bathtub when you first got to the house?" asked Howser.

"Uh-huh. See, Jamie Danielson thinks he's the smartest guy around. He thinks he's a fucking genius—which he's not. He tried to scare me," said the girl, straightening up. The hair fell away from her eyes. "He went out and killed some of his old man's chickens and drained the blood into a couple of paint cans and took it to the old lady's house and splashed it all over her kitchen. Then him and his friends brought me in there through the back door thinking I was going to freak out or faint or something and do anything they told me to do. It looked so stupid I laughed. Then, 'cause I didn't freak, Jamie got pissed off and grabbed my hair and dragged me up the stairs into the bathroom where the old woman's body was and told me they'd cut her throat that morning and that they'd do the same thing to me if I said anything to anyone about Sarah."

"And you believed him," said Beef.

She frowned at him and bit her lip. She shrugged again. "I don't know. I mean, I could tell the kitchen thing was a joke just like that big mess they made in her bedroom, but the old lady was cold and smelled pretty bad and they had me touch her to see that she was really dead, and Jamie even stuck Ernie's knife into her boob just to show me how they'd done it when she was alive. How was I supposed to know they'd made it all up? He's crazy enough to do it."

Howser went to the file cabinet and opened it and flipped quickly through the dividers for the autopsy report on Amy Johnson. He found it and drew it out. *Superficial knife wounds shallow and nonfatal.* He turned back to the girl. "So, you say it was Ernie Long's penknife that made those cuts in the old woman," said Howser. "Right?"

She nodded.

"You're sure?"

"Uh-huh."

Howser handed the report to Corey, then walked back behind the desk and sat down. He scribbled Ernie's name next to Annie's and made a note about the penknife. He wrote in Jamie's name and Amy Johnson and drew a circle around it. Then he asked, "What happened after that?"

"Jamie took out some rope and pushed me into the bedroom and tied me to the bed. He said he was going to come back and fuck me after dark. Then they all left."

"Did he come back?" asked Corey.

Before she could answer, Beef said, "See, Chief? I told you we should have busted those little fuckers two weeks ago. I knew they had something to do with this."

Howser leaned back onto his elbow and stared at the girl. He nodded for her to continue.

She blinked the sweat out of her eyes and said, "Only Ernie came back. I don't know where the others went. He wouldn't tell me. He just crawled onto the bed beside me and blew in my ear like a fucking idiot and told me I should kiss him, but no way was I going to do that. I told him to go jerk off somewhere." She grinned. "I guess that's just what he did because when he came back, all he wanted to do was talk about his stupid brother. I just fell asleep. I don't know when exactly. There wasn't any clock in there."

"Was it Ernie who told you that the old woman was already dead when they cut her?"

"Yeah. He was mad because Jamie wasn't helping him look for Howie. He told me he didn't care what happened anymore. He said he'd let me go if he could, except that if he did and Jamie came back, we'd both get killed."

"But Jamie never came back?" asked Howser.

"To screw me? No. Only Roy showed up the next morning, but he didn't come upstairs. I heard him in the backyard talking to Ernie. He sounded scared. They both did."

"Scared of what?"

"Scared of either getting caught by you guys or getting killed by the tramp they said wasted Calvin and Ray and Danny. They were both freaking out."

"All right, so there's an old woman dead in the upstairs bath and you're in the next room tied to the bed and Ernie Long's somewhere nearby. So, what happened?" asked Corey. "How'd you get away?"

"After Roy left, Ernie came back upstairs and I told him I had to pee and could I please be untied so I could go to the bathroom. I promised I wouldn't try to escape. He untied me and let me go to the bathroom down the hall. No way I could pee next to a dead person. Ernie tried to follow me into the bathroom—I think he wanted to jump my bones when I pulled my pants down. What a twerp. I just shut the door in his face. Then, when I came out again after peeing, it suddenly got real quiet. I went out into the hall and listened for Ernie. I thought he went outside, but when I got to the top of the steps the front door slammed and I heard Ernie come running through the downstairs, yelling his stupid head off. I didn't know what the hell was going on so I crawled into the little closet there by the stairs and pulled some sheets and towels down over me and just laid there. Then I couldn't really hear anything except what sounded like people running through the house and all these doors opening and closing and after that nothing at all for a long time. It felt like I was in that closet for a week. I thought I was going to suffocate."

"Annie, tell me something," said Howser, shifting in the chair again. He let the pencil tumble onto the desk and asked the question both of his officers obviously had on their minds as well. "Was Officer Cox in the house while you were there?"

The girl's face flushed. The question seemed to blank the expression she had worn half a moment earlier, but she did not appear surprised to hear it asked. Her eyes closed almost reflexively.

"I don't know. Maybe. I'm not sure."

Corey said, "You're not sure whether you knew Alfie was getting himself killed three feet from where you were hiding?"

"I didn't know he was there. I told you, all I heard were some noises like people walking around. I was too scared to see who it was."

The intercom buzzed. Howser raised a finger to the girl, then opened the line to Jane.

"Yeah, Jane."

"We just got another call in from the Longs. They say Ernie didn't come home last night and nobody's seen him today, either. What do you want to do?"

Howser looked down at his notepad. It was rapidly disappearing under a series of scribbles and names. He picked up his pencil and added one more.

"Send Craig out there to take a report."

"Okay."

"And don't put any more calls through until I get back to you, all right?"

"Yes, sir."

He shut the line off and made another note beneath Ernie's name, then turned back to the girl.

"Go ahead, Annie. Tell me what happened next."

She trained her eyes up at Corey who was hovering there over her shoulder.

"I told you I was in that closet for I don't know how long, and hiding under those sheets I could hardly breathe and it was so hot I was getting claustrophobic. I wanted to get out of there but I was afraid. And then I heard someone walking in the hall, going one way then the other, and coming back to the stairs again. And then, I don't know, it was like I freaked, and that's when I pushed the door open and ran. I just wanted to get away. I was so scared."

Her voice cracked and nothing else came out. She drew a shallow breath and whispered a response that was missed somehow by all three men.

"What was that?" asked Howser.

Then she said, "I didn't know it was him. I thought maybe it was Jamie. So when I heard the footsteps outside the closet, I just opened the door and pushed. I didn't know who it was until I saw him fall."

Howser felt the blood rushing into his face. Both of his officers looked stunned.

"*What?*" yelled Corey.

"It happened so fast I didn't have time to look. I didn't care who it was, I guess. I just wanted to get away."

"*You pushed Alfie over the banister?*"

"I swear it was an accident. I didn't know who it was until it was too late. God, I was sick when I saw him."

The girl's heart was pumping furiously and her legs trembled. Her face was puffed and swollen. The three men continued to stare at her, shock clearly drawn on their faces.

Howser said, "You just burst out of the closet and rammed Alfie over the railing?"

She nodded. "I heard him land on the floor below. I knew right away he was dead."

"What'd you do then?"

"I ran out of the house."

Corey shouted, "*Did you even bother checking to see if maybe he was still alive?*"

Annie squirmed in her seat, unsure of how much more she ought to say. She knew she was already in trouble and she didn't want to make it any worse by saying the wrong thing. "I don't know. Maybe I did. I don't remember. All I know is that I was scared shitless and I wanted to get out of there as fast as I could."

"And he didn't say anything to let you know he was there with you in the house?"

She shook her head.

"Where'd you go after that?" asked Howser.

"I'm not exactly sure. I just remember running outside into the orchard and getting as far away from there as I could. I just ran until it got dark and then I stayed out all night."

"And after the first night?" asked Howser. "Where'd you hide?"

"In the mill."

"Why the mill?" asked Beef.

"It was the only place I knew Jamie wouldn't look for me."

"Christ!"

"All right," said Howser. "That's enough." He grabbed the tape recorder and punched the stop button. He could see the girl was dead tired. They all were. Whatever else she had to say could wait until morning. She wasn't going anywhere and Howser knew he'd need a few hours anyway to go over the details in everything he'd heard from both her and the tramp down in Curry. He waved his officers toward the door and said to the girl, "Wait here. We'll be back in a few minutes."

Corey and Beef walked out into the hall. Howser followed, closing the office door behind him. A draft from an open window somewhere down on a lower floor cooled the dark air in the hallway. The two policemen leaned up against the walls facing each other like odd-size bookends on an empty shelf. Howser walked a little farther down toward the rest rooms, then stopped and stood there in the shadow of the office light. In a low voice, Corey said, "Jesus Christ! I don't believe it. How the hell could she've killed him?"

Howser tapped the toe of his shoe on the lower wall tile. "It makes sense. Consistent with how we found him. It also explains the old woman, and the way Jamie and his buddies have been acting all week."

"What're we going to do with her?" asked Beef, lighting up a Winston and blowing the smoke back in the draft toward the office.

"Well, there may be involuntary manslaughter here," replied Howser, "and even if there isn't, we can't let her go until we bring Jamie and his friends in. So, I suppose we'll just hold on to her and see what happens. In the meantime, we'll put a warrant out for the boys, and keep looking for the tramp." He looked at them. "Is that all right with you guys?"

"Sure," answered Corey. "Sounds good."

Beef nodded in agreement.

"Okay then," said Howser. "Take the girl downstairs and put her in a safe place. I don't want anyone knowing where she is just yet. One of you call Judge Hindley to get the warrants taken care of and we'll all meet up here at, say, eight-thirty."

Howser went back to the office. The girl was sucking on a long strand of hair and had her bare feet up on the desk again.

"Annie."

She rotated in the chair, letting her feet fall back to the floor. Howser walked to the desk and picked up the reports and the notepad he had left lying there. He tore off the top sheet, then put the notepad and the reports back into the top drawer and shut it.

Howser said to the girl, "You're going to stay downstairs tonight and we'll see you again after breakfast in the morning. We're not going to file any charges right now, although I think you'll be better off visiting us for a few days than you would be going home. It'll be safer here. We'll call your folks and let them know where you are."

The girl nodded. Howser folded up the sheet of notepaper and stuck it into his shirt pocket. Then, after ushering Annie out of the office to where Corey and Beef stood waiting in the doorway, he switched off the desk lamp. Searching for the office key in his pants pocket, Howser listened to the footsteps of his officers escorting the girl downstairs. As the last echo faded away, he walked out, locked the door and headed off into the empty corridor toward the back staircase, wondering as he went how much, if anything, even Annie Connor knew about what still remained hidden somewhere out there in the summer dark.

23

Ernie Long woke blind lying on his back on a dirty iron-and-wood floor. His face burned with pain and felt broken and caved in and his senses flooded with vertigo. In the black heat surrounding him he did not know up from down. Slumped in a wooden corner with his neck bent forward at an awkward angle, he moved his arms outward and found walls with the backs of his hands, yet he could not tell where his legs were nor whether they were even attached still to the rest of his body.

He was somewhere indoors. Coming to consciousness, he guessed he was no longer outside because above him no stars shone in the seamless dark. There was blood still wet in his mouth and his ears buzzed. He was in a small room, humid and black. There was a ceiling he couldn't quite see and a hard rough-paneled floor beneath him and at least two side walls he could feel. The room smelled like the bottomhole of an outhouse: sweat, excrement, mildew, all hanging together in the stagnant air. The smell would have been worse but for Ernie's nose shattered and swollen up like a potato on his face. He sucked air into his lungs through a mouth half-open. It was all he could do to breathe. Ernie tried to move. He lowered his elbows to raise himself up and got as far as his lower back when vertigo wrenched his gut and blood and snot spewed from his nose and mouth. The pain and shock that ensued made him lose his balance and he slumped backward, banging his head on the wall behind him. Abandoning the idea of getting up, at least for the present, he shut his eyes and let the walls and floor fall away while he floated nearly insensate in a black void.

A vibration rumbled across the wooden floor. He stared into the blackness and felt it again. Somewhere out beyond his toes the fabric of shadow suddenly rippled. *Is that you, Howie!? Is that you? Down in the basement, the lights are out and Ernie is the bogey-man hunting on hands and knees for a victim to catch and devour. The victim is always Howie. Where is he hiding? The rules say he has to whisper and giggle but he makes no sound at all. Ernie searches and searches. Howie, where are you? The game is no longer fun. Ernie is tired and wants to quit. Howie, where are you? Please come out!* The floorboards trembled again and Ernie Long, still lying motionless on his back, steeled his eyes and stared into the black for movement.

And the suffocating odor of the place moved, too, like a rank draft swept up out of nowhere, and the subtle vibration became a sound as the floor under Ernie quaked loudly. The room shrunk. Ernie's eyes watered and his vision, what there was of it, began to blur. The wooden floor creaked again and the ripple in the black became a wave and it rose up over him and hovered there like a dark mannequin, breathing. It was not Howie. An image of cold black water flashed in Ernie's brain. Bailey's Reservoir. His brother was dead. He was not hiding in a dark basement. This was somebody else. Who? There had been a voice at the reservoir, a voice and then the black water. He remembered now. Where was his knife? As he felt around for it, the narrow floor seemed to sag and yaw beneath him and the mannequin became human and breathed directly into Ernie's face and uttered a word that had no meaning.

24

The window blinds in Howser's office were drawn open to the morning light above Main Street. They were open because Howser needed the glare off the pavement and storefronts to keep himself awake. Yesterday had lasted a lifetime and he could no more stay awake sitting in a dark office than he could lying flat on his back in bed. Besides, he had reports he hadn't even seen yet stacked up in manila folders on his desk: interviews and rap sheets and Indentikit sketches on tramps and transients from Stockton, Fresno, Bakersfield, Marysville, Sacramento, Visalia and six dozen other smaller towns having connecting lines anywhere close to the railroad. Even though there was no way he could read through them all and expect to catch the killer before Christmas, he had a certain obligation to go through at least a couple of dozen or so before turning them back over to Jane and Susan, both of whom had gone to a lot of trouble gathering the information for him. The blinds were going to have to stay open for a while.

Howser grabbed one of the folders and opened it up. He was only halfway down the first page when he heard footsteps in the hallway outside. There was a knock at the door. He looked up at the clock. Eight-thirty. Well, this is a switch, thought Howser. He yelled, "Come in!" and the door opened. His officers filed in, Corey and Beef followed by the reserve squad: Randy, Al, Craig, Dennis and Archie. They brought chairs with them from the conference room on the second floor and set them down in an uneven half-circle around the desk. Howser smiled. They were right on time. Maybe they were finally making an effort to justify the trust put in them by the town when it handed them their badges. Well good, he thought, better late than never.

"You going to tell us how to catch the killer today, Chief?" asked Dennis, sliding onto one of the chairs. Howser slipped the report he'd been skimming into the nearest stack of folders and shoved the whole pile off to the side. Now that he'd finally been given a copy of the rules, he wanted to make this game as short as possible. He started with their favorite word: *arrest*.

"Guys, the arrest warrants are already sworn out and waiting for you. I want Jamie Danielson, Roy Lee, Jerry Hardisty and the Long twins brought in. Before lunch if possible, but absolutely by suppertime. I don't want any of us having to run around out there in the dark again, so let's try to get this taken care of while the sun's still shining, okay? You can pick up your papers from Susan. We're going to put an end to at least some of this crap once and for all."

"Now you're talking," said Al, with a large grin.

Randy raised his hand. "Who gets who?"

"I don't care," answered Howser. "Why? Who do you want? You have a preference?"

"Well, yeah," said Randy. "I sure as hell don't want Jamie Danielson. His old man hates me. Always has. And the Longs are both nuts. I don't want to go near that place."

Howser looked at Corey who shook his head. "Then, by all means take Roy or Jerry. Makes no difference to me who you bring in as long as you do it quickly."

"Then I'll take Roy," said Randy.

"Jerry, here," said Al.

Nobody else spoke up. Howser waited. He waited a little longer. When he still did not hear another voice, he said, "No other volunteers? Well, that's okay because this isn't a democracy, anyhow. Dennis, you and Craig have the Longs. Now, I know they're reported as missing, but stop in on their folks just the same. You might get a line on where they've gone. Archie, you got Jamie. Don't worry. We're going to call ahead and warn the old man you're coming. He might take it a little easier that way. I hope. If you have any problems tracking these kids down, call in right away. There's always a chance they might rabbit on us, but I doubt it. There's no place for them to go. And listen, no clowning around on this one, understand? The warrants are for suspicion of rape and suspicion of kidnapping. No joke. We're not just inviting these kids to lunch."

The officers nodded. Howser got up and walked to the window. He opened it a crack. The noise level outside was rising with the temperature. He looked down and saw that commerce on Main Street had picked up considerably from what it had been at the beginning of the week. Traffic was heavy enough to be stalled temporarily at the light in front of the State Farm building at Main and Elm, and the pedestrian crosswalks were occupied by morning shoppers doing what they did best: passing time on the sidewalks. Just another day in small-town America.

"What're we going to do about that tramp?" asked Craig. "You got a warrant for him, too?"

"Yeah. Suspicion of ugliness," said Al. "It's all signed and everything. The judge issued it this morning, didn't he, Chief?"

"Not exactly," said Howser, turning away from the window. "That one'll have to work like a regular APB—you see him, you call for a backup and the rest of us come out and help pick the guy up. And I'm trusting you guys to make the call on the right guy. He shouldn't be that hard to identify."

"Somebody big and weird-looking, huh?" said Dennis. They all laughed.

"Look, just make sure you don't try to take him on your own."

"You think he might be armed?" asked Randy. The idea of someone that big carrying a gun or even a hunting knife erased a few grins in the room. Howser shook his head. "I doubt it. That's not the impression I get. On the other hand, if he's as strong as we think he is, then he doesn't need a weapon. He's dangerous enough without one. But let me tell you something here: If at all possible, I do not want him hurt. Got that? If you do run across him, use a little caution and protect yourselves, but, listen to me, do not under any circumstances fire on him. I mean that. Don't shoot this guy. I want him back here in one piece and still breathing. That's an order."

"Well Christ, Chief, the fucker might've killed three kids, maybe more," said Randy. "What if he decides he doesn't want to take a ride with us?"

Howser crossed the room to the door and opened it. The hallway was empty but he could hear the secretary typing downstairs in the mayor's office. He flipped the starter switch on the electric fan sitting on top of the filing cabinet. The metal blades began to rotate slowly, drawing air in from the hallway.

"Listen, guys," said Howser. "We don't know for certain *who's* responsible for any of these killings. We have a lot of stories floating around now, a lot of fingers being pointed, but not many facts and even less hard evidence."

He walked a line in front of his officers, playing like a lawyer laying out a case before an attentive jury. He paused every other step to look one of his officers in the eye. The idea of him putting on this routine might have struck them as ridiculously funny were it not for the fact that things had become distinctly humorless in the last three days. Alfie's death was particularly disturbing since he'd only gone out to make a routine call on an eccentric old woman and had ended up coming back to town on a gurney—DOA. Who would have believed something like that even a week ago?

"The kids say it was the tramps who beat and raped Sarah. Well, Doc didn't get any cross matches with the tramps they identified. And while Jamie would like us to believe that the big tramp who got away at the railyard stuck around to break Danny Williams's neck up in Stuart's Mill, did he see him do it? Nope. Did anyone see him do it? No sir. Meanwhile, the tramps themselves maintain that they didn't touch anybody at all in this town, not the girl, not the kids, nobody; although they do admit they've been sheltering a deranged idiot for the past year and a half.

And then just last night Annie Connor crawls out of the woodwork and confirms at least part of the tramps' story by claiming that it was Jamie and his friends who raped Sarah and threw her in the river. This case is crazy and it's dangerous and I'd sure as hell like to solve it, but more than that I don't want anybody else hurt. That's the bottom line. No more bodies. All right? Enough fooling around. You guys get out there and bring those kids in. Get it done as quickly and quietly as you can. And listen, after we get the kids picked up? No more singles. We do the rest of our investigations, arrests, calls, whatever, by twos or threes. You got that? No more Lone Rangers. Like I said before, I don't want to lose anyone else. Another thing: I'm going to suggest a curfew to the mayor this afternoon. We can't be keeping track of everyone wandering around after dark, and I won't have anyone else in this town turning up in Doc Sawyer's back room. It's bad for tourism."

He walked to his desk and sat down. Then he smiled and said, "Now get the hell out of here."

The reserve squad gathered up the chairs they'd brought in with them and left the room, heading downstairs to pick up the arrest warrants from Susan at the front desk. Beef and Corey waited behind. When the fourth floor became quiet enough that the blades on Howser's electric fan hummed in the air, Corey pushed himself off the wall and pulled a chair up to the desk and sat down. Behind him, Beef lit up a cigarette and strolled over to the window where the draft could draw the smoke away into the blue daylight.

"So, where are you going to look first?" asked Corey.

"The mill," said Howser. "Where else?"

"You're going up there alone?"

"Yeah."

"I thought you just said . . ."

"That was for their benefit, not mine." Howser cracked a half-smile. "I think I can handle it."

"Yeah, okay. So, where do you want us to go?"

Howser opened the drawer in front of him and took out a map of Rivertown and the adjacent area. He drew an arc from Green River through the railyard and the mill all the way up to the orchard and out into the valley. Then he slid the map across the desktop to Corey.

"Why don't you start with the yard and move on out to the river. It's a lot of territory to cover but I'll have Jane send the other guys out your way as soon as they get back in."

"You mean, *if* they do," said Beef, flicking ash off into the breeze.

"They will," said Howser. "Don't worry about it. Those kids aren't going to hassle this. There's no point. We got 'em, they know it, and that's all there is to it. If anything, they're going to shit on each other. Just watch. I've seen it happen a thousand times."

"You're the expert," said Corey. He reached into his shirt pocket and drew out a pair of metal-rimmed Ray-Bans and put them on. The sunglasses were new and Howser could see himself reflected in the polished lenses. Corey stood up and turned to Beef. "Let's go, partner. We got a job to do."

Beef snuffed the cigarette out on the windowledge and left the butt there for the birds to play with. Pausing in the doorway, Corey said, "Give us a call, Chief, if you find anything up there. We'll be close."

Howser nodded. Beef gave Howser a salute off the bill of his cap and followed Corey out of the office. As soon as the door closed, Jane's voice came over the intercom.

"Chief, I just called out to the Danielsons."

"And?"

"Nobody's home."

"Or nobody's answering."

"Whichever. You want me to keep trying?"

"Give it one more shot then have Archie check in when he gets out there. Have him open the line before he gets out of the unit. All right?"

"Will do."

"Soon as I finish up with these reports I'll be taking a ride out to the old mill."

"I'm off at noon but I'll have Susan call you when she comes in."

"That'll be fine."

Howser switched off the intercom and pulled his notes

back out of the desk drawer. *Danielson*, he wondered. *Now, where the hell did he take off to?* He stared out the window. The heat was coming on strong again. He could feel it under his uniform. It was going to be a long day.

The phone rang upstairs at the Walcott where Jack Clayton sat in a sunlit and empty third-story window, daydreaming about a place thirteen years and seven hundred miles away, somewhere cool and distant and blue. The phone rang again, echoing through the pink floral wallpaper behind him. Two black flies buzzed in tandem at the screen by his face. The lawn sprinklers in the arbor below spun water into the rose beds, though there was no draft to carry the warm morning air past the screen and into his room.

Clayton picked up the receiver on the fifth ring and listened to a voice he hadn't heard since twilight a day and a half ago at Parker School.

"Are you awake?" asked Jane.

He pulled up a chair and sat down. The image of blue waters rippling in the summer sunlight off the Newport pier faded in his mind, replaced by a memory of another kind, one more immediate and visceral.

"Of course," he said. "What do you think I do, sleep all day?"

She came back quickly with an answer characteristic of their relationship.

"I don't know," she said. "I haven't figured it out yet."

The light in the room changed subtly as a draft came through from the trees outside. Jane spoke again, softer this time, asking, "Do you want to have lunch with me?"

A morning scent of jasmine rising off the arbor followed in the draft, then faded as quickly as it had come. Did he want to go to lunch with her or not? It wasn't a complicated question.

"I suppose," he said. "Where?"

"Sutter Park?"

"Forget it. It's too hot downtown."

"All right, how about taking a drive out to the river?"

"When do you want to go?" he asked.

"I'm the only one around to take calls until Susan gets

361

in at noon. So it'd have to be after that. Everyone else is out for the afternoon."

"Where's Howser?"

"Stuart's Mill."

"What's he doing up there?"

"Working."

"Any news?"

"Not yet." There was a pause. "Do you want to have lunch with me, or not?"

"What time are we talking about?"

"Twelve-thirty."

Clayton glanced across the room at his old alarm clock perched on a square shelf of the nightstand by the bed. The black hands read a quarter after eleven.

"All right. Can you pick me up here? I'm a little low on gas."

"Sure," she said, and hung up. He held the phone to his ear until he got the dial tone. Then he hung up, too, and went back to the window where the morning heat was rising in the trees. His daydream was gone for the moment but he knew it would return, coming back again like an old love song on the radio played over and over just for him. He left the window finally and went to the closet to begin sorting through everything he'd collected during his stay in Rivertown. After lunch, he decided, he would start packing.

Howser put the unit into reverse and backed into the shade under the sycamores a few yards past the old wire-and-iron gate to Stuart's Mill. He shut the engine off and got out, his attention focused past the shade trees up to where the noon sun glared off the white dust in the open yard at the front of the mill. The sticky odor of tarweed was strong in the heat and millions of summer insects droned in the thickets and the long grass or shot past in the dry blue air overhead. Up ahead in the mill yard, the dark façade of the structure rose against the sky.

The yard was empty. The mill was open up above where dozens of bluejays gathered in the broken windowframes on the fourth floor, but there was no indication of anyone human around. He shielded his eyes to the sun and looked up. Even sagging slightly to the west as it did, Stuart's Mill impressed him as being larger even than he'd pictured it in his mind. He could see why the kids came up here to hang out. Miles from town, isolated and invisible even from the county road a quarter of a mile below, it must have made an amazing clubhouse.

The main doors had been chained and locked shut a week earlier by Corey and Beef, so Howser went around to the east side. The weeds were taller there, pressing up against the steep brown walls. Howser picked his way along, taking care to avoid walking over anything capable of punching a hole in his foot. He had stepped on an old rake when he was a kid and had not found the experience of tetanus booster shots very pleasant. The open door Annie had told him about earlier in the morning was there. Originally a fire exit, it was jammed open now by a thick growth of milkweed growing in the doorjamb. Howser kicked some of the weeds away and stepped inside. He gave his vision a minute or so to adjust before moving around. He was not sure what he was looking for yet; he just assumed he would know when he found it. The air was five or ten degrees cooler in the mill's interior and right off he noticed the familiar stink of animals and wood rot, though not half as bad as the kids and his officers had made it out to be. He'd smelled worse—apartment houses in the valley where people had died alone in the middle of the summer with their TV sets on, or had been murdered in the last act of a drug deal or love affair gone sour, their bodies left to putrefy until the smell got so bad someone finally bothered to call it in. Ratcrap and mildew had nothing on decomposing Homo sapiens.

He shoved his toe at an empty gallon can of industrial stain and sent it rolling. He shook his head. The place was a mess. Someone ought to have organized one big flea market years ago and gotten rid of everything, then hosed out the entire ground floor. What attracted the kids to the mill these days, he had no idea. You'd have to be horny as hell, he thought, to even consider coming in here to get laid. The flatbed of a pickup truck might be roughing it a little, but still. . . . Then he remembered his own experience in that old chicken shed out back of Velasquez's the summer after his senior year, and it struck him that probably atmosphere doesn't play much part in romance when you're that young. He grinned, remembering the girl and the shed, feathers and shit everywhere. But it hadn't been all that bad. Neither of them had even noticed the smell. Or, if they had, they'd pretended not to. It must've been love.

He found the stairwell leading to the second floor a few minutes later and considered going up for a quick look around, then changed his mind. The mill appeared empty and harmless enough, but then so had that 7-Eleven store, and Howser saw no good reason to confuse duty this time with foolishness. Without a flashlight and a partner in the immediate vicinity, he had no intention of poking his head up there into the shadows. Maybe he had left his balls for the job back there in that 7-Eleven, but neither was he the stupid cop he'd been two and a half years earlier, and being humiliated in San Jose was one thing, getting killed in Rivertown was another. He listened a few moments at the bottom of the stairs, then moved off slowly and picked his way back through the debris to the entrance again.

On his way out, in a cluttered corner a few yards to the left of the door and behind some large shipping crates marked for Stockton, Howser found an old wool blanket bundled up on the floor next to the wall. He bent down and picked it up, shaking loose a couple of dirty candy-bar wrappers from underneath. He studied the blanket for a few moments. *Was this Annie's? Is this where she slept?* He brushed some of the dirt off and gave it a good looking-over. It was frayed around the edges and smelled awful. He brought the blanket outside with him and held it up to the sunlight. It was moth-eaten in several places and had a large dark stain on one side. It was not the sort of blanket a young girl would've carried around with her. *She might've used it, but it wasn't hers. So who'd it belong to?* He stopped playing with the blanket to listen a second, imagining he'd heard something off in the brush. Coming out alone to the mill wasn't the smartest thing he'd done all week. He knew that. But with the limited personnel available to him, he hadn't much choice. He listened a little longer. Just bugs and birds. Not even much of a breeze. Howser folded the green blanket under his arm. It appeared as though he still had the mill to himself, which was good because he had one more thing to look at.

The hole Jamie had punched in the side of the mill had been enlarged by Corey and Beef on their visit, so Howser had no difficulty climbing in off the ladder. The floor creaked slightly beneath him as he brushed some sawdust from his clothes. He strolled back into the shadows. It was just as Jamie had described—the table saw and tarpaulin, shipping crates, sawhorse, the short length of pipe he'd used to break through the wall. Howser walked over to the freight platform and looked down the shaft. The elevator was almost invisible beneath the junk pile of shattered crates. The kid did a hell of a job of covering his ass, thought Howser. He glanced back at the hole in the wall. Had Jamie really been chased out of here by the tramp? Everything he'd heard in the past thirty-six hours made Jamie's story sound a little more believeable. If it *was* true, then how long had the tramp been staying up here? Since the night of the shooting? And if he *had* been here, was it Jamie Danielson, Danny Williams, or Corey and Beef who'd scared him off? Or somebody else?

Howser crossed back into the light and stood at the hole in the wall. Outside, the heat shimmered in the trees. Bluejays soared and dove swiftly on the noon sky. Looking down at the footprints in the dirt at the bottom of the ladder, he thought *At least three people, excluding my officers, have been up here in the last week or so, and one of them didn't get out alive. And one of the two who did knows why the third didn't.* Howser shaded his eyes and glanced up at the sun burning relentlessly overhead. When had it moved last? The middle of June? He looked down at the footprints again—*and one of the two who did knows why the third didn't*—and wondered: When would he show his face?

"This is a waste of time."

Beef sat down at the base of a willow. He leaned his

head back and wiped the sweat from his brow and closed his eyes. "Nobody's hiding out here."

"We got to keep looking," said Corey, still scouting the bluff overlooking Green River.

Beef looked over at him and frowned. "Why are you always so goddamned responsible? No one gives a fuck how far we look. Howser isn't out here. If he was, he'd have given up an hour ago. Hell, I could've told him there wasn't anything to find."

"You know what he's going to say, though: 'I don't care how long you guys looked. Get the hell out there and turn something up for me.' "

"Fucking flies," said Beef, chasing one off his collar. He rubbed the back of his neck. Corey gazed down at the river flowing south below the bluff. They'd gone over more than two miles of its length now and had nothing to show for their effort except an empty ice chest and an old pair of laceless brown patent leather shoes left in the bushes along the riverbank half a mile back. And that was more than they'd found in the railyard. No tramp, no kids, no killer, no clues. Just garbage, sweat, and a touch of sunstroke. A typical summer's day on the job—all pain and no gain. Corey watched the river run and wished he was down there on it, paddling along in his daddy's old canoe like he used to when he was a kid.

"Let's go back to town," Beef said, under the tree. "We'll just tell Howser we couldn't find anything. He'll understand."

The sunlight sparkled on the surface of the river where the water bubbled and swirled. Corey's eyes were still locked on the dark current. The blackbirds in the trees across the river yakked distractedly at the empty sky. He bent down, dug a large rock from the dirt and hurled it in a sluggish arc toward the river. The splash drove several birds off in a squawking flurry.

"What're you doing?" asked Beef, with a cough.

Corey turned away from the river and shrugged. "I don't know," he replied. "Thinking, I guess."

"Well, while you're at it, start thinking about us going back in. It's fucking hot out here."

"You don't want to catch the killer then, huh? Be a hero?"

"I don't want to catch heatstroke," said Beef. "We can start looking again at sundown."

"Can't see anything after dark," said Corey.

"Then fuck it, let the guy go. I don't care. The only ones getting killed are the assholes, anyhow. Why should we bust our butts to put a stop to that? Christ, somebody out there's doing us a favor and we're killing ourselves trying to run him in. That's bullshit!"

"Then don't think about it," said Corey. "Just do your job and let someone else worry about who's taking it in the shorts."

Beef grunted as he rolled over onto his side. "This heat's making me crazy."

"No shit."

His partner closed his eyes again and Corey turned back to the river, drifting lazily on to the south without him. The ripples shimmered and swelled in the summer sun. The shade under the trees fluttered briefly and fell still. Twenty minutes went by. The birds he'd chased off earlier returned.

Corey nudged his partner in the rear with the stiff toe of his boot, waking him. Then he walked on ahead to the unit and opened the door.

"Come on," he yelled. "Let's hit it. I just got an idea."

Beef struggled to his feet, using the tree trunk for balance. He rubbed his eyes and gazed drowsily in Corey's direction.

"What's that?" asked Beef, dragging himself back to the car. "You figure out a way to get us home in time for dinner?"

"I tell you, we should've thought of this sooner. It makes sense. Makes a lot of sense." Corey banged his fist on the car's roof. "We must be jerks."

"Speak for yourself."

Corey slid into the driver's seat and started the engine. Beef climbed into the passenger seat beside him and pulled the shoulder belt down and buckled it. Corey slammed the transmission into drive and swung away from the river bluff. They drove back down to the county road, hung a left and barreled down the highway to the south, driving half on the pavement and half in the dust on the shoulder of the road, sending a voluminous cloud of dirt into the blue air behind them. Three miles later, Corey slammed on the brakes and jerked the car into a narrow service road slicing east through the weedy edge of the same underbrush they had been tramping in all afternoon.

"Where the hell are you taking us?"

"Just shut up and think for a second. Remember when you were just a runt running away from home 'cause your folks wouldn't let you keep that scrawny goat."

"I never had a goat."

Corey twisted the wheel and whipped the car around a tight bend, down through the middle of a dry creekbed and back up again into the gravel and manzanita.

"That's right. You didn't have a goat, because your old man told you to get it the hell out of your bedroom. And you said, no, that you were going to keep the mangy old thing. And he whacked you across the mouth, loosening that big tooth in front. Remember now?"

Beef licked his tongue across the front of his mouth where one tooth bent back at an odd angle. It had been that way since he was eleven. His father . . . yeah.

"You ran away for a week after that," said Corey, jerking the car away from the brush. "Don't you remember?"

"I remember getting punched, yeah. That asshole."

"Well, where'd you go after he hit you? The mill? Nope. It was still open in those days. The quarry? No sir. It was flooded by the river back then. Where then? Think about it. Where'd you run off to that you knew nobody'd find you unless you wanted them to?"

"Oh shit. I don't know. Christ, that was a long time ago."

"The circus trains, you idiot. You ran away and hid in the painted boxcars on the old nine track by the river. No one used them anymore. Hardly anyone even remembered they were there. It was perfect."

"The circus trains?" asked Beef, trying to recall something he'd obviously buried a long time back.

"Yeah, the boxcars with the animals painted on them.

368

And the cages? Remember? Out in the north woods by the river."

Corey gunned the engine up a slant in the road, skirting a fence overhung with sunflowers while Beef struggled to locate the boxcars in his memory.

He found them. "Okay, yeah. I remember now. Up where the old tracks used to be. All right. God, I was just a kid."

"That's right. But you sure as shit knew where to go when you didn't want anyone to find you. Someplace where nobody'd ever think to look."

Beef picked at the shoulder belt, trying to free it from the tangle it was making under his armpit. The black-and-white lurched over a deep rut. Beef thought about the old circus cars sitting there in the deep woods half-buried in underbrush.

"That train sits in about as remote a spot as there is in this county," said Corey. "You can't even drive in there anymore, so nobody bothers with it—unless maybe they're someone looking for a place to hide. Like our tramp."

"We should've thought of it sooner," said Beef, grinning.

The road ended in a clearing ringed by live oaks and brush. Corey pulled the car to the edge of the long grass then backed it around, facing out toward the road. He called their location in to Susan, then turned the engine off. He stared at the ignition a second and then started it back up again.

"All right," he said, getting out of the seat. "Let's go take a look."

"You going to leave it running?"

"Yeah."

"Why?"

"I don't know."

Beef looked at him, then nodded. "Okay."

The two patrolmen climbed out of the car. Corey walked around to the hood and watched Beef struggle to get the shotgun loose from the mounting. He jerked it free and slid outside. He pulled a handful of shells from his vest pocket and jammed five of them into the breech.

Corey asked, "What's that thing for?"

"Never mind."

"You're going to blow your goddamned foot off, you know. Probably mine, too."

"You don't trust me?"

"Just take it easy."

"I promise," said Beef. He watched Corey head off under the trees. Then he hoisted the shotgun up onto his shoulder, the barrel pointing off into the west where the sky was beginning to whiten, and followed Corey into the brush.

The rails were easy to follow even half-buried as they were under thirty summers of long grass. Less than four hundred feet from the end of the service road where the police cruiser sat idling, the old cross-stitching of redwood and iron could be found marking a perfect line in the rumpled ground. The tracks themselves had darkened with rust and dirt from three decades of disuse, but the planking ties between them had only broken here and there, resisting for the most part the upward surge of the grass and weeds which claimed this place. The river slunk by only three hundred yards to the east but the thick brush made it invisible from the tracks.

The patrolmen found the first boxcar in the dense woods a hundred yards up the tracks. Its colorful sides, painted up in the rainbow hues of an African delta, had faded almost entirely to browns and grays. What little paint was left cracked and curled and gave the car a leprous appearance. They walked around it and looked underneath. Grass growing between the rails rose to the bottom of the car. Beef slipped the shotgun off his shoulder and waved it under the car, fanning back the grass and thistles from the floorboards so Corey could get a better look.

"I don't think anyone's been sleeping under this thing for a while," said Corey. He watched a small bluebelly lizard scurry off into hiding.

"Well then, let's open her up."

Corey pulled on the lever hanging free from the door. It wouldn't budge. The catch was rusting heavily. He tried jerking on it, managing only to bang and cut his knuckles. They bled lightly and swelled.

"Shit! Get this thing open."

Beef aimed the gun stock at the lever, then slammed the butt end into it. Chips of rust and flaking paint flew off, and a gash was cut into the red metal. He banged it again, then pulled on the lever. It slid a little and stopped. He jammed the stock under the lever and pushed up, several short pops at a time. He pulled on the lever. The door slid free back along its rollers and slammed against the bulkhead of the siding. The roar echoed out into the underbrush and back again through the dark interior of the car. A swallow flew out. Corey let his right hand fall to the butt of his revolver and leaned in. Lying in the center of the car was a tattered magazine. He climbed up inside. A tickling shiver ran up his neck and made his back twitch. He flashed a quick look to either side. The magazine was soiled with waterspots and grime, but the colors had hardly faded at all. The cover read: ADVENTURE: BURMA * MIDDLE EAST * SOUTH SEAS * WEST with artwork depicting a soldier, circa 1940s, gallantly raising Old Glory on a simple rope standard under withering enemy fire. Corey picked up the magazine and opened it. A page from the end dropped out. It was an advertisement for International Correspondence Schools, showing a man standing disconsolately with his hands pulling the lining out of empty pockets. The heading in bold black arrows read, "This empty means this empty" with the first arrow pointing at his head and the second at his pocket.

"That's me," mumbled Corey.

"Huh?"

"Nothing. It stinks in here."

"Stop talking to yourself," said Beef, leaning into the car. "You're making me nervous."

Corey dropped the magazine and looked around. The corners were steeped in dirt and just as empty as the rest of the car. His eyes followed a thin ray of light to its source in a corner of the roof where rust had eaten a fist-sized hole away.

"There's where the birds get in."

Beef moved closer and peered up into the car. "What'd you say?"

"I said there's a hole here in the ceiling where those birds are getting in."

"Oh, yeah?"

Corey walked over to the southeast corner of the car where a pile of what appeared to be clothes of some kind lay bundled up. He pushed at them with his shoe, turning them over, and saw they weren't clothes at all, just some old oily rags. He returned to the entrance and climbed back down into the sunlight.

"Well?" asked Beef, trying to sound optimistic. "You find something?"

"Nothing. Just a pile of grease rags. Thing's empty. Nobody's camping in this one."

They both turned to look up the tracks. Four flatcars sat end to end with an old cage car used for hauling big cats and bears. They connected to another boxcar whose side door was slid open. The rest of the train was hidden at that point by two trees bending together and intertwined over the front of the second boxcar.

"All right, let's check the others."

They proceeded slowly past the flatcars, stopping every few feet to look underneath, then moving on. The bars on the cage car were bent slightly, though not enough to admit anything larger than a squirrel. Beef walked on one side, Corey the other, both trying to pretend they were searching for something other than evidence of a huge and incredibly violent killer.

They came up to the second boxcar. Enough blue paint remained on one side to reveal part of a lagoon drawn across the lower right-hand corner of the siding. A palm tree curved around the edge. Corey approached cautiously and leaned slowly in the open side door. An old newspaper and a torn brown paper bag lay open on the floor. Corey craned his neck to look into the shadowed corners of the car. It was empty and stunk badly of ratshit and grease.

"Anybody in there?" asked Beef, tightening his grip on the shotgun.

"Nope," replied Corey. "It's as clean as the other."

"This is ridiculous."

Corey ran his hand over the wood, scraping off flakes of paint. "Remember how long it took your old man to find you out here? And he knew where you were hiding."

"Thanks to you, old buddy. Ratfink of the week."

"He threatened me. I had to tell, you know that."

"Yeah, right." Beef grinned at his partner. "Asshole."

They followed a last set of flatcars and a single cage car leading up to the arch of oaks. Beef broke a tight path through some overhanging branches with the butt of the shotgun. Beyond the trees, about a hundred feet ahead, were two Pullman cars and a single boxcar linked together under a dense green canopy of weeping willows and mossy oaks. The remaining circus cars sat stranded in splintered sunlight, separated from the rest of the train by a thick oak root that had severed the rails at a perfect forty-five-degree angle.

"I don't think we're going to have time to check all three of them," said Beef. He was getting fidgety. Corey stared at him. *Does he know something I don't?*

"Shut up and get going," said Corey. "I don't want to be out here any longer than we have to."

"Ladies first," said Beef, stepping aside and showing the way to the next car.

Corey frowned. "Coward."

"Hey, I'm backing you up," said Beef. "I got the heavy artillery, remember?"

Birds screeched invisibly in the trees overhead and the surrounding underbrush buzzed with insect life. The air felt warmer by the minute and sweat had soaked into their shirts. Corey walked up to the spot where the tree roots had snapped the rails. A large irregular mound heaved up under the railroad tracks, tipping the first Pullman car slightly to the right. Coming up beside him, Beef kicked at the ground covering the root until he unearthed part of it. He thumped the butt of the gun on the bark.

"Sturdy little fucker, isn't it? Be a hell of a job digging it out."

Corey climbed around the overgrown root and strode up the tracks to the back of the old Pullman car. All of the windows were a smoky-black from the grime, opaque and impenetrable. The car itself was colored a dull yellow and painted with lifesize circus characters in marching poses along the sides. There was a clown drawn in blue and green grinning at him from the door. Like the rest of the figures, it was mostly chipped and peeling. Only the red on the clown's nose and lips remained fairly bright and intact. Corey wiped the glass to the right of the clown's face with his elbow and tried to look in. The fabric shades behind the glass had been drawn down flush to the frame. It was too dark to make anything out. He turned to Beef, standing in the long grass at the bottom of the steps, and whispered, "Go around to the front and come in the other door."

Beef nodded and disappeared to the left. Corey waited. All about him, the brush shook gently in a soft breeze. Or was someone there, stalking him? His own nerves were playing tricks on him now. Waiting until he heard Beef on the iron stairs at the front of the car, Corey put his hand into the clown's fist and went in. As he released the door, it slammed closed behind him.

It was like entering a long blackened tunnel: he could not quite see to the far end of the car. With the dirt on the windowpanes and the shades pulled down, only the faintest movement from Beef's silhouette up the aisle disturbed the dark. At each row Corey stopped just long enough to search the seats on either side, then moved forward again. The first six rows of seats on his end of the car were empty and the old blue velvet cushions were worn in places and covered with dust. In the seventh row, he found what looked like part of a newspaper lying under one of the seats and knelt down to retrieve it. As he drew the paper out and held it close to his face, trying to make out the date, a large hand clamped down on his shoulder. Corey jerked upward, hitting his head on the back of the seat. He dropped the paper and it skittered away. Beef stood beside him in the aisle, grinning.

"Jeez!" whispered Corey. "You scared the crap out of me!"

"Look at this." Beef thrust a red five-gallon gasoline can into Corey's hands. The contents sloshed softly inside. In a hushed voice, he said, "I found it next to the door."

His partner ran his fingers over the surface of the can. It felt smooth and clean but damp. He sniffed his hands: they smelled of gasoline. Beef whispered, "Stinks, huh?"

Corey nodded and wiped his hands on his pantleg. Beef slipped in beside him and released the shade and tried to wipe the glass clean with his elbow. "Check this out. It's paint. That's why it's so dark in here. Now why the hell would you want to paint over the glass?"

Corey located the newspaper on the floor across the aisle. He leaned over and picked it up, then held it in front of his partner's face. "Think that's funny, look at the date on this."

Beef squinted to read the number in the upper right-hand corner of the paper.

"It's last month's paper," said Corey. "That means somebody's been out here recently doing who knows—"

"Hold on a second." Beef grabbed Corey's wrist, cutting him off in midsentence. "Did you hear that?"

Corey jerked his arm free of his partner's grip. "Hear what?"

"I don't know. Listen!"

After a few seconds, Corey shook his head. "I didn't hear anything."

Beef chipped at the glass with a fingernail while Corey slid out into the aisle and headed toward the front of the car. When he got there, he smelled gasoline where he was standing and bent down and dabbed his fingers over the floor. It was wet. He smelled his fingers: gasoline again. *What the fuck?* He drew his revolver. Beef came up from behind and tapped him on the shoulder with the butt of the shotgun.

"Hold this," said Beef, passing his gun over to Corey. "Somebody's out there."

"How do you know?"

Corey listened at the door but couldn't hear a thing above his partner's breathing.

"Shhh!"

Then Beef drew his revolver and with his free hand reached for the door. Corey slipped a finger into the trigger guard of the shotgun, and in the same instant they both heard an unmistakable stomping noise on the stairs just outside the door. Turning the handle, Beef thought: *Maybe this day isn't going to be a complete waste after all.* Then the door, kicked violently from the outside, slammed open into the patrolman, driving him backward into Corey whose shotgun exploded in Beef's face, blowing his head apart. His body flew sideways into the window shades and landed clumsily upside-down on one of the seats ten feet from the door, quickly staining the velvet cushions.

The collision knocked Corey straight over backward where he lay flat on the floor, ears ringing loudly, six rows up the aisle. The smell of cordite and wet blood was strong in the air and, dazed as he was, Corey wasn't even sure what had just happened. He craned his neck and looked forward over his chest. Beef was gone and the door was open; Corey could see clear through to the rear door on the next car. It, too, was open. He rolled over and felt around on the floor for the shotgun and discovered he'd lost it in the fall. Then the door in front of him closed with a bang, dumping the Pullman car back into darkness. Corey crawled under one of the seats and reached frantically into his holster for his revolver, only to find it empty. A few yards away, near the door, something was dripping or leaking onto the floor from a row of seats. The can of gasoline. Where was it? Jesus Christ, were they going to be burned alive like that tramp? Then, realizing he'd lost track of his partner, he sat up and looked for him. Where the hell was he? Corey crawled forward a foot or so and stared out toward the door and saw the stains on the window shades and realized where the dripping was coming from. Then the color ran out of his face and Corey knew not only that his partner was dead but that he would be, too, soon enough, if he didn't try to get back to the unit and radio for help.

The sunlight blinded him as he burst out onto the rear stairs. Ahead, the trees fluttered in the checkered shadows and the woods were quiet and clear. He vaulted the railing and tumbled down into the dust, then got up and ran, hurtling over the root and stumbling on past the old train car trapped so hopelessly in the tangled wood. As he hurried by the boxcar where he'd found the magazine, Corey heard an iron door bang closed back behind him. He cut immediately to his right, entering the dense brushline to take a shorter line to the cruiser. Thorns and branches cut at his face and hands as he tore his way through, bleeding now but feeling no pain. Half a minute later he angled off to the south and came out of the brush on a dirt path somewhere above the clearing where he'd parked the unit. His shirt was torn and sweat stung in his cuts and the sun burned hotter on his face than it had all day, but he could hear the car engine idling nearby. Shoving his way through a thicket of manzanita, Corey stumbled into the clearing above the unit and ran for the door. As he jerked it open and grabbed for the radio inside, the brush rustled harshly and came apart twenty feet behind him, and he heard the sound of running footsteps sliding to a stop in the dirt and then the grating pump action of a shotgun ejecting an empty shell. Corey dropped the mike and spun around. For an instant he stared incredulously into the face of his pursuer, then ducked and threw his hands up reflexively to shield his head and cried out, "God, Tom . . ." and took the full load of .00 buckshot square in the neck. The impact threw him across the fender and into the dirt by the front wheel. He was dead when he hit the ground.

Danielson worked the pump again and the spent shell flew off into the dust. The blast echo faded with the blue smoke in the air. He walked up to the car and laid the shotgun on the front seat then stooped to take a closer look at Corey's body, now soaking a dark pool of blood into the dust. He felt the patrolman's wrist for a pulse. Finding none, he straightened up again and walked to the cruiser's rear door and swung it open. Then he went back to the front, grabbed Corey's ankles, and dragged the body through the dirt to the rear of the car. When he got there he raised the body up by the armpits and shoved it into the backseat, head first, then kicked the door closed. The toe of his boot left a dent in the metal. He picked the shotgun up again and looked around. The birds, invisible in the treeline, heckled him mercilessly. He didn't notice.

Danielson squinted as he swung about in a full circle, searching the brush for something. Except for the blood drying in the dirt beside the car there was no longer any color in the clearing. The sun had bleached it all away, leaving just a blinding whiteness in the heat. Danielson walked back to the patrol car, got in, released the emergency brake, and slipped the transmission into drive. Then he brought the car around in a tight three-point turn and backed it right up to the brushline and held it there with his foot on the brake and the transmission whining while he checked the mirror and adjusted it for a clear view to the rear. Lifting off the brake, he slammed his foot into the gas, blasting the car backward through the brush until it struck a tree and stopped. Danielson shut the engine off and got out. Carrying the shotgun in his right hand, he disappeared north again into the woods.

Howser heard the radio in the unit while he was down in the thicket away from the gate attending to some personal business. It took him half a minute or so to finish up and respond.

"RP1 to RP base. Go ahead," he said, sliding into the front seat.

"Chief, it's Randy."

Howser struggled with the fastener on his belt buckle. "Where are you?"

"Courthouse."

"What're you doing there?" asked Howser. "Did you find Roy?"

"Not exactly."

Howser pulled the sun visor down to cut the glare from the windshield. "Well, tell me what you're doing then."

"Chief . . ." There was laughter in the background. "We got some good news and some bad news." More laughter. Howser held the mike down in his lap. Jesus Christ. Good news and bad news. It was too hot for that crap. He raised the mike again.

"Just get to the point."

"Roy's gone."

"Where'd he go?"

"Out of the county, down south somewhere—L.A. maybe."

"Who told you that?"

"His folks. He left them a note."

"What about Jerry?"

"He went with Roy."

378

Howser rolled his eyes. They should've known someone was going to rabbit eventually.

Randy said, "Chief?"

"Yeah?"

"Want to hear the good news?"

"I thought that was the good news," he said.

"No."

"Go ahead."

"Jamie's here. Archie brought him in twenty minutes ago. He gave himself up."

"Out at Danielson's?"

"Yeah, he was just waiting there at the back door."

"Was Tom there?"

"Arch said his truck was gone."

"And Jamie didn't give Archie any trouble?"

"Nope, he was a perfect gentleman."

"That figures."

With half of his friends dead now, thought Howser, and the others missing, Jamie'd obviously come to the conclusion that the safest place in Rivertown now was a jail cell. That's why he'd surrendered so quietly. Howser squeezed the mike and asked, "Did he say anything yet?"

Randy answered, "He confessed to forcing the two Long boys into raping Sarah."

"Yeah?"

"But he said it was just a misunderstanding."

Now that was the Jamie they all knew.

"Some confession," said Howser. "He must've known we talked to Annie."

"I don't know."

"What did he say about killing her?"

"Says he didn't do it."

"That's a surprise."

"He thinks his father killed her."

"He said that? Tom killed Sarah Miller?"

"Yeah."

Howser looked out the window and sighed. What next? This was getting ridiculous. Danielson murdering his own son's girlfriend? For what possible reason? He wondered

379

if Corey and Beef had turned anything up. There were still another good six hours of daylight left. Now they had someone else to run down.

Randy interrupted his thought. "Chief?"

"Yeah?"

"Jamie says that tramp's out there somewhere, waiting to kill him."

"So?"

"That's all he said. The kid's kind of strung out, you know what I mean?"

"I'm sure he is," said Howser. "What's happening with the Longs?"

"Denny and Craig said they went out there but nobody was home so they just stuck a note on the front door and came back in."

"Did Corey call in yet?"

"Haven't heard anything."

"All right, well, I'll be back into town in half an hour. Tell Denny and Craig I'd like them to go back out to the Longs' and wait there until somebody returns. You stay there at the courthouse with Jamie, and let Al and Archie go back out on patrol. And if Corey calls in before I get back, patch him straight through. I'll take care of Tom."

"Sure thing."

Howser signed off and stuck the mike back on the console. Tarweed was all over his shoes and pants from his short hike in the brush, and the sticky odor it carried was made even stronger by the heat. He took a swig of water from the bottle on the seat beside him. Then he fired up the engine and steered the unit out from under the sycamores and down through the old gate again toward the county road and away at last from Stuart's Mill.

The first explosion woke Ernie Long from the delirium he'd been floating in for the past ten hours. It rung in his head like a great bell, then waned. The second explosion came as a distant echo of the first. He threw open his swollen eyes. The monster was still there with him in the dark room, just across the floor, sitting up against the far wall and breathing loudly into the wood. It hadn't killed him yet, but he was expecting it to any time now.

Ernie's face was still fat and bloody, though the pain had diminished somewhat. Either that, he thought, or the feeling had gone out of his body and he was dying and didn't know it. Ernie watched the monster rubbing its own ugly face up against the wall. Every so often it snorted and coughed. It never seemed to sleep and only twice did it get up on its feet and walk: once, when he saw it for the first time, and then again when it dropped a half-eaten candy bar by his foot. He kept expecting the monster to roll open the wall and jump outside and go kill somebody, but it never did. It just stayed in there with him, making peculiar noises and shuffling about in its own dark corner. Maybe it was trapped now, too.

The chocolate was the only food Ernie had eaten in three days yet he wasn't hungry. With Howie gone, and his own death awaiting him, he just felt dried-up and hollow. He wasn't even aware that he was lying in his own filth. His nose was broken so badly, and his tongue so swollen and bruised, that neither tastes nor smells were getting through to his brain. He just lay there in the dark on the wooden floor feeling awful. Then the explosions woke him and his blood stirred.

A shuffling noise from outside followed the echo from the second explosion by a few minutes. Ernie shifted his head to listen at the wall. Somebody was there nearby, walking around. He looked across the room at the monster and saw that its head, too, was pressed to the wood, listening as he was. The shuffling seemed to circle the room, passing in and out of the wood. Then it stopped, and something splashed on the walls outside. And again. And a third time. And Ernie heard a soft trickling from the wood, like rainwater dripping from the guttered eaves outside his bedroom window. The monster rolled onto its knees. And there was a loud *pop!* from beneath the floor and then the crackling of long grass burning everywhere at once.

In the dark, the smoke rose like a shadow on the wood. Ernie crawled to his knees and huddled in his own corner.

The monster stood up and the floor sagged underneath. In a few short minutes they were both choking in the failing air. Splinters on the outer walls of the old boxcar ignited while the flames in the grass scorched the bottom. Then it was burning, and the heat from the floorboards singed the skin on Ernie's knees. He forced himself up against the wall and looked down at the fire coming through the wood at his feet. The paint on the outside of the boxcar peeled off and melted away into the air with millions of bits of ash rising now from the flames raging through the other train cars and off into the trees on both sides of the tracks. The monster bellowed in agony and hurled itself at the dark wall, shaking the car thunderously and knocking Ernie to the floor where his skin made contact with the burning wood and cracked instantly and blackened. Then the walls and floor split open at the seams and the dark was erased by a searing light and the hair on Ernie's head disappeared in a puff of smoke. The monster shrieked idiotically and beat its fists against its own smoldering skull, and from the burning floor Ernie watched in awe as it thrashed wildly about, howling furiously, then grabbed its head and plunged through the fiery side of the boxcar in a blaze of cinder and sparks. As it went, the skeletal frame of the boxcar shuddered violently and collapsed and Ernie followed the monster out into the air.

Standing on a dirt embankment overlooking Green River, Jane first saw the smoke rising in the blue sky to the north. She watched it drift and darken above the trees in the distance. Down below, Clayton was waist-deep in the river current, wading in his cutoffs.

"Look at that," said Jane, pointing at the smoke fanning out now in the air a mile or so away. Clayton came out of the water on the opposite sandbar where he could see farther upriver. "What do you think?"

Clayton shrugged. "Controlled burn?"

Jane shook her head. "Not in this weather. Besides, nobody lives over there."

A breeze tossed at Jane's hair. Birds chattered incessantly nearby in the trees. Clayton cupped a hand over his brow to shade his eyes as he scrutinized the widening smoke. "I don't know, then."

They both watched a little longer as the smoke billowed and deepened.

"I'm going to call it in," she said. "It looks like it's spreading."

Jane left the embankment and hurried down the short path through the brush to the end of the access road where they'd left the police car she'd borrowed for the afternoon. She slid into the front seat, grabbed the radio and patched straight through to the courthouse.

"Susan, this is Jane. Jack Clayton and I are out here at the river off Frazer Road and it looks like there's a fire about a mile due north of here. You'd better call Forestry."

"Okay."

"Is there anybody out here now besides us?"

"Hold on a second."

While Jane waited, Clayton waded back across the river and toweled off on the sandbar beneath the embankment. Then he climbed up to where he and Jane had eaten lunch in the grass, changed clothes, and began gathering up everything they'd brought out with them.

Susan came back on the radio. "It looks like Corey and Beef are right around there now. The last location they called in was Mockingbird Lane, so they should be close."

Jane looked north again toward the river. The smoke was heavy now. Clayton came out of the brush carrying the small plastic cooler and two backpacks. Jane raised the mike again and asked, "How long ago was that?"

"Corey calling in?"

"Yes."

"About forty-five minutes or so."

Clayton opened the rear door and dumped everything in the backseat. Then he closed the door and came around to the front. As he climbed in on the passenger side, Jane said to Susan, "Try raising Corey again and I'll call the chief. Jack and I are on our way up the road right now to take a closer look."

She hung the mike back on the console and pulled her door closed, then started the engine and wheeled the unit around and down through the underbrush toward the county highway. Brambles scraped the sides as she navigated the dirt access road just slowly enough to avoid bottoming out the suspension in the deeper ruts. When they came out of the brush, Jane turned right up onto the pavement and headed north in the direction of the smoke.

"What're we going to do when we get there?" asked Clayton, as they accelerated up the highway.

"I don't know," said Jane. "I suppose it depends on what we find. I better call the chief." She picked the mike up again. "RP2 to RP1."

A moment later, Howser's voice came on the radio. "Jane, what're you doing in Alfie's unit?"

"I had to borrow it for the day. My battery's dead."

"I thought you had the afternoon off."

"I do," she said.

"Where are you?"

"Out by the river."

"Not by yourself, I hope."

"No, Jack's here."

"What're you doing out there?"

"Well, we *were* having lunch," said Jane, "but it looks like there's a fire burning in the woods about a mile up the river from here. I think it's a bad one."

"You called it in?"

"Yes, but here's the problem: it should've been Corey's call. I'm down here off Frazer and the fire looks like it's near Mockingbird Lane, where he gave his last location. If he and Beef are out there, why didn't they call it in themselves?"

The speed draft from the highway dried the perspiration on Jane's forehead.

"How far are you from the fire right now?" asked Howser.

"I'll be there in two minutes."

As the unit passed under the spreading edge of the smoke, Jane saw the blue sky disappear above her.

"Okay, I'm another five minutes behind you. Stay in the unit until I get there, understand? And keep Clayton with you. Don't let him run off anywhere. And be careful."

Six miles to the south, Howser switched on the light bar and the siren, jerked the car into a screaming 180-degree turn in the middle of the road, then jammed his foot into the gas and gunned it back up the highway toward Green River.

"RP1 to RP3."

He waited a few seconds for Corey to pick up. Nothing. He tried again.

"RP1 to RP3."

Silence. Nothing on the scanner. He patched back through to base. Susan came on.

"Chief?"

"I want Al and Archie to set up roadblocks a mile apart to the north and south of Mockingbird Lane. Copy that?"

"Yes, sir."

"Send them out Code Three. I want them here now. Doc, too."

"Yes, sir."

Howser could see the smoke above the treeline, rising everywhere in the northeast by the river. He was closing quickly. Jane was right. It was a big fire. A bad one.

"And listen, tell them this: I don't want anybody except Doc and the forestry people going in or coming out. Tell them that. I don't care who it is. Understand?"

"Yes, sir."

"All right. Pull Denny and Craig off the Longs and send Craig out here with Randy. Denny can go back on patrol. I'll be at the river in about five minutes. Have Doc look for me when he gets there. And keep trying to raise Corey until you hear from one of us, okay?"

Howser signed off and stuck his foot harder on the gas. He knew what was going on. Not the specifics, but he had a general idea. He tried raising his two missing officers one more time.

"RP1 to RP3." Static on the scanner. "RP1 to RP3." He waited a few moments. Nothing. He tried again. Still nothing. He gave it up with the feeling that Corey wasn't going to be answering any more calls. Not today, not tomorrow. Howser angled off the main highway onto Mockingbird Lane. The smoke was drifting east from above the river, hiding the summer sky. Halfway up the narrow side road, Howser could smell it in the air. He slowed the unit to fifteen miles an hour and switched on his high beams. The sun was gone now and the smoke was getting thicker. Howser looked for Jane's unit on both sides of the road as he brought his own around a slight dogleg to the left and up a slope. Where was she?

"RP1 to RP2."

He slowed to ten miles an hour. Visibility was decreasing by the second and the heat inside the unit had become almost unbearable.

"RP1 to RP2."

No answer. Where was she? He ran the windshield wipers to clear the glass of ash. Then Clayton's voice came on the radio.

"Yeah, is that you, Howser?"

"Clayton? Where are you?"

"Uh, hold on a sec. Let me ask Jane."

Smoke drifted out over the road ahead and Howser brought the car to a stop. A light gray ash was raining down onto the front hood and windshield. He ran the wipers again and looked out through the glass. His eyes were beginning to burn.

"Chief?"

It was Jane.

"Yeah."

"Chief, we're in a clearing about three hundred yards from the river off Mockingbird Lane. Did you come in from the south?"

"Yeah, but I haven't seen any turnoffs yet."

"Just keep going north and you will. Take the first right. It's a dirt road. You can't miss it."

"All right."

Howser eased his foot off the brake and the unit moved forward again up the lane. The wipers were running continuously now and Howser had to squint to see where he was going. Another fifty yards and he spotted Jane's road dropping off to the right through a stand of oaks ringed in purple wildflowers. He entered slowly and drove up the middle of the dirt, just to be safe. The fire hadn't spread yet to this area of the brush but he knew it couldn't be that far off. He was afraid of getting trapped within the fireline and wondered just how far in Jane had driven. He couldn't imagine her being so careless as to get herself caught. Howser followed the narrow dirt road into a clearing where he found the black-and-white parked at the entrance, facing out. The fire was still beyond the treeline and the breeze was blowing, at least for the moment, toward the river. Howser brought his unit around in line with Jane's.

As he shut the engine down and switched off the siren and the light bar, he saw Jane emerging from the smoke to the east. She was coughing and waving her arms and yelling something. Howser climbed out into the heat and the falling ash stung in his eyes and made them water and close. Jane ran up to him.

"We think we found Corey."

Her face was dark with ash and her hair soaked in sweat. She shoved it back off her forehead with the palm of her hand. Her pupils appeared dilated in the shifting light.

"Where?"

She swung back around to the east and said, "This way."

Then she led him through the smoke to a spot in the woods bordering the fireline where Corey's unit lay trapped and smashed at the trunk of a large oak. Clayton was waiting there by the open rear door. His skin, like Jane's, was black and filthy, and droplets of sweat trickled down his face. He pointed Howser to the backseat, then stepped away from the battered car. Howser moved up and looked inside.

"My God."

One glance was all it took for Howser to know who it was (only Corey wore the uniform that way) and what had happened (he had seen bad shotgun wounds before). The backseat looked (and, in the heat, smelled, too) like the inside of a slaughterhouse, and, for a moment, the sight of it disoriented him. How could those dark stains belong in any unit he commanded, or that officer, butchered from the shoulders up, resemble anybody he'd ever known? *Sonofabitch!* Howser jerked his head out of the car. A few feet back in the drifting smoke, Jane stood beside Clayton—the two of them watching, stony-faced, like a pair of ghosts. Behind them, the fire raged in the long grass and ignited leaf to leaf in the trees above. The heat scorched Howser's face, but the unit was not in danger. Not just yet. Howser stared at the approaching flames.

"Whoever did this expected the fire to move faster," he said. "We weren't supposed to find it like this."

Jane circled away from Clayton to the other side of the unit.

"What are we going to do?"

Howser looked into the front seat at the steering column. The keys were still in the ignition. He noticed, too, the shotgun mounting. It was empty. Was Corey killed with his own weapon? Good God.

"We'll have to try driving it out."

"I'm not sure we can," said Clayton. "It looks stuck."

Howser got down on his knees and looked underneath the rear wheel assembly. The suspension was sunk into the dust up to the floorpan. He said, "Maybe we can free it up."

Clayton walked around to the back of the unit and slipped a hand under the bumper.

"We can try."

"Whatever you're going to do, make it quick," said Jane. "We're running out of time here."

Howser got up and looked at Jane. "You get behind the wheel and we'll lift from the back."

She nodded and climbed inside and started the engine while Howser went to take a position beside Clayton along the rear bumper. As he searched for a clear grip, he yelled, "Don't put it in gear until I say so." Then he turned to Clayton, "You ready?"

They could both feel the fire moving closer in the brush behind them. Clayton winced and tightened his grip.

"Okay, Jane. Hit it!"

The back wheels spun hard into the dirt, churning grass and dust out the sides of the wheel wells. Howser and Clayton strained to lift the rear end a few inches up from the dust. Jane pressed down a little harder on the gas while the two men dug in with their toes and heaved.

"In low!" yelled Clayton. "Put it in low!"

Jane dropped the gear lever into low and shoved her right foot into the pedal, racing the engine until the car shuddered hard and lurched away from the tree. She drove straight through the brush and out into the clearing, then rolled to a stop next to Howser's unit and shut the engine off. Climbing out of the car, she could hear sirens wailing on the highway in the distance. The fire trucks were only a couple of miles to the west now, and closing. A few seconds later, Howser and Clayton came out of the brush behind her, both of them filthy in sweat-soaked dirt and smoke.

Howser went straight to the radio and patched through to base. When Susan came on, he gave her his location and asked if she'd gotten hold of Doc Sawyer.

"He should be out there any minute," she answered.

"Does he know how to find us?"

"He said he did."

"Okay."

Susan asked, "Did you find Corey?"

Howser looked at Jane, waiting there by his shoulder, listening to the conversation. She blinked some sweat from her eyes and stared back at him. He shook his head, "No, we haven't seen him at all."

He signed off and stuck the mike back on the console. He knew what Jane was thinking but there was no point in trying to explain. Instead, he climbed out of the unit and said, "We got to find Beef."

Jane turned toward the smoke rising in the trees only a few dozen yards away.

"I don't know where he'd be," she said. "If he's behind the fireline . . ."

Her voice trailed off. She stared at the fire just coming visible in the brush. The heat pushed at her face.

"If he's behind the fireline," said Howser, "he's probably dead. But if he's not, we've got to try to find him while we still can."

"There's a path up there," said Clayton, gesturing to

the north. "It runs parallel to the fire. If he made it out of the brush, maybe . . ."

Clayton kicked at the ground where a thin layer of ash hid the dirt. Up above, the smoke darkened further in the air.

"Someone's got to stay and wait for Doc," said Howser. He looked at Jane. "Okay?"

She lowered her eyes. "Yeah, I'll stay."

Climbing into Alfie's unit, she watched Howser and Clayton disappear into the smoke to the north. On the scanner she could hear Archie and Al monitoring the road-blocks on Mockingbird Lane. They'd just let Doc Sawyer pass through. Forestry was arriving now, shutting down their sirens and preparing their equipment. The smoke had extended west to the highway and visibility there was di-minishing by the minute. Jane looked in her rearview mir-ror. The fire was burning now through the spot where they'd found Corey's unit. Another ten minutes or so and it would be at the clearing. She rolled the windows up in the black-and-white and started the engine.

In the thickets to the north, smoke was so dense Howser lost track of Clayton immediately and had to work his way through alone. For the first few minutes he kept the fire on his right and tried to maintain as straight a line forward as possible. Then the temperature in the brush rose and the heat seared his skin wherever it was exposed and Howser lost direction in the smoke. He wandered blindly for a couple of minutes then stumbled across a broken tree branch and fell to his knees. The grass there was already smoldering and it singed the palms of his hands. He got to his feet, ash swirling in his face, and clawed forward another few yards through the thicket. Smoke burned in his lungs and eyes. The fire arched over him from the east, roaring loudly in the trees above. He knew he had to keep moving but the heat was so intense he found it impossible to locate the fireline in the smoky brush. For all he knew it was on top of him and he'd already run out of luck.

He shouted for Clayton, waited a few seconds, then crashed forward through the brush. Everywhere above him leaves and moss crackled and exploded into flame. Burning ash fell onto his uniform. Howser shouted again and looked around. Nothing but smoke, swirling now in the fire wind. If he got himself lost now, he was dead. He looked around, trying to find his bearings. It was then he saw the figure through the corridor of smoke. Just a dark shape, standing maybe forty yards away, silhouetted in the firelight beneath a burning tree. Howser stared in disbelief. *What the hell . . . ?* As he watched, the figure seemed to turn toward him and its face became visible in the firelight. *A dark face . . .* Then the smoke swirled again and the figure vanished. He stared into the smoke. The apparition was gone and the smoke was thickening. *Was that . . . ? Christ almighty!* Choking badly now, Howser drew the handkerchief from his breast pocket and folded it over his nose and mouth. Which direction was the highway? He had to make a decision right now but, Christ, if he went the wrong way . . . Deciding that going anywhere was preferable to standing still, he started blindly into the brush. As he did, a shout echoed out of the smoke behind him. He stopped and spun around and heard it again—a voice, Clayton's, calling him.

"Howser!"

The voice filtered through the roar of the fire and Howser answered back with a yell. Clayton called again and Howser broke toward the sound, plowing a path violently through the thicket as he went. He found Clayton a dozen yards away stooped beneath the low branch of a large oak. He had a small lateral cut on his forehead that was bleeding into his eyes. The expression on his face was flat and passionless but his eyes were open wide. At his feet, in the long grass, was a small boy's body huddled up against the base of the tree. As Howser moved in under the tree himself, Clayton said, "I found him."

The boy was blackened virtually head to toe. The fingers on his right hand were clenched into a fist and one side of his face was swollen and featureless. There wasn't a trace of hair left anywhere on his body. Howser stared at him. The boy's eyes were shut. He leaned down and stroked the boy's arm with a forefinger. The skin was wet and bloody and warm.

"He's dead," said Clayton.

Howser studied the boy's face. Smoke filled the heated

air. Less than ninety feet away, the fire hissed in the trees, dissolving leaves into ash by the thousands. Clayton glanced down at the boy, then shifted his attention to Howser.

"Who is it?"

Howser met Clayton's eyes. "I'm not sure."

The police chief backed out from under the tree limb and twisted to look at the fire. As a blast of heat caught him in the face, he straightened up. The two men stared at each other across the dark body in the grass.

"We've got to get him out of here," said Howser. He looked down again at the boy. "We're just going to have to pick him up and carry him out. That's all there is to it. We can't leave him here."

Clayton coughed harshly, and nodded. The fire, crawling steadily closer, ignited another foot of grass and brush. Large smoking flakes of gray ash flew everywhere. The sun vanished overhead.

Then Jane yelled out from somewhere nearby.

"Chief!"

Howser moved a few steps out from the body and called back, "Over here!"

Then there were other voices, too, filling the woods, and five figures walking out of the smoke to the west. Howser watched them approach—Jane and Doc Sawyer in the lead, followed on the flanks by three county firefighters, stomping through the brush in full gear.

"Forestry's down on the road. Did you find Beef?" asked Jane, coming up to the tree. She saw the boy in the grass and stopped. "Oh my God."

Howser moved aside to give Doc Sawyer access to the body. One of the firefighters began unfolding a stretcher. As Doc crept in under the tree to examine the boy, Clayton looked at Jane. There was an incendiary light reflecting in her eyes from the fire rising in the woods. Howser watched Doc go over the body while two of the firefighters laid the stretcher out in the grass. The third wandered in the smoke near the fireline relaying information into a walkie-talkie. Doc stood up quickly and caught the attention of the firefighters waiting with the stretcher.

"We have to move him right now." Then he shouted

through the smoke to the one with the walkie-talkie, "Billy, tell them we're on our way back!"

The fireman acknowledged with a wave, and Doc turned to face Howser. "This boy's alive."

Howser shot his eyes back to the body. He searched the boy's face for some sign of life, and saw none. The skin was still black and broken, hair gone, lips and eyelids seemingly melted shut.

"You're kidding," said Clayton, staring now, too, at the same burned and lifeless body he'd stumbled upon in the smoke only a few minutes earlier. He turned to Jane. "God, how can he be alive?"

"He won't be much longer," replied Doc, "unless we get him out of here right now." He turned to the firefighters waiting with the stretcher. "Guys?" They moved in beside him under the tree and, with Doc's help, lifted the boy from the grass and onto the stretcher. They raised him up and backed carefully out from under the oak. Then they covered the boy with a flame-resistant blanket and prepared the stretcher for transport. Howser watched them fit the straps.

"Do you have any idea who it is?"

Doc Sawyer stood up and removed his glasses and mopped the sweat from his face with a handkerchief. The smoke had stung and blackened his skin as it had everyone else's.

"Yeah," he answered, dabbing his eyelids. "I sure do." He blinked until his vision cleared and he replaced his glasses. "It's Ernie Long."

The fireman with the walkie-talkie came up beside Doc and Howser.

"The wind's changing. We better go."

Doc nodded, and wiped his face again. Howser watched the firemen with the stretcher start off into the smoke. The moss on the upper branches of the oak smoldered as the fire neared. The tails of the rattlesnake grass darkened and sagged twenty feet away. Jane hurried out from under the tree; she'd felt the heat singeing her eyelashes and was certain her hair was going to catch fire any second. Doc followed the two firemen with the stretcher into the brush. Clayton walked a few feet after Doc, then paused to wait there in the grass when he saw that the others weren't coming just yet.

"What are we going to do about Beef?" asked Jane, brushing ash from her hair.

"I'm not sure," replied Howser. The light was changing now, brightening as the fire surged into the trees above them. Howser backed toward the fireman with the walkie-talkie. "There's nowhere we—"

A hollow blast sounded in the distance from the direction of the river. Four heads turned as one. The echo followed in the air. An instant later, the moss on the oak they had been standing under exploded into cinder and flame up and down the length of the tree. The heat seared the skin on Howser's face and neck, and he stumbled backward with the others into the thicket, scrambling to get out from under the fire as it shot through into the long dry branches above them.

"That was a shotgun," yelled Howser, slowing in the thicket to look up at the trees. Nothing but smoke and leaves. He caught up with Jane and grabbed her arm. "That blast back there was a shotgun!"

She stopped and stared back at him, her face swollen now and red. The leaves overhead began to hiss, and the fireman crossed into the brush behind her, parallel to the fire, alternately coughing and shouting into the walkie-talkie. Howser spoke directly into Jane's face.

"Do you understand what I'm saying? I've got to get over there."

She blinked and dark water ran from her eyes.

"You can't," she said, glancing to the east toward the river. "Even the old train's probably burned to the ground by now."

Leaves flickered and charred high up in the trees around them. Clayton ran up out of the smoke, shouting, "We got to keep moving!"

Howser ignored him, keeping his attention focused on Jane.

"What train? What're you talking about?"

"The circus train," she said. "On the old nine track. River line."

Howser coughed and drew his handkerchief out again.

Over the roar of the fire he yelled, "Nobody told me anything about a train out here."

The grass on the trailing edge of the thicket sparked and flared up and Clayton moved off a few strides into the brush, then looked back. The fire gave his face a peculiar shade in the smoke. He shouted, "Come on, we've got to go!"

Jane watched the flames crossing into the trees overhead. She felt the heat surging, even through her clothing.

"How far would I have to go to get around it?" yelled Howser.

"Around the train?" said Jane, distracted by the inferno roaring toward her from above.

"Yeah, how far do I have to go to get around the train?"

"I don't know," she said. "Three hundred yards? I'm not sure. I don't remember exactly where it is."

Howser grabbed her by the arm and pulled her forward through the brush just as a flurry of burning cinder and ash rained down from the upper branches blown free by a hot wind in the air. They escaped into the thicket. Another fifteen yards and they ran into the fireman evading the burn from the south. Then the three of them yelled for Clayton and waited, keeping their eyes on the fire, until he came out of the smoke from the northeast, choking.

"I need to get on the other side of the fire," said Howser, turning to the fireman. "How can I do it?"

"He's got to get past the old circus train to the river," said Jane. Smoke billowed in heavily from the east and the air began heating up again. "But we're not sure exactly where the train is."

"I could see a section of it from the fireline a few minutes ago. But it's burning like crazy in there. There's no way you can get through from here."

"I know that," said Howser. "But what about around?"

The fireman looked at Jane. She shrugged. Water welled up in her eyes and she blinked them clear. Clayton paced anxiously in the tall grass a few feet away.

"How about to the north?" asked Jane. "You guys came in that way."

The fireman watched a fragment of burning ash flutter

down into the grass at his feet. He stamped it out with his boot.

"Yeah," he nodded. "That's a possibility."

"How far would I have to go?" asked Howser. The fire in the trees was lighting his face again. They were going to have to move any moment now.

The fireman turned to Jane. "What do you think? Maybe another couple hundred yards?"

"I don't know," she answered. "Maybe less."

"Or more," offered Clayton, looking back over his shoulder at the brush becoming incandescent that very instant.

"I'll take you there," said Jane, as the fire blew into the grass behind her. The four of them started to separate in the smoke.

"No! You get back to the clearing," yelled Howser, moving off into the brush at a tangent from the other three. "Send Randy and Craig, if they think they can get a unit in there. Otherwise, have them wait for me out on the road."

Then the others were gone, their voices passing quickly out of earshot, and Howser was alone again, hurrying through the hot smoke. He ran hard in the thicket, fending branches off with his hands, keeping an eye on the fireline as he went. Glowing bits of ash fell in his path and his lungs burned both from the smoke and his own furious breathing. The hot wind was increasing now, blowing thousands of sparks ahead into the treetops, but the roar of the flames wild in the thicket dulled the farther Howser ran and the smoke thinned visibly around him.

He came out of the brush onto a dirt access road running east and west between the river and the highway, similar to the one he had taken to reach Jane's clearing half an hour earlier. The road looked empty in both directions. Howser stopped for a few seconds to catch his breath, then went east through the smoke toward Green River. Fifty feet up the middle of the road he heard the second shotgun blast. It sounded so close that Howser's first thought was to look for cover but when he heard the echo following in the distance, he realized the shot had come from somewhere farther up on the river bluff and he started running in that direction. The road ended another forty yards ahead where the ground dipped to form a shallow basin in the heavy brush. A red Chevy Blazer was parked there with its lights on and the engine running. It was a familiar vehicle, one Howser had seen already too often that summer. It belonged to Tom Danielson.

He drew his revolver and reached inside the cab and switched off the ignition and palmed the keys. As he slipped them into his pocket he heard a third shot, this one echoing away down the river canyon. It was followed by the sound of a blown shell being ejected from a pump action shotgun. Howser clawed through the brushline and into the long grass 150 feet from the river bluff. For the first time since Stuart's Mill he found himself standing under a silver-blue sky, the smoke having been driven off by the wind, while ahead of him, leaning over the edge of the bluff, twelve-gauge shotgun in hand, was Danielson.

The wind rippled quietly through the grass: Howser could hear his own shoes crunching in the dirt as he walked toward the bluff. The air was clear above the river. The haze had all gone into the west. Halfway to the river, Howser was close enough to smell the water and Danielson still hadn't noticed him. He'd caught him by surprise. Thirty feet away, he stopped.

"What're you looking for, Tom?"

Startled by the voice, Danielson nearly lost his footing. Howser walked a few feet closer and brought a sleeve across his eyes, wiping away the sweat. Danielson straightened. He saw the torn, filthy uniform and smiled, letting the shotgun barrel tilt slowly toward the ground.

"You look like hell, Chief."

Howser ran his eyes over the surrounding area. He needed to know they were alone. The trees stirred soundlessly in the wind. Even the birds had gone off somewhere. It looked as though they had the bluff to themselves.

"What're you shooting at, Tom?"

The grip on Howser's revolver was becoming sweaty; he held it stiffly at his side. Danielson's fingers tightened on the shotgun.

"The tramp was out here all this time and we didn't even know it. He was hiding in one of the old train cars."

"Yeah?" Howser imagined he could hear the river flowing lazily below the bluff, but maybe it was only the wind passing in the trees. "Where's he now?"

"He attacked me and I shot him. I knocked the son of a bitch into the river. He's gone."

Keeping his eye on Danielson, Howser walked through the grass to the edge of the bluff and looked over.

"You won't be able to see him," said Danielson. "I told you, he's gone." He slipped his free hand into his shirt pocket while Howser watched the river swirling by sixty feet below. He drew out a fistful of .00 shells. "I'm pretty sure he set the fire, too. Probably to cover his tracks."

Howser cocked his head in Danielson's direction.

"The tramp set the fire?"

"Yeah."

Howser took a step back away from the river. "Tom, how about putting the gun down? All right?"

Danielson stood motionless, five .00 shells in one hand and the shotgun in the other. Howser stared into the empty afternoon sky. He frowned and kicked the grass at his feet.

Danielson lowered his right arm until the barrel of the shotgun was touching the dirt.

Howser asked, "Where's Beef?"

"How would I know?" Danielson answered. "He's your responsibility, not mine."

Howser wiped the perspiration from his eyes again. "Isn't that his shotgun you got there?"

Danielson looked down at the elaborate circle pattern custom-carved into the stock. His expression changed, and the smile went away. "You're right. I suppose it is."

"So where is he?"

Danielson looked off down the river to where it curved into the southwest. The sun lighted his face and he had to squint. Beads of sweat shone on his skin. "It's funny, isn't it, the way the heat makes you feel."

His eyes brightened in the light.

"We found the unit in the woods," said Howser.

"Good work."

"We found Corey in the backseat."

"Is that right?"

"You must be crazy, Tom. He was a police officer."

"You know, Howser"—Danielson loaded a shell into the shotgun and strolled to his right—"I always thought it was a mistake bringing you here to this town, giving you that badge, letting you think you were somebody important."

Howser moved a few steps too, maneuvering the sun away from his eyes.

"Your kid's in jail, Tom. He gave himself up out at your place an hour ago. He admitted forcing his friends into raping the Miller girl." The gun in Howser's hand was becoming heavier by the second. "But you know what? He told us you killed her, Tom."

Danielson loaded in another shell and looked up.

"He said that?"

"Yes, he did."

"My son's an idiot."

The wind gusted in the dry grass, surging through the trees above the river. Danielson rolled the last three shells between his thumb and fingers. Howser watched, his eyes fixed hard on the shotgun.

"Why don't you tell me what all this is about, Tom?"

The wind blew through Danielson's hair from behind, ruffling his shirt. He loaded another shell and angled his face away from the sun.

"The girl was a little slut. I told my kid to stay away from her. I told him she'd be trouble, but he wouldn't listen to me. He still went sniffin' after her every night."

"Sarah Miller was raped by her own friends, Tom." Howser felt the long grass fanning his legs. "And four days later she was beaten to death. Why?"

Danielson looked off into the northwest where the sky was still clear and blue. His fingers flexed around the trigger ring of the shotgun.

"Did you know there are people in Sacramento willing to come down here and put together a development along this part of the river? Did you know that? Six months ago not one of them had ever heard of Rivertown. And now, in a few weeks, they're going to come here and spend a whole lot of money. They're going to do us all a big favor. And you know why? Because I asked them to. What do you think of that?"

"I don't know what to think anymore, Tom," Howser answered, blinking furiously to clear the water from his eyes, "because I don't know what any of this is about. Half an hour ago I found another one of my officers dead. He was shot in the face. Can you imagine that? And there's a boy back there we just carried out of the woods. He's burned half to death and his head looks like somebody's clubbed him pretty good. What kind of person does that to a kid?"

"You're the expert, Howser. Figure it out."

"I'd rather hear it from you."

"You know, Howser, you're the worst kind of phony. We both know you didn't like those kids any more than I did, and the only reason you came out here today was because you were worried about losing your job. Well, it's too late for that now. By tomorrow morning, we'll be hiring your replacement."

"You killed the Williams kid, too, didn't you?"

Danielson laughed. "Hell, I killed all four of the little shits! If the whole story on that crap they pulled at the railyard had gotten out, it would've queered my deal with Sacramento. Reputation's half of business. You ought to know that."

"So that's why you've been murdering transients out on the river for the past twenty years, huh? Business?"

Danielson rubbed the fourth shell along the stock on the shotgun. He frowned. "Every one of them was trespassing on my property. I don't allow trespassing. I was brought up to respect private property. People who don't understand that get themselves into trouble. I warned Lou Hudson. He made me put some signs up. They got ignored. So I handled it myself. I've got my rights."

"You've hurt a lot of people, Tom, just to protect your privacy."

Danielson shoved the fourth shell into the shotgun. "You have no idea what I've done."

Howser's uniform felt cold and wet now in the wind and his face and hands stung from the burns he'd suffered in the brush.

"Put the gun down, Tom, and step away from it."

"Don't tell me what to do."

"You're under arrest."

"Sure I am."

Howser brought the revolver up to shoulder level and pointed it at Danielson.

"Put it down."

"You're going to shoot me if I don't?"

"Those were my men you killed, goddammit! I won't ask you again."

Danielson lifted his eyes and watched the smoke drifting white on blue above the woods, and shook his head. He jammed the last shell into the breech and loaded it.

"Go to hell, Howser."

He raised the shotgun.

And Howser shot him through the chest.

25

The room was empty now. Linen stripped away. Closet and floor space exposed. Windows and drawers thrown open to summer light and air. A television set down the hall played into the emptiness, filling it in the same way as did the breeze in the weeping willow outside the south window or the slow voices on the front porch downstairs. Jack Clayton stood in the middle of the floor letting his eyes detail the changes two hours of moving had brought about. He made a single sweep of the room. It was more or less how he had first seen it in June, with the roseate wallpaper rippled and sunfaded on the east wall and the ceiling plaster fractured overhead and the hardwood floorboards warped on the closet and hallway thresholds and the dust (and ash now, too) heavy in each bottom storm-screen runner. He searched for some obvious difference, something to indicate he had been there for a month, but found nothing. The impression he had made on this small corner of Rivertown had apparently been slight.

A woman's laughter rung through the arbor below. Clayton walked to the south window and looked out. It was already late in the afternoon. The drive west to Santa Cruz would take at least four hours, which meant he wouldn't get there now until after dark—just as he'd come into Rivertown. There was a dream he remembered from that first night, a peculiar dream about dry grass-swept hillsides and silent winds in tall houses and a child's ruffled bedspread and the light at the end of the day. It had caused him to wake into the blue shadows of his room feeling hollow and depressed, completely disoriented by a meaningless dream. Now, he was feeling only distracted, perhaps a little restless. *You were wrong, Mick. This wasn't a good place for me to hide away in. I would've been better off going all the way home instead.* He came away from the window, back into the sunlit middle of the room. He went over everything carefully one last time, in and out of the closet and each of the drawers, checking to see that he hadn't forgotten anything. Then, when he was done, he walked to the west window, pulled the long canvas shade down flush with the sill, tied it closed, and left.

Downstairs, Jane kicked her feet into the air, gently rocking the porch swing into motion. The chains creaked in the wooden sockets. Howser sat on the railing in the sunlight nearer the front door. The burns he had suffered in the woods showed a week's worth of healing. Most of the pain had gone. He had just that morning been able to take a shower without cringing under the hot water. Though Jane's burns had not been nearly as severe as his, she had taken care that her skin not become infected and had stayed out of the sun for the first few days after the experience on Green River. Now she sat in the shade of the porch and rocked with the passing breeze.

When she was a little girl, her father had taken her walking one day out beyond Sturgeon's lumberyard on the south side of town to a trailer court in a cottonwood grove just off the old highway. Why he had chosen that place as the terminus for their walk she did not know but he had brought her with him in under the green shadows to a dingy trailer in the center of the court and then left her sitting on the doorstep while he went inside. She waited perfectly still with her hands folded in her lap, counting as high as she could, which did not take her very long. Then she recited the alphabet forward and backward and when her father still did not come out of the trailer she got up and knocked on the door. There was no answer. She called for her father but the door remained closed so she went looking for him, down

*the steps and off between that trailer and another, scuffing
her tiny black shoes in the dirt as she went. She heard voices
chattering in the trailers around her. Some of them sounded
like her father's, most did not. She walked along calling
out for him, repeating his name like a prayer. The back
end of the trailers opened up into a small dirt yard. She
found children playing a game there. They were naked and
dusty or wearing dirty corduroys and old denim. When she
walked out from between the trailers and the children saw
her, their game stopped and the yard went silent. Her mother
had dressed her that day in a white dirndl skirt with a puffy-
sleeved blouse and a crinoline petticoat peeking out under
a hemline trimmed in rickrack and a big pink bow in back.
It looked like a birthday dress, but it was not her birthday.
She stopped at the side of the yard. The leather ball they
had been playing with rolled to a rest in the dirt by her feet.
She picked it up and looked at them. Their eyes were cheerless and gray. She told them her name. They stared at her
in silence. None of them spoke. She set the ball back down
in the dirt. Her father called and she said good-bye politely
with a smile. They did not say a word. Even when she was
struck in the bottom with a dirt clod as she ran off, not one
of them laughed or called out an obscenity after her. She
reached her father's arms by the roadside, humiliated and
distraught, and cried most of the way home. Later on, when
she was older, the route the school bus took in the afternoons
brought her past the same trailer court in the grove of cottonwood trees by the old highway. The children were still
there, hollow-eyed and filthy, but her bus never stopped to
let any of them on board. And then, one afternoon, there
was no trailer court at all. Nothing under those cottonwood
trees but dust and shade. When she asked her father where
the trailers had gone and the people who had lived in them,
all he would tell her was, "Somewhere else, honey. They
just all went somewhere else."*

Jack Clayton came out onto the porch from the lobby. The
sun was in his eyes. He walked past Howser and lifted
himself onto the railing, sitting with his back to the light,
halfway between the porch swing and the stairs. He looked

over at Jane, rocking slowly in the shade. She smiled at him.

"How was Porterville?"

"Slow," he said, "but friendly. A lot of produce."

"How were your friends?"

"Doing pretty well."

"You missed some news here while you were gone."

"Oh, yeah? What happened?"

"They caught Jerry and Roy."

"Where?"

"In a parking lot next to Disneyland. They were arrested by the Anaheim police last night just after closing time. Dennis left this morning to go pick them up."

"What were they doing down there?"

Jane looked at Howser and laughed.

He leaned out and looked back at her, then laughed, too.

"What's so funny?" asked Clayton.

"Tell him," said Jane.

"The two of them beat up Mickey Mouse last night in Fantasyland."

"You're kidding."

"Nope," said Howser. "Apparently they attacked the kid in the Mickey Mouse suit outside of Snow White's Castle as the park was closing. They knocked him down, tore his suit up, and then took off. The security people chased them into Tomorrowland, where the kids jumped the fence somehow and got out of the park. Three city black-and-whites caught up with them in a hotel parking lot a couple of hundred yards away and nailed 'em. When their ID's were run on the computer, Orange County got a hit and gave us a call."

"Why'd they beat up Mickey?"

Jane laughed again.

"I suppose because they're a couple of idiots," said Howser, "I can't imagine any other reason."

A water truck rumbled past on the street, raising the dust again and rattling the beveled windows in the front door. Clayton watched it pass. As it rolled out of view, he asked, "What happened with that kid we found in the woods?"

"Doc had him sent to the burn unit in Sacramento. He's still critical but hanging in there."

"And his buddy's in jail?"

"Yeah, though Jamie's getting moved to Stockton tomorrow. His lawyer's hoping for a change of venue. They're trying to get him as far away from here as possible."

"Think it'll make a difference?"

"Nope," said Howser. "They'll be lucky to find either a judge or a jury anywhere in this state sympathetic to a kid who gave his own girlfriend over to be raped by his friends. And he's got the Annie Connor kidnapping and the crap he did in the orchard house on top of that. He wouldn't even get off in San Bernardino County. They'll probably try him as an adult and send him away for the rest of the decade."

"His mother flew up from Glendale yesterday," said Jane. "She's been camping out in the courthouse lobby, tying up the phone lines with calls to lawyers all over the state. And Jamie's older brother Luke's in town now, too, staying out at the ranch, looking after things."

"They must've been thrilled to hear about the old man," said Clayton.

Jane shrugged. "Neither of them has said a thing about it since they got here."

"Maybe they weren't surprised."

"His kid wasn't. Before we went out to search his house," said Howser, "Jamie told us to look in a cardboard box in his father's bedroom closet. That's where we found Sarah Miller's clothes, bloodstains all over them. Apparently Tom had killed her in the barn, then stripped the body, dumped it in the river and hid her clothes."

"Why?"

"Why'd he kill her?"

"Yeah."

"That's hard to say. Killings like this sometimes steamroll. At first, it just seems to happen, you don't really know why. Then you begin doing things because you think you have to, and after a while you're doing them just because you can. I'd like to be able to give you an answer about all those tramps it looks like he murdered out on the river, but I can't. I'm no psychiatrist. All I can say is that he told me they were trespassing, violating his private property, so he felt within his rights to kill them. Yeah, it's crazy, I know, but that's how he saw it. Now, as to the question of how he was able to get away with even one homicide, much less fourteen, well, that's something I plan on spending some time looking into. There's a certain deep-sea fisherman in Florida I'd like to talk to. Retired or not.

"Regarding the teenage kids, I'm sure the initial idea was to protect his son which would also, in his mind I suppose, save his own reputation. Maybe he felt that the people he was dealing with in Sacramento wouldn't tie their money up with a family that had a rape prosecution pending. That's just a guess. Who really knows? We got lucky and it didn't work out for him. Annie Connor was the key. Once she decided to talk, it was all over. Things just sort of unraveled on him, fell apart. Annie gave us Jamie and he turned over his old man. What happened out by the river only finished it. I'll tell you something though, that girl's incredibly lucky to be alive. If Danielson had found her before she came in to talk to us, there's no doubt in my mind she'd be as dead right now as her friends."

Another truck, an old flatbed Ford, drove by. The dogs two doors away ran out after it into the street, barking crazily in a dusty draft. The bougainvillea rippled lightly on the trellis.

"And the tramp?"

"I don't know about that," said Howser. "We've guessed from talking with Ernie, as much as he *could* talk, that Danielson had them both locked up in one of the circus boxcars. As for why, we're not sure, but possibly he hoped the tramp kid would kill Ernie, then Danielson could step in and kill the tramp and use him as a cover for his own killings. He'd be the hero and the case'd be closed. My officers probably surprised him out there near the boxcar and he couldn't think of anything else to do but kill both of them and set fire to the train. The autopsy on Officer MacAlister's body showed it'd been soaked in gasoline there in that Pullman car before the train even caught fire. Same thing with the boxcar Ernie Long and the Kid had been locked up in. I suppose after he set the fire Danielson spotted the Kid getting away and tracked him down and shot him. As for how he found the Kid initially, and where the Kid was between the night of the shootings at the railyard and the fire, we don't know. We do think it was the Kid who was responsible for the trashing of Redmon's Garage, but that's just speculation at this point. We don't have any real proof."

"So you haven't found the tramp's body yet either, huh?" asked Clayton.

Howser looked away into the sun and closed his eyes. The light still stung where his skin had been burned. He thought about the promise he'd made to a skinny tramp named Robinson that afternoon at Curry Station. *Nobody's going to shoot anybody. I'm sorry about what happened to the old man, but it's not going to go down that way with the Kid.* He thought about it because six days ago Danielson had made a liar out of him.

"No," said Howser, "but we will eventually. Or somebody else will. It'll probably turn up downriver. Give it a few weeks."

"That's a cheery thought," said Jane.

Howser raised his eyes. She was looking at him.

"Jane watched us drag Howie Long's body out of the old reservoir on Friday," he explained to Clayton with a grin, "and it ruined her whole morning."

"Most gruesome thing I've ever seen," she said, rocking the swing now with one foot. "I was sick for the rest of the day."

She slowed her rocking and repositioned the pillow on the seat. Then she kicked the porch swing into motion again and the breeze blew softly in her hair. Howser stepped back down onto the porch.

"Well, he'd been in the water since the Fourth and when we finally pulled him out he was looking pretty bad."

He walked to the lobby entrance and looked in.

"Bad," said Jane, "is an understatement."

It was quiet inside the hotel. The ceiling fan was circling slowly over the front desk and the lace curtains in the east window were open and fluttering. A square clock on the desk read half past six. The television set on the third floor that had been going all day long was silent now and most of the upstairs guests had either gone out for the day or were lost in late-afternoon sleep. For a few moments Howser studied the old rose strip carpet, light-faded and worn at the bottom of the staircase, then shifted his attention back to Clayton, still sitting there on the railing with his face in the sunshadow.

"I hear you're on your way to the coast."

Clayton nodded, fighting off a yawn. "It's too hot around here. I don't do well in warm weather."

"We cool off in September," said Jane, "just in time for school." She smiled. "Usually."

"Well, I have friends on the coast in Big Sur I haven't seen in a while and this just seems like it might be a good time to give them a visit. And my father called me from Huntington Beach the other night. He asked me to come home for the holidays this year." He slipped down off the railing. "I promised him I would." He looked across the porch at Jane. "I've been away a long time."

She brought the swing to a stop. The sun was strong in the west and as she stood she brought a hand up to shade her eyes. She heard Howser walk off down the stairs, leaving Clayton in the center of the porch, waiting patiently in the light. When she came up to him, he slipped an arm around her waist and they walked together down into the yard where his van was parked in the gravel.

Clayton played with the keys in his right hand. As they reached the van, he said to her, "I didn't get a chance to say good-bye to Ellen."

"I know. She had to take off early. Her sister wanted her up in Grass Valley by noon. She told me to say good-bye for her, though. I promised her you'd send us a postcard."

"Okay."

He turned to Howser: "What about you? I hear you'll be helping Jane run the hotel while Ellen's gone."

"He'll be handling our dirty laundry," said Jane, slipping her arm around the police chief, giving him a light squeeze. "It's a perfect job for him."

Jack Clayton looked up at a sky fading steadily into

sunset. The long shadows from the fenceline were already creeping onto the front stairs from across the yard.

"Well, I'd better get going," he said. "It looks like I'm running out of light."

"Take care of yourself, Clayton," said Howser. He added, "Drive safely. Keep an eye out for the loonies."

"I will."

They shook hands then, and Clayton kissed Jane and gave her a long hug and another kiss. He said good-bye with a promise to remember—essentially the same promise he'd made to everyone he'd met, every place he'd been. The getting-around part of traveling was easy; keeping the promises he'd had to make in all those places was always more difficult. Everybody takes something away with them from wherever they've been. And, of course, they also leave something behind. In this case, Jack Clayton knew it might be a long while before he fully understood what it was he had taken. And when he drove out of Rivertown, all he'd left behind were a few barking dogs.

Epilogue

There is a man sitting in a car on a dark road near the river. He is alone and has the windows rolled down to let the cool air in off the water. There is a radio in the car and it is tuned to a music station but the volume is turned down low and the music is drowned out by the wind moving through the stars overhead. And he is not listening to the music anyhow; he is watching the lights of traffic passing on the interstate in the distance. He has been there a long time. Longer than he can remember. And the traffic has been there with him, and the river. Every so often he falls asleep and in sleeping he dreams, and in these dreams he sits by a roadside where butterflies float in the dusty twilight. He sits alone waiting for a ride that never comes, but he is older now and so he understands: The farther we have to go, the stronger we will always be. There's still a lot of traveling to do.

MYSTERY PARLOR

☐ **THE DEAD PULL HITTER by Alison Gordon.** Katherine Henry is a sportswriter—until murder pitches a curve. Now death is lurking in her ballpark, and she's looking for a killer on the dark side of glory days and shattered dreams.   (402405—$3.99)

☐ **HALF A MIND by Wendy Hornsby.** Homicide detective Roger Tejeda had an instinctive sense for catching criminals. But now he's working with a handicap: his last case left him with a skull fracture, black-outs and memory lapses—which make it that much harder to figure out who sent him a gift box holding a severed head....   (402456—$3.99)

☐ **THE CHARTREUSE CLUE by William F. Love.** Although a priest with a murdered girlfriend wasn't exactly an original sin, the irascible, wheelchair-bound Bishop would have to use leads that included a key, a letter, and a chartreuse clue to unravel the deadly affair.   (402731—$5.50)

☐ **MRS. MALORY INVESTIGATES by Hazel Holt.** "Delightful ... a British whodunit that works a traditional mode to good effect." —*Cleveland Plain Dealer*   (402693—$3.99)

Buy them at your local bookstore or use this convenient coupon for ordering.

NEW AMERICAN LIBRARY
P.O. Box 999, Bergenfield, New Jersey 07621

Please send me the books I have checked above.
I am enclosing $_____ (please add $2.00 to cover postage and handling).
Send check or money order (no cash or C.O.D.'s) or charge by Mastercard or VISA (with a $15.00 minimum). Prices and numbers are subject to change without notice.

Card #_____ Exp. Date _____
Signature_____
Name_____
Address_____
City _____ State _____ Zip Code _____
For faster service when ordering by credit card call **1-800-253-6476**
Allow a minimum of 4-6 weeks for delivery. This offer is subject to change without notice.

There's an epidemic with 27 million victims. And no visible symptoms.

It's an epidemic of people who can't read.

Believe it or not, 27 million Americans are functionally illiterate, about one adult in five.

The solution to this problem is you... when you join the fight against illiteracy. So call the Coalition for Literacy at toll-free **1-800-228-8813** and volunteer.

Volunteer Against Illiteracy. The only degree you need is a degree of caring.